BATTLING AGAINST SUCCESS

BATTLING

AGAINST

SUCCESS

For Ann Pierson, with regards and regrets we did not get to meet you with Don this evening

Neil Davis

Aug 27, 2004

NEIL DAVIS

MCROY & BLACKBURN, PUBLISHERS
ESTER, ALASKA

OTHER BOOKS BY NEIL DAVIS

NON-FICTION:

Alaska Science Nuggets, 1982
Energy/Alaska, 1984
The Aurora Watcher's Handbook, 1992
The College Hills Chronicles, 1993

FICTION:

Caught in the Sluice, 1994

©1997 by McRoy & Blackburn, Publishers
P.O. Box 276
Ester, Alaska 99725
All rights reserved.

Book and cover design by Paula Elmes,
ImageCraft Publications & Design
Fairbanks, Alaska

ISBN 0-9632596-6-0 (paperback)
ISBN 0-9632596-7-9 (casebound)

Printed in the United States of America

CONTENTS

AUTHOR'S NOTE

THIS BOOK'S DEPICTION of persons and events is based on reality in much the same fashion as are the several computer-processed images that accompany it. These images derive from actual photographs mostly taken long ago by me or members of my family, but they have undergone modifications, some slight, some severe. Like the images, the text's portrayals of events and people ranges from memory-filtered total truth to composites of manipulated truth and fiction. Not all here is strictly factual, but I have tried to make it truthful. (For those interested in such matters, my processing of the photographs has relied much on the Adobe™ Photoshop 4.0 Sketch Filter used in Graphic Pen mode, but some of the creations and modifications were accomplished freehand or by machine-driven applications of various other Photoshop tools.) Thanks go to ex-Wien Airlines pilot and boyhood friend, Douglas G. Millard for providing me with information on the DC-3 aircraft and old Weeks Field in Fairbanks. My wife Rosemarie contributed a great deal to this work by reading and discussing the material as we went along through revision after revision over the course of several years. I also am deeply grateful for the guidance given by Carla Helfferich of McRoy & Blackburn.

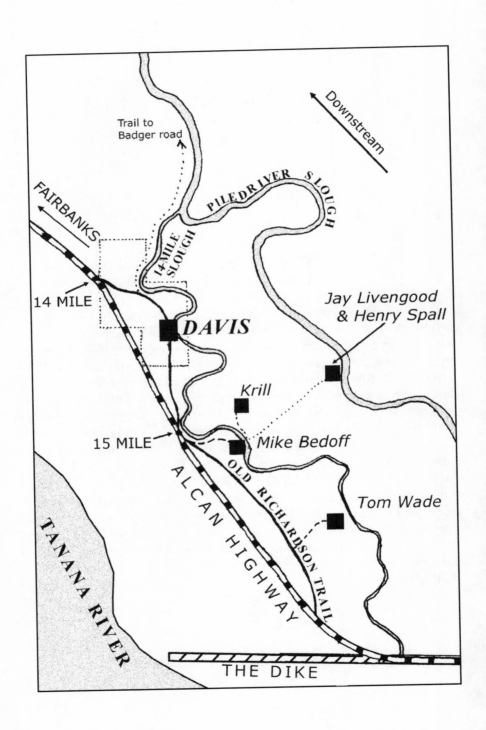

FAIRBANKS AND THE MODEL CAFE

10:00 P.M. TUESDAY, AUGUST 6, 1944

I'M FEELING A LITTLE QUEASY myself, but Lewie is looking real green, his eyes are rolling, and he's hugging his stomach with both arms. "Hang on, Lewie, you can do it; we're almost down," I tell him as I hold the stiff white bag under his chin. It says "Courtesy of Pan American Airways System, the Line of the Flying Clipper Ships" on its side. At the same time I am trying to look out the window over his head at the ground slowly coming up beneath us. Lewie had started getting sick almost as soon as the pilots lowered the flaps to slow the plane for landing. That makes the airplane shudder and sway, and that's what makes Lewie want to woof his cookies. This is the sixth landing we are making in the twin-engined Lockheed Lodestar, and I know from our experience with the first five that if we can get through the horrible jerk and noise of the landing gear popping down into position, we are going to be OK. Exactly when the gear dropped, Lewie threw up during our first landing, the one at Prince George yesterday morning, and he did it like that again when we came into Juneau earlier today. But he'd gotten through the landing at Annette Island where we stopped for fuel, and three others, including the last just a few hours ago at Whitehorse. I'm sure hoping he'll make it through this very last one because when he tosses I come close to doing it too. That's a kid thing, and it'd really be embarrassing for it to happen to someone who is as grown up as I am. Most people think I'm even older than twelve because I'm bigger than most boys that age, and since I've been around a lot and done a lot of things I'm sure I act older than that, too.

1

But with Lewie it's different. For being eight, he's awful small and skinny. He really looks like a little kid, but since I've been taking care of him so much these last few years I know just how tough the little twerp is. He is a nervous kid, but I don't know why he is having so much trouble with these airplane landings unless it's because what is happening to us is so darn exciting, this being our first airplane trip and our first trip to what's going to be our new home in Alaska.

Dad went to Alaska early in the war, back in 1942 when I was ten and Lewie six. Then Mom went a few months later, and of course we haven't seen them since. Mom and Dad will be meeting us this time when we land in Fairbanks, so it's no wonder that these last few minutes Lewie's been almost out of his gourd. Maybe it'd be a good thing if he did throw up and get it over with right now.

Then we feel the airplane jerk upward as the landing gear releases and the quick hard thud of it locking down. Lewie's elbows come out as he slaps his tummy, holds the pose a few seconds, and then smiles up at me. "Hey, you did it. That's swell," I tell him. "Look, we're about to land." Checking my pocket watch, I see that it is just after nine o'clock at night, but since the sun is still shining right in our eyes, we can't see very well. I can tell that we are coming down right on the edge of what must be Fairbanks.

A horrible clattering noise comes from below as the Lodestar's wheels hit down and bang across the potholes in the gravel runway, and now I can see hangars and a whole bunch of parked airplanes out beside us. It seems to take forever for the plane to slow down, turn around and then roll in toward a hangar where we see people standing around waiting to meet us. There aren't many because even though this airplane can carry fourteen passengers, only five of us and the two pilots are still on it.

The plane finally comes to a stop, but we are sitting on the wrong side to see Mom and Dad. "What if they aren't there?" Lewie says, and I feel his fingers digging into my arm.

"Don't worry, they'll be there," I tell him. Boy, they better be there. It's been a long haul for Lewie. He went to live in the orphans' home in Chicago that summer after Dad left there for Alaska, and I went off to Iowa to stay with Aunt Phena and Uncle Irwin on their farm. He didn't see much of Mom that summer because she was working in the bombsight company way over on the other side of Chicago. It was better for him when I came back and went into the orphans' home

2

with him. Then when Mom went to Alaska, too, Lewie and I both went back to the farm. I got along well there because I really liked the farm and my aunt and uncle. I think Lewie liked it there too, but he was so darn ornery that they rode him a lot—seemed like he was always in some kind of trouble. And this trip sure has taken a long time, too, three days on the train from Iowa to Seattle, a week of waiting there for better weather, and then two days of flying across most of Canada. I'm glad it's finally over, and Lewie is just bonkers over thinking about being able to live with Mom and Dad again. I'm pretty happy too to finally get to Alaska, and I'm looking forward to living on our new homestead down the Alcan Highway from Fairbanks. That is something extra-special because, except for our clothes and sometimes an old car, this homestead is the first thing our family has ever owned. I've been wanting to have a home for a long time, and I feel good every time I think about the homestead. I don't think Lewie cares; he just wants to be with Mom and Dad again. Yeah, they better darn well be out there, or Lewie will bust into tears for sure.

We are moving out onto the ramp now. Great, there they are! Mom and Dad are right in front of us, standing side by side, arms linked. With her prematurely gray, almost white, hair Mom looks even prettier than I remember, but Dad still has that gaunt hungry look of a man who has worked a lot and not smiled very much.

Of course Dad is smiling now, and Mom is too. In fact, we are all wearing the biggest smiles you'd ever hope to see. "You boys sure have grown," Mom says as she hugs us and Dad shakes our hands.

"Yeah, feel my muscle, Mom," Lewie says proudly, flexing his arm. It is pretty funny, because his arm is so skinny you can't feel hardly anything. Uncle Irwin and I taught him to do that, and Lewie is so dumb he does not realize it is a joke. He actually thinks he has a muscle in there, and that it is getting bigger every day.

"Well, as fast as you are growing, I think it's time for you to eat again," Mom says. "We'll go down to the Model Cafe right away, and you boys can eat whatever you want." That sounds good to me because I'm really hungry. I haven't had anything since the sandwich and apple that was in the box lunch the copilot handed out between Juneau and Whitehorse.

As we stand waiting for our baggage and I look around at the other people and the nearby buildings I begin to realize how strange it is here. Now, at ten o'clock, we no longer see the sun in the northwest, but the sky there is bright and it casts everything in a soft gentle light. I feel a sense of things not being real, like we are all taking part in a black and white movie. I'm in it, but I'm sorta also out in the audience watching.

Soon Dad and I are loading the two suitcases—they contain everything that Lewie and I still own—into the back of the family car, a slightly battered gray 1936 Ford pickup. We all pile in and the pickup moves away from the Pan Am hangar onto a dirt street lined with birch trees and a boardwalk on one side. Dad drives slowly, hunched over with both hands high up on the steering wheel, and I suddenly remember that he always drives a car that way, as though it were a horse about to run away.

Already I can see that Fairbanks is different from any town I've been in before because it has so many log cabins. The street we are driving along has some houses of the regular kind, too, squarish sturdy-looking ones made out of boards and with painted wooden siding. I like the log cabins best, though, they look like they belong. Some have bushes and flowers all around and low-pitched roofs that stick way out over the walls and in front, and that makes them look sort of like old broody hens that have fluffed out their wings and dug themselves into their nests, planning to stay forever.

The street leads straight down to the river where Dad turns to the right on what the sign says is First Avenue. Several big metal and wood warehouse buildings face out onto the street and the riverbank, where ramps and gangplanks lead out to two paddlewheel riverboats. From some of the letters Mom sent to us in Iowa, I know it's called the Chena River, but for a moment being there on First Avenue between those paddlewheelers and warehouses makes me think it's a long time ago and I am riding in a horse-drawn wagon beside the Mississippi River in some place like Keokuk, Iowa. Of course the Chena is a lot smaller, and the riverboats aren't very big either, but you can sure tell Fairbanks is a river town.

On beyond the warehouses, we roll past the big wooden block-long Northern Commercial Company store. "That's the N.C. where we buy almost all our groceries and other things," Mom says. "We've got an account there." Dad drives on another two blocks, makes a couple of right-hand turns and we come onto Second Avenue, which has a lot of stores and people on it, but only a few cars. Dad eases the pickup's front wheel up to the cement curb, almost right in front of the Model Cafe.

Gosh, this is supposed to be night, but people, mostly men, are everywhere, some walking, but most just standing around talking. Right in front of the pickup are two old men with beards, one of them with a backpack on. A lot of other older men stand around, and people of all sorts walk past them. A little dark-faced man with legs so bowed he seems crippled hobbles along with a group of women wearing long cloth dresses with fur-rimmed hoods laid back over their shoulders. They have dark faces like the man's, so I know they must be Indians or Eskimos, but I can't tell which. Up and down the street are quite a few more, and many soldiers, some of them Negroes.

I feel just a brief twinge of fear when I see a fierce rank of men approaching. They are wearing stiff gray uniforms with wide black belts and big, polished black boots. On the shoulders of each uniform is a red epaulet, and each man's cap has a round red symbol of some sort just above the brim. "Russian pilots," Mom says, seeing my stare. "They pick up airplanes here in Fairbanks and fly them over through Siberia to the Russian Front." I am glad to learn that these guys are on our side; still, they look awfully stern and serious as they march past, silent and erect. It makes the American soldiers seem slouchy as they saunter down the street laughing and joking with each other.

Over in a doorway, almost hidden in the shadows, stands a little white-haired woman dressed in black. As we watch, she reaches into a greasy paper sack she is holding to pull out a partially eaten T-bone steak. After inspecting it briefly, she takes a bite. "Mom, is that the funny woman you wrote about, the one...?" I ask.

"Yes, that's her," Mom says. "That's Mrs. Ford. Would you like to meet her?"

Mom wrote us all about Mrs. Ford, who was one of the people she got to know while she worked as a waitress in the Model Cafe. Mrs. Ford came in to pick up food scraps that people saved for her and which she said were to feed her cats. Mom said that Mrs. Ford did have a lot of cats but that she highgraded the scraps for herself like we had just seen her do. Funny thing, though, is that Mrs. Ford is rich. She owns a whole bunch of houses in town, but since she will not let people live in them, they are mostly empty except for the cats.

Mom tried to rent a house from her, but when Mrs. Ford found out that Dad would be staying there too, she refused. She does not like most men, and from what Mom said, Mrs. Ford really hates powerful ones like businessmen or government men. She especially hates one man, one of the town's bankers. Mom wrote the story she'd heard that one time a miner tried to borrow money from this banker. He said he'd loan the money if the miner could get Mrs. Ford to cosign a note. When the miner asked Mrs. Ford, she said, "You go tell that old S.O.B. that if he will cosign a note, I'll loan you the money."

Having read that story in Mom's letter I got the idea that Mrs. Ford must be a big tough woman. That makes it a shock to see her for the first time because she is so little. Her narrow shoulders slope down beneath her worn black coat, making her look extra fragile and delicate. Her tiny, unsmiling face is almost regal, and she sure doesn't look like the kind of lady who would tell a banker off.

Mom leads Lewie and me up to her. "Mrs. Ford, these are my boys," she says proudly. Mrs. Ford does not say anything, but she nods as her eyes sweep over my face. Yet I feel like she is looking right through me. She sure is different than most people.

Of course I am really fired up anyway tonight, but Mrs. Ford and all those new people out on the street seem especially exciting. It is strange—this is Tuesday evening, but here on Second Avenue in Fairbanks it is even busier than on a summer Saturday night back in Panora, Iowa. That's the town near Aunt Phena and Uncle Irwin's farm where Lewie and I have been living these past two years.

Saturday nights there are big deals. All the farmers dress up and go to town where the women shop and gossip in the stores and the men go to the pool hall or stand on the street talking to each other. The women all dress pretty much alike and so do the men. If you hear them talking it's always about the same things: their crops, who people are related to, and who has died. Except for the men's slow drawling and the women's rapid twanging, the voices sound mostly alike, too. And while their parents visit, groups of young girls saunter up and down the two blocks of main street giggling and twirling their full skirts each time they meet the groups of boys who carefully pace themselves so as to always be going the opposite direction. About eight o'clock, the band begins playing in the square, and everyone sits on the grass around the bandstand to listen.

Saturday nights in Iowa are fun. They are sad, too, because everything is so predictable. It makes you wonder if anybody is going anywhere except home after the band concert—and then only to come back next Saturday night and all the rest of the Saturday nights of their lives.

Maybe it's just that everything is changing for me on this bright Tuesday night that I think the crowd on the street seems so exciting. The many different kinds of clothing help, and so does the contrast in voices. The rough, sharp words of soldiers from eastern cities cut across the soft tones of those who have lived here a long time: the Native people and the old Sourdoughs. Drifting in and out are foreign sounds and those not identifiable but different from the others. The symphony of voices on the street sings out that, like me, almost everyone here is from someplace else. We are all headed someplace, too. You can sense it in the air, and it feels good.

We go inside the Model Cafe, and it, too, is different, a kind of street scene all by itself because its one main room runs all the way from the door we entered on Second Avenue to the one on First Avenue. The room is so smoky and so long that you can barely see the far end. A counter faces the door and curves around to run down the middle of the whole cafe. Behind the counter is the cooking area, and on the opposite wall are many tall wooden booths. Most booths are full, and so are almost all of the stools at the counter. Cooks and dishwashers work away behind the counter, some chatting with the customers, and waitresses scurry everywhere. Meat sizzles away continuously on the big metal grills.

We get a lot of attention as we come up to the counter. "Hey, they finally got here," the nearest cook calls out loudly, and customers sitting nearby turn to look at us.

"Yes, these are my boys," Mom says, again with a tone that makes you feel good.

"You're Neil, and you're Lewis. I'm Ben," the cook booms out again with a friendly smile. I guess Mom knows just about everybody here, going by all the other pleasant greetings and smiles from waitresses and customers.

As we eat our supper, so many people stop by to chat with Mom and say hello that we hardly get a chance to talk to each other. We talk enough though for me to learn, much to my disappointment, that we won't be driving out to the homestead tonight. That's because Dad goes to work at midnight. He is the baker at Zehnder Camp, just across the river from the main part of Fairbanks, where every night he makes bread, about fifty pies, and a bunch of cakes and other stuff. Along with all the construction workers who live there, Dad has a room at the camp where we can all stay the night.

7

After eating, we are back out on the crowded street again where we immediately run into a strikingly tall and handsome man. "Maury, meet my two boys," Mom says, again proudly. "Boys, this is Mr. Smith. He's the town's best newspaper reporter, and he's on the radio too." I can see why he is on the radio because when Mr. Smith speaks to us it is with about the deepest, most pleasant man's voice I'd ever heard.

Mr. Smith asks us how we spell our names and he jots them down in his notebook along with a few details of our trip to Fairbanks. "You'll be in tomorrow's paper, boys, maybe even on the front page. Be sure to look," he says as he heads off down the street. Wow, I think, this is incredible. I can't believe how much attention we just got in the Model Cafe, and now we are going to be in the newspaper, too. Never before have I been anywhere where people pay this kind of attention to young kids like us. Maybe it's because not many people live here, so everybody is important. Or maybe it's just that there aren't many kids—I sure haven't seen many women so far, and if you're gonna have kids you got to have women.

GOING TO THE HOMESTEAD

AUGUST 7, 1944

THE FIRST THING I SAW when I woke up in Zehnder Camp this morning was this naked light bulb hanging down out of the green ceiling by a twisted pair of wires, and for a scary moment I thought I was back in the orphans' home in Chicago. Lewie actually liked it there, I guess because he had so many kids his age to play with. I didn't like it though, and I'm glad this is Zehnder Camp and that today we're going to the homestead.

Zehnder Camp is just like all those army bases you see in the war movies. It's a bunch of drab olive-green bunkhouses all lined up in rows along two or three short streets. The streets and the spaces between the buildings are just dirt that looks like it was scraped bare with a bulldozer not long ago. Except for our pickup, the only vehicles around are army trucks and jeeps and a lot of buses. Mom says that the buses are to take the construction workers who live here to their jobs. Most of them work on Ladd Field, the Army Air Force base just the other side of Fairbanks, the place where the Russian pilots get their airplanes.

While Dad sleeps, Mom takes Lewie and me over to the mess hall for breakfast. We get to eat as much as we want of anything there. They even have steaks you can eat with your eggs, and some of the pies that Dad baked last night are laid out on the counter. You just help yourself, and it's all free.

Lewie doesn't eat much, unless it's ice cream, so he finishes up early and says he wants to go outside and play with the three young husky pups that hang around the building. A cook who has come over

9

to have coffee with us winks at Mom and says, "You boys like those dogs, do you?"

"Yeah," says Lewie, "they sure are furry." Lewie likes anything that is soft and furry, so of course he likes the dogs. I do, too. It would be fun to have real sled dogs like that, and I mention that I've been thinking that now I'm in Alaska it'd be fun to have a dog team.

"Looks like you got a dog team then," the man says, grinning. "Lew, go over there and get three of those big steaks to take out to feed your new dogs."

I can't quite believe this is for real, but Mom tells me it is, that she and Dad have talked it over, and that all the men around the camp have agreed to let us take the three dogs to our homestead. "But not today," Mom says. "You've got to get collars for them and we've got to haul a lot of groceries out to the homestead. Now, while Dad's sleeping, we'll go over to the N.C. store and do some shopping."

I've never been in a place that has as many things in it as the N.C. Walking through the front door, we see counter after counter of clothing going all the way to the left and back walls. Mom leads us over to the grocery section stretched along the right-hand wall from the store's front to what appears to be the back wall. But then as we walk along the edge of the grocery area we realize that what I thought was the back of the store is just a middle wall. Hidden behind it is the hardware section that has stack after stack of just about everything imaginable—including all sorts of things hard or impossible to buy back in Iowa because of the war, things like car tires, electric fans, toasters and appliances and tools of every type.

The only thing missing, and I notice that just walking past the groceries, is that the price tags on things don't tell how many ration stamps you have to use. I ask Mom about that, and she laughs and says, "We don't have rationing; that's just for back in the States. Here in Alaska, if you've got the money, you can buy as much of anything as you want. The only thing we've had trouble buying is lumber for the cabin at the homestead."

"Even gasoline?"

"Sure, it's expensive, but all you want."

Wow, I think, that is something. Back in Iowa, the people who live in towns can't get much gas. Of course the farmers like Uncle Irwin have all they want for their cars because they have a huge ration for their tractors. Uncle Irwin is always careful not to let his farm neighbors see him put tractor gas in the car, even though he knows they are doing it, too.

I remember that in one of the letters Dad wrote us when we were in Iowa he said that rationing business is pure nonsense. The government does it just to keep everybody fired up about the Japs and the Germans. People won't go along with a big war like we're in now unless you con them by doing things like rationing, Dad says. He is kind of a socialist or something because in his letters he is always talking about the bad things the government and the army does, and how the rich people like the Roosevelts, the Krupps, the Rothschilds, the Morgans and the Carnegies like wars so much because they can make lots of money, no matter who wins. Dad does not like the Catholic Church either because he says it is rich and takes so much advantage of poor people.

Of big interest to me in the N.C.'s hardware section is the huge display of chains, dog collars and harnesses hung up on one wall. The harnesses are neat. Each one has a collar that looks like it was made for a tiny little horse. From the collar, two webbing straps run back past the dog's sides to a little wooden stick that goes crossways behind the dog's tail and hooks onto the tow rope. The trouble is that they are so expensive, about $20 each, so I'm sure not going to buy any of those real soon. Mom and I just pick out some collars and chains for our new dogs, and she puts them on the account. "Just this time, though," she says, "You'll have to pay for everything else if you're going to have a team. Of course as long as Dad works at Zehnder Camp you'll have free food for the dogs."

A few minutes later I am wandering around the store while Lewie goes with Mom to get the groceries, when in the clothing section I come up behind a bunch of the Russian pilots who are standing at a counter jabbering away at a lady on the other side. Standing there in a row like that in their big black boots and fancy gray uniforms, the fierce group of Russians looks almost like a firing squad about to shoot the woman behind the counter. Then I walk up beside a man who is watching all this from the side and I see why he is smiling. The saleswoman looks flustered because one of the Russians is holding a brassiere up toward her chest, and the others are all laughing because the lady looks real embarrassed. The counter below is loaded with a jumbled pile of women's brassieres, and beyond it are others containing women's panties, stockings and slips piled high in disarray. One of the Russian soldiers has about ten brassieres of different sizes looped onto one arm, and in the hand of that arm he is clutching what looks to be a dozen or so pairs of panties.

"Quite a sight, eh?" the man beside me says. "Hell, they buy so much underwear to take home with them that the store just dumps it out in piles like that. Those frilly undies are worth a fortune in Russia. Bet those guys have a heck of a good time with the ladies when they get home." Like the saleslady, I am embarrassed, so I head back to find Mom and Lewie, and my mind is reeling with all that's happened and the strange new things I've seen since coming to Fairbanks. Boy, you'd sure never see men in Iowa go into a store to buy women's underwear.

I'd almost forgotten about Maury Smith and his newspaper until we finished up at the N.C. and went to the drugstore on the corner by the bridge over the Chena River. A pickup dropped a bundle of papers off just as we went in, and soon Mom was reading aloud to us, "New residents Neil Davis, 12, and Lewis Davis, 8, arrived on yesterday's Pam Am flight. The boys and their parents, Bon and Bernice Davis, will be living on the family's new homestead near 14-Mile on the highway south of town. They are fine-looking boys, and Fairbanks welcomes them."

"Read that last part again, Mom," Lewie says with a big grin, and I'm glad he asks because it sounds pretty good to me, too.

By early afternoon, Dad is up, so we leave Zehnder Camp for the homestead. Oh boy, I can hardly wait to see it! Of course I think I've got a pretty good idea what it will be like because I already know a lot about the homestead and about Alaska. That is because of Mom's and Dad's letters to us in Iowa, and the sketches they sent. Ever since last March, when Dad first wrote about the homestead, I have been imagining what it will be like to live there, and in Alaska.

Mom's and Dad's earlier letters came from various places I'd mostly never even heard of before, places like Juneau, Excursion Inlet, Whitehorse and Destruction Bay. We weren't even supposed to know about those places because of the war. Everybody's letters were censored to stop people from telling where they were or about anything else useful to the enemy. The postmarks on the letters didn't help either 'cause they just read "APO Seattle." We knew, though, because when Dad went to Alaska he and Mom had a code to outfox the censors. When Mom went to Alaska a few months later, she continued to use the code when she wrote to Lewie and me. All you had to do was pick out the first letter of each new paragraph in a letter and if it spelled anything, that's where Mom or Dad were. The first letter from Dad was funny because he had to write fourteen paragraphs to spell out "Excursion Inlet," and the second paragraph began with the sentence "Xmas was good this year, wasn't it?"

I always looked forward to those letters. The cellophane tape on the end where the censor had closed each one up made the letters more than just notes from Mom or Dad. They were secret messages from faraway foreign places that you had to ponder over to understand. You had to figure out what Dad was really saying when he wrote something like, "My life has undergone substantial improvement lately. Subsequent to my coming here, I wanted to base my life on building a fortune, but that was an excursion into fantasy, and now I am content just to construct a base of happiness for the family's future."

Dad never really talked like that so we knew he was sending a special message, and the message probably was: "Here at Excursion Inlet we are building a submarine base." Sometimes I think the censors caught on because some pages of Dad's letters had whole chunks cut right out of them.

Later on, the censorship stopped, or maybe it depended on where the envelopes were mailed. Anyway, the letters from Mom and Dad were more normal, and usually full of plans for what was going to happen. In the beginning I got pretty excited about some of those plans, but after a while I learned not to get too excited because another letter would come along saying something different. A letter telling that Dad would be taking a teaching job on the lower Yukon next week was followed by another saying the job had fallen through. That letter said that Dad was thinking of going into business with another man on the Kenai, and the next told of a different idea. Not long after we got the letter that said Mom would soon be coming to visit us in Iowa we got another saying that she was not coming. These plans all changed so fast you wondered after a while why Dad even bothered to tell us about them.

One consistency in the letters from Mom and Dad was discussion of money. Almost every letter said that a money order would be on its way before long. Sometimes the letters mentioned the expected amounts, $25, $50 or even $100. This money was intended to help pay for Lewie's and my keep or to repay money Aunt Phena and Uncle Irwin had loaned earlier.

I guess that was always the way it had been with Mom and Dad. No matter what was happening, Dad was always scrabbling for enough money to pay a bill owed, while also developing a new plan for the future—one that usually required borrowing more money. I thought maybe that's why our family never had a home and always moved around so much and did so many different things, but I also wondered why it was still this way. Mom and Dad ought to have plenty of money because they both had good jobs that paid lots of overtime, and they got their board and room free. I guessed that they must have built up some really big debts before the war.

Then one day we got this amazing letter from Dad that, instead of promising money or describing what might happen, actually contained a big money order and told us about something that had already happened. The letter came from a new place, Fairbanks, and it said that Dad had just taken out a homestead not far away. Also, Mom was quitting her job in Whitehorse and was coming to Fairbanks, and as soon as it could be arranged, Lewie and I would move to Alaska too.

From the letters following, we learned that the very next day after Dad arrived in Fairbanks, he applied for the homestead. He had gone to the Land Office and learned that he could homestead land many places north of Fairbanks or almost anywhere beyond six miles south of town. He rented a car and drove down the Alcan until he got to 14-Mile. Although everything was covered up with snow, he thought the land there looked less swampy than what he'd seen so far. It had a lot more big trees, and a pretty stream, too. The man at the Land Office had told Dad not to take the first thing he saw, but Dad liked this place so much he went right back to town and filed on the most he could get, 160 acres.

I think that the homestead is going to change everything. We now have land, and that is bound to make things more stable—like in Iowa where everybody stays in one place and makes a living on the land. Of course I don't want it to be that stable, but I don't think there's much danger here in Fairbanks where everything's so active and different. Just think how much has already happened today, and now we are on our way to see the homestead for the first time.

Just outside Zehnder Camp we drive past the Alaska Railroad's end of track, the hospital, the Catholic Church and Sampson's Hardware before climbing up onto the steel bridge across the Chena. The bridge's decking sings and clanks as we roll across and on down into the intersection of First Avenue and Cushman Street where a newly painted white wooden post reads Mile 1523, Alcan Highway.

Heading directly south, Cushman Street stretches out in front of us. The pickup rolls smoothly along it, past the Federal Building just the other side of Second Avenue, and then a few blocks later we drop off the blacktop onto rough road filled with potholes. I soon discover that Fairbanks does not have any outskirts; it just stops at 11th Avenue. There, Cushman Street truly becomes the Alcan Highway, and off a ways down a street called Gaffney Road that turns to the left, you can see the guardhouse into Ladd Field. Out in front of us as we cross Gaffney we see a greenhouse and a little field full of cabbages. Beyond that, the road just stretches off into the wilderness. We sure as heck haven't gone very far to get from downtown Fairbanks into the wilds of Alaska, less than half a mile.

The road runs straight south for another mile, and then curves around to the left. This is Big Bend, the last place for quite a ways to have a name, Mom says. Beyond that, everything is "Something-Mile," the "something" being however far it is from Fairbanks.

As we near Big Bend, I notice off in the distance some of the tall, snow-covered mountains of the Alaska Range that Lewie and I saw up close yesterday as we flew in from Whitehorse. They don't look like much from here, and as we round Big Bend we lose all sight of them. The only things to look at now are the swamps, brush and scraggly little trees alongside the road.

We are getting plenty of chances to see what is out beside us because Dad is a slow driver. He's always been that way as far back as I can remember. Even on paved roads he'll never drive faster than forty, and he doesn't like to go over thirty on dirt or gravel roads because he says it is too hard on the tires.

In most places the Alcan is rough with rocks and gravel, so we are moving along at about twenty, and sometimes far less. Dad just crawls along when we come to the really bad places that he says are frost boils. It's strange to see gooey mud like that mushroom right up in the middle of the road. When I hang out the window I can look down at the leathery-looking ground beside the boils and see how it moves up and down and how the mud oozes out as the pickup rolls past.

The ditches alongside the road are so steep and raw that you can tell that the road is new. Over beyond each of them is an ugly berm of tangled moss, brush and trees pushed up by the army bulldozers that built the road two years ago. In some places the berms are higher than the pickup, so they block the view of the bushes and trees beyond. The trees here sure aren't much. None of them are very tall, and the three kinds of them we see—what Mom says are black spruce, birch and tamarack—are all skinny. These trees reach for the sky instead of bushing out like the big elms and walnuts in Iowa, or the smaller junipers and cedars up high in Colorado. For some reason the trees here are mostly strung out in long, irregular stands, and between these it's all just bushes and swamps, lots of bushes and swamps. With all that water on the ground you'd think the air would feel wet and muggy, but it doesn't. The air is so crisp and clear that even the distant trees stand sharp against the blue sky. The land here looks lush, but it feels stark.

Not having been around Mom for a long time, I have forgotten how much she likes to play with words and names of things. It all comes back, though, as she tells Lewie and me about the kinds of the bushes and trees out alongside the road. Mom can be funny, but sometimes what she comes up with is just embarrassing. It's kinda both ways when she says, "See that smooth grassy area over there by that pond? That's muskeg. It's all full of little mossy mounds called niggerheads." Her eyes flash and she emphasizes "niggerheads" with the impish low tone she uses when she knows she is saying something wicked, and of course nobody in our family would ever call anybody a nigger. "It's hard to walk through the niggerheads 'cause if you try to step on top of them they fall over, and if you step between them they'll rub up against your fanny and give you a soggy bottom." Mom laughs and then says, "They're called tussocks and hummocks, too, so maybe you could call them hussocks or tummocks. Or," and Mom giggles again, "how about tussyhummocks or hussytummocks?"

That is kind of funny, partly because the niggerhead idea causes me to picture hundreds of dark bushy-haired people standing in a swamp with just their heads and shoulders showing, and that thought causes Mom's "hussytummocks" to come out in my mind as a whole bunch of naughty women who have gotten themselves pregnant and are lying on their backs with just their big rounded stomachs sticking up. Of course I'm not about to tell anybody ideas like that because they might get mad or maybe think I'm strange.

One odd thing I notice about what we are seeing out on the other side of the berm piles is that no dirt or rocks show anywhere. The ground everywhere is covered with moss, bushes and water, and no car tracks run across it, or any trails you might walk on. If this were where we lived in Colorado, Wyoming or Utah, you'd see lots of dirt and rocks, and car and cow trails leading off the road everywhere. Or if this were Iowa, you would see plenty of dirt and places to drive off the road into the pastures and cornfields. Even back where we lived in West Virginia, many paths and car tracks led off the roads back into the hills, and there was plenty of dirt to see between the trees. But here on the Alcan in Alaska it's pretty obvious that the only places you're gonna go are where the road takes you. You might be able to walk out there in most places, but it sure wouldn't be any fun, and it's so flat you'd probably get lost real quick.

Another interesting thing we see is that some of the trees are just gray-black trunks two or three inches in diameter sticking up about twenty feet, with no branches on them. "That's black spruce firekill," Dad says, "Best damn firewood in the world." Dad always says things like that, "Best damn..." whatever it is that he is talking about. "Those trees were killed by a forest fire a long time ago, and they've been standing there drying out ever since. Best damn firewood there is."

It seems like we have been driving a long time when we finally come to something different. Alongside the road is a post with a white-painted, tapered top and a black "5" on it. "That's the 5-Mile post," says Mom. Heck, we got a long ways to go to get to the homestead.

A mile farther along, at 6-Mile, we come to the first building we have seen since leaving Fairbanks. It is a little white guardhouse just big enough to hold one man, and he controls traffic onto Badger Road because that road allows entry to the southeast end of Ladd Field. A soldier with a rifle comes out, but he goes back inside when he sees that we are not turning off on Badger Road.

"Boy, there's not much traffic on this road," says Lewie. "We haven't met a single car so far."

"No, and we probably won't see any either," says Dad. "The road goes on like this for hundreds of miles and hardly anybody uses it. This whole Alcan's just a big boondoggle, a way to spend lots of money. Soon as the war is over, the Alcan will sink back into the tundra because nobody at all will use it then. A road like this will never be a useful means of transportation to Alaska from the States." I suppose Dad's right, him having been a school teacher and all.

The Alcan tracks on southeasterly through the swamps and brush, curving left or right to avoid crossing the worst of the wet places. These are mostly little mossy oxbow swamps that show where streams used to flow. Dad says that everything is so flat here because all the ground has been deposited by meanders of the Tanana River, which he says is now off a mile or two to the south of us.

Every once in a while, out away from the road, we see tripods that look like the remnants of Indian teepees. Most of them have an insulator near the top and some of those have wires hanging from them. Dad says they were what used to hold up a telegraph line that ran to the coast, hundreds of miles away. By using tripods, the builders of that line did not have to dig any holes in the frozen ground, Dad says, and that seems clever to me. A brand new telephone line with normal poles and crossbars runs along the Alcan, and where its poles are set in wet places they are already starting to tip over. Around some of them are rock-filled timber cribs that help to keep the poles upright. Another new army construction alongside the road is a pipe about six inches in diameter that Dad says runs all the way from a place on the ocean coast called Haines to bring gasoline to Ladd Field for all the airplanes that go through.

That's about all we see until we come to the post marking the location of 10-Mile. Then, not far off the road at 11-Mile, we see the next building, a little log cabin with its roof mostly fallen in. Dad says that it used to be a roadhouse on the old Richardson Trail. The Richardson Trail runs about 350 miles from Fairbanks to Valdez, down on the coast. The Alcan coming in from Canada meets the trail at Big Delta, about 100 miles up the Tanana from Fairbanks. From there, the new Alcan more or less follows the trail, but in most places the new roadbed is a lot straighter. Since leaving 6-Mile we have been seeing little loops of the old trail, some only a few hundred feet long, angling in and under the new road.

We are nearly an hour out of Fairbanks by the time we get beyond 13-Mile. Out ahead and off to the left, a long stand of tall dark-green trees rises above the horizon. "We're getting close now," Dad says with excitement in his voice, and I can see that Mom is happy and excited, too. "Those trees over there are white spruce," Dad says, "They're good trees, not like these scraggly black spruce we've been seeing so far."

Then at 14-Mile we angle left onto a loop of the Richardson Trail, headed right for that stand of trees. "Now we're on the homestead," Dad says, and we then come alongside a beautiful stream. "That's 14-Mile Slough," he continues, "and they also call it 30-Mile Slough because if you go upriver from Fairbanks on the Chena River and off on Piledriver Slough, it's 30 miles to this stream."

This is as exciting as all heck. What a wonderful place, way out in the wilds like this. We have driven an hour and not seen another human, car or house, except of course for that old roadhouse at 11-Mile and that guard shack with the soldier back at 6-Mile. Now we are not even on the highway anymore, and we are driving on this neat old corduroy road alongside this really fantastic stream.

The pickup comes to a stop about half a mile in. Right alongside is the cabin, and on the other side, an open bank leads down to the slough. Boy, what a swell place.

Our new home is a genuine log cabin, built by Mom and Dad with their own hands, using no tools except an axe, a hammer and a crosscut saw. I can tell they are really proud of having built it themselves, "And it's all paid for too," says Mom, "though of course we don't really own the land yet."

One thing I notice right off is Dad's bear protector arrangement, an idea he got years ago from a cabin he'd seen in the mountain wilds of Colorado. Beneath each window is a two-by-four with about twenty big 60-penny spikes sticking out of it. Boy, nobody is going to lean their arms against those windows. "Best damn way to keep a bear out there is," Dad says.

We are soon inside having the first home-cooked meal we have sat down to as a family in two years, and it is cooked in the first home our family has ever owned. The cabin sure seems comfortable and cozy, like one of those old-time cabins the settlers built when they went out west, but of course this one is fancier because it has a board floor and a really good cookstove. Right now, because of the war, no factories are making regular kitchen stoves that burn wood, coal or corncobs, so Mom says she feels lucky to have found this one. She bought it and a steel double bed from a second-hand store even before she and Dad began to put the cabin up.

They talk about that while we eat, even though they'd written a lot about building the cabin in their letters. As soon as Dad had taken out the homestead claim he had begun work on the cabin, going out early in the morning right after getting off his baking shift at Zehnder Camp and coming back in time to get some sleep before work. He was on a seven-day week, so every day was like that. Dad started out by clearing off four feet of snow from the cabin site and then cutting down all the

nearby spruce trees that were big enough to make cabin logs. He moved the logs by scooting them through the snow, doing it the way he learned when he was young and had to move timbers on his job in the Kansas oil fields. He straddled the log facing backwards and locked his hands under it while lunging back hard. Unless the log was too heavy, it would move two or three feet, and then he could take a couple of steps backward and do it again. It was a big job because most of the nearby trees were smaller than Dad wanted to use, less than four inches. He was having to drag some logs as far as two hundred feet, and since he was building the cabin sixteen by twenty feet, some of the logs had to be more than twenty feet long.

Dad laid out his first round of logs on the still-frozen ground and went at it. All the cabins that he had seen around Fairbanks were made from peeled logs, but Dad found out that peeling was a lot of work, so he gave up on that. He claimed that the rough bark would help hold the moss that he planned to use for chinking between the logs. He notched the logs where they came together at the corners to maintain what he figured was enough spacing for moss. Where log ends came up against door and window frames, which he made out of rough two-by-fours, he used nails to hold the logs up so that the cracks between them would be the same as near the corners. Some people flattened the logs on the top and bottom, but that too was a lot of work, and Dad knew that if he did flatten the logs, it would take more of them to get the cabin up. As soon as the snow began to go, it was Mom's job to collect sacks of moss and stuff it in the cracks between the logs.

Because the military was taking all lumber available, Dad couldn't buy one-inch boards in Fairbanks and so he made the slightly sloping shed roof of the cabin out of small black-spruce poles covered with more moss. Soon after he and Mom got that finished, Dad was able to buy one-by-ten rough boards from the Independent Lumber sawmill in Fairbanks so he got enough for flooring and to put a board roof over the moss. He bought rolls of tin roofing to go on top, and that made Mom happy because she said the pole and moss roof had not kept out any water at all the one time it rained.

The cabin is nice and roomy inside. It has one door in the middle of the south wall. Inside and to the left is the double bed, and beyond it on the west wall a cot is set up for Lewie. Its head is up against a clothes closet in the northwest corner built by draping two bedspreads around a spruce pole bar hung from the ceiling by wires. Down under it is a bunch of Blazo boxes stacked up on their sides for shoes and all the other clothes that do not go on the hangers up on the bar. I see now what Mom meant last night at the airfield when she said, "Look at that pile of Blazo boxes over there. I sure wish I had them." I had to ask her what Blazo boxes were, and she told me that those particular boxes each had two square five-gallon cans of aviation fuel in them. "Everybody calls them Blazo boxes because Standard Oil Company sells Blazo that way too, and that's just a brand name for the unleaded gasoline people use in Coleman lamps and stoves. Blazo boxes are great because you can sit on them, use them for shelves and make all kinds of furniture out of them." Yeah, I can see what she was talking about because I can see about ten Blazo boxes right now.

My bed is on the north wall between the closet and the cookstove. The rest of Mom's kitchen area is on the east wall beneath and around the window that looks out over the old Richardson Trail and 14-Mile

Slough just beyond. Dad has used some of the boards to build a few shelves, but mostly the food and dishes are stored in shelving made out of Blazo boxes laid on their sides. The bucket for carrying drinking and wash water sits on the counter by the window, alongside Mom's dishpan. Then around the corner on the south wall is the table Dad built out of some of the two-by-fours and one-by-tens, and around it three chairs and a taller stump. As we sit down to eat Mom winks at me and tells Lewie that I probably want to sit on the stump but she'll give him first choice if he wants it. Dumb Lewie of course takes the stump and is happy to have it.

Dad has built an outhouse just across the old Richardson Trail from the cabin, just between the road and 14-Mile Slough. Alders and young spruces that have sprung up along the Trail block the view so the outhouse does not need a door. To get rid of dirty water used for washing dishes and other stuff Mom carries it to the door and heaves it out in the moss on the other side of the path going to the road. It will be Lewie's or my job to carry water for her from the stream and to get rid of garbage. We can do both these things on the same trip because Mom and Dad have started a garbage dump down on the bank of 14-Mile Slough, right below the outhouse and just upstream from where we get water. It's handy, because standing there in one place you can both dip the water and throw the garbage out.

Supper is over and Dad starts talking about what we were going to do. He is full of exciting plans. In order to prove up on the homestead, we will have to clear 20 acres of land and put it in cultivation. We will start on that right away, as soon as the new tractor arrives. Some of that clearing will provide firewood which we can sell. Dad says that almost all the houses in Fairbanks burn wood for cooking and heating, so you can sell all the wood you want. It is worth ten dollars a cord right here on the homestead, and seventeen dollars if delivered in town. Dad also has talked with the War Production Board about getting permission to buy a new sawmill, and he says there will be no trouble because lumber is so scarce in Fairbanks. You can sell lumber for $100 per thousand board feet.

Dad says that the homestead itself does not have all that many trees, so he has taken out a timber permit on the heavily forested school section that adjoins the homestead. It's lucky that the homestead is right there up against this township's school section because that square mile of trees is almost free for the taking. Dad just has to pay the Land Office twenty-five cents a cord for the smaller trees and about fifty cents a thousand board feet for the ones big enough to saw up into lumber. He figures we can get at least 2000 cords of firewood, plus a lot of big saw logs. Just the cordwood alone will bring in $20,000, and gosh knows how much we can make from the lumber. The money is going to be rolling in right away, because Dad already has orders for four cords of wood that he and I will get ready during the next few days. We will just go out and collect some of the dry firekill that is standing all over the place.

Then we will clear as much land as we can, maybe as much as twenty acres, and next spring we will plant that to potatoes and pea-oat hay. "Pea-oat hay ought to really grow well here," Dad says. "It's the best damn hog feed there is, and so next year we will get a boar and a sow and begin raising pigs."

And while we are doing that, we will build an addition on the cabin just as big as the original structure. The first cabin can then be the kitchen and Mom and Dad's bedroom, and the new one will be the living room and Lewie's and my bedroom.

I can see that we are going to have a busy, exciting fall. I haven't worked with Dad since I was a little kid back in Wyoming and

Colorado, when we had the gold claims and then the uranium mine. Of course I was too small then to do much, but now I am almost as big as a man, and with Dad, I'll be doing a man's work.

GRANDAD THE INVENTOR

EVENING, AUGUST 7, 1944

T'S BEEN A FUN DAY, and now tonight Zehnder Camp and Fairbanks seem like a world and a long time away. Dad has driven back there to go to work, Lewie is asleep, and Mom is across the room on her bed reading a detective magazine. As I lie here on my new bed I feel good, and my mind flits around over lots of things. For some reason it settles in on Grandad Davis, maybe just because he's really the reason all of us got to Alaska. He was a swell guy, so I think about him a lot. Even though he died when I was six, I got to know Grandad pretty well, and he was almost a famous man because of his inventing things like the Greeley Washer.

Grandad spent a lot of time with me and he taught me things like how to play checkers when we used to visit Grandma's big boarding house in LaSalle, Colorado. We called it Grandma's house because it really was hers. By feeding and boarding railroad workers, she made enough money for her and Grandad to live, and to make the $6 payment on the mortgage every month. She worked real hard most of the time, doing things like cooking meals, washing clothes and cleaning rooms. One thing that helped was that Grandma's meals were so good the Lions Club always met there each Wednesday noon for chicken dinner. They paid fifty cents apiece and Grandma said it took that extra money to make ends meet. She was happy to have them, too, because the Lions could go any place they wanted, and their meeting at Grandma's told everybody in town that she had the best food in LaSalle.

Grandad spent his time inventing things in his shop out back, sitting around on the front porch smoking his pipe, and playing checkers with me or talking to the boarders. The boarders and Grandad sat out on the porch a lot because Grandma would not let them smoke inside her boarding house. Her own mother had smoked a pipe, but Grandma never had. She said she thought it was a nasty habit; anybody who smoked was almost as bad as a man who chewed tobacco and spit it all over everything.

Playing checkers with Grandad was a lot of fun when I went there to visit, but being with him out in his inventing shed was the most fun of all. His inventing shed was really a greenhouse, so it had that pleasant half-wet, half-musty greenhouse smell. Out there, Grandad had all kinds of things he had built out of electrical wires, steel and wood. I could not understand what most of these things were, but they sure were neat. When I was little I wanted to be an inventor like Grandad. So one time after I went home from a visit to Grandma's house, I tried to invent something by nailing a bunch of boards together so that they stuck out in all different ways. It was a pretty neat invention, but, like a lot of Grandad's inventions, I never could figure out what it was for.

Over the radio I had heard about something called an electric chair that somebody was going to put a man named Bruno Richard Hauptman in because he had kidnapped and killed the Charles Lindbergh baby, so I decided to invent one of those. I found an old broken chair in the dump out back of our house, some big hinges and other pieces of iron and some electrical wires with a plug on one end. I nailed the hinges and other stuff to the seat and the arms of the chair, and I hooked up the wires. Mom saw me just as I was sitting in the chair and trying to plug it into an outlet for a test. That was about the only time she ever screamed at me that I can remember, and it was a heck of a scream. A man who I guess was working on something just outside the house heard Mom and came running in. He looked at my invention and said I was lucky to be alive, so Mom made me tear my electric chair apart, and promise not to mess around with electricity any more.

Grandad had done lots of other things besides inventing, too. When he was real young back in Kansas he was a politician. My dad said his dad had joined the Populist party—a group that Dad said was always trying to change things and make them better. Grandad got himself elected to the Kansas legislature in 1896. He made enemies right away because he was always fighting against big business. He wanted the state of Kansas to publish its own school books to avoid paying so much money to the book publishers. The book lobbyists told him to shut up or they would make sure he did not get re-elected. It didn't matter because right in the middle of his term, in 1897, Grandad went off to the Klondike in the gold rush. He stayed there one winter, floated down the Yukon River on a raft to St. Michael, and there took a boat back to Seattle. On the same boat was the famous writer Jack London, and he and Grandad got to be such good friends they wrote letters to each other up until Mr. London drank himself to death in 1916.

So that was why my family went to Alaska. Grandad did not get rich there, but he had a lot of swell adventures he told about, so as long as I can remember, Mom and Dad talked about going there someday when they could afford it. They never managed, but then the war came along and they got their way paid when they got jobs in Alaska.

When Grandad left Alaska he went back to Kansas and married my Grandma. Grandma did not like to talk about that because she was his first cousin. There were reasons people did not marry their cousins, I guess, things like having kids and especially grandkids who were not too smart or who had things like six toes. This time I don't think it hurt much because I'm perfectly normal, Lewie is only a little bit weird, and we both have five toes on each foot.

Like Grandpa, Grandma was really swell, and boy, was she tough, too. When she was a young girl she once walked behind a covered wagon all the way from eastern Missouri to western Kansas, just about the same time that dummy Custer got killed by those Indians on the Little Bighorn in Montana.

I liked to hear about things like that, and I liked the story about Grandma not knowing where she was born. It was either in Iowa or Missouri, that is for sure, because when they surveyed the boundary between the two states it came in one window and ran crossways right across the middle of her mother's bed. If the head of the bed was in Iowa, Grandma was born in Missouri. But it's also a fifty-fifty chance she came out the chute in Iowa.

Grandma's grandma must have been tough, too. She was born in Kentucky way back in 1804, and she had ten kids. Her husband and three of their boys went off to the California gold rush in 1850 and had all sorts of adventures. They made big money running cattle from Texas and Iowa to California to sell to the miners, fighting a lot of

Indians along the way. There were some neat stories about them. One I never got tired of hearing about is how on the way home to Missouri they got into a fight with Nicaraguan soldiers dressed up as bandits and got robbed of $80,000. One of the brothers carried $40,000 in his money belt and he was a real fighter. He killed three of those soldiers before they lopped his head off with a sword. Then they cut him down the middle to get his money belt off and took another $40,000 away from another brother and his dad without killing them. That was good for me because the brother that lived was Granddad's dad, and if he hadn't gotten away I wouldn't be here.

Another neat story was when Grandma was walking from Missouri to Kansas. The wagon train stopped by a river one night, and the Indians were camped on the other side. When one of the maidens came down to the river for water, a young man with the wagon train raped and strangled her. That made the other Indians mad as heck, and they came to the wagon train and said they would kill everybody unless they gave up the young man. So the wagon train let the Indians have him. Right there in front of them all, the Indians made a knife-cut around the man's stomach, peeled his skin up and tied it around his head so that he smothered to death. You don't often hear better Indian stories than that, especially from your grandma.

After Grandad married Grandma, he took out a homestead near Pueblo, Colorado, where it was so dry almost nothing would grow. Later he got himself a college degree and started teaching. He also had a shop for casting machinery, but the great Pueblo flood of 1924 destroyed that, so the family moved to Greeley, Colorado. Grandma ran a boarding house there, and Grandad invented things. One of them was the Greeley Washer.

There used to be sort of a naughty saying, "I ain't had so much fun since Ma caught her tit in the wringer." That sounds funny, but back in the days before Grandad's Greeley Washer, those things really happened. It hurt like crazy, too, I guess, because the first powered washing machines had wringers with rollers locked tight together. Women were always getting their hands and arms caught in the wringers, and they were so unfamiliar with machinery they would panic and not shut the washers off. Some of the women with big bosoms were afraid even to run the machines.

Grandad pondered about this, and he had noticed that women in pain tend to jump up and down a lot. This was the main idea behind

the Greeley Washer. It had a wringer with rolls held together by stand-ing on a foot pedal. Grandad figured that even if a woman forgot about the pedal, she would start jumping up and down if she got caught, and that would release the wringer. In 1928 Grandad started selling stock in the T. C. Davis company that would manufacture the Greeley Washer. His advertising brochure showed Grandma almost smiling as she stood with about half of one arm sticking right through the rolls of the washer.

It was a heck of an idea, but the T. C. Davis Company failed when Maytag brought out the quick-release wringer that washing machines have used ever since. That took the heart out of Grandad, and almost none of his later inventions were quite so good as the Greeley Washer. I say "almost" because Grandad invented another thing that was really swell. This was a kite made entirely out of steel, and it actually flew.

The day that Grandad invented the steel kite, he and I started out by playing checkers, but it didn't go very well. Since Grandad always beat me when playing regular checkers—and that was no fun—we had worked out a special deal. We would play three regular games, and of course Grandad would win those three. Then we would play a game called "give-away" where the idea was that the person who lost all his checkers first won the game. Grandad did not like this game because he said the idea of checkers was that you were supposed take away the other person's checkers. To give checkers away on purpose was just not right, said Grandad. Grandad disliked giving checkers away so much that he could not play give-away even well enough to beat me. I always won those games, and while I was winning Grandad sat frowning, wagging his head back and forth, and repeatedly saying, "It's not right." But he'd manage to complete the game, and then we would go back and play three more games of regular checkers. We did it over and over, day after day. Even though I never did beat Grandad even once at regular checkers, he taught me to play so well that I could beat almost everybody else except my own dad, 'cause Grandad had taught him too.

But on the day that Grandad invented the steel kite, we played only three games of regular checkers. As usual, Grandad won those games, and then we began playing give-away. I set him up real fast so that he had to take about five of my checkers in one move, and all of a sudden while he was jumping and taking my checkers Grandad got awfully red in the face, and his hands and his head started shaking. "This game's not right. I won't play any more," he said, pouting like a little kid. He seemed awfully sad, so we put the checkers away and I went outside to play.

The wind was blowing hard enough to raise little whirls of dust and bounce tumbleweeds across the big open space across from Grandma's house, between there and the railroad tracks. That gave me the idea to build a kite. I was going to make it out of brown wrapping paper glued with flour paste onto strings stretched across the ends of two crossed sticks tied together. I asked Grandad to help because my kites were not very good unless Mom or somebody else worked on them too.

At first, Grandad said no, but then I think he was feeling badly about getting mad over the checkers. Then as I told him how I built a kite he said, "I've got a better idea. I'm going to make you a real kite." We went out to Grandad's inventing shop where I watched him build what he called a box kite, using a pair of shears and a soldering torch to cut and glue together thin sheets of tin and light steel rods. I figured Grandad did not know much about kites if he was making one out of metal, and I told him so, and that the kite he was building could not fly. That irritated him some, but he got over that and told me to wait and see.

By the time Grandad got finished I was getting excited about seeing if his kite could really fly. I was awfully disappointed when he said we would have to wait until the next day because he needed to go to the store to buy some lighter string than he had in his shop. "Aw heck," I said, "let's try it with the heavy string. It should work." Grandad said no, but I kept insisting until he started shaking again. His shoulders sagged and looked sad, sort of like a beaten puppy.

"Oh OK," he finally said, "but it won't work, and the wind is too strong. We should wait until tomorrow." Grandad got his roll of heavy twine and hooked the metal kite to it. We went out on the street beside Grandma's house where Grandad laid the kite on the ground and then ran just a little ways while holding the string. The wind was blowing really hard, and suddenly that steel kite left the ground and flew like a scared duck. It climbed steeply up above the street until it was high as the top of a tree. Then suddenly the kite plunged straight down like a rock and mashed itself flat in the middle of the street.

For a moment all was quiet and unmoving—even the wind had stopped blowing—as Grandad and I stared at the flattened kite. "I told you it wouldn't work," he said, and as I looked at him he seemed especially sad and small, like he was shrinking away from the inside of his clothes. He turned and walked slowly into Grandma's house.

I felt terrible because I knew that I should not have insisted on flying the kite when Grandad didn't want to. This was about the first time any adult had given in to me like that, and somehow that made things even worse. It was hard to forget what happened because just a few days later Grandad collapsed, and an ambulance took him up to the hospital in Greeley where I had been born. Because his heart was going bad and he was bleeding a lot inside, Grandad was dying, Dad told me. Grandad would be gone in a few hours, and he wanted to say good-bye to me.

Dad almost pushed me into the room, and then he stayed outside the open door. There in the brightly lit white room, lying on a bright white bed, was Grandad. The whiteness everywhere stunned me because I expected that since Grandad was bleeding so much that bright red blood ought to be gushing from his nose and mouth, and that it would be all over everywhere. But there was no blood at all, and the other thing that surprised me was that Grandad was smiling kindly at me. How could he smile like that when he knew he was dying? Our conversation was short.

"I want you to be a good boy, Neil."

"I will, Grandad."

"Good-bye, Neil"

"Good-bye, Grandad," and I left the room determined to always be a good boy forever.

That happened a long time ago, and in a place a long way from Alaska, but even as I drift off to sleep this first night on the homestead I feel like Grandad is here with me. I still see those little hairs sticking out of Grandad's nostrils and the glint in his eyes each time he leans over the board to jump one of my checkers.

EXPLORING

AUGUST 1944

THE FIRST FEW DAYS we have on the homestead are fun for Lewie and me because everything is so different from what we've seen before. We've got the dogs here now, and it's all new for them, too. Since they were born at Zhender Camp and grew up there, they've never been out in the woods before. It's funny watching them poke their noses into the moss and then jump backwards when something scares them.

One of the first things we do is go out exploring to find out what is here. It's slow because the homestead is so flat and covered with brush and trees that in most places you can't see very far. Back in Iowa, or in Colorado or Wyoming, it would be easy because all you'd have to do is go up on a hill or a mountain and you could see out everywhere, maybe for miles.

Lewie and I work our way out from the cabin like a spider building out his web from its center, first running out in a couple of directions with long stringers and then filling in the net later. Our first stringers go out along the Old Richardson Trail to its 14-Mile and 15-Mile connections with the Alcan. The Trail is easy walking and we can see out through the alder and willow bushes or the stands of spruce as much as fifty feet or more. Our other pair of stringers are on the game trails running up and down the near bank of 14-Mile Slough. Game trails are fun because they wind in and out, and you sort of ooze along them without thinking where you have to go next, just like you imagine a fox, a wolf or a moose might do. The trail along 14-Mile Slough runs up close to the water where the bank is cut steep so you can look right down into the pools and see the grayling resting in the deep water. Then the trail usually scoots off into the spruce timber away from the stream on the shallow banks because the willows and alders out there are tougher to get through. It doesn't take Lewie and me long to figure out how the animals like to move, so if we foul up and lose the trail we know how to get back on real quick.

Little by little, Lewie and I roam out in other directions from the cabin, but here there are no trails and we have to keep remembering what the trees and bushes look like and how they fit in with the low mossy swales and humps formed where streams used to flow. These wind around some, but they mostly run in directions close enough to 14-Mile Slough to help when you think you're almost lost. Of course Lewie and I never really get lost, we just sometimes are not quite sure which direction to go.

Part of the time Lewie and I take out with us the .22 rifle Dad bought for shooting grouse. The grouse are all over the place, and they sure are dumb. If you scare them up they just walk or fly off a few feet, so shooting grouse is about like shooting pigeons in a barn. Rabbits are something else, though. When you see them they are moving so fast you could never hope to shoot one. Once in a while we see or hear a moose on the road or out in the bushes, and they leave lots of tracks and piles of what Mom calls moose nuts lying around. The moose are pretty skittish so they don't hang around much. We even see bear droppings once in a while but no bears yet, nor any of the caribou or wolves, foxes and lynx that Dad says come around here sometimes.

One thing that is always around is mosquitoes, just about all the time, and every time you step out into the moss. Mom says that they were a lot worse earlier in the summer and that a big help now is the new Formula 612 mosquito dope. It's something the Army has developed, and Mom has been able to buy some. She and everybody else calls it "Six-Twelve."

This noon, Lewie rubbed a whole bunch of Six-Twelve on his face and hands before lunch, and then while he was eating his bread and jelly, he tried to get funny by sticking the jelly side to his chin before eating it. The dumb kid nearly choked to death when he tasted all that Six-Twelve on his bread. Mom just laughed and said, "You should have thought that through a little better, Lewie." I'd heard that remark from Mom about thinking things through a long time ago, and I still believe it's about the best lesson I ever learned.

It's funny how kids learn things. I'm not sure adults always understand how it goes. Some things are real hard to learn and take so much time maybe you never do learn them. Other things come so fast and easy that you wonder why you didn't learn it sooner.

That thing I learned from Mom about thinking things through was kind of a one-two lesson. The first part of the lesson came one morning when we were living at Grandma's house in LaSalle while Mom and Dad ran a cafe about a block away during the summer. Dad was teaching school but school was out for the summer, and since Dad couldn't find another job he had borrowed some money to start up the cafe.

I was just over three years old that morning when Mom took me to the cafe with her. I sat around for a while watching her work, and then asked if I could help. Mom said I could fill the salt shakers setting on the counter. I filled one or two and then came to one that was about half-full, so I did not put salt in it. Mom jumped me about that, and I said that this one didn't need any. "Now," she said, "What is the purpose of a salt shaker?"

"It's to get salt out of."

"That's right. Now think it through. A salt shaker on the counter with no salt in it is worthless. You must make sure the shaker always has salt if it is to do any good. Think it through."

Her words struck me hard. The idea they carried jabbed into my mind like none ever had before, as if Jesus or God or somebody like that had spoken to me. Yes, I suddenly realized, this is what it's all about! You do have to think it through—everything that you do.

The idea got strengthened in my mind a short time later when we were back in Hanna, Wyoming, and while that was happening I learned a good lesson about Mom, too. It was that she was a real calm person, and you couldn't put much of anything over on her.

That night, she was giving me a bath in the big tub she had set up near the kitchen stove. She was washing my back when I got an urge to do a number-two. What the heck, why not, I thought, I bet that sure will surprise Mom, and make her holler, too. I was watching Mom's face real close when this great big turd came floating up out of the soapy water.

Mom didn't say a word or even bat an eye; she just kept right on washing me, swirling the water around in a special way that made the turd keep rubbing up against my chest. It was terrible, and I was wishing I had thought things through better before I let that turd in my bathtub. I knew then that I was never going to do that again, and I learned right then that there was no point in trying to agitate Mom just for the fun of it.

As young as I was, I was already seeing that Mom was not the kind of mother like some I'd run into who swatted their kids or yelled at them when they did something wrong. Instead, Mom had a special quiet way about her that made a kid know that when he did something nasty he could expect it to turn around and bite him. Having a mom like that took a lot of the fun out of doing things I knew I shouldn't.

Lewie and I have been pretty lucky with our moms: Mom and Aunt Phena, who is like a second mom since we've lived with her so much in Iowa. Aunt Phena is like Mom in that she is not one to swat or holler, but Aunt Phena is different; when you do wrong things she preaches and pouts, and of course you can ignore that. It is like Aunt Phena is willing to take over your conscience, but Mom makes you deal with it yourself.

I guess the fill-the-salt-shaker-and-don't-let-turds-in-your-bathtub lesson was just about the all-around best one I ever learned when I was young. Of course you don't always do it, but if you will just pause a moment when you go to do something and think it through, you can sometimes save yourself a lot of trouble. Kids like Lewie are worst about this. They will do all sorts of dumb things like getting Six-Twelve in their mouths because they tend not to think ahead enough. But you see some adults that are like that too, and it makes you wonder if some people ever really grow up. Every time I see a salt shaker without much salt in it, I think about that day in Mom's cafe, and that makes me think about the turd in the tub, too. It reminds me that a job only partly done is not worth anything, and that it's best not to do some jobs at all.

INTO THE WOODS WITH DAD

FALL 1944

As Lewie and I spend these first few days getting familiar with those parts of the homestead easy to walk over, I keep hoping that the tractor will come in so we can do some real work. Earlier in the summer Dad wrote to us in Iowa saying that he was going to get a tractor so we could farm the homestead, and he asked what kind to buy. His letters like that one were addressed to me because he knew it made me feel good to be asked important questions.

Uncle Irwin uses an Allis-Chalmers on his farm, a rubber-tired tractor with the front wheels close together so that they fit between the corn rows. Uncle Irwin and I talked about it, and I wrote back to Dad that we recommended he get an Allis-Chalmers, too. Instead, Dad has ordered a new International Harvester tractor called a Farmall H. His decision makes me wonder if Dad really knows what he is doing, going against our advice like that. Of course, I am happy that he is getting a tractor, any tractor, because I sure know how to drive one and am looking forward to it. I can drive a team of horses or mules and a car too, I tell Dad. That's what comes from living on a farm.

Actually, I have not driven Uncle Irwin's tractor very much, and a car only once and never on an actual road, but Dad does not need to know that. Changing parents like I have just done is a good deal. Mom and Dad do not know about any dumb things that I might have done, and it is easy to convince them that I am a man of experience about a lot of things, things like driving tractors and cars.

I am glad that they did not know about the dumb thing I did just a week before leaving Iowa. I forgot to loosen the reins that were hooked tight to the mouth of Uncle Irwin's left mule. He tied the reins tight

37

like that when he left the mules standing by themselves. That way, if they tried to move, they would just go around in a circle. The mules were hitched to a big harrow when I said "Giddup." Away they went in a circle so tight it tipped the harrow upside down and badly bent all its adjustment handles. That is real embarrassing to a person who knows as much about farming as I do.

This past year I've pretty much settled in on the idea of becoming a farmer, and even though I am now in Alaska where I can do all sorts of things, I am still planning to be one. During our exploring, Lewie and I have found a dirt bank pushed up to make a drainage ditch that runs more than a quarter mile all the way from the Alcan over to and under the Richardson Trail and into 14-Mile Slough. This bank is steep and it faces south, so I think it will make a good garden. Besides, it is about the only part of our 160-acre homestead that is not covered by thick moss. On our first trip to town I buy some seeds and plant them in that bank. Since it is already mid-August, I realize that the pumpkins might not make it, but the lettuce, radishes and other things ought to do swell. Back in Iowa, you can plant stuff like that almost all summer long. What I need is a little cow manure to mix in, but of course we don't have any, so I gather up a whole bunch of moose turds that are lying out on the Richardson Trail.

Finally, the big day is here, and we are off to town this morning to get the new tractor. As we come down to the end of Cushman Street and go up over the bridge across the Chena River, we can see the tractor sitting there out in front of Samson Hardware. That's next to the International Harvester place, which is right at the end of the Alaska Railroad's track. The tractor came in on the train from Seward, at the other end of the railroad, and it got there by ship from Seattle.

As soon as I see it, I think that except for its pretty red color, the tractor looks kind of disappointing. Of course I guess I am prepared to be critical. Dad should have got an orange Allis-Chalmers like I recommended. As we drive up, several people are standing around looking at the tractor, maybe because International Harvester mostly sells caterpillar-type tractors in Fairbanks, and wheeled tractors are rare things. New machines of any kind are not available to just anybody because of the war, and I suppose only a farmer or a homesteader can buy a wheel tractor like the Farmall H.

One thing that disturbs me right away about the H is the arrangement of its wheels. They are made of steel, and the front wheels are set

38

way out wide, just like the back wheels. How can you farm a homestead with a thing like that? Nor does the tractor look like it will have any traction because those big wide rear wheels are perfectly smooth.

But it turns out that the tractor comes with a set of V-shaped steel lugs about six inches long that are to be bolted to the rims of the rear wheels. The lugs have been left off so they will not cut up the ships and the railroad cars during shipment. I remember now about those signs I have seen beside the cement roads back in Iowa that say "No Lugs." Dad says we will wait until we get the tractor out to the homestead before putting the lugs on. That makes sense because the tractor does have to go up over the Chena bridge and down the pavement on Cushman Street before getting onto gravel road.

On the way into Fairbanks I mentioned to Dad that maybe I should be the one to drive the tractor home. As we stood around the tractor I suggested the idea several more times, but I saw that Dad was getting irritated with me, so I shut up. Maybe he was just flustered and out of sorts because of the people gathered around watching him and the International Harvester man try to get the tractor started. I think they used too much choke and were flooding it, but they finally got it running. Then as Dad got up on it and practiced with the gears, it looked to me like he had never driven a tractor before. I know I can do better—and that Dad would have been smarter if he had bought an Allis-Chalmers on rubber tires.

Finally we're off, with Dad on the tractor and Mom driving behind in the pickup with Lewie and me. Dad heads up the long metal ramp of the bridge and gets almost to the level part before the H spins out. Those smooth steel wheels just do not have any traction on that ramp. Dad is getting really flustered now, and he backs the H into the guard rail as he tries it again. We get out of the pickup and go over. "Maybe if we all push it will help," Mom suggests. That just makes Dad mad; I guess the idea of people watching him drive up the bridge on a tractor being pushed by a woman and two boys is too much for him.

"Goddamn tractor is no good. It ought to go up that bridge by itself," he retorts. I am not about to say anything, but I agree. Of course if Dad had bought an Allis-Chalmers on rubber he wouldn't be having this problem. But I do think Dad is acting a little childish, because you can't expect a tractor without lugs to have much traction. I suggest that we go over to the N. C. Store and get some rope and wrap it around the wheels like tire chains, but that seems to make Dad even madder. He fumes and fusses awhile, and finally backs the tractor down and gets it started up a part of the steel ramp that is not so slick, and he makes it onto the level part of the bridge.

Dad really should have thought it through more, and he should have accepted my idea of using rope, because the steel ramp on the south end of the bridge is about twice as steep as the one on the north end, and a heck of a lot smoother. Dad and the H make a real spectacular entrance into the intersection of Cushman Street and First Avenue, with a lot of people watching. The H starts sliding sideways before it is halfway down the ramp, and it careens over into the other traffic lane and comes to rest against the sidewalk on the far side of the street. Dad's face is almost as red as the paint on the Farmall H.

Dad backs up, gets into his proper lane and heads down Cushman Street, moving very slowly because it is a rough ride on those steel wheels. He would be holding up a lot of traffic if there were any, but as it is, the H is one of the few vehicles on the street. It takes Dad nearly an hour to get out to Big Bend, and he still has thirteen miles to go. Mom and Dad abandon the plan for the pickup to run along behind the H, so we drive on. Dad and the H arrive at the homestead in time for a late supper.

The next morning Dad and I bolt the lugs onto the H's big rear wheels, and we also build a choker out of a piece of cable, a steel hook and some cable clamps so we can hook onto logs and other things with the H. Dad lets me do the driving and we quickly discover that it will go anywhere. The rear wheels are so wide that even if the front wheels sink down into the mossy wet places, that H churns right on through, even pulling a load.

I'm having a heck of a good time driving the Farmall H and I'm surprised that it turns out to be such a wonderful machine. It's for sure no rubber-tired tractor could do what the H can. Those wide-set front wheels are great, too. A tractor with narrow-set front wheels can tip over sideways real easy, but that H is rock-steady on any kind of slope. I'm starting to think that Dad has done the right thing after all, because that H sure could drag Uncle Irwin's Allis-Chalmers all over Alaska.

Now that we have the tractor, our next job is to build a go-devil—Dad's name for a log sled, and what some people call a stone boat—to carry the firewood and the trees behind the Farmall H. "Best damn way to move heavy things around," Dad says, "better than a wagon

because it's low and easy to load; we always used go-devils in the oil fields." So we cut down some trees and use them to build the sled. While we are doing that, Dad gets to thinking about how much work it is to cut trees, and we do have to cut a lot of them to build the new addition on the cabin, and also to make up the 2000 cords of firewood he plans to sell during the next year or so. Being a sort of inventor like his father, Dad figures out a way to make the Farmall H do most of the work for us. As we work on the go-devil he sketches up some plans and then delivers them to the Northern Commercial Company's machine shop in Fairbanks.

In the meantime, to fill the order Dad has for four cords of firewood, we go out after fire-kill, that being the only dry wood available to sell. Sometimes you can just push on a fire-killed tree and it falls right over. Others you have to cut with an axe. Most of these dead trees are only about two or three inches in diameter, so we are beginning to see that it sure is going to take a bunch of them to make four cords. Before we have collected even one cord, we know we are not going to get rich real quick selling this stuff. We have to take all the dead trees off of about five acres of the homestead just to get two cords. Only some parts of the homestead have fire-kill, so Dad soon realizes that we'd best just try for the four cords and not take any more orders for dry wood to be delivered this fall. Whatever other fire-kill we might bring in can go into Mom's kitchen stove.

By the time we get the four cords of fire-kill collected, the N.C. machine shop in Fairbanks has completed the parts for Dad's new invention that will allow the Farmall H to make tree-cutting easy. While we are bolting the machine together, Dad talks about the possibility of getting a patent. The device consists of a vertical axle that hangs by a metal frame on the front of the H, and has a three-foot diameter buzz saw on its lower end, about eight inches off the ground. A twisted 6-inch flat belt delivers power from the power-takeoff pulley on the side of the H to another pulley mounted on the upper end of the vertical axle. We get it all assembled, and crank up the H. Boy, that buzz saw really screams. It looks wicked, too, like it is just begging to chop your leg off. Dad warns me to stay well away from the front of the tractor, but he really doesn't have to tell me that.

Dad should have thought this through more than he did. The first problem is to get that buzz saw up against the tree you want to cut without hitting anything else. Dad's initial attempt throws moss and brush all over the place. Next, he runs into a downed log, stopping the saw, but not before the drive belt slips off and into the saw's sharp teeth. An hour passes before we have the four belt pieces patched back into a continuous loop.

The first tree actually cut falls over on the H, not causing any damage because it is not a big tree. That incident gives Dad the idea of carrying what he calls a pike pole on the tractor so he can push on a tree. The pike pole is just a piece of fire-kill about fifteen feet long with a nail sticking out the end. Dad drives at the next tree holding the pike pole held under his arm. With that pole angled up over the front of the H, he looks like one of King Arthur's knights jousting aboard a red horse on wheels. This next tree is a lot bigger than the first one, more than a foot in diameter. As planned, the pike pole and the buzz saw hit at the same time, but just then, one of the H's front wheels falls into a little hole. Dad jerks backward in his seat, and the saw chews into the tree about halfway through before smoke boils out and the blade sticks tight.

Dad and I both recognize the main problem: his invention is going to work only if every tree has a nice smooth cement pad around its base to keep the tractor level—and if there is a better way to keep the trees from falling on the tractor. We get the saw unstuck and drive back to the cabin where we reluctantly disassemble the rig. We know it is going to be axes and hand saws all the way from now on, and I try to envision how many trees it is going to take to get 2000 cords of firewood.

This business of cutting trees is a lot of work, for sure, and I'll be glad when we can get more directly into farming. That is something I really want to do. When I was young and around Grandad a lot, I wanted to be an inventor when I grew up. I'd also thought about maybe being a schoolteacher too, because Mom and Dad were schoolteachers and so were Aunt Phena and Uncle Irwin. Then when Dad quit teaching school and went into mining I thought I might become a miner. That is the way it goes with young kids. From reading the Buck Rogers comic strip in the Sunday paper, some us even talked about being space pilots when we grew up. We knew of course that it was just a dream because Buck Rogers was not a real person, there really weren't any space ships, and there never would be. Still, when we were little, we had a lot of fun holding spark plugs in our hands and flying them around in mock fights like they were real space ships.

Farming, though, is something you can really do. All those other things I'd thought about being when I grew up were just passing kid ideas—like wanting to be a fireman when you saw a fire truck go by, or wanting to be a policeman when you saw one in his uniform. I know that in farming I have really settled on something permanent. I learned a lot about it in Iowa, and now that we have the homestead to farm, it is a sure thing.

Dad is enthusiastic, too, and he thinks he has an idea that will revolutionize farming in Alaska. He says that the people who are into farming near Fairbanks mostly just raise things like potatoes and cabbages. They have not figured out yet that the real way to make money is to grow what Dad calls pea-oat hay and feed it to hogs. "Pea-oat hay is the best damn hog feed there is," he says, "and I'm sure it will grow well here. Soon as we get enough land cleared we'll plant it to pea-oat hay. Then we'll get a sow and a boar and begin raising hogs."

That sounds darned exciting to me, and I am eager to get started. Along with the new tractor, Dad has bought a plow. Before it can be used, however, we have to clear the land. Dad has a scheme for doing this using his newest invention, a brush-cutting machine. He thinks it will work so well that other homesteaders will want to hire us to clear their land, too. We can make some extra money that way.

Dad draws up the design for the brush-cutter and gives it to the N.C. machine shop. We bring it home in the back of the pickup a few days later. And it's so heavy the two of us can barely pick it up. The brush-cutter looks like one of those paddle wheels you see on the back end of a river boat. The paddles are made of the steel cutting blades used on road graders, each ground to razor sharpness. The idea is to drag the cutter behind the tractor, and when the device rolls along over the brush it will chop the stuff up in little short pieces that can be plowed under. It's like using a disc to cut up straw and cornstalks the way they do back in Iowa.

Dad picks out a spot of about five acres near the cabin. It is mostly covered with alder and willow bushes, but it has quite a few trees too big to drive the tractor over. At first we try to get rid of the trees by pulling on them with a cable attached to the Farmall. No bigger than these trees are, Dad says, we ought to be able to pop their tap roots right up out of the ground. He's seen people do that back in farming country using just a team of horses. We find out right away that the H has no trouble tipping the trees over because none of them have any tap roots like trees do back in the States where the ground is warm. Instead, each tree has a big shallow root system that lies mostly in the moss atop the ground, so when the tree tips over, huge blocks of roots and moss come up. Some of these tangles are 20 feet across, and all interlocked with the roots of other trees and bushes. We can't figure out what to do with them. Dad decides that we'd better leave all that moss and roots there for the plow to turn under, so we cut all the trees by hand.

Dad has one of his worst temper tantrums ever when we hook the brush cutter up for its first try. It goes along behind the H just fine, rolling along like it is supposed to. However, those sharp blades have no effect on the brush at all. They just ride up over the top of it, making little marks in the bark here and there. Dad is really disgusted because he has run up a bill of more than $300 to have the thing made, and I bet this is another of those things Dad wishes he had thought through a little better. We disassemble the brush cutter and bolt the blades flat onto the bottom of a big V-drag we build. Sometimes when this drag goes between two clumps of alder brush just right it will pop one of them out of the ground. But it works so poorly that we end up cutting the brush by hand.

The new plow also is a disappointment. It bites down into the moss and turns it over, but the moss flops right back where it has been. We never can get a furrow opened up so that moss from the next cut will have a place to go. Also, the moss is so thick in some places that the plow will not even cut through it. But Dad is not about to give up. He has heard that a farmer in the hills north of Fairbanks, a man named Henry Grutberger, has something called a "breaking plow" which Dad thinks will work a lot better, so one day we drive out to look at it. The man who told Dad about it said that Mr. Grutberger is kind of odd and highly religious, but if Dad goes about it right he probably can rent the plow for a few days. Dad is not into religion much; just the opposite really, and he is always saying that you can never trust anybody who seems to be overly religious.

As Dad drives the pickup off the Steese Highway onto Mr. Grutberger's farm we see several cars parked there and a whole bunch of men, women and children digging up potatoes in a field. Most of them are picking up the potatoes by hand after they have been turned up with a walking plow pulled by a team of horses. Only three rows are turned up, so it looks like they have just started the work. Dad stops the pickup and we go over to see which one is Mr. Grutberger.

"Henry's sick, and he's in bed over at his house there," a man says, nodding over to a little A-frame shack on the far side the field, "We're members of his church come to dig his potatoes for him. Just a minute, I'll take you over to see him; I need to show Henry some of these potatoes."

The man picks up a bucket of potatoes and we three walk over to the A-frame, going past a lot of junky-looking farming equipment, except for one big plow on wheels that looks almost new. It is the breaking plow, for sure. "Henry's been sick in bed most of two weeks now, and he lives alone," the man tells us. This is a warning, I realize when we go into the A-frame behind him. The A-frame is just a shack partly dug into the ground; the place is a mess and it does not smell very good, either. Over in one corner on his bed is Mr. Grutberger, a skinny old man in a dirty pair of longjohns, and mostly covered up with an army blanket. He raises up on one elbow and stares at us out of watery blue eyes that do not seem to focus very well.

"God bless you all, brothers, for helping a friend in need to harvest his crop. Oh the Lord does provide," Mr. Grutberger calls out and then falls back on his pillow.

"Henry," the man with us says gently, "I brought in some of your potatoes to show you," and he holds the bucket near Mr. Grutberger's bed. The old man stares down into the bucket, then reaches in to pick up a scabby, misshapen potato not much bigger than an egg. Mr. Grutberger rolls it around in his fingers, peering at it.

"It's not a very good crop is it, Wilbur?" he says.

"No it's not, Henry," says our guide.

Mr. Grutberger drops the potato into the bucket then leans back on both elbows and stares at nothing with a sort of thoughtful look on his face. "You know," he says, and his voice sounds like he is giving us a sermon, "A man works hard in his partnership with God to till the soil and bring forth the bounty of the land. A man provides the labor and the seed, and the good Lord makes things grow. I have done my best and I think that if this is all the better God can do for me, He can stick those potatoes right up His ass."

I am standing a little behind Dad and I can see his shoulders hunch up and his head bow. "We'll come back later," he mumbles, and as he turns and leads me out the door I can see that Dad is about to explode. He bursts out laughing when we get outside, and he giggles to himself most of the way back to town. "Just like old Ira Emerson," he snorts, and starts laughing again when we got home and he tells Mom about it. We know what he means because the Ira Emerson story is one of Dad's favorites about religious people.

Ira Emerson was a wheat farmer back in Kansas, a member of the same threshing run as Granddad Davis and who was always spouting religion when working with other men. That particular fall, the run's farmers had everyone's wheat in except Ira Emerson's, and they were just starting on it when a terrible hailstorm began. The hailstones were so big that everybody crawled under a wagon for protection. Ira Emerson lay there watching the hail destroy his crop and then he leaned out from the wagon and looked up saying, "Lord, is this the right way to treat your loving children?" Just then a golf-ball-size hailstone hit him right on the end of his nose. Ira shook his fist at the sky and yelled, "Why, you old Son-Of-A-Bitch!"

The next day we go back and get Henry Grutberger's breaking plow, and it works pretty well. It rides on wheels and has such a wide blade that the moss turns over and stays put, at least most of the time. We are surprised to find that in some places the ground is still frozen just below the moss, even though it is now the fall of the year. Funny, some of the things you run into. Dad figures it will be OK, though. Once the moss is broken up, the ground will thaw fine, and it will grow a great crop of pea-oat hay next year.

Even with Mr. Grutberger's big breaking plow, the work goes slowly. We go at it more than a week, and we get only about three acres cleared and plowed up. Dad says we are running out of time and so we will wait until spring to do more. In order to prove up on the homestead we will have to get at least twenty acres planted and inspected.

I am beginning to see that this farming in Alaska is a lot like cutting cordwood to sell. You can make a lot of money doing these things, but almost everything takes more time and is harder work than you expect when you start out.

But so's we can feel like we're getting into farming more this fall, Dad says that when he takes the breaking plow back he is going to try to buy six laying hens and some chicken feed from Mr. Grutberger. I'm not real enthusiastic because chickens are just about my least favorite farm animal. What's worse, Dad's talking about chickens reminds me of what happened with Mrs. Wilson's chickens in Seattle last month when Lewie and I were on our way to Alaska. It's the kind of thing I'd rather forget.

MRS. WILSON'S CHICKENS

EARLY AUGUST 1944

WHEN LEWIE AND I GOT TO SEATTLE we had been on the train for three days and nights, all the way from Perry, Iowa. Every seat was filled, mostly with soldiers and sailors, so there was no room to move around. Some of them had been traveling even longer than us and so the train everywhere had that real thick sweaty, woolly, close smell that comes from a lot of people crowded together in a warm place. It's even worse if people are excited like everybody was when we approached Seattle, where most of the soldiers and sailors were getting on ships to go fight the Japs. Riding on this train with all those men in uniform made me feel closer to the war than I ever had before, even though we were hearing a lot about it over the radio, especially since D-Day, when things began going good for the Allies. It was pretty exciting, and instead of being just twelve I was wishing I was old enough to be in the army or navy like all these guys on the train so I could fight in the war and be a hero. But it sure had been a long trip, and Lewie and I were really glad when the train finally rolled into King Street Station.

Mr. Wilson, the Pan American Airways ticket agent in Seattle, was there to meet us. I was hoping he would take us to the airport so we could fly to Alaska right away, but that's not the way it worked out at all. Instead, Mr. Wilson drove us to his house which was down south of Seattle on Highway 99.

Mr. Wilson was not much for talking, but he said we might have to stay in Seattle several days because the weather was too bad for flying, and it might not change. The clouds and fog were so thick as we drove along that we saw almost nothing, but we did see one neat

49

thing. As we went up a long hill that goes past what Mr. Wilson said was the Boeing plant, Lewie and I saw that the airplane factory was all covered up with netting of some sort, and on top of that were a whole bunch of fake trees and houses. Mr. Wilson told us it was camouflage so that the Japs couldn't find the place when they came to bomb it. This was about the most interesting thing we'd seen since we left Iowa.

A few miles farther south we came to the Wilsons' house, a little place right alongside the highway with a small yard and a garage out back. Mr. Wilson told us his wife kept chickens in the garage. "Until the rationing is over," he said, "the car can stay on the road." After we met Mrs. Wilson and her two little kids, I took Lewie out in the yard and chased him around awhile and wrestled with him. You have to do this, what Grandma Davis calls "blowing the stink off him," to Lewie almost every day or else he drives everybody nuts. He is eight years old, but not much bigger than Mrs. Wilson's five-year-old girl Winifred. What he lacks for in size, though, he makes up for with activity. He can be an awful pest.

After several days at the Wilsons' I was getting pretty bored because not much happened. Mr. Wilson went off to work every day before we got up, so we didn't see him until supper time or even later because he worked so much. By the time Lewie and I got up, Mrs. Wilson was usually sitting at the kitchen table having coffee while her three-year-old boy Sammy tugged at her housecoat, jabbering or crying. Just to myself, I called him Sammy the Screamer. Winifred was Winny the Whiner in my mind, although I had to admit that she was not much worse than any other little girl. By and large, I thought Mrs. Wilson had two fairly nasty little kids, and that this is why she seemed so flighty and nervous. She was not a bad sort, and aside from always looking frazzled, Mrs. Wilson acted like she did not know much about a lot of things. She didn't know about farming and animals, that's for sure. Not like me anyway. Mrs. Wilson was polite, but as each day passed I more and more got the feeling that she was going to be happier to see us leave than she was to have us come to stay at her house. I wanted to leave, too, but Mr. Wilson sure was right about the weather not changing. Even if it wasn't raining, the clouds were so low you couldn't see anything.

After breakfast, if it wasn't raining, we'd usually send Lewie and Winny the Whiner out to play, although as the days went by, Mrs. Wilson or I tended more to go out to keep an eye on them. The first day, Lewie taught Winny how to make mudpies, and Mrs. Wilson was not happy when she saw the results. The thing that bothered her more than all the dirty clothes was that Lewie and Winny had tried to feed the pies to Sammy the Screamer, and he had thrown up all over himself.

A day or two after that, I had to pull Winny from a tree that Lewie had helped her climb, and the next day, we heard Winny crying because Lewie had tied her arms and ankles around the tree with a rope. Lewie also taught Winny to stand on her head. Mrs. Wilson made Winny go inside right away after she walked around the corner of the house and saw Winny with her dress over her head and the rest of her almost bare body sticking straight up in the air, partly supported by Lewie's hands on her ankles. Lewie had a big grin on his face.

I tried to make it easier for Mrs. Wilson by helping keep an eye on the kids, by mowing her lawn, and by telling her stories. I had a lot of good stories to tell her because Mrs. Wilson had never lived outside the Seattle area, and she didn't know near as much about the world as me. She had a hard time believing that in my twelve years I had lived all the places I have and have done so many things. She listened skeptically when I told her things like about the pet bear named Bear we used to have in Colorado, about seeing the rings of stones the Indians had used to hold their tents down when we went to our gold mine in Wyoming, and about how big the rattlesnakes were there. I told her about seeing the woman in the circus who wrote beautiful penmanship with her toes because she was born without arms, about the time Lewie fell twenty feet down a coal chute onto a steel spike and didn't get hurt, about the time he fell over backwards off a chair and bit his tongue off, and how the doctors had sewn it back on perfectly. I keep telling her lots of things like that, about things that had happened in Colorado, Wyoming, Utah, West Virginia, Ohio, Chicago and Iowa. I'm not sure that Mrs. Wilson really believed the pet bear story, even though I showed her the scar on Lewie's arm where Bear bit him and the other one in the corner of his eye where Bear clawed him. That was too bad because Dad killed Bear for doing that, and he was about the most fun thing we had to play with when we lived up on the mountain in Colorado.

I told Mrs. Wilson a lot about farming too, because having lived on an Iowa farm for more than a year, I knew almost anything anybody needed to know about farming, and I especially knew a lot about chickens. My aunt raised a thousand of them on the farm every year, and I had to help take care of them. Which is the main reason I don't much like them. Mrs. Wilson was impressed when I told her about the chickens because she had fifty of them herself in the garage out back, and collected eggs from them every day.

We'd been there four days when I got this idea on both how to pass some time and help Mrs. Wilson out. I told Mrs. Wilson that she was not doing too well with her chickens, and that we should do something about it. Those chickens were all leghorn hens, flighty birds not much good for eating, but darn good layers. I told Mrs. Wilson that since each hen should lay an egg every day, she ought to get about 50 eggs a day instead of the two dozen she was finding. What we needed to do, I told her, was cull out those that weren't making eggs so she could make stewing chickens out of them. Mrs. Wilson saw the merit in that idea. But how, she asked, could you tell which chickens laid the eggs? I was expert at that, I replied: "You just catch a chicken and see how many fingers you can stick in between the bones near her hind end. If you can get three fingers in, she is a layer; if she takes only one or two, you should kill her and eat her." Mrs. Wilson got kind of red in the face when I told her that, and then she pointed out that if I was wrong about how to cull chickens, then some of the layers would be killed.

I thought that through overnight and I figured out a way to prove I was right. When we sat down to breakfast I told Mrs. Wilson, "What we'll do is build a fence down the middle of your chicken house. We can do that today and then tonight we'll catch the chickens and cull them. We'll put all the layers on one side of the fence and the bad hens on the other. Tomorrow all we have to do is gather the eggs, and if they all are on the one side of the fence you will know I am right."

"Well...yes, that does sound reasonable. All right, we'll do it," said Mrs. Wilson, but she still had a skeptical tone to her voice.

Mrs. Wilson and I worked away on the fence much of the day amidst a lot of squawking chickens and screaming kids as Lewie, Winny the Whiner and Sammy the Screamer kept busy chasing each other and the chickens around. By midafternoon we called it quits because we had the fence up at least eight feet high, just a foot or two short of the garage's peak.

Mr. Wilson was again working late, so after supper we put the kids to bed early and Mrs. Wilson and I went out to the garage, grabbed some roosting hens, and culled them. Mrs. Wilson was a little reluctant at first, but she soon got the hang of it. Before long I think she was having as much fun as I was checking out those chickens. She was impressed that we were getting almost equal numbers of three-finger jobs and losers, and that the final count of 24-26 was just what I had predicted. We stuffed them all in gunny sacks temporarily and then turned them loose in the two sides of the garage and went in the house for cocoa.

Sitting there drinking and listening to some of the new songs on the radio, ones like "Swinging on a Star," "Sentimental Journey," and "Accentuate the Positive," Mrs. Wilson and I felt about as close to each other as we ever had. It was good to share an accomplishment like this one, and I was feeling extra proud of how well it worked out. Truth was, I'd never seen positive proof that laying your fingers to a chicken's butt really worked because back in Iowa we'd always killed the ones culled out before they got a chance to show that we might have been wrong. For all I knew, this was the first careful test, and so maybe Mrs. Wilson and I were making agricultural history.

But the next day was not a good one for either me or Mrs. Wilson. When we went out to the garage, we discovered that the hens were all together on one side of the building. The fence we had built had not been quite high enough, so all those on one side had flown across to the other. The worst thing though was that none of hens laid any eggs that day, nor the next. Mrs. Wilson was noticeably cool toward me by the end of that second day. That night I overheard her ask Mr. Wilson how much longer it was going to be, and I was pretty sure I knew what she was talking about.

I was just as eager for it to be over as Mrs. Wilson was. She was getting more pinch-faced all the time, but on the third eggless day we finally got the word. The clouds were not so thick as they had been for all of the last week, so Mr. Wilson drove us to Boeing Field where we got on the airplane and flew toward Alaska. I sometimes wonder if any of Mrs. Wilson's chickens ever laid another egg, but mostly I'd just as soon not think about it all. Of course now that Dad is talking about getting chickens here on the homestead, there's no escaping it.

OFF TO SCHOOL AND BACK TO WORK

EARLY SEPTEMBER 1944

TIME IS GOING BY FAST. School is about to start in Fairbanks, and Mom and Dad have decided that Lewie and I will go. Their plan hinges around my telling them I can drive a car. Not only did I learn all about farming back in Iowa, I told Mom and Dad, I also learned to drive a car pretty well. They are inclined to believe me because I have demonstrated ability as a tractor driver. Now, Dad is letting me drive the H during almost all of our farming and tree-cutting operations. I am getting doggone good at it—much better than Dad.

Actually, I have driven a car only once when a neighbor of Uncle Irwin's hired me to help him stack hay. My job was to drive an old car tied to a rope that pulled a hay fork up and down under a tree where the neighbor was stacking his hay. I just drove the car back and forth about fifty feet. It was tough at first, but I was doing fine by the end of the day so I am not exaggerating much when I say I can drive pretty darn well.

Like some states with rural populations, the Territory of Alaska has a law that lets a person who is twelve or older have a school driving permit. The permit makes it legal to drive to and from school only. And of course since I can drive, Mom and Dad have decided that I will get a permit and drive Lewie and me to school in Fairbanks. Mom takes me to the Territorial Trooper office in Fairbanks where the man in charge types on a little piece of paper and hands it to me. "Now, son," he says with a deep, stern voice, "this is a standard driver's license. It allows you to drive a regular car or a truck any time. But if we ever once catch you speeding or doing anything at all wrong we will take it away and you'll never get another one."

Wow, that is swell! I'll never in my life ever do anything wrong again, I promise myself. I am really proud to have that license, and it occurs to me that when I drive to school probably some of the girls will see me drive up, and they will be impressed.

On the first day of school, Mom goes with us, but she lets me drive. I am tickled silly, and I do real well most of the way. But along the straight stretch between 6-Mile and Big Bend I guess I get to concentrating on too many things. I am pretty good at concentrating on things. When you go to a one-room school like I did back in Iowa, one thing you learn to do is concentrate. In that school I learned to concentrate so well I would not know what was going on around me. The little kids could be reading aloud to the teacher or she could be instructing another grade at the blackboard, and I would not even be aware of it as I worked my own problems or read a book. To get my attention the teacher sometimes had to come to my desk and shake my shoulder.

I can do the same thing while out working or driving the tractor. I am always concentrating and thinking—all sorts of thoughts, or maybe about how fun it would be to have some girl come up and see me working just like a full-grown man. I guess I am concentrating like that on the straight stretch beyond 6-Mile. Suddenly, Mom yells and shakes my shoulder, and I realize that the pickup is in the ditch. Luckily, the ditch is not very steep, and with Mom's help I get the truck back up on the road. I think, though, that my ability to concentrate like that bothers Mom some.

Actually, it bothers Mom so much that Lewie and I go to school in Fairbanks only for one week, and Mom goes along, spending her time during the day downtown doing something or other. Mom also talks with Mr. Frank Ryan, the head of Alaska's schools, and learns that Lewie and I can take correspondence courses. A course costs $140, and Mr. Ryan will pay half of that. Furthermore, when you finish a course at the end of the year, you get your $70 back, so it really is free. Mr. Ryan must be a pretty fine man to do that for us. So Mom takes us out of school, and Lewie and I are released from any more education until early November, when the correspondence materials should arrive.

Lewie isn't very happy about leaving school because he really likes to be around kids, but I am glad to get out of there. These few days in school have been pretty scary because all the other kids seem to be way ahead of me, and the teacher, Mrs. King, a large, wide woman, is tough as nails. She showed us that the second day of school when, while she was out of the room briefly, a boy named Walt put about six thumbtacks on her chair. I thought that was a terrible thing to do to a teacher, and I certainly would not have done it. We all watched her face when Mrs. King settled her big behind down onto the chair. She didn't even blink or anything, and after sitting there for a minute or two she got up and walked over to the blackboard. We could see the shiny thumbtacks sticking into the dark red knit dress stretched over her butt, and then we heard "plink...plink...plink" as one after another they dropped out on the floor. Mrs. King turned around toward us, scanning every face in the room. How she knew who it was I don't know, but with great calm and no expression she said, "Walter, obviously you are unaware of the fact that I wear a very sturdy girdle under this dress." She turned back to the board without saying or doing any more about it, and we all knew that nobody was going to mess around with her.

Getting out from under Mrs. King has put me back to work on the homestead, and that is fine. I enjoy doing whatever work Dad wants me to do, and it is pretty invigorating out here in the wilderness where we can see that rapid change is underway. Fireweed's purplish blooms are shrinking up into wispy shreds of old woman's hair, and the cottonwood leaves are starting to yellow and curl. A few willow leaves are falling, and the reddening of raspberry and currant leaves is broadcasting intricate crimson patterns across the dark green moss on the more open parts of the forest floor. Each day the air seems crisper, and as it moves it carries the musty smell of rotting mushrooms mixed with the sharp, biting tang of overripe high-bush cranberries. Earlier in summer, the squirrels dawdled in the sun and stopped to scold when the mood struck. Now they chatter on the run as they rush up into the trees to store spruce cones and mushrooms in the branches. They keep their red-brown coats, but the snowshoe rabbits below are turning white.

It's fun when things are changing like this. I like change, and I think Dad does too. Both of us are working hard, and we're getting a lot done now. Sometimes I have to work closely with Dad, like when we use the two-man cross-cut saw or work together at rolling a log, but at other times I am working by myself and always have to figure out what to do next. I don't always know exactly what job to do or how to go about doing it, but even Dad is having problems like that with all the new things he is trying to do on the homestead. As good as he is at inventing ways to make work easier, some of those things have not worked out, things like the tree-sawing machine and the brush-cutter.

But that is the way it goes when things are changing, and I am starting to see that being young on a homestead in Alaska is a lot different than being young on a farm back in Iowa. Uncle Irwin and the farmers there all know what to do when they farm. Their work each spring and fall is just the same as the work they did last spring and fall, and the spring and fall before that. They all have a pattern to follow, one that they have learned from their fathers and grandfathers. Things have changed a little bit with time, like when the farmers started using tractors instead of horses. Still, the crops are the same year after year, and for generations people have known what crops to plant and when. By the time a farm boy gets as old as me, he at least knows what the pattern is, and all he has to do is learn how to do each job that farming involves.

Homesteading in Alaska is not like that at all. Everything is first-time. I can't learn to do the things that Dad has learned to do because he hasn't yet learned how himself. And since none of us have ever lived this far north before, we do not even know how much day and night changes with season, or what the change of season will bring. That in itself is exciting, not knowing how soon winter will come and how cold and dark it will be. It is fun, too, getting used to so many things that are different. In Iowa, people always go north, south, east or west so many miles because that is the way the roads all run, and there is a road every mile. In Alaska, directions mean nothing; it is all up or down, along a stream or along the highway. People sometimes even use hours to tell you how far away a place is. In Iowa, you can tell what time it is by looking at the sun, but that sure does not work in Alaska. The homestead and the land around is a whole new world, kind of all the same in a way because it is full of not much else but moss too wet to sit on and stretches of swamps, brush and trees that block out the distant view. The homestead does not even have any rocks other than the large rounded pebbles in 14-Mile Slough, and only where the stream or the road or the plow have cut through the moss can you even see any dirt.

I am learning some from Dad, but we are learning together about a lot of things, like how to clear land, plow up moss and cut trees down. That means that I sometimes do almost as much figuring as he does about how to do whatever job we face. He is the boss, of course, but it sure is fun to beat him on something. Maybe I work out a new trick on how to move logs easier, or see something that he has missed, and it makes me feel real good. I try hard to do as much work as he does. Too bad some girl cannot just happen along and see me doing so well on everything.

About the only really humiliating thing I have done this fall was on the night of the first hard freeze. Both the tractor and the pickup were filled with water instead of antifreeze, so when Dad saw that it was going to get cold, he sent me out to drain them. I knew where the drain was on the tractor but had to search for the one at the bottom of the radiator on the pickup. When I got back inside, Dad asked me if I was sure I had gotten both drains. "Yeah, I got them both," I told him. Not until the next day when Dad started up the pickup and water ran out of a crack along the full length of its engine block did I remember that Dad had earlier told me that the pickup had two water drains. I had forgotten that, and that was what Dad meant when he asked me if I got both drains. Dad saw how bad I felt about doing such a stupid thing that was going to cost a lot of money to fix, so he just said, "Well, I guess you learned something, didn't you?" He is like that; no matter what I do wrong, he never speaks harshly to me. When your dad is like that you know it's your own responsibility, so you try hard not to do things wrong.

Dad has a terrible temper, though. He does not seem to get upset with people unless they are parts of organizations, but if something goes bad with machinery, Dad usually gets red in the face, curses a lot, and bangs on things. When he gets like that, I feel very uncomfortable, as if it is all my fault. I guess maybe that is because of what used to happen when I was small, about six years old. In addition to his job then in the Union Pacific coal mine, Dad was mining for gold in southern Wyoming, and it was my job to stand by his air compressor so I could shut off a valve that sent air to his jack hammer when it got stuck in the rock. That happened often, and I had to shut off the valve real fast so that the jackhammer would not get stuck tighter. Each time it did get stuck, Dad would get mad and start swearing. That made me feel like I was causing his trouble.

Somehow I cannot really get over feeling guilty when I am around somebody who flies off the handle like Dad does, even though I know I am not at fault. I have already made up my mind never to be like that.

This idea really came to me one day when I was nine, and Dad put on the worst, longest temper tantrum I had ever seen.

That was in the early spring of 1941. Dad had been working a uranium mine on a mountain along the Colorado-Utah border, but had decided that uranium mining was a losing proposition, although he thought something funny was going on. The summer before, several strangers had been nosing around like they were interested in buying mining property. Dad said as near as he could figure, the war in Europe must be creating more demand for the vanadium content in the uranium ore we were mining because the vanadium was used in hardening steel. The uranium ore had a lot of radium in it, too, and maybe more of that was needed for watch and instrument faces that you could see in the dark. Dad said that the uranium itself wasn't useful for much of anything.

So we moved from the uranium mine down to a ranch near Gateway, Colorado, carrying as much of what we owned as we could on our backs. We had to do that because the road to the mine would not be passable until all the snow was gone, and that was still months away. A few days later, Dad borrowed a pack horse, and we returned up the canyon to the mine to get the rest of our belongings. By the time we had climbed up the ten miles of dangerous trail and loaded the pack horse, it was getting dark. We had to have light to go back down because in some places the trail ran along rock shelves so narrow that a wrong step could take you straight down hundreds of feet. In those places, the trail was too narrow to ride a horse. The packers who worked the trail in summer always unhitched the ropes that tied the pack-train horses together so that if one horse fell off he would not drag all the others away.

As we got ready to leave, Dad took a carbide lamp and a can of carbide from the mine. If we stuck together, that would give us enough light to get down the trail. All went well until the carbide lamp needed refilling. To do that you unscrewed the base of the lamp and filled it with carbide lumps. Then you put water in the top of the lamp, and it dripped down through a small hole to release the carbide gases that rose up a passageway to the burner. Dad put the carbide in, and then he said, "Oh heck, I meant to bring a can of clean water, but I forgot." He then found a puddle of melted snow water in the trail and dipped some up. Since it was now dark, he did not realize that the water was dirty, so dirty it soon plugged up the carbide passageway, and that caused the lamp to go out. Dad swore viciously. He emptied out the lamp and tapped it on a rock. The lamp worked a few minutes and then went out again. Dad swore more loudly and longer than before, and then he threw the lamp hard against a rock. I could not see him in the darkness, but he sounded like he was jumping up and down. That was when I decided that I was never, ever going to lose my temper like Dad was doing.

After several more bad times like this, each involving furious swearing and lamp throwing, Dad ran out of matches. He knew I had some because he insisted that I always carry them with me when I was out away from the house. He was very careful to give me instructions about what to do if I ever got lost or got in trouble in any way. He was really good about that. I had two little boxes of wooden matches, so I gave him one. Dad was still so mad he was almost shaking as he took the box of matches. That caused me to think that maybe he had lost all his reason, and that I'd better do some planning ahead.

Two miles farther down the trail, he ran out of matches again, so I gave him the other box, but before handing them to him I slid out two matches and put them in my shirt pocket. We were not going to get much farther that night, I thought, and now that heavy snow was falling and the wind starting to blow, we were going to need a fire. My two matches would take care of that.

Dad ran out of matches again just as we got through the most dangerous part of the canyon. By this time he had just about sworn himself out, so now his cursing was more a grumpy whimpering. Dad put the horse out in front to lead the way, held onto his tail, and I followed behind. Soon we were on level ground, the snow turned to rain, and we had but two miles to go. Dad was calmed down now, but he said, "I sure would like a smoke. Wish I had a match."

I knew we were going to be all right then, so I got my last two matches out and gave them to him. He was stunned. "Ohmigawd," he said in a soft voice that told me he realized what had been going on. When we got home Dad told Mom all about it, how he who had preached so much about being careful on the trail and yet had foolishly lost his temper and his reason, over and over again, and how I, a nine-year-old kid, had remained calm and had saved the last two matches for emergency use. When Dad bragged on me to Mom he seemed proud, and I felt good about it, too. Yes, never would I let myself get mad like Dad, I decided. No matter what happened I would always stay cool. Somebody could come up and cut my arm off, and I'd just stand there, calm and collected, maybe even until I bled to death.

Dad is still having temper tantrums every once in a while as we work around the homestead, but now they are short-lived. When he hits his finger with a hammer and starts swearing, I just stand by calmly with a superior, disdainful expression. He sees that, and I bet it reminds him of that night on the trail, just as it does me. He then cools down right away, and we go on about our work as if nothing has happened.

Except for those times, Dad is pretty good to work with, and we both sure are learning a lot about how to do things we've never done before. I am a better tractor driver than him, and I am almost as strong, but I guess I know down deep that he is smarter about a lot of things than I am. For one thing, he knows how to build a bridge, and that is going to be one of our big projects this fall.

THE BRIDGE OVER 14-MILE SLOUGH

SEPTEMBER 1944

DAD IS MOVING AHEAD with his plan to build an addition on the cabin so that Lewie and I will have a separate place to sleep. We can cut enough logs for the addition from the homestead and from the part of Dad's timber permit that lies on our side of 14-Mile Slough, but the best trees are on the other side. Dad still is hoping to cut those 2000 cords of firewood to sell, and most of that is across the slough, too.

So Dad decides that we will build a bridge, one strong enough to carry the Farmall H and a go-devil loaded with logs. Dad plans to haul a lot of trees over that bridge during the next year or two, so he says we have to do the job right. Dad's plan is for the bridge to be 130 feet long with crossways log decking atop bigger logs that will rest on gravel- and rock-filled cribs every twenty feet.

This is a big project, but 14-Mile Slough is a formidable obstacle. At the bridge site the stream is about 80 feet wide, and more than three feet deep near the far bank. The water flows so fast here—Dad calls the place a riffle—that it will sweep you away if you try to cross, and this is one of the easier places. The near bank is just a gently sloping gravel bar, but the other is a steep rise being cut away by the swift water. Every few hundred feet up and down the stream, the water surges over other riffles like this one. In between lie deep pools of fairly still water, some nearly ten feet deep. About the only place we can walk across 14-Mile Slough is where a fallen tree floats on one of these deep pools, its roots still attached to one bank.

People call 14-Mile a slough rather than a river because some tens of miles southeast of the homestead it starts in the Tanana River. The slough then empties into another, much larger slough named Piledriver Slough less than a mile down below the homestead. Piledriver Slough, in turn, empties into the Chena River that flows through Ladd Field and Fairbanks, and then into the Tanana River a few miles below town. So the sloughs are really just links between rivers.

This is a pretty tricky layout, it seems to me. Water flows out of the Tanana and then back into it far downstream, but only after going through three other streams: 14-Mile and Piledriver sloughs and the Chena River. The network was handy in the early days, Dad said, because it allowed people to cut logs on the Tanana River and the two sloughs and then float them down to sawmills in Fairbanks each spring when the water was high. He said that this is how Piledriver Slough got its name; it was a good stream to float logs down. That also explains why we see so many big tree stumps around the homestead, but not many big trees. The best of the trees went down to the mills in Fairbanks long before I was born.

Piledriver and 14-Mile sloughs caused a lot of trouble for Fairbanks, though. Each spring when the snow melted, the Tanana rose so high that the waters flowing through the sloughs and the Chena River flooded Fairbanks. Dad said that old-timers claimed that every spring people could row boats down First and Second avenues and that all the basements in downtown Fairbanks got flooded. Ladd Field had the same problem, and for that reason, the military had built Moose Creek Dike.

The military engineers built the dike with big rocks blasted out of Moose Creek Bluff, near 20-Mile on the Alcan. They placed the rocks in a long bank that started at the bluff, cut across a clear-water stream named Moose Creek, then across Piledriver and 14-Mile sloughs out past 18-Mile on the Alcan toward the main channels of the Tanana River. From about 18.5-Mile to 20-Mile, the Alcan sits right on top of the dike. The idea, Dad says, is to make enough of a barrier to keep the high spring waters from flowing down into Ladd Field and Fairbanks.

We drive up to the dike and see how muddy the water is in the sloughs above it. Dad says that is because a lot of glaciers run into the Tanana and fill it with silt. The rocks in the dike are so big that a lot of water still flows between them into Piledriver and 14-Mile sloughs. But by the time the water has flowed down to the homestead, it is far less murky than up near the dike. Dad says that is because the muddy

Tanana water is mixing in with the clear water from Moose Creek and with clear runoff water draining into 14-Mile slough below the dike.

Dad and I start building the new bridge right after Lewie and I finish our one-week stint in the Fairbanks school. A big part of the job is cutting down trees and hauling them to the bridge site. Just getting the deck logs seems to take forever because we need over 300 of them, each 12 feet long. Three weeks we have been at it now, and I think both Dad and I are wishing we were using all these logs to build the addition on the cabin instead of putting them into the bridge.

As it turns out, we should have done that because something strange is going on. Each day, the water flowing under the bridge is becoming less murky, and its level is dropping. I guess this happens in most streams in the fall, but what Dad and I are seeing is going way beyond that. We are almost done with the bridge and the work is going faster because now we can easily walk across the stream beside the bridge without any danger of being swept away or even getting our knees wet. We can see that, except for that cut bank on the far side, the H would have no trouble crossing the stream without a bridge because the water is so shallow and the bottom is solid rocky gravel.

Dad seems especially quiet and thoughtful these last few days, and now finally we are finished. As Dad and I are standing on the bridge admiring what we have done when he says, "Let's take a drive up to the dike." We get in the pickup and head up to where 14-Mile Slough flows through the dike. Dad gets out his sighting level and has me go down on each side of the dike with a long pole so he can measure the ground level. "Yep, it's just like I thought," Dad said, shaking his head, "The damn thing is silting up. The ground is already about a foot higher on the upper side of the dike, and it's going to get higher as time goes by. We won't be seeing near as much water in the slough any more. That dike is going to make a lot of changes around here, and I think we just built a bridge across a raging torrent that is destined to become a trickle. In another year or two we'll be driving across the slough just about any place we want. We'll see the day when what was a beautiful stream is nothing but a stagnant swamp. And that dike is the beginning of the end for Fairbanks as a riverboat town. Already, the big boats have quit coming up into the Chena River."

As we drive back home, Dad and I talk about it some more. "You know," he says, "I'm not sure it ever pays in the long run to try to change the way water flows. What seems like a good idea at the time

can turn into a bad one later on because you can't foresee all the conse-
quences, no matter how much you think it through. For one thing, the
world keeps changing, too often in ways you can't predict."

THE WARM NEW CABIN

OCTOBER 1944

I 'VE BEEN CHECKING MY GARDEN every day or so while we've been building the bridge. Everything I planted has come up, but most things have not done very well. The carrots are barely out of the ground, and the few radishes I have picked are not much bigger than the peas. We have been able to eat some of the leaf lettuce, but the big surprise is the way the pumpkins have grown. The vines have spread out several feet, and the seven pumpkins that have formed are about the size of oranges. I think now that I might have been a little foolish to expect a garden planted so late to do well, but it's been worth it anyway, just to see what happens here in Alaska.

Also, my garden on the ditch bank is a great place to watch the Lend-Lease airplanes from Great Falls, Montana, go by on their way to Russia. The ditch bank is right on the flight path and it faces south, the direction the planes are coming from. Across the ditch, the trees are low, so the planes show up sooner and better than at most places on the homestead. With the bombers it doesn't make much difference because they fly high, I'd guess at least 500 feet and maybe even up to 1000. They tend to come in groups, some in tight formation and others in ragged bunches. The fighters are the fun ones because they usually roar in just over the treetops, and if they are off to the side a hundred yards or so the pilots and I can see and wave to each other. Some pilots peer intently only straight ahead, I guess trying to see Ladd Field where they will soon land. The more relaxed ones look everywhere and when they see me they wave their hands or wiggle their wings. They seem happy and surprised to find me out there, and I might be the first person they have seen since their last take-off

in Whitehorse. Watching them go by makes me think that being a pilot could be almost as much fun as farming—and a lot less work than cutting all these trees down to build the bridge and the addition on the cabin.

But the bridge is finally done now and so Dad and I start in on the construction of the cabin. We have a few days' delay when Dad decides we ought to dig a partial basement under the addition. Down about three feet, right where a big clump of alders was, we run into frozen ground. Dad says it is permafrost, which is ground that will never thaw unless we help it some. Luckily, the frost layer is only about six feet across and we only have to dig two feet deeper. Dad attacks the frozen ground with a pick, but gives up on that idea real quick. He thinks dynamite might work, but before he gets around to buying any, the permafrost thaws out almost by itself. Each day we remove the few inches that melts, and soon the problem is gone.

That little lens of permafrost is funny. It sure shows how fine the line is between having permafrost or not. All around that clump of alders the mossy layer atop the ground is only an inch or two thick, and in places on the homestead like that the ground is thawed all the way down in the fall. But the alder clump made just enough shade in summer to keep the sun from thawing all the ground that froze last winter. Only twenty or thirty feet away is a strip of black spruce trees growing out of a spongy layer of moss more than a foot thick. If you dig down there, your shovel hits frozen dirt right at the bottom of the moss. Yet off in the other direction is a stand of nice big white spruce trees, and the ground beneath them is not frozen.

A good way to keep Lewie occupied is to have him count rings on stumps and logs, and he never seems to get tired of doing it. He's a strange little kid. From all his counting we discover that the big white spruce and the scraggly little black spruce trees near the cabin are all about the same age: 50 to 150 years old. We don't know if it is the permafrost that makes the black spruce so small or if it was the black spruce that makes the ground stay frozen all year. Whichever way it is, the two things sure do go together, and you can see that old forest fires must have had a lot of effect on where the permafrost is now.

One afternoon while we do battle with the permafrost layer we hear a loud "Hallou," and we see a tall man in a big black hat come striding briskly up the Old Richardson Trail from the direction of 14-Mile. Following behind with the listless walk of the very tired is a girl, smaller than me but bigger than Lewie. As they come up to the cabin I see that she has jet-black hair but I can't really see her face because of her turned-up collar and the scarf draped around her neck.

"I'm Calvin Cornwell," the man says loudly as he and Dad shake hands, "and this is my daughter Shiela. She's a little tired because she's only ten years old and we've walked up along the Piledriver, all the way from the end of Badger Road. Must be about eight miles, and we've been blazing out a route to extend the road here to your homestead."

Soon we are inside the cabin where Mom is preparing coffee for the visitors. I sit on my bed, and Mr. Cornwell and his daughter sit across the room at the table. Mr. Cornwell continues to talk, loudly and nonstop, but his words lose all meaning for me when Shiela takes off her scarf and lays down her collar. She has big dark eyes, long lashes, high cheekbones and a perfect mouth. Wow, she is the most beautiful girl I have ever seen! As I stare at her she looks briefly into my eyes and then bows her head. Gosh, I wish she were older, I think to myself, I know I'd like her a lot.

69

For me, the next hour is a blur as Mr. Cornwell talks on and on about the wonderful developments that are going to take place in this part of Alaska. He is planning to erect a huge building on his homestead, which he says is located out beyond the end of Badger Road, and up along the Piledriver in our direction. This big building—it will be 400 feet long and three stories high—has some special purpose that we will learn later. We will be amazed when we find out, Mr. Cornwell hints, and we will be glad that a road will be built between Dad's homestead and his.

During Mr. Cornwell's tirade I sneak occasional glances at Shiela, but quickly look away if it seems like she might catch me doing it. Then she and her father are gone, and neither of us has spoken to the other. I wish she were older, but I don't think it matters because I don't think she hardly knew I was there in the room with her. As soon as they are out of hearing Dad snorts and says to Mom, "That guy's nuttier than a fruitcake. Did you ever hear of such nonsense—a road from here down the Piledriver to Harry Badger's place. It'll never happen, and we'll probably never see that guy again."

The visit from Mr. Cornwell and his daughter gives us things to think about as we finally get rid of the permafrost layer and start putting up cabin walls. We are doing a far better job of it than Dad did in March on the original cabin. Back then, his idea was to get the cabin up as quickly and cheaply as possible. Also, I think that he figured a log cabin would be warm by definition, no matter how it was built.

One big improvement is that we are not using any moss for chinking the logs or on the roof. A bad thing about moss is that mosquitoes tend to crawl or fly right through it. Until they are gone this fall, we've been killing them off every night before going to bed by burning Buhach powder on the stove. Also, as the moss dries out, it tends to fall out from between the log walls and, worse yet, drop down through the pole ceiling. Mom always has to wipe the moss off the table before setting it for supper, and she has strung a strip of oilcloth above her stove to keep the moss out of her pots. So even though it is expensive, Dad has bought a bunch of oakum to use for chinking. Any mosquito is going to have to be a tough cookie to crawl through that stuff, and if he tries he'll probably die from the oakum's creosote odor. It's a funny smell, sort of nasty but pleasant in a way, too.

Dad has now seen enough other cabins around Fairbanks to know that we ought to try to do a better job in general than he had done on the original cabin. So one improvement is to use bigger logs, some up to sixteen inches in diameter. They are heavy, so in the corners of the cabin Dad stands up what he calls gin poles to which we rig a block and tackle to move the big logs into place. We do not peel the logs, but we use an axe to flatten them on both top and bottom. Then by using a saw instead of an axe, we are able to make tight fits at the corners. Before each log finally goes into place, we lay oakum on the log just below, and we carefully lay more oakum in the corner joints. Dad says we are doing a good job all around because as we lay the last logs up we find that we have the wall heights the same everywhere within four inches. "Anybody who can come within four inches is damn good," he claims, and I can't tell if he's kidding or thinks it's true.

We hurry as best we can toward the end, spending only one day to lay up the two-by-six rafters, sloped in a shed roof that matches the gentle pitch of the first cabin's shed roof and meets it at the top. Dad has managed to buy some 3/4-inch tongue-and-groove boards to put over the rafters, and we get those nailed down in another day. He also has bought rolls of roofing paper, but now it is too cold to put them up. "I wish we could have gotten that roofing on," he says that night, "but that's OK. We'll do it next year when the weather warms up. That tongue-and-groove is good stuff. It fits tight together, so it will do just fine until then. All we'll have to do is scoop the snow off it next spring."

That night Dad heads into town where he will stay while working at his new job as cook for the Pioneer Hotel. We are down to the wire on money again because of all the things Dad has bought for the cabin. He and Mom have a big bill at the Northern Commercial Company store, too, for food and for the construction of the brush-cutter and the tree-felling machine. He also still owes money on the Farmall H.

We have been lucky on the weather up until this last week, when the thermometer has regularly gone down below zero every night. The new cabin is great, especially because it is heated by a big barrel stove that sits almost in the middle of the room. Seeing how warm it is, Mom is going to move her bed into the new cabin, and we will keep the door closed between it and the old room. We can fix most of our food on the barrel stove, and when Mom wants to bake something, she can put on her overshoes and coat and go into the kitchen where she can use the oven.

SETTLING IN WITH MOM

WINTER 1944–45

IT SURE SEEMS LIKE THINGS have been aw
ful hectic and unsettled these past three years.
The last really peaceful time we've had was back in the winter of 1940–
1941 when we were snowed in up at the uranium mine near Gateway,
Colorado, where we had no radio or ever saw any newspapers. Of course
it's wartime and that changes things, but now that Dad is working and
staying in town, living here on the homestead is a lot like it was back at
the mine. It's cold, and the snow is getting deeper all the time, just like
it was there, but mainly I guess it is because we are alone and don't see
anybody else. Another sameness is that time doesn't mean much of
anything, except that at some times it is light and at other times it is
dark. Mom, Lewie and I are settling into an easy routine. We eat when
we get hungry, and we put more wood in the fire when it needs it.
Every day I have to get water from the slough, feed the dogs and saw
up some wood and carry it inside, but it doesn't matter what time of
day I do that.

I think Lewie gets a little bored because he doesn't have anybody
to play with except me, and I'm usually wanting to do something else.
Mom is happy though, and she is spending almost all of her time
reading love story and detective magazines and books that she bought
second-hand in town. That is really good because somehow I think
Mom has mostly had a sad life. She never says anything to give you
that idea, but I can sense it, and I have some memories that kind of
hurt when I think about them.

When I get to pondering over things like that, one day in particular comes up again and again, I'm not sure exactly why except that

something sad happened to me that day and maybe that made me pay better attention to how things were going with Mom. It was a late-summer day in Gateway, just before Mom, Lewie and I left the little town to go to Dad's mine on the mountain to the west. Mom was working at a ranch just outside town, and since school was out, I was taking care of Lewie during the days while Mom was away. He was easy to take care of because there were other kids around and we joined them on hot days for swims in an eddy of the Dolores River. I had not learned to swim yet and so stayed in the shallow water, but Lewie caught on right away and would go out in the deep water with the other boys who swam. At first, they kept an eye on him just in case he got out of the eddy and started getting swept downstream, but in a few days it was obvious he could take care of himself. Of course it was embarrassing to have my little kid brother out swimming with the rest of the boys while I splashed around in the shallows.

That morning as Mom left to work at the ranch she said, "We will be going up to the mine on the mountain in a day or two and we can't take all those kittens, so you better get rid of them." She was talking about the litter of kittens mothered by a stray cat that had come to live with us. Mom had said Lewie and I could keep her. Lewie was tickled silly over the kittens when they got big enough to play with because he loved cuddly things. I could see that this was going to be a problem, so the first thing I had to do that day was to figure some way to get the kittens away without him knowing about it.

While I was thinking about that, Lewie went out to play near the creek. Down there he found a whole bunch of furry brown caterpillars which he stuck in all the pockets of his bib overalls. Then he fell down on his stomach and flattened most of the caterpillars stuffed into the chest pockets of the overalls. Lewie came back sobbing hysterically because he had squished all those nice cuddly little worms, and boy was he a mess. Getting up, he rolled over on his side and mashed another bunch of caterpillars in his side pocket, so now he had several pockets full of brown fuzz and gooey green slime. I thought it was funny in a way, but I knew that Lewie was awful sad over what he'd done to the caterpillars so I felt sorry for him too.

I got Lewie mostly cleaned up and then took him over to the school yard and left him to play with some other kids whose older sister said she'd look after Lewie until I got back. At the house, I rummaged around and found the stuff I'd need to take care of the kittens: a gunnysack and a cookie tin. I put all the kittens on the cookie tin, and held them up over my shoulder as I walked down to the river. On the way, I walked past the Post Office, where two old men were sitting on the porch.

"Where you going with all those kitties, sonny? Down to the river, I betcha," one of them called out.

"Hey, don't he look like a waiter walking along with that gunnysack over his arm and those kittens up on that cookie tin?" the other one said.

I sure was not happy about what I had to do, and I would have chickened out if it had not been for those men. I knew they would razz the heck out of me if I walked past them again carrying the eight kittens back home. As it was, I cried a lot as I sat there on the riverbank petting those cute little kitties and popping them in the sack, one by one. Then I put a rock in with them and heaved them in the water. I was still feeling pretty bad as I walked past the men again, this time carrying only my empty cookie tin. I felt even worse when Mom got home late that afternoon, far sooner than usual. I told her about Lewie's accident with the worms, and she laughed some over that. Then I told her about the kittens.

"You drowned the kittens? My word, I didn't expect you to do that," she said, "I just meant that you should try to give them to somebody." Nuts, why didn't she tell me that to start with; it would have been a lot nicer day for the kitties and me both.

Mom knew I was feeling real bad about it, so after supper when Lewie was again off playing somewhere, she said, "Let's go for a walk." We headed off up the road toward Grand Junction, moving slowly but still kicking dust that the heavy uranium ore trucks had ground up out of the roadbed. Those trucks usually barely slowed down at all as they roared through Gateway with their loads of sacked ore concentrate produced at the mill in Uravan. The truckers always waved, though, and usually would stop if a person flagged them down for a ride. Since almost nobody in Gateway had a car, people rode the ore trucks if they needed to make the fifty-mile trip to Grand Junction. It was on the sly because the company said that nobody except the drivers was supposed to be in the trucks.

We heard a truck coming up behind us, and it slowed down almost to a stop as it came up beside us. "Hello, Mrs. Davis. How are you doing?" the trucker called out with a big smile and a wave.

"Just fine, Joe, thank you." Mom called back and returned his smile as the truck moved on ahead and picked up speed. Mom told me that this was the trucker who had picked her up the day she was having so much trouble with asthma that she had to get to a doctor. Joe was a really nice guy, she said. He had taken her directly to the hospital in Grand Junction. Then the next morning after unloading his truck at the United States Smelting, Refining and Mining Company facility, Joe had detoured back to the hospital to bring Mom home. Mom said Joe could have lost his job over doing that.

We came to where the road swung in close to West Creek, the little stream that flowed down the Uniweep Canyon through Gateway and into the Dolores River at the other edge of town. "That's a pretty spot over there," Mom said. "Let's go sit; I've got something special to show you." We settled down on the bank of the little creek at a place where Mom could lean her back against a tree.

"Since Dad will be coming to get us soon, today was my last work day at the ranch," Mom said, and then with a extra-happy lilt to her voice she continued, "and look at this." She reached into the pocket of her dress and when her hand unfolded before me it was full of coins, all quarters.

"Wow, how much is it?"

"Eight dollars and twenty-five cents, and it's all ours to keep. It's to be our secret, just yours and mine," Mom said. I could tell she was proud of what she'd done, and I was proud that she was sharing the secret with me. This money had not come easy; it was all from her job at the ranch. Each of the men who worked there earned a dollar a day and keep, and Mom got fifty cents plus meals for herself and enough food to bring home for Lewie and me. She went to the ranch early enough to cook breakfast for the ranch hands, she cooked their dinner and supper, and in between, she and the ranch owner's wife canned fruit. About the only time Lewie and I saw Mom not working was when she would come out and play baseball with us after finishing the supper dishes at the ranch.

All the while Mom had worked at the ranch she would not let Lewie and me have any money for pop, and about the only money she spent was for Bull Durham cigarette makings which she did not like but which were far cheaper than real cigarettes. The result was that $8.25, more money than Mom had owned for several years. I could remember the years back in Wyoming when Mom sometimes could not write letters to her mother and Grandma Davis because she did not have money for stamps—and that was one thing she couldn't get on credit at the Union Pacific company store. She'd be down to just writing post cards because they only cost a penny to send, and letters cost three cents. I remembered once when she had written a letter to her mother and then reached up on the shelf where she kept stamps, only to find none there. "Oohh," she had moaned softly, and I had seen a tear come down her cheek as she turned away, mashed the letter in her hand, and then dropped it in the kitchen stove.

For me, Hanna had been an interesting place to live, but for Mom it was not so good because of not having money. That's what made her eight dollars and twenty-five cents so special. We had stopped talking and Mom had leaned back against her tree, listening to the sounds of distant meadowlarks and nearby running water, and with her eyes staring off into the distance, seeing nothing. I'd seen her do that a lot and I always knew then that Mom was all inside herself with thoughts that I or no one else probably would ever hear. The few times I'd seen her father before he died I noticed that he, too, sometimes got that funny, far-away look. I thought Mom was like him in lots of ways. Her dad had a terrible name, Cornelius Blueford Sappenfield, but he had a nice gentle face and a soft voice. He was so tall and thin that he looked almost ghostlike. When I was small I thought that if I ever was going to see a saint like they talked about in Sunday school he would look just like Grandad Sappenfield.

The first time I ever remember seeing him was when Mom took me to her parents' house in a stand of big spreading trees just east of Boulder, Colorado. Grandad Sappenfield had a big garden there where he raised vegetables to sell in the summers when he wasn't teaching school. He'd always been a teacher even back when he had lived in Indiana before he had to move to Colorado in 1903 because of having tuberculosis.

On the day Mom and I got to Boulder, Grandad went off to the store and bought me a sack of roofing nails and a little hammer. He gave me a big block of wood and showed me how to use the hammer. Before the day was over I had all of those nails driven into that block of wood. That was just about the nicest thing anybody had ever given me, so I knew that Mom's dad was really swell.

Mom's mother, though, was my least favorite grandparent. She was pretty like Mom; she had hair so long when she took her braids

77

out that she could sit on it, and she always wore a nice little smile—even when she was telling me to do something. When we visited, she was always telling me to do something, too. It was mostly having to do with religious things like saying prayers, returning grace and keeping myself clean. I think maybe that's all she ever thought about and wanted everybody else to think about. Grandma Sappenfield pushed her religion so much that I always looked forward to going home. I had the feeling that Grandad Sappenfield was truly religious in the best sort of way, but Grandma was religious in a way that was not real good for other people. If she wasn't my grandma I would have suspected that she was one of those kind of religious people you couldn't trust, the kind that Dad sometimes talked about.

Mom began playing the violin when she was about ten years old, and she spent so much time at it that she later became the first violinist for the Boulder Symphony Orchestra. I figure Mom spent so much time on the violin as a way of putting up with her own mother, although Mom never said anything about it. She tried to teach me the violin when I was about six and I got good enough to play "Pop Goes the Weasel" and "Silent Night." One day I said I'd rather go out and play than practice the violin, and Mom said I could do what I wanted. I figured Mom let me off the hook because she didn't want to be a pusher like her mother. Of course I was so poor at playing the violin that Mom might have thought I didn't have enough talent to make it worthwhile.

From little things Mom and her younger sister Virgie said, I know they were both so happy to get away from their mother and home that they went sort of wild. Mom once told me rather proudly that when she went to college she spent almost all her time partying. She said the only time she would study was all night long before a test. She could usually get a good grade on the test but then she would forget almost everything she learned. Most mothers I know would not admit stuff like this to their kids, but Mom is different. She is awfully honest, and she has always seemed to trust me to make the right decisions no matter what information I have had about how badly she or others did things. Even when I was young and Mom was making me do things like all mothers make their kids do, she usually made me feel like it was my choice to do whatever it was I was supposed to. Maybe it wasn't like that all the time; I sure will never forget the time in Hanna, Wyoming, when Mom got so mad that she gave me no choice at all.

This happened in early afternoon, on a normal baking day, Wednesday, when Mom made all the bread, cakes and pies for the week. She washed clothes on Mondays, ironed on Tuesdays, and we took baths on Saturday nights. All this was done in the kitchen where we also ate our meals. It was a big room with plenty of room for tubs and a big work table near the stove where Mom heated her wash water and our bath water on the coal stove. The kitchen was extra big because before we moved there the building had been a boarding house for single mine workers, and then the Union Pacific had built a wall down the middle of the building so that two families could live in it. We ended up with the kitchen on our side and the other family had an even bigger room that used to be the dining hall.

Our two families shared another thing left over from the boarding house, the biggest toilet in town. It was about the size of a large garage with its far end perched on two stilt-like legs out over the open sewer ditch out back of our house. You needed to carry a light to go out there at night, but when you opened the door in the daytime enough light came in through the cracks to see what was on the back and side walls, which was a single U-shaped bench containing sixteen holes. Sometimes when I was out there alone I wondered what it must have been like in the old days when sixteen coal miners were sitting on those holes, all at the same time.

Our part of Hanna had a whole network of ditches like the one that ran under our sixteen-holer. Most boys and some adults called them the "little shit creeks" because they led into the town's main sewer ditch called Big Shit Creek, or in polite company, Big Stink Creek. It was about twenty feet wide and it separated Main Street from the Union Pacific railroad tracks. You could jump the little creeks in lots of places or cross them on boards or little bridges, but Big Stink Creek was a serious obstruction with only two bridges and a place near our house where you could usually cross on some wobbly boards if you were careful.

One day Mom got a telegram saying her father was desperately ill and might die. She just might make the next train if she hurried. I helped her pack, and we ran out of the house just as the train was pulling into the station directly across Big Stink Creek. I suggested that the only way Mom could catch it was to take the shortcut across the boards, something she'd never tried before. She made it almost all the way before one foot slipped off. Mom was in the blue-green mire up to her knee, and I saw the agonized look on her face as she tried to decide whether to keep going or come back. I wished then that I hadn't suggested she cross Big Shit Creek on the boards. Suddenly, Mom yanked her foot out and ran for the train. It was the right thing to do because Grandad Sappenfield died right after she got to Boulder.

Anyway, on that particular baking-day Wednesday afternoon I had gone to visit a friend whose father was the town banker. I really liked to go there because my friend Joey had an older sister and brother and a mother who were nice to me, and the family had a set of books called *Book of Knowledge* which had lots of fun pictures, like of people and places far away, and even of other planets. The family also had running hot water and a flushing toilet. Joey's house was as neat and nice inside as was the white-picket fenced yard outside, the only one in town covered with mowed grass. Joey couldn't play for very long so I went back home, having to cross two little shit creeks on the way and kick through a lot of coal slack because the Union Pacific used it to pave all the streets. Our yard was mostly paved with the waste coal fines, too.

I guess I was feeling disgruntled about how our house compared to Joey's when I walked into the kitchen and saw Mom bent over looking into the oven at her bread. That day Mom was doing her usual baking and also her Monday wash because something had stopped her from doing it either on Monday or Tuesday—she might have been down with her asthma. I looked around the room at all the dirty clothes strewn on the floor, and then I said, "Why don't you clean this place up; it sure looks a mess."

I got a far bigger reaction from Mom than I had expected. Her head came flying out of the oven as she spun around, and I could see fire in her eyes. "Well," she said with vigor, "if you don't like it here you can leave." She paused a moment and then said, "You are leaving. I'll pack your bag."

In silence I followed her into my bedroom where she took down the brown valise and threw a bunch of my clothes in it. She did not pack them well, she just jammed them in there, and she forgot to put any socks in. She snapped the valise shut and led me into the kitchen. Saying nothing, she picked up from the counter a dried piece of bread and put it in a little brown paper sack, along with a dill pickle. Then she led me to the outside door and opened it. As I walked out on the little stoop, Mom handed me the valise and the paper bag and said, "Which way are you going, east or west?"

East and west were the only possibilities: the Union Pacific Railroad ran east-west and Highway 30 paralleled it. Rawlins was a long way east, Rock Springs a long way west, and between Hanna and those towns was nothing but sagebrush and sand. Tears came to my eyes as I thought about that and the fact that I was starting out with no money and nothing to eat except that dry piece of bread and a dill pickle. I didn't even like dill pickles. My shoulders started to heave up and down as I began crying and burst out with, "I don't want to go."

"Hmpf," Mom said, still looking terribly stern, "I suppose you can stay, but I don't want to hear any more nasty remarks from you about my housekeeping." She said it with a gentleness in her voice that let me know things were all right again. Mom had always been able to do that: make things right again for someone else if they'd gone bad. She'd sure done it for me that day there on the bank of West Creek, and sitting there with her I couldn't help but think how pretty she looked with the low evening sun shining on her face. I'd wished then that it could always be like that, and wondered why bad things had to happen. Why was it that little boys had to fall down and kill caterpillars; why did bigger boys have to drown cats, and why did pretty women like Mom have to work hard sixteen hours a day for only fifty cents while the cowboys rode around on their horses for ten hours and got a dollar? Why did Mom have to have so much trouble with asthma, and why had she had live so long in a house surrounded by coal dust and shit creeks and not have enough money to write to her mother just so that the Union Pacific Railroad could have cheaper coal?

All that's in the past now that we've got the homestead. I can see how happy Mom is to be here in her own home with nothing pressing and nothing to worry about. One thing that makes it easy for her is that we don't have any furniture or other stuff to clutter up the cabin. I guess it's always been that way really. Mom still keeps some things like family photographs and cloth things like hand-made rugs and fancy pillowcases in Grandma Davis's attic in Greeley, Colorado, but everything else has traveled along. When we left Hanna, Wyoming, in the middle of the night, everything we owned was packed in the car and in the trunk lashed to the back. Coming down off the mountain to Gateway we had only what the family and a horse could carry, and when we went on to Cheyenne, to West Virginia, Ohio and Chicago, everything easily fit in the car. When we split up in Chicago, Dad and Mom going to Alaska at different times, and Lewie and I to Iowa, each of us took one or two suitcases, and Mom always took her violin. As Grandma Davis would say, "We got shuck of everything else."

So now here at the homestead we have only the clothes that each of us has brought and whatever Mom and Dad have bought in Fairbanks, just those things that a homesteading family has to have. Some women aren't happy without lace curtains and frilly doilies all over the place, but Mom's not like that at all. She is happy as long as she has coffee to drink, cigarettes to smoke and plenty of things to read. She's got all that now, and in her own house, too, and it makes me feel good to see how happy she is. It's for sure that things have not always been this good for her.

BABICHE

OCTOBER 1944

SINCE OUR CORRESPONDENCE COURSES have not arrived, Lewie and I have much free time. About all I have to do each day is carry drinking water up from the slough and saw up wood with a crosscut or Swede saw and bring the pieces in for the stoves—and that barrel stove does burn a heck of a bunch. The wood cutting takes about a third of each day. My one other have-to chore is to use the Farmall H to plow the road open to 14-Mile when it snows. Then if the weather is warm enough for Dad to get the pickup started, he can bring supplies out from town.

One of the things I am doing on my own hook is putting out snares for rabbits. Now that the snow is deep enough for them to run along the little trails they have packed down, they are easy to catch. I just rig six-inch loops of soft picture-hanging wire in the rabbit trails near where they cross the old Richardson Trail leading out to the Alcan at 15-Mile. Since I learned the right height to set the loops, about two inches off the snow, I have been catching one or two rabbits nearly every night. We have all the rabbit meat we want to eat, and Mom is using some of the skins to make mitten liners for Lewie and me.

My main effort, though, is making furniture for the new cabin, using birch poles and babiche. I had to learn about babiche because I got an old broken dog sled, one I bought for almost nothing at the used goods store in town where Mom got her stove and bed. The store owner told me that all the sled needed was babiche and a few slats. Babiche sure is wonderful stuff for holding things together. I sometimes don't do too well with a hammer and nails, but my babiche joints all work great.

The babiche I am able to buy from Smith's Hardware on Second Avenue is not really good stuff. The babiche strips are irregular and some of them still have a lot of hair on them because they were quickly made by some Eskimo who had just laid a reindeer hide down on the floor and sliced with knife cuts outward from near the center of the hide to the edges. Each bundle of babiche looks sort of like a brown octopus with about a hundred tangled-up legs sticking out.

When I need to make something, I cut off some of the strips and soak them in water until they are all slimy and limp. Then I just wrap them around the joint I want to make and let them dry. That babiche shrinks up so much it really locks things together.

A man who knows told me that Indian babiche is better than Eskimo babiche because the Indians cut it out of moose hides in a way that produces long strips of uniform width. The man said that an Indian will start at the edge of a moose skin and carefully cut a continuous strip about one-quarter inch wide until the entire skin is gone. He then wraps the strip around two trees spaced maybe twenty feet apart, making many wraps. The Indian hangs rocks from rope tied to the wraps to make them stretch. If he keeps pouring water on the strips and keeps relashing them between the trees, the Indian can make the babiche strips as thin as he wants, and get a huge length of very uniform babiche from one moose hide.

Even if Eskimo babiche is not very good, I really like to go into Smith's Hardware to get it. Besides all the normal hardware and tools, Smith's sells many exotic things that an Alaskan might need. You have to be in there for a while to see everything because the store is down a few steps below street level, and its only windows face out on the street, under an overhanging part of the building above.

They keep the babiche in the back of the store, right near the bales of dried salmon sold for dog food. Odors from these seep forward through the crowded aisles, picking up the scent of tobacco and of oiled leather and metal from stacked or hanging arrays of guns, fishing poles, snowshoes, traps and dog harness, and an additional tang from the beautiful fox and wolf pelts hung on one wall.

By the time the growing mixture of smells reaches the front door where I enter, it has a pleasing pungency that flares my nostrils and carries me away to another time and place. Pausing there by the front counter, I am no longer a twelve-year-old boy standing just across the street from the Model Cafe in downtown Fairbanks in 1944. I am a grizzled old trapper back before the turn of the century, who has just come off a tough wilderness trail to walk into a remote Hudson Bay post.

"Well, what will it be today, Sonny?" says the trader, bringing me back to where I really am. And so I buy my babiche, some snare wire and a box of little .22 shells, and I go out to meet Mom or Dad in the pickup in time for the drive back to the homestead.

I spend most of late October and early November building the furniture: beds, tables, shelves, all lashed together with babiche. I leave so much birch sawdust and bark shavings on the floor that Mom says there is no point in her doing any cleaning until I finally get done. Mom spends most of her time reading and making clothes for Lewie. He is hard to buy warm clothes for, so she even makes him a pair of boots out of an old sheepskin coat. We play a lot of cards, too. Lewie prefers checkers, but he is getting old enough to play three-handed auction bridge, our favorite game. Mom, Dad and I had played a lot of that when we lived that winter at the uranium mine up on the mountain. Now when Dad is around, he, Mom and I usually play cards after Lewie goes to sleep, sometimes for most of the night.

We also have a battery radio which is always tuned to Fairbanks' only radio station, KFAR, so we can listen to Tundra Topics every night. During that program, the announcer reads messages to people about who is going where and when.

"To Cecil John at Hess Creek from Mary in Fairbanks: Annie had a baby boy yesterday. Everybody here is fine. I will be in on the Wien plane on Thursday. Please meet me with the dogs; I have lots of groceries."

"To Edgar Charlie at Venetie from Janice in Fairbanks: The doctor says I have to go to the sanitarium in Sitka. I go tomorrow. I will come home when I can. I love you."

"To Bernice Davis at 14-Mile from Bon: Will drive out Friday night. Have Neil make sure the road is open."

That last message is the one Mom wants to hear because she is out of cigarettes, and making do with Bull Durham. She rolls terrible-looking cigarettes out of that, and she says that it is not all that much better than tea leaves, Mom's smoke of last resort.

Saturday nights are the most fun for listening to the radio because Rueben Gaines comes on to tell neat stories about Alaska, and we can listen to the schottisches and polkas on a show called Alaska Dances.

Once in a while, we listen to the news about the war, but we don't care about that much because none of our family is involved and we know the Allies are winning anyway.

It is mid-November, and today is the big day. Dad brings home two large boxes that came in the mail from the Calvert School in Baltimore. It is time for Lewie and me to go back to school.

THE CALVERT COURSES

WINTER 1944–45

N EW BOOKS ALWAYS LOOK and smell so
nice, and it is exciting to open up a big box
filled with new school books. Then I discover that the Calvert School
has made a mistake. I am supposed to be in the eighth grade, but these
books are for both the seventh and eighth grades. Mom says that the
Calvert School combines those two grades into one year, and the letter
to her that comes with them said I really only have to do the eighth
grade part. I am happy about that until Mom says, "I think we will
have you do the whole thing. It won't hurt you any, and you've got
plenty of time if we get to work right away."

Heck, oh well, that's the way it goes. My schooling has always
been mixed up anyway. I've missed a couple of grades, so I guess doing
one twice is not too bad.

Before I went to the first grade in Hanna, Wyoming, Dad was
teaching school, and he was teaching me arithmetic at home. He made
a bunch of flash cards which we went through almost every night. By
the time I got into the first grade, I could add and subtract numbers, I
knew all my multiplication tables by heart, and I could divide some
too. Since my birthday came at the wrong time of year, I was older
than almost all of the other kids and was way ahead of them in almost
everything except writing. I could print my name but I couldn't write
it or anything else. I was so good at most subjects that it sure hurt
when I found out that nearly all the girls in the class were learning
how to write more quickly—and better—than me.

I spent almost a whole year in just that one school, except for the
month or so when Mom had to stay with her family near Boulder,

87

Colorado, because her father's sickness made him need help. Her sister was teaching in a school near Denver, so they put me in that school. All the kids there spoke Spanish, and except for one blonde girl who also spoke Spanish, I was the only one who was not Mexican. None of the teachers spoke Spanish, and most of the little kids could not speak English. Big girls who spoke English and Spanish always sat in our class to tell the kids what the teachers wanted them to do.

It wasn't much fun going to that school because I'd already learned everything they were teaching, and the kids all spoke Spanish during recess. I could not understand them, and they did not seem to like me much. Instead of calling me by my real name, they called me "Gringo," and some of them had a funny tone in their voice when they said it, like maybe they were laughing at me. After a while some of the boys started being nicer to me, and one day I asked one of the friendliest ones what Gringo meant. He looked real embarrassed, and then he told me, "It means fair-haired boy." I couldn't understand why it bothered him to tell me that; I thought it was a nice name to give me.

I was back in Hanna when second grade started, and went most of the year there. By then Dad had quit teaching school and gone to work in the coal mine because he could make more money. The Union Pacific Railroad owned the mine and the whole town, so everybody worked for them. Right after Dad started in the mine, the company cut the mine shifts to three days a week, so it did not work out well. Dad was not getting any paychecks at all because the company subtracted the bill for rent and food at the company store before they wrote the checks. He had worked for fourteen months without a paycheck when one night he and Mom put Lewie and me to sleep in our car. Just before I went to sleep I saw them turn the house lights off and carry out our big trunk which they tied on the back of the car. When Lewie and I woke up the next morning, we were crossing the Wyoming border into western Colorado and Dad was saying to Mom that we'd made it without seeing a single patrol car. He was worried that the company might send the police after us. We soon stopped in a little town in western Colorado for gas, and there Dad sent a postcard to the Union Pacific Railroad apologizing for skipping out while owing them money. On the card he said he would pay it back when he could.

I finished second grade in Gateway, Colorado. The next winter we were up on the mountain at the uranium mine, so I could not go to school. Mom had borrowed some third-grade school books for me to use, but we spent so much time reading other books and playing cards that I didn't use them much. Toward spring, Mom got to feeling guilty about it, so she made me do a little bit of work.

We moved to Cheyenne that summer where Dad got a job cooking in the Union Pacific Railroad station there. Things had changed a lot while we were living on the mountain, and now jobs were real easy to get because lots of working men were getting drafted. The Union Pacific was so happy to have Dad go to work that they didn't even care about our skipping out on them in Hanna, and of course Dad was paying them back out of his wages.

Dad was not happy about what was going on, though. He'd even get mad just reading advertisements in the magazines like *Life* because they had so much warlike stuff in them. "Dammit, look at this!" he would say, showing a Chrysler Corporation ad to Mom. "They are supposed to be making cars, but the product list starts out with 'army tanks, anti-aircraft guns and army vehicles.' Down near the bottom it says 'passenger cars'...Damn, here's another one from Du Pont. 'In the interest of national defense, conserve anti-freeze so there will be enough to go around,' it says." Dad turns a few pages and sees an ad from a farm tractor company. 'Plowshares *are* Swords,' it says in big letters. "Damn, that rich bastard Roosevelt is doing everything he can to get us into the war, and these companies are all for it too—the sons of bitches."

But Dad was making enough money to pay the company off, and also to buy a car, an early-thirties Dodge for which he paid fifty dollars. I was starting to like school in Cheyenne but after I spent only three weeks in the fourth grade Dad and Mom packed up the car and we headed for West Virginia. That was kind of exciting because Dad was going to a little coal-mining town called Sabine as a spy for Mom's brother, who owned part of that town and its mine. We stopped in Chicago to see him.

Mom's brother Mathew was about the richest person I ever knew. He lived in a big house with lots of grass around it, and he owned parts of seven different companies. He was married to a woman whose parents owned a big golf course in north Chicago and she had a daughter, Susan, about my age. Susan wasn't really my cousin because Mom's brother wasn't her father. Before Uncle Mathew married her mother, Susan's father was killed while riding in a big black car down Michigan

Avenue when another big black car came up alongside and shot him full of holes with a machine gun. I'd seen enough Dick Tracy comic strips to know that only big-time crooks get killed that way, and I think Uncle Mathew might also have been sort of a crook. For one thing, Mom once told me that her brother worked his way through college by writing bad checks, ones that Grandad Sappenfield somehow managed to cover. Anyway, Uncle Mathew had bought this coal company in Sabine and was beginning to think the mine there didn't have much coal. So he hired Dad to go there to find out.

Sabine was a company town like Hanna, but a much worse place. The town was mostly only about one or two houses wide because it was in a small, steep-walled valley through which a tiny stream flowed, really sluggish in places because of the greenish- yellow slime it soaked up from the coal mine dumps upstream. The company put us in a house in the center of the town, the only house occupied by whites that was next to the Negro houses. The Negroes all lived up-valley from us, and the whites down. Everybody bought what they needed at the company store near our house, but the Negroes were allowed to go there only on Wednesday and Saturday mornings. They could come to the Saturday night movies in the theater up over the store but they had to sit on the left side of the aisle, and if they laughed or talked too loud they would be thrown out. Those movies were the only times the blacks and whites ever were together, except maybe at work down in the mine.

Another exception was that William, the boy my age next door, and I got together whenever we could. His mother was not happy about that, and she'd scold William if she saw us together. "William, you stay 'way that po' white trash, you hear," she'd call out. That embarrassed William and me both, but we still did things together when she wasn't looking.

I liked William a lot, and that made what happened to William's older brother James seem extra terrible. It happened because of the bad water in Sabine. The water everybody in Sabine used for washing clothes and bathing came out of the stream and I think it irritated most of the whites that the Negroes got to use it first because they were upstream. All the whites carried drinking water from a spring down below the white end of town, except that the spring sometimes ran dry and then we had to go up and dip water from a shallow open well that the Negroes had in their part of town. The first time Mom sent me up there for water it really bothered me because the three

Negro women who were there dipping water quickly backed away when they saw me. It was strange because they were adults and I was just a kid. Besides, it was their well so I thought the Negroes ought to have first crack at the water, but that is not the way it worked in Sabine. Not until I got my water did the women come back for theirs.

I understood a lot better why those women backed away after what happened to William's brother James. He had a job cutting trees for a farmer who lived down below the town, and late one hot afternoon when he was coming home he stopped to take a drink from the white spring. Two women saw him do it, and before James could get through the white part of town their husbands and some other men battered him with clubs, breaking both his arms. William and I were playing marbles in his yard when James came staggering home, one eye closed and both arms hanging limply down. William had to open the gate for him and the door of the house, too.

I felt sick when I saw James, and I was really sick and furious the next day when I found out how James got hurt. I hated Sabine and was happy that we would be leaving soon because Dad's spying job was over. The only good part about living in Sabine was what had happened to me in school. Both the fourth and fifth grades in the white school were in one room, taught by one teacher. Things went slowly, so after I finished my fourth-grade work each day, I kept busy doing what the fifth graders did. None of the other kids did any homework, but I did all that the teacher gave us. One day she gave us a bunch of three-digit by three-digit multiplication problems as homework, and that night I did them. The teacher did not expect students to do that, so she made us go to the board each day to work the problems given us the day before. She sent me to the board and called out a problem to be written on the board and solved. I happened to remember the answer, and so I wrote just that on the board instead of the problem. The teacher gruffly insisted that I write the problem out and then solve it step by step. I figured she thought I had cheated somehow, and I was scared and shaking so much that I was barely able to do the problem right for her.

She looked real thoughtful as she sent me to my seat. Then about a hour later she came to my desk, exchanged my fourth-grade books for a fifth-grader set, and told me to go sit in that part of the room. So having already avoided the third grade by living on the mountain the year before, I now also got to skip the fourth grade.

We got out of Sabine in late November and Dad tried to find work in Charleston, West Virginia. He didn't get a good job right away, and the only thing I really remember about Charleston was sitting in our second-floor apartment above one of the main streets when we heard a big noise out there. Dad opened the window and we looked down on hundreds of people milling around and shouting. The only word you could make out was "War" because newsboys were shouting it out loudly and the papers they were selling had the word printed in red ink on the top half of the front page. We turned the radio on and heard President Roosevelt tell about Pearl Harbor. Despite Dad's many nasty statements about Roosevelt and about the country being already at war, Dad listened intently and with respect as Roosevelt spoke, and when he finished Dad seemed as excited as everybody else about what was happening.

I did not go to school at all in Charleston, and then we moved to Dayton, Ohio, where it did look like Dad would get a job. Mom put me in school, but that very night the job fell through, so I never went back. We drove to Chicago, arriving on Christmas Eve. Dad now had no money at all, so he went out and sold the car for $20. With that, he paid $6 for an apartment, bought food, and also came home with a Christmas tree. The apartment was in south Chicago, just across the street from the University of Chicago.

Lewie woke up crying soon after we went to bed. Mom and Dad checked us over and found we both were badly bitten by bedbugs, so they washed us and put us to sleep in our own blankets on the floor, and they sat up that night. Dad insisted that the place get fumigated on Christmas Day, and it was.

Now that the war was underway, Dad quickly got a job in a factory, and before long Mom got one too, in a plant that made Norden bombsights. The Chicago schools were much better than others I had been to, so it was tough sledding for a while. I had usually been the best in my class—except in English and writing—but not any longer. By the time school was out that spring, I had caught up with the other kids, but then I moved to a new school in Chicago that fall, and started the sixth grade.

Dad had already gone to Alaska, and Mom was working long hours in the bombsight factory. I baby-sat Lewie most of the summer, spending endless days at the beach because he liked to swim, and in movies that we got into for a dime, also getting a comic book to boot. We saw a few good movies like "Sergeant York" and "King's Row," but I was getting really tired of the Three Stooges always fooling around, of Gene Autry's singing to his horse, of Ginger Rogers' dancing and Esther Williams' swimming, so we began spending a lot of time in the Museum of Science and Industry. The thing that Lewie liked most was a lathe which a person could turn by hand to shave tiny little slivers of metal off a steel bar. I could leave him there by that machine for hours while I went off to look at more interesting displays. The best exhibit, one that I never got tired of, was a whole series of real babies in bottles, all different ages from just a few days old up until the time they were born. They had a pretend working coal mine there too, but they would not let Lewie or me go in it because kids had to be with adults inside the display.

One neat thing about living there by the University of Chicago was that we were close by a library that I could go to in the evenings when Mom was home. It had a kid's room lined with books that was sort of my own private room because nobody except me ever went into it. Before long, I had read all the books in that room—except for the picture books for little kids, and then I began to work on what the librarian called the 'intermediate section,' for high school students. When I started checking books out of that section the librarian thought I was stealing them or something. The first time, I remember her looking at me very sternly and saying, "You don't want those books. You can't read them." She let me have them, but she was right—some of them were too much for me.

When school started, Lewie went only half days and so I could not take care of him well enough any more. Mom decided the best thing to do was put us in an orphan's home up closer to the Loop, and she got a place to stay nearer her work. Most of the kids in the orphans' home really were orphans, but several others had one or two parents nearby, just like Lewie and me. Lewie liked the home a lot because he had so many other kids to play with. I did not like it much, but the school we went to near there was fun. Instead of working in a class, you got to do work by yourself on special lessons, and you could go as fast as you wanted to.

Then Mom went to Alaska, and so Lewie and I went to live on the farm in Iowa with Aunt Phena and Uncle Irwin. We walked one mile to school, which wasn't easy on cold days because the school was north of the farm so that the wind blew right in your face. Coming home was better. This school had only one teacher for all eight grades. I was alone in the sixth grade, one girl was in the seventh, and the fifth and fourth grades had one or two girls apiece. Altogether, we had about fourteen students, most of them just little kids like Lewie. Being the only older boy was interesting in some ways, but the girls were always doing things to embarrass me. Things like pinching each other's legs and fannies when I was close, and then all pretending that I did it. One girl even tried to catch my head between her legs when I pushed her on the swing at recess. After I finished the seventh grade and got to Alaska, I thought about that, and I wished I had not been so shy. I know I could have had a lot more fun in that school than I did.

It's too late for that since there are no girls around now that I am taking correspondence courses. That is just as well because as I dig into the Calvert course I find that it is a lot of fun, and I am pleased to discover that Calvert's seventh grade is so different from my work last year back in Iowa that I do not feel like I am repeating anything. I really like the Calvert way of doing things. The course is arranged into five separate topics, and each topic is organized into a six-week unit. If I work an hour a day on each of the topics, I am expected to complete a unit for each topic every six weeks. We then mail the unit to Baltimore for grading by a teacher there, and when she finishes she mails the materials back. In the meantime, I am supposed to continue with the next set of units. Acting as supervisor, Mom gets a separate set of papers which contain timed tests that I do for each unit.

Mom has agreed to let me work on only one topic at a time, rather than all five simultaneously. It is so much fun being able to concentrate on one thing that I go at it hard. Sometimes I can complete a six-week unit of one subject in one day, or in two or three days at the most. When the first set of units come back, I am tickled to learn that I have received top grades on all except English. That is my bad subject. The teacher who grades that course says I am going to have to work hard on my grammar. She also says that when I write themes I need to stick to the point better. I tend to ramble around a lot about things that are not necessary, she says.

The best and worst days are the ones when the graded units came back in the mail. They are good days because the grades I receive usually are all "1"s, the same as "A"s, and it is fun to see what the teachers have written on my papers. I can tell that they are nice people, and that they work hard. But those days are bad, too, because no matter how well I have done on each unit, the teacher always finds some mistakes that I have to correct to Mom's satisfaction. Sometimes the teachers even make me send back to them papers that I have worked over—especially the ones on English.

English isn't much fun, but I work hard on it, and as we go along, the teacher says that she can see that I am doing better. Even so, I have a terrible time trying to read and write reports on Shakespeare's plays. I really hate Shakespeare, and I can't make any sense out of the plays. I struggle away manfully at "The Merchant of Venice" until Mom finally lets me off the hook. She takes over the reading of it and the other Shakespeare stuff, and tells me gist of the stories. I then write the required themes on each play.

When the grades come back from Baltimore on that part, they are very good. The teacher writes that she is impressed by my work because she has rarely seen students my age show such good comprehension of the meaning of Shakespeare's works.

COLD WEATHER

WINTER 1944–45

THE CORRESPONDENCE SCHOOL WORK is keeping me busy, and now that we are getting some really cold weather I am thinking that this first winter in Alaska is going to be the most enjoyable I've had since we lived up on the mountain at the uranium mine in Colorado. Up there at the mine, we were all alone, except for a rancher named Bart Scott who lived six miles away and a trapper named Charley Smith and his wife who lived three miles away. Charley was now a trapper, but he had not been one very long, and "Smith" was not really his last name, either. Dad said Charley was a former newspaper reporter from Chicago in hiding. He carefully watched the trails leading to his house, and if he saw some unknown person approach, Charley grabbed his gun and sneaked out the back to a hiding place in the rocks up above his cabin. Dad figured that Charley had gotten in bad with gangsters back in Chicago, or maybe with something like the FBI. He was a good neighbor to us, though. He gave us all the deer meat we wanted to eat, and that was the only meat we ate that winter.

Living on the homestead is like living on the mountain. Almost the only person Mom, Lewie and I see is Dad when he comes out from town to stay with us for a day or two while he is off work. We do get into town once in a while and we sometimes go out to see Nellie Kelly at 23-Mile. Once past the guard shack at 6-Mile, hers is the first occupied structure you see along the road going down the Alcan from Fairbanks.

Nellie Kelly is about the biggest, strongest lady I ever saw. She used to have a roadhouse at 18-Mile, but when the army built Moose

97

Creek dike it flooded her out. She tried to get the army to move her roadhouse for her or build her another one, without success. Finally she got mad and moved the place all by herself. Without any help from anyone, she took down all the logs, hauled them to 23-Mile, and put them back together again alongside the highway there. Nellie Kelly still calls her place a roadhouse, but it really is just a bar. This is a good location for a bar, since it is right alongside 26-Mile Camp, the emergency airfield where quite a few construction workers stay.

Nellie Kelly is as strong as most any man, and she does things that you wouldn't expect a woman to do. She even has her own motor boat, and because of it she has the only saloon I'd ever seen that, in addition to all the bottles, has a special set of elegant matched books from the Smithsonian Institution up on the backbar. Nellie told me that one day she got her boat motor tangled up in some vines hanging down into the creek from the Moose Creek Bluff, and when she swept them away there was a whole bunch of Indian hieroglyphics. She sent word about them to Washington. In appreciation for her reporting the find, the men from the Smithsonian who came to inspect the hieroglyphics gave her the set of books, and she sure was proud of them. I asked her to tell me where the Indian figures were but she said that they are gone because the army blew them up with dynamite when they built the dike.

Nellie Kelly not only works like a man, she talks more like a man than most men do. She can hardly say anything without using swear words, and some of them are pretty bad. The first time when we went there, she was throwing a drunk out of her bar, and she was saying some really nasty things to him, using just about every bad word I'd ever heard, and even a few new ones.

Nellie Kelly can be nice, too. She has a pretty Samoyed female dog that the famous dog musher Leonard Seppala gave her. The dog whelped two pups that ran loose around the roadhouse, because, as Nellie Kelly claimed, "Some goddamn wolf came in one night and screwed her right on her chain," except she didn't say "screw."

Nellie said I could have the pups if I could catch them. While she and Mom had coffee, Lewie and I went out and tried to grab the pups. They were so wild that neither of us could get anywhere near them. Finally, Nellie came out to help, but I did not think her method of catching them was likely to get results. She just ran around swearing at the pups while throwing whiskey bottles at them, ones that were laying around on the ground outside the roadhouse. But one pup tried to get away by running into the open door of a shed. "Gotcha now, you little sonofabitch," Nellie yelled, slamming the door on him.

The pup fought like crazy when I went in to put a collar on him, and his eyes were green as could be. We never did catch the other pup, but I have this one home now. I call him Wolf, and I think when he gets bigger he is going to a great addition to a dog team.

Even with all the schoolwork I am doing, I get outside a lot, and it is interesting to learn what it is like to be out when it is really cold. Sometimes when Dad is home, we go out and cut trees. It is surprising how warm we can stay even if it's forty below. I do not have a coat, and instead wear shirts and sweaters under a heavy woolen shirt on which Mom has sewn pieces of wool blanket to make it warmer. That outer jacket has to come off if we are working at temperatures much warmer than forty below. We have decided that twenty below is the perfect temperature for working out in the woods. If it is warmer than that, you tend to sweat all over and get your clothes wet, even when stripped down to just one sweater.

I find that if I am careful I can stay outside for hours at 60 below without getting cold. At that temperature, you have to keep moving so that your feet do not get cold in your moccasins, and you cannot hold onto something like an axe for very long without getting cold hands.

One day when it is sixty-five below, Dad and I go out for a while to cut down green trees. You can drop them with a sledgehammer as easy as with an axe because the frozen trees just shatter where you hit them. Sometimes I can cut a six-inch tree with just two blows. After about a half hour, our hands get too cold to keep going, but it is fun while it lasts.

We've heard that when it is cold like that you can throw a cup of water up in the air and it will not come down because all the water freezes into little ice particles that stay in the air. Lewie and I try it, but we can't be sure. We think we might be hearing pieces of ice hit the snow.

Even when it is really cold, Lewie and I do not dress up to go out to pee at night. Lewie is so lazy that sometimes he does not even put his shoes on. It is pretty funny watching him out there squirting ev-ery-whichy-way while jumping up and down to keep his bare feet from sticking to the snow.

The only trouble with not putting your clothes on when you go out like that is that the northern lights might be playing. If they are especially pretty, you want to stay out to watch, but if you are just in your underwear you cannot do that very long.

Even aside from the cold, winter here on the homestead is different from anything I've seen before. One curious thing is that it never really gets dark at night like in Iowa, Colorado or other places like that. One reason I guess is that everything is covered with snow, but you can tell that there is more to it than that because even if it's cloudy the sky itself glows with a soft light. I talked with Dad about this and he says that he has read that the air high up has a glow to it something like the aurora borealis, but very weak. Dad says it gives out about as much light as the all stars do in places farther south, but up here nearer the North Pole the glow is much brighter. Dad is smart about stuff like that, probably because he used to read so much when he was in college and was a school teacher.

Anyway, you never need to carry a light when you go out at night here, and if the moon is out or if the northern lights are bright it can be almost like day except that everything is more blue. This is a night like that so I go out snowshoeing on my trail up 14-Mile Slough just because it is so much fun being alone out where everything is so beautiful. Even if you've got a good trail packed down like this one it is more fun to be on snowshoes than just to walk on your moccasins. The hickory and the babiche in the snowshoes somehow join together to give a little extra springiness that causes you to take those long swinging steps that feel so good as you glide along. The snowshoes also make that neat crunching sound that echoes back from the trees when it is extra cold out.

When I make a new trail that I might use again I try to make it just a little wider than it would be if I am just passing by once. To do it right and make a really good trail you have to go back over it before the packed snow freezes, and if you do that you end up with a trail that is sort of like a square trench in the snow. Then later you can speed along without watching the trail because it guides you and the snowshoes along and lets you watch for other things.

One of the strange things about winter here is that the air is always so still, and once the snow falls it never moves around. I don't think we have had a breath of wind since the snow first came last fall, and that is why all my snowshoe trails are still there. If this was Wyoming or Iowa or some of the other places I've lived my trails wouldn't last very long because of the wind. But now, out on the limbs of the spruce trees to either side of 14-Mile Slough, the snow stands about six inches deep, and that is one of the things that makes it so pretty at night on the homestead, and the best time of all to be out on the trail.

It's like that tonight, and except for the creak and crunch of my snowshoes, everything is dead quiet as I speed along. I think I am the only living thing out here tonight until I hear the horrible piercing scream over in the trees. It is a high-pitched "EEeeeeee" like a woman screeching in agony, and it tells me that three of us were here along the frozen slough just a moment ago. But now we are just two, because the rabbit is dead and only the unseen snowy owl and I remain. The rabbit's death call is really terrible; I sure hope they don't shriek like that when they get caught in one of my snares.

Then, just as though the rabbit's screech has called it over, one heck of an aurora borealis starts coming in fast above the treetops. It is a brilliant green double curtain with red at its bottom. One end of it suddenly curls around and it becomes a woman's pleated, red-hemmed skirt with matching inner petticoat that swishes out over my head as she dances closer. Oh boy, now I can see right up her—all the way to her wasp waist that all the pleats point to. She is fabulously beautiful but she is empty, I think, for she has no upper body that I can see, nor any feet. Yet on those unseen feet she trips along, swirling her skirts here and there across the sky until she gives the hem one last fling that throws it out of sight over the trees. Like the rabbit, she is gone and the sky looks very black. Then up there in that black space between the treetops a new aurora forms in place and this one is really strange because it has no pleats and is deep red all over. It starts at one end and grows as though some giant hand is painting the sky with a wide, bloody brush, writing a big symbol that finally looks just like a perfect question mark that is missing its dot. The red aurora stays there just a few seconds and then fades away to nothingness. Wow, I've seen a lot of northern lights so far this winter, but never anything like that!

Suddenly I feel very cold, and I realize that I have been standing stock still in my trail watching all this since the owl dug his talons into the rabbit's back. I shudder, turn around, and start moving fast to get warmed up again, not quite sure if my feeling of being cold is all due to the temperature. I don't believe in signs and stuff like that, but it is weird that so much has happened here all of a sudden and that it has ended with a big red "What?" This is the sort of thing a person is not likely to forget.

All of us are learning a lot about living in the cold this winter, and we can see that people tend to exaggerate when they tell about how bad it is. Really cold weather is not much different than slightly cold weather—you just get cold a lot quicker. If you do not have to fiddle around with anything made out of metal, living in the cold is not bad at all. The worst metal objects are those that have engines, machines like cars or tractors. Dad and I have been learning a lot about that fairly quickly. My first lesson was that one I learned the night I forgot to drain the pickup properly and broke its engine block.

Dad bought enough expensive antifreeze to fill the Farmall H, but we soon learned that we could not start the tractor in the cold unless we drained the antifreeze, heated it on the kitchen stove and then poured it back in the tractor. Each time we drained the tractor we lost some of the antifreeze. Dad decided that if we were going to drain the tractor before every use, we might just as well use only water and then drain it out at the end of each work session.

This method worked well until one day, when it was about 20 below, the tractor started to heat up. Dad realized that the radiator was frozen because the fan was pulling cold air into it. Something had to be done fast, so Dad made a heating torch out of a gasoline-soaked rag on a stick. He held this in front of the radiator until we could see that the radiator was beginning to thaw. He wanted to make sure all the ice was gone, so he put more gasoline on the torch, and held it close to the radiator. All of a sudden, we heard the metallic clatter of half-melted solder pellets going through the fan, and a three-inch hole appeared in the middle of the radiator. All the rest of the water in the tractor quickly ran out on the ground.

This experience led to a trip to town for repair of the radiator, and it taught Dad and me to beware of hot torches around radiators. A side lesson learned that day was always to block off a water-filled radiator completely with cardboard to keep it from freezing. By doing that we have been able to continue to use water as a coolant even when it gets down to sixty below.

For the H we have worked out foolproof starting and operating procedures that are successful no matter what the temperature. First, of course, we heat water on Mom's stove. A few minutes before pouring it in the tractor's radiator, we begin heating the oil pan with a gasoline-soaked torch. We have learned that no fumes come off cold gasoline, so we do not have to worry about explosions. In the beginning, we were draining gasoline from the tractor's tank—which sits directly over the engine—into a can, and then pouring gasoline from the can onto a torch before lighting it. We progressed to pouring gasoline from the can onto a burning torch with no trouble at all because really cold gasoline does not even burn well in a direct flame. So now we don't even use the can at all, and just hold the burning torch under the gas tank and open the drain cock. Flames may move an inch or two up the stream of gasoline, but never as far as up to the gas tank itself.

Once the oil pan is heated and the hot water poured in, we transfer the torching operation to the carburetor and air intake pipe. Finally, we start cranking and soon the engine will start—well, most of the time. If it does not start within a few minutes, we have to drain the tractor again before its radiator and engine freeze up and break.

One trick we use is to put a block of wood on the pedal to open the clutch out when we shut the tractor down at the end of a workday. If the weather is extremely cold, the clutch will not move when the next starting operation commences, and it is not possible to crank the H on a cold morning with its transmission engaged. Even with the transmission disengaged, we cannot budge the engine crank before pouring in the hot water and torching the oil pan.

Now that the cabin is finished, we have little use for the tractor except to haul in firewood and drag snow off the old Richardson Trail out to its intersection with the Alcan at 14-Mile. But each start is a cold start, and we are doing enough of them that the torching is rapidly turning the front end of the tractor black. It's still new on the inside, but the poor H sure looks old on the outside.

Christmas rolls around, and it too is like the Christmas we had when we were snowed in up on the mountain at the uranium mine. That year, making presents was a have-to thing, but this year we do it from choice. I've tanned some of the skins of rabbits I've caught, so with Mom's help Lewie sews up rabbit skin to make nice little fur purses for our grandmothers and Aunt Phena. Using birch bark, willow twigs, babiche and clothes-hanger wire, I put together what I think are pretty nice lampshades for everybody. Mom doesn't need one because we have no electricity, and so for her I build a little set of bookshelves to put up over her bed. It's harder to think of useful things to make for men, but then I remember that both Dad and Uncle Irwin like to play cribbage. So they get cribbage boards that I make out of a moose horn I found, using a hacksaw and a hand drill. That is a slow proposition, and I'm not too happy with how well I get all the holes lined up. I barely get Uncle Irwin's done by December 1, the last day for mailing Christmas presents to the States.

We have thousands, maybe millions, of spruces to pick over for a Christmas tree, but it is hard to find a decent one. The small trees on the homestead are so scraggly that Lewie and I shake snow off dozens of them before we finally give up and take a tree we aren't too happy with. After we get it in the house, I drill a few holes in its trunk and stick extra limbs in them, and then the tree looks pretty good. Mom and Lewie thread up wild cranberry and popcorn on strings to hang on the tree, and at the NC store Mom buys two packages of those metal icicles to drape all over the limbs. The tree looks darn good when we are done.

Two big boxes arrive from Iowa just before Christmas, and one of them is a real disaster. Had Aunt Phena asked first before sending that box, Mom and Dad would have told her not to do it, but of course Christmas presents are supposed to be secrets. The box looks just like an egg crate, and that's because it is an egg crate full of what used to be eggs. Only one egg out of the twenty-four dozen Aunt Phena packed in the box came through unbroken. Boy, what a mess, and it cost her a bundle to send the crate, too.

The other box contains some neat presents, including a fine pocket knife for me and a bow and arrow set for Lewie. Of course Lewie loses all his arrows in the deep snow the first day after Christmas, but we know we will be able to find them again in the spring.

Winter moves along and now it's early February. The weather's been colder than heck these past few weeks. We've been doing fine living mainly in the new cabin, although that barrel stove has a fierce appetite. I work every day for two to three hours to cut wood for it, a stack about three feet high and five feet long, which we store right alongside the stove beneath a window.

The roof gives us no trouble at all, but it is strange that the tongue-and-groove boards remain bare of snow almost all the time. Even during a heavy snowstorm, not much snow piles up, and it is all gone within a day or so. None of it seems to melt, it just magically evaporates away.

One night Lewie goes to sleep fairly early and Mom and I continue to read in bed. Each of us has a kerosene Aladdin lamp by our beds, up on the stacks of Blazo boxes we use for magazine and book shelves. "Guess I'll quit," says Mom, blowing out her lamp. "Better make sure you load the stove up again before going to sleep; it's about 35 below out."

I am into this really neat book called "The Other Side of the Mountain" so I read for another hour, slip on my boots for a quick trip outside and then fix the fire and drift off to sleep. And then I guess I am dreaming...it's a terrible dream, too, because I am lying on my back and very, very slowly sinking down through the ice out on 14-Mile Slough getting wetter and colder by the moment.

Hey, this is no dream! I am soaking wet and cold as the ice in my dream; my whole bed is wet, and water is pouring down through the ceiling all over me. Mom wakes up, too, and she's got the same problem. We get a lamp going and then we see that it is raining like crazy outside. Going out to check the thermometer, I discover that it is forty-five above. The air is moving; it smells good, and it feels warm and soggy. "We're having a chinook," Mom says as she comes outside, too. "I've heard of them; it's warm air blowing up from the coast."

Lucky Lewie sleeps through it all because for some reason no water comes down onto his bed at all. Mom and I think about moving into the other room, which has a roof that doesn't leak. The trouble is that our bedding is wet so we just decide to sit by the stove until the rain lets up. As we talk about it over cocoa, Mom and I realize that this may be our chance to put the roofing on, so I go get it from where it is stored in the other cabin and bring it in near the stove.

The rain lets up well before dawn, so at first light I go up on the roof and nail down roofing as fast as I can. Mom carries the rolls out one at a time and hands them up to me. I quickly unroll each one to get it flat before it breaks up because the wind is down and the air is getting colder again. It is strange up there on the roof looking out over all the naked trees and bushes. Yesterday they had snow all over them, but the rain and the heat has removed it all. By four o'clock I have the job done, just in time, too, because darkness comes and the temperature drops down almost to zero and is headed lower. I barely get that last roll stretched out before it stiffens up.

During the week after the chinook we discover that we do not have to go out to the thermometer to tell how cold it is. The roofing nails that Dad bought are so long that some of them have come right through the roof boards, and if it's below zero outside, some of them over in the corners of the cabin get frost on them. I've penciled in on the ceiling near each nail what the temperature has to be for frost to form on it, so we've got a sort of inside thermometer now. It doesn't work perfectly because it depends on how well the stove is doing, but in the mornings when the fire is down the nails are accurate to about five degrees. I get the feeling that the cabin is warmer now than before the chinook, too. I guess it should be some because we've added a good eighth of an inch or more of roofing to the tongue-and-groove boards, and they are just three-quarters of an inch thick.

MOM'S PET MOUSE

ONE WINTER DAY

DAD IS ALWAYS PRETTY SERIOUS about most things, and he does not joke around much. He has always insisted that Lewie and I use good table manners and that we behave when we are inside the house. He has spent a lot of time telling us stuff like how to get along if we ever get lost and how to find our way home. Even when I was a little kid back in Wyoming and Colorado, I knew how to build a fire from things you could find wherever you were, and if you got lost you always went downhill until you found a stream. Then if you followed the stream down you would always come to a road or a house. That's maybe even more important here in Alaska where we don't have hardly any roads.

Dad also makes sure that Lewie and I know all about guns. He has established all sorts of rules that we have to follow when we carry a gun. The main rules are that guns are always loaded even if they're not—but we do keep our guns loaded all the time—so you never let one point at another person. If Lewie and I were out with a gun, the one who is carrying it always has to walk in front. Dad says you should have a special place in the house for a gun, and that you should not touch the gun unless you are going to take it outside right away.

All this is second nature with me now because my training began four years ago, back when we lived at the uranium mine in Colorado. Uncle Irwin gave me a single-shot .32 rifle that I carried everywhere when I went out away from the mine. One of the first lessons Dad gave me was how to get through a fence with a gun. He said a lot of people shot themselves or those with them when going through fences. Colorado had fences everywhere, but the lesson is not of much use now because I haven't seen a fence since I got to Alaska.

Dad's gun-handling lessons cover just about every situation, and it goes without saying that a person must never—absolutely never—let a gun go off inside a house. If that were to happen it probably would be the last time the kid who did it would ever be allowed to hold a gun again. Guns are not playthings, Dad says, and he makes sure Lewie and I understood that careless handling of guns is just as bad as playing with them.

Dad's serious ways, and especially his seriousness about guns is just part of the reason this has been such a strange day. Winter is well along now, and of course we have abandoned the first cabin and have moved Mom's bed and all the canned good into Lewie's and my room. However, whenever Mom needs to bake something, she fires up the kitchen stove and goes at it. While doing this, she has become acquainted with a little mouse that lives down under the floorboards beneath the stove. The floorboards were green when Dad put them down, and they now have dried out enough to leave good-sized cracks for this mouse to crawl through. He is a cute little thing who has been sticking his head up through a crack near one leg of the stove whenever he hears Mom. She's been feeding him little bits of bread, and he's been coming out to eat, even while she is baking. Sometimes when I am doing schoolwork, I can hear Mom in there talking to the mouse like he is a little kid. She obviously likes this little mouse.

Today Mom was busy cleaning up after baking bread as Dad and I came in from working. Dad's feet were cold, so he sat on a chair in front of the stove with both his feet in the warm oven. Dad seemed in high spirits and he was sitting there happily sipping a cup of coffee and warming his feet when Mom's pet mouse comes out from under the stove wanting a handout. I watch as Dad looks down at him sort of askance. Then his eyes twinkle and a smile spreads across his face as he reaches for the loaded .22 rifle that stands in its usual place behind the stove. "You silly little bastard," Dad says gently as he lays the end of the rifle barrel down against the mouse's head. Dad is just playing of course, but that sure surprises me. Now the cute little mouse is peering directly up the gun barrel. "Kerblouie!" the gun goes off.

My jaw drops as I hear it. My word, Dad has just intentionally fired a gun off inside the house, and of course it blows the mouse to smithereens. I hear Mom give out a long low "Oohh," and as I watch her face I see it express agony, then anger, and finally a terrible sadness. Tears roll down her cheeks as she quickly walks into the other room. Seeing this brief but intense burst of anger aimed at Dad is almost as shocking to me as Dad's firing the gun. I have never seen Mom direct that emotion toward him before. I felt terribly sorry for her, having lost her pet mouse like that, but on the other hand, what Dad has done is so unexpected and out of character that it seems funny, too.

We've had supper now, a quiet one without much talking, and Dad is on the way back to town to work a late shift. I've been thinking about his shooting the mouse ever since it happened, and I know Mom has too because she is doing something she doesn't do very often. She is sitting across the room with her eyes closed playing on her violin, playing the solo to Mendelssohn's Concerto in E Minor like she used to do on stage with the Boulder Symphony Orchestra before she married Dad.

Listening to her sad music, I am deciding that what Dad has done is not funny at all. At first I just thought it was not like Dad to do such a thing, but as I listen to Mom play I can see that, in an odd sort of way, his action was in character. Dad always has been pretty thoughtful and considerate of other people but sometimes with the family, especially with Mom, it is different.

It seems that in Dad's mind, the family is part of himself, and Dad is the kind who throws himself all the way at whatever he is into at the moment. Mom seems not to mind or to think she is being put upon if Dad does something like come in and grab a blanket off her bed to put around a tractor or car radiator. Some women probably would object to stuff like that, but it doesn't seem to bother Mom, or if it does she is not going to let anybody know.

Of course things like homesteading and cabin building have to be family things where the family works together as a unit, and we have to use whatever is available without worrying about who it belongs to. Even when we have been separated, like when Lewie and I were in the orphans' home in Chicago, I have always thought of us as a unit, and I know Mom and Dad think that too. Still, the four of us are not really equal parts of the family unit, because we actually have a unit within a unit, with Mom and Dad being the tighter inside unit to which Lewie and I are attached. It's something like the helium atom I was reading about this morning in my Calvert course. My book says that a helium atom has a nucleus containing two protons tied to each other by some strange force that nobody really understands. That nucleus is Mom and Dad, and hooked to that inner unit but not exactly a part of it are Lewie and I. We are the two electrons that kind of wheel around the nucleus to make up the rest of the helium atom—and sometimes break away. Someday Lewie and I will break away, and the nucleus will still be there as a helium atom that will behave differently without its electrons.

Maybe this isn't exactly how it is, but it's close enough because one thing that almost never happens is that the nucleus breaks apart. Sometimes it does, but that is pretty rare. The one family I know of that had broken apart was Mom's sister Virgie and her husband Dillon, but that was because he was sort of a nasty guy who couldn't hold a job, and Aunt Virgie was not about to keep on supporting him forever. Our family will never fall apart—but I guess it could someday if Dad pulls any more tricks like shooting Mom's pet mouse.

A NEW VENTURE

SPRING 1945

THE SNOW IS NOW BEGINNING to melt and we even see a few pussy willows coming out along the northern side of the Old Richardson Trail and other places that get the most sunshine. Even though we did not start the Calvert correspondence courses until mid-November, I have easily finished mine already even though April is not quite over. Except for the Shakespeare part, I am pretty happy with everything I have done, and I think I have learned more this winter than during any other part of my schooling. It makes me realize how much time is spent in a regular school on things not having anything to do with actually learning what you are supposed to.

I received "1"s in all my subjects, and I am especially proud of the grade in English and of the final letter the teacher wrote me. She says that my grammar is much improved, and that my themes are far better than they were when I started. Lewie has not done badly either, although he is still working away at it. Like most young kids, he will try most anything to avoid doing his schoolwork. Mom has to force him to work nearly every morning, but she lets him off the hook about noon, and gives him one day off each week.

Mom is pushing hard on Lewie to finish up now because great plans are afoot. Dad is quitting his job, and Mom will be going to Fairbanks to take a waitressing job. That switch is but one element of the overall plan. Dad is entering the sawmill business with our closest neighbor, Mike Bedoff. He is an old Russian who came to Alaska because of the 1917 revolution, mined for a while, and then acquired a place that another man had homesteaded. This homestead is two miles

111

upstream along 14-Mile Slough and is reachable from the highway by another loop of the old Richardson Trail, one that starts near 15-Mile and comes out again near 17-Mile.

With great enthusiasm, Dad explains to us that Mike says his homestead is loaded with big timber, and Mike is willing to put up the money to buy a used sawmill which Wien Airlines has previously operated down on the Yukon River near Ruby. Dad will own the operation, and he will repay Mike's investment in the sawmill by overly generous payment for the logs taken from his place. Mike will also help in the logging by cutting trees down and telling other people which trees to cut.

Dad has seen sawmills operate, but he has never worked on one. That is no problem because Dad has hired a sawyer, Earl Hirst. "Hirst's the best damn sawyer in the country," Dad brags. "He's expensive; I'll be paying him twenty-two dollars and fifty cents a day plus providing him with a place to live, but he's sure worth it. He knows all there is to know about sawmilling. And I've got several other good men lined up for fifteen dollars a day plus board and room."

Dad says that we will use the Farmall H to haul the logs into the mill, and he is buying another new tractor from International Harvester. This is going to be a Farmall M, bigger than the H, and with a 40-horsepower engine that can better power the sawmill. First, Dad says, we'll use the M on other tasks, just to break in the engine. Dad is not really happy with the way this new tractor is built, but it is the only one available. Like the H, it has steel wheels, but instead of sitting out wide like the H's, the M's front wheels are right under the engine. The rear wheels of the H are 14 inches wide with lugs mounted right on their faces. The M, however, has rear wheels only two inches wide, and its lugs stick out to either side like a moose's ears. Part of the reason why Mom is going to be working in town is to help pay for this new tractor. As with the H, Dad is buying it on credit.

But money will soon be rolling in, and there will be plenty of it because Mike has a lot of good timber, we have the best damn sawyer in the country plus a good crew of men lined up. Dad has done most of the figuring in his head while he worked in town this winter, and he is seeing a high profit from the summer coming up. Not counting in his own labor, he estimates a net of about $20 on every thousand board feet sold, and the operation ought to easily put out two thousand feet a day. By fall, Dad should have a bunch of money saved up, at least three or four thousand dollars.

Dad plans to have the hired help do most of the work, but he will be busy too. Since Mom is going to be working in town, Dad will be up early to cook breakfast for the crew and pack their lunches. He'll be able to go out and work with the crew on some days, and he will also handle all the lumber sales. That is going to be the easy part because of the high demand for lumber in town. Dad will also cook suppers for everybody unless Mom is working a shift that lets her be home in the evenings. It sure does sound swell. I am so excited about this new venture and so eager to go to work that I am there the first day the sawmill and Earl Hirst arrive over at Mike's place.

Earl Hirst is a short, big-stomached man with reddish-white hair and a grumpy expression most of the time. His hair does not lie down quite right, and he always wears an old wide-brimmed World War I army hat pinched in at the top. In that funny hat, Earl Hirst looks a lot like an oversized elf, but his bearing is that of a superior being. As sawyer, he knows he holds the most important position. Dad seems to hang on his every word, and Mr. Hirst does truly seem to be an authority on most everything.

Mr. Hirst is not sure at first that he wants a kid around, but as he begins to assemble the sawmill I watch and help whenever I can. Before long, he is accepting me, and I am doing some of the assembly work under his supervision.

While we work, Mr. Hirst tells me stories about how he used to mine up in the Nabesna country where a lot of Indians lived. He tells me things like how the Nabesna Indians keep mosquitoes away by burning the fungus disks that grow on birch trees and how they hunt for moose. A good hunter never follows a moose's tracks, Mr. Hirst says. If an Indian finds a track, he will walk out in a half-circle away from it until he comes back to the track again, then continue with another half-circle. Finally he will walk a full circle without seeing a track, and then he knows where the moose is. Mr. Hirst claims he has seen Indians go out and kill moose this way using only bows and arrows. Mostly, though, they use guns, but they always get real close to a moose before shooting it to avoid wasting ammunition. Nobody should have to use more than one shot to kill a moose or a bear, Mr. Hirst says.

He does have some neat things to tell about the prospecting and living over there with those Indians, but I think maybe Earl Hirst is a BSer too because some of the things he tells me are wild. A lot of his stories probably are made-up lies, and when he tells them to me he is just having fun with what he thinks is a gullible kid. Like one of the first stories he told me, the one he said explained why his hair is so funny. He said that he was riding a horse along the ridges over in the Nabesna country when a big grizzly bear came up behind him and pulled him off the horse. The bear bit the top of Earl's head off, just the scalp part though, and then ran away when some other people came up. They picked up Earl's scalp and tied it back on his head with a piece of cloth. Several days went by before Bob Reeve, the bush pilot from Valdez, could take Earl out to the doctor. The doctor then discovered that the men had put Earl's scalp on crossways and that it had started to grow back on his head. So Earl claimed the doctor just cleaned some of the moss and rocks out and left the scalp that way, and that's why his hair is funny. No way am I going to believe something like that.

But that was before today, and now I am on my way back from town thinking that I am going to have to pay close attention to Earl Hirst for a couple of reasons. I've gotten new information while on an errand for Dad. He sent me to the Independent Lumber Company's sawmill alongside the Chena River for a special sawmill pulley. When the man there gave me the pulley he said, "I hear your dad has hired Earl Hirst for a sawyer; he could have done a lot better, you know." What is this? Dad said Hirst is the best in the country, so I asked the man what was wrong with Earl Hirst. "Well, he couldn't work here, that's for sure. He wastes too much lumber by cutting off slabs that are too thick." I asked the man if he knew anything else about Earl Hirst.

The man laughed and then said, "Oh yeah, I learned a lot about Earl from a friend of mine who prospected one summer with him over in the Nabesna years ago. Ol' Earl is a character, and he was one of the first white men to spend much time with the Indians over there. Back then he was quite a man with the ladies—and you know that red hair of his—well when the anthropologists from up at the university finally got into the Nabesna country they found lots of young Indians with red hair. Ol' Earl sure had himself a good time over there in the Nabesna." The man laughed some more and then said, "And speaking of Earl's hair; did you know that his hair is crooked? One time a bear tore the top of his head off, and when my friend and another guy put it back on Earl's head they got it crosswise. Ha, ha, ha; it's been like that ever since!"

Well, so I guess Earl Hirst really isn't a BSer after all, so maybe all his stories are true enough to listen to. But what the guy said about Earl not being the best sawyer in the country bothers me, so when the time comes to start sawing I will watch to see if he really does waste lumber.

That time comes in a few days. We have the mill all assembled and have hooked its shaft up to the Farmall H's power take-off pulley with a long, flat belt. Earl has me speed up and slow down the H's engine until it is going at just the right pace. Every saw blade is different, Earl says, and unless it runs at just the right speed, somewhere between 400 and 600 rpm, the blade will take on a dish-like shape. He sure is right about that: this blade is sixty inches in diameter, and when it is not turning just right you can see a curve in it when you put your eye close to the spinning teeth. To help the blade run true when it is cutting, the sawmill has a U-shaped guide clamp placed near and just below where logs enter the blade. This guide holds two wooden blocks that press against the sawblade near its outer rim, just inside the teeth. Earl shows me how to adjust that guide, and also how to sharpen the teeth with a file and reshape their cutting edges by placing a steel forming device called a swage against them and banging on it with a hammer.

It takes three men and a boy to run this sawmill at full speed. Two men stand down behind the saw blade carrying away the slabs and boards as they come off the mill. They walk in a narrow space formed by the sawmill's track on one side and the long belt running back to the Farmall H on the other. Earl, as sawyer, stands on a small platform at the head of the saw with one hand pushing on a wooden handle that controls the motion of the log carriage up and down the track. He also operates another handle on the carriage that moves the log sideways to determine where the saw will cut it, and he helps the log turner standing behind him set and unset the sharp hook-like steel dogs that dig into the top of the log to hold it in place. When the saw is actually carving through the log, Earl holds his one hand up to shield his face from splinters of wood and bark that catch in the teeth of the sawblade, and then spew out like water coming from a rotating sprinkler. Green logs, the kind he is sawing, also cast out a stream of watery pitch that clings to Earl Hirst's reddish-white beard and whatever else it strikes.

Earl is always in the direct line of fire because he holds his head so that he can sight along the saw cut to see that the blade is running straight.

My job as chief log turner puts me behind Earl, where I can watch him operate the mill. When all is going well, the smoothly repetitive motions and sounds make it seem like I am up close to a comic ballet duet performed by a dumpy little elfin prima donna wearing an old army hat and her mechanical partner, a large machine totally subject to the diva's desires. Earl's sawyering motions—a series of arm outstretchings, torso twistings, and risings up on toes to draw the log closer to the saw—are so ballerina-like that I can almost see the front of his tutu standing out beyond his round belly and the back of it jutting out past the suspenders that hold his stiff brown canvas pants up over his scrawny butt. Earl leads the dance and the mill responds, all to the accompaniment of a mechanical orchestra that features the intermittent high-pitched whine of the big saw as it slices through the logs. Metallic clinks and clanks from various parts of the mill come in on cue, as do the leathery slaps of belts against pulleys and the deep-throated rumbles of the Farmall H's engine each time its governor reacts to the call for more power that transmits down through the long main drive belt. Out in front of Earl, the two men in supporting roles pick up boards or slabs and then dance away to place them off-stage beyond the H. As Earl's understudy and helper, I stand a log-length behind him with peavey in hand and at the ready whenever the score calls for a log-turning.

It doesn't take long to learn that Earl mentally sizes up each log as I roll it onto the carriage. He is making the important decision what boards to go for because that determines where various saw cuts have to be placed to minimize waste, always keeping in mind that the very last board has to be at least two inches thick, even if you want only one-inch boards. Part of the fun of the job for me is to keep score on how well I can second-guess Earl's cuts. And as time goes by, I decide that what that other man had said about Earl is true: he does cut thick slabs. If I were the sawyer, I'd make them thinner and get more boards out of the logs.

If all goes well, and if a log is small, its conversion to sawdust, slabs and boards maybe takes only about three minutes, or if the log is bigger, as much as ten minutes. Earl figures that if he can saw 60 logs a day he is doing fine. These logs mostly range in top diameter from

about eight to fourteen inches so they each produce 40 to over 100 board feet of lumber. Thus, a proper day's sawing yields 2000 to 3000 board feet, worth $200 to $300.

Of course the mill can't run all day because Earl has to sharpen the saw teeth about every two hours, a job that takes him fifteen to twenty minutes. While he does that, the rest of us occupy ourselves by rolling more logs up on the ways ready to go on the mill or in working at scooping sawdust or dragging slabs away. A sawmill like this produces huge piles of slabs and an immense amount of sawdust. If the mill is making primarily one-inch boards, nearly 20 percent of every log goes into the sawdust pile. An endless belt carries the sawdust from a pit beneath the saw to a pile some twenty feet away, but even that is not enough to keep the sawdust cleared out. To help with that, Dad designs and builds what he calls a buckboard. It looks like a small billboard with two handles sticking out its top and has a loop of cable attached near its bottom so the Farmall M or H can pull it. Two men hold onto the handles striving—sometimes without success—to keep the buckboard vertical as the tractor drags its through the sawdust.

Pushed by the buckboard, the yellow-brown pile of sawdust spreads out like a sand dune encroaching upon the nearby forest.

We have been sawing a month now, and the crew has cleaned all the saw timber from the school section. The men begin work on Mike Bedoff's place. "Got lotsa big trees, maka lotsa boards," Mike had said in his broken English, but the men quickly discover otherwise. Mike's property does have many trees but practically all of them are too small for making lumber. Much expensive crew time is spent following Mike through the woods looking for a tree big enough to cut.

Dad is now wishing that he had walked around on Mike's property before entering into the agreement with him and building the mill near his house. Another problem is that the two-inch boards are piling up. Dad has been able to sell all the one-inch lumber we can make, especially after he bought a used planing mill that allows converting the rough boards to shiplap. Nevertheless, Dad is having a tough time meeting the payroll every week. Whenever he can come up with enough money from lumber sales to pay salary owed to them, he starts laying men off. The crew drops one by one from a maximum of six, until only Earl Hirst, Dad and I are left.

Dad is feeling real low then, thinking that he might have to fire Earl Hirst and go back to town to work in a restaurant. Then, suddenly everything turns around. Dad has come up with an exciting new scheme that is going to pay all the bills and give a cash surplus by the end of the summer.

BERRY CREEK

SUMMER 1945

DAD HAS PULLED OFF A REAL COUP. He has managed to buy 150,000 board feet of logs, already cut and stacked, for only $225. The reason the logs are so cheap is that they are so far out of town, 143 miles down the Alcan Highway from Fairbanks, some forty miles beyond Big Delta. Three years ago, when it was building the Alcan, the army built a logging camp at a place called Berry Creek, right alongside the new highway. The army put up a Quonset hut and several small bunkhouses, and built a sawmill there. Crews had gone into the woods and brought in the logs, but just as the army began to saw them up, it abandoned the plan. Now, Dad can have those logs for a ridiculously low price, which also allows use of the sawmill and the camp.

We of course have to get to Berry Creek, and have some way to get the lumber sawn there back into Fairbanks. Dad contracts with a trucker named Ed Blair to haul the lumber from Berry Creek for $20 per thousand board feet, and with Fairbanks Lumber Supply to buy it for $100 per thousand. Dad drives to Berry Creek to look things over and discovers that the army sawmill is much bigger than ours, and it lacks a power source. Dad decides that we'd best tear our sawmill down and take it to Berry Creek along with our two Farmall tractors. As soon as the engine on the Farmall M can be broken in, Dad plans to have it power the mill.

On Earl Hirst's recommendation, Dad hires two new men who have such unpronounceable last names that they are just called Oly and John, or sometimes "the Swedes." These two are the best damn loggers around, Dad claims. He has not hired them before because

Earl says it wouldn't work out to have them be as close to town as the homestead. If Oly and John have any money at all, they get drunk and stay drunk until the money is gone. They are excellent workers, Earl says, but you have to keep them away from liquor. He says they will do just fine at Berry Creek if Dad will take them out there and not let them leave until the job is over.

I soon learn that Oly and John seem to be happy with their way of life, and John at least is good-humored about it. Oly is small and quiet, John large and talkative. I like the funny way he speaks; some of his words are sorta goofy but roll out like music. "Ve always get dronk ven ve got money," John says with a big smile. "Ve stay dronk vor veeks soomtimes, und ven der money all gone ve go to vork. Ve gudt vorkers. Oly, he little, bot he damn gudt vorker. I'm big und strong. Yah, I trow dem logs 'round like tootpicks."

Mom and Dad decide that we really can't put up with the dogs at Berry Creek so I take them to Mike Agababa's dog kennel on the riverbank in Fairbanks, right near the Independent Lumber Company sawmill and the cemetary. He keeps many dozens of dogs there, so it's a pretty noisy place when feeding time comes each day. He charges a lot for each dog, I think, but since Mom and Dad are paying I don't mind too much. Except for Wolf, this is really the first time the dogs have had to be tied up all the time, so they are not very happy about it.

On the trip out to Berry Creek, Oly and I ride up high in the air atop Ed Blair's heavily loaded truck. Beneath us are the Farmall H, the disassembled sawmill and a big supply of groceries. After an hour and a half we stop for lunch at Silver Fox Lodge, fifty-five miles out from Fairbanks.

Silver Fox Lodge is a pretty nice place. One interesting thing about it is that a man named Mr. Fox runs it, and since he has pure white hair the name Silver Fox really fits. The lodge is set well back off the road in an attractively open stand of tall white spruce trees, with a few bushy-topped birches mixed in. The main lodge building is a beautiful structure made of large spruce logs oiled golden brown with linseed oil, and the low-pitched sod roof above is sprouting a bright green covering of new spring grass. The grounds are neat; no whiskey bottles lie around like at Nellie Kelly's bar back at 23-Mile, and the path up to the heavy-hewed wood front door is lined with stones painted white. Beside it stands what looks to be twenty years' worth of moose and caribou horns all stacked up and laced onto a vertical pole.

Because of several big multi-paned windows, the inside of the lodge is pleasantly bright. Up back of the bar at one end of the main dining room is a glaringly white and very big silver fox painted on a rug of black velvet. It isn't a very good painting, but it sure shows up well. Mr. Fox himself serves us our food, and it really is good. I can see why Ed Blair always stops here.

Like most truckers, Ed loves to eat. He is not any taller than Earl Hirst or Oly, but his love of food has made his belly about twice as big as Earl's and maybe ten times bigger than Oly's. Ed Blair is an ex-prizefighter, and he has a curious nervous condition that he says dates back to his fighting days. Any time he is surprised by a sudden noise, his eyes go blank and he suddenly drops into a crouch and raises his closed fists. At first I thought he was faking some of this stuff but I guess he really isn't. Both he and Dad have warned me never to come up behind Ed without letting him know I am there because he might punch me out. I forgot about that one time when Ed was carrying a long two-by-six, and he knocked me down with it.

From my vantage point up on Ed's truck I see a lot of trees and hills on the way out to Berry Creek, but little else because low clouds are everywhere. I begin to realize how big Alaska really is, and how empty of people. We meet only one other truck before we get to Big Delta, and no other traffic from there on out to Berry Creek. On past Silver Fox Lodge, the only other place on the road out to Delta is Richardson Roadhouse right near Banner Creek, and a few abandoned miners' cabins. Beyond Delta, not a single cabin or any other sign of humans comes into view, and of course the road through this area is new, less than three years old.

That last part of the trip is a little miserable because rain begins to fall. Oly tucks himself under a corner of loose tarp, but I get worried about the cardboard barrel of coffee that rides at the very top of the load. I can see we are going to have a terrible mess if that barrel gets wet enough to fall apart, so I crouch over it on hands and knees for the better part of thirty miles.

After five hours of driving, not counting the stop for lunch, we finally get to Berry Creek, and Earl supervises the unloading. We stop first at the cookhouse, composed of two round-topped wooden Quonset huts stuck together in the form of a T, and with but one door at one end of the structure. This whole end of the building is covered by scratch marks. "Bear," says Earl Hirst. "Some of them look recent, don't they?" They sure do; I am impressed because some of those scratches go clear up to the top of the building. The bear that did this must be as big as a horse.

We unload all the groceries, a huge pile of them. Earl tells me to put them in the cookhouse while the others go down to the sawmill area some hundreds of feet away to unload everything else. Keeping an eye out for bear, I get my part of the job done. I am hoping to hear our pickup drive up at any minute because, along with Mom, Dad and Lewie, it is carrying Dad's bear gun, the single-shot 30-30. Dad said that they would be coming along about two hours behind us because he had to run into Fairbanks before starting out.

After the unloading, Ed drives off, headed back to Delta. From there he will drive down the Richardson to Valdez for a load of gasoline to take to Fairbanks. His plan for the coming weeks is to fold in trips to Valdez for barrels of gasoline whenever our sawmill is not turning out enough boards to haul. Ed says that unless he loses a tire he can clear about $100 per trip hauling the gasoline, not bad for three day's work. He will do even better hauling boards, because he can make a round trip in one day, grossing $60 to $80 per load. Having heard how much Dad figures to clear at Berry Creek, I can see that Ed is going to do about as well. Except for loading and unloading, he'll be sitting on his butt all day, too. Nor will he have to worry about feeding and paying any hired help.

As supper time approaches, we still have seen no sign of Mom and Dad. Earl tells me to do what I can to fix supper for the crew. Earl, Oly and John busy themselves settling into two of the little bunkhouses nearby, Earl in one, and Oly and John in the other. Earl takes the best one; it is rigged up with a stove and a supply of food for emergency use by anyone who might get stranded at Berry Creek. That, Earl says, is standard practice in remote areas of Alaska. If you use any of that food, you are supposed to replace it if you can. If not, you should at least leave some food in another cabin someplace else for people to use in an emergency.

I fire up the huge army cook stove that sits in the cookhouse, and begin to fix something to eat. Then as I sort through our food pile, I realize that all of the cooking and eating utensils are in the pickup. I do the best I can, though, improvising as I go along. For salt and sugar dispensers, I set out on the eating table the two halves of a two-pound cheese box. I open enough small cans of vegetables so each of us will have a coffee cup after the vegetables are eaten.

We eat our simple meal while water heats for coffee. After rinsing out the vegetable cans, I serve everyone a cup of coffee, something that Oly and John are especially waiting for. When not drinking liquor, they do like their coffee.

"Damn! Those cans are hot," Earl says, " I guess I'll let mine cool down some." Oly likes his coffee hot and black, so he begins sipping his right away, while John uses the one big spoon we have to ladle out four heaping spoons of sugar into his coffee. Then he gives the spoon to Earl, who puts a spoonful in his and stirs to help cool the coffee down. In the meantime, John begins drinking his coffee, and I notice that he has a strange look on his face. He says not a word, but Earl makes up for John's silence as soon as he takes the first sip. "Goddamit, kid, that's salt! Why in the hell didn't you label those boxes with what they had in them? That is a terrible thing to do to people. John, throw that coffee out, and, kid, get that goddamn salt off the table."

"Yah, dat coffee not good stuff," John replies, but it is obvious that he was prepared to suffer through his entire can of heavily salted coffee in silence. I think John and Oly are both like that; they can put up with whatever life hands them without any thought of complaint.

After the men finish their coffee that first evening at Berry Creek, they go to their bunk houses and I prepare to spend the night, still expecting to hear the pickup drive in at any moment. I know that our family will be sleeping in the Quonset hut attached to the cookhouse Quonset, which has no door except that leading into the cookhouse. Instead of bunking in the back Quonset, I decide it will be wiser to stay close to the food. It sits in a big pile beside the stove, so I set up my army cot crossways between it and the door. That way, if a bear does come along, he is bound to wake me before going for the food. With any luck, I can scare him away.

The first sound I hear is early the next morning, when Earl walks in to find me still asleep. "Humph," he grumbles, "Still in bed; you sleeping there so you can get out the door real quick if a bear comes along?"

Since that was not my intent at all, Earl's remark bothers me even more than his stinging words about the salt and sugar mix-up the evening before. I say nothing, but Earl's superior airs are really starting to get on my nerves. I make myself feel better by thinking inwardly that he talks too much and saws slabs that are too thick. To hell with Earl Hirst.

But then I am glad I haven't said anything, because as he walks out the door I see just a slight upward twitch at the corner of his mouth. Heck, he knew all along why I was sleeping in front of the door.

The pickup rolls in about noon that day. Dad had car trouble, fortunately just when he was in town the day before. Everybody is happy to see Mom because she is the cook. She scurries around and gets everything organized, cooks supper, and the family all goes to bed back in the second Quonset. Mom has seen all those bear marks too, so just before lying down she lashes the door shut with a great length of heavy string. Dad also puts his bear gun, the single-shot 30-30, beside his bed, at the opposite end of the Quonset from where Lewie and I sleep.

I wake up in the middle of the night to hear Mom yelling, "Bon! Bon! Get up; the bear's here."

I raise up to see Dad coming up out of his bed with a blank look on his face, saying, "Where? Where?" He is still half asleep, but he grabs his gun and runs out into the other room where Mom is. Not wanting to miss anything, I am running along behind him, thinking that he looks pretty funny stumbling along with the back of his long johns open so that his bare butt is sticking out. Then, I stub my toe on the doorway. Instantly, Dad wheels around, and I am looking right down the barrel of that 30-30. "It's me, It's me," I stammer, trying to jump backward while curling up to make myself as small as possible. Dad then comes fully awake. I know I have just had a close call, but the startled look on his face as he almost shoots me is pretty humorous.

Meanwhile, Mom is trying to open one of the wire-mesh windows high up on the sloping wall of the Quonset, the kind all covered with plastic so you can't see through them. Just as she gets the window open, the bear sticks his nose in, and there they are, face to face, staring into each other's eyes. Mom backs off real quick, and she and Dad run over to the door. They frantically work at trying to undo all the string Mom has wrapped around the door handle. It is taking them so long that I am glad that I have not had to go out to pee during the night; I would never have made it.

Mom finally gets the door open, and Dad sails out through it. He would have been better off to have eased out more cautiously, because the bear has just run around the corner of the building and is standing sideways in front of the door. When Dad pulls the trigger, the bear's side is just inches away from the end of the gun barrel, and that gunshot reflecting off the bear's side sure makes a terrible noise. The bear goes down, his back broken by the bullet. We get outside in time to see Dad fumbling around trying to get another shell in the gun, finally managing the task, and then finishing the bear off with a second shot.

Dad is proud as all heck at having just shot his first wild bear, and we all are excited, except for Lewie, who has slept through the whole thing. By then it is almost time to get up, so Mom fixes the fire for coffee. Dad is drinking his second cup when Earl walks in.

"I shot a bear last night, " Dad says, with pride in his voice.

"Yeah, I heard," replies Earl with his usual superior lilt. "What was the second shot for?"

The plan for the day is to begin assembling the sawmill over near the big army mill. Then Dad gets an idea. "You know, it just might be worth a try. I'm going to hook the H up to that army mill."

"Won't work," says Earl, "that little tractor hasn't got enough power even to run the carriage up and down the track, never mind turn the saw."

"I'm going to try it anyway," Dad says, and soon he has the H lined up and the long drive belt attached to the army mill. Slowly, slowly, the mill begins to turn, and after a while its massive main shaft is up to speed. "Let's put a log on it," Dad says with glee.

"Won't work," says Earl says again, shaking his head and frowning at what he considers a ridiculous waste of time. But he is wrong; the saw chews down through the log at least as fast as our own mill could. Dad is elated. "Hell, we're going to start sawing logs today," he says. The thing that he had correctly suspected is that the turning parts of the army mill have so much momentum that, even when underpowered, the mill will work reasonably well.

Within a few days Dad decides that the Farmall M is broken in enough to put on line. Its engine is half again as big as the H's and so it has no trouble powering the mill.

The whole operation goes like that. During the next six weeks—almost with no down-time at all—we convert that stack of army logs to a huge pile of sawdust, an even more impressive pile of slabs, and many truckloads of boards that go off to Fairbanks on Ed Blair's truck. Dad and I spend most of our time moving logs over to the mill, dragging slabs and sawdust away, and planing the one-inch boards into shiplap. Big John takes over the dog-setter duties while little Oly, sometimes with help from me or Dad, carries off all the boards and slabs that the mill produces. Other than Lewie, Oly is the smallest person in the camp, but he is the one who has the hardest job.

John lives up to his words: "I trow dem logs round like tootpicks." He is highly skilled at the use of a peavey, and his great strength is an asset. However, as I watch him work, I see that he has a deep understanding of the mechanics of log rolling. He uses momentum and leverage at every opportunity. When he sees that I am trying to copy what he does, he gives me hints and demonstrations of special tricks he knows.

One is to sink the point of a peavey in the end of a log just inside the bark, and then apply pressure to roll the log along, much as a driver rod on an old steam railroad engine makes the engine's wheel roll. This method is far faster than any other for moving a log along the rolls.

John's most spectacular trick is a way to stop a run-away log if it gets out in front of you. I secretly practice John's trick for days until I can succeed on most attempts. My chance to demonstrate comes one day when Dad and I are up on top of the log stack rolling logs down on a go-devil for transport over to the mill. "Watch out," Dad says, "that one log looks like it will roll down and go right over the go-devil."

"Don't worry; I'll take care of it," I say boldly, and give the log a big push to get it started. As Dad has predicted, the log picks up speed, careens down the pile and heads over the top of the go-devil. At just the right moment, I throw my peavey like a spear, in the fashion I have been practicing. Its point slides under the back of the log, and its hook comes over the top and grabs hold. The turning log spins the peavey's handle over until it strikes the ground on the far side, braking the log to a sudden stop, precisely where wanted, directly atop the go-devil. Not having seen this trick before, Dad is mightily impressed. I give him my silent "I told you so" look, but never again do I have that much success with the trick.

When, in early August, the last log is sawn up, Dad lays off the crew. Mom hauls them back to Fairbanks, and she and Lewie return to the homestead. Dad and I stay on to plane what lumber is left. During the evenings, while Dad is relaxing, I go out near the camp and cut down a few big birch trees, then put them on the sawmill and practice running it. Were Earl around I could not do this because he is the sawyer, and no one else can touch his sawmill, even if it belongs to the army. Since I have to be my own dog-setter and board-carrier-outer, the sawing goes slowly. Never mind that, I have a lot of fun playing with that big machine, and I get enough birch boards to build some furniture and maybe a few dog sleds, my excuse for the endeavor.

The wild geese know that winter is rapidly approaching. Huge flocks of them wheel around overhead each morning. They hardly move their wings as they ride the air pushing up here because of the hills all around except downriver to the northwest. The geese all seem to know about this place because each flock grows larger by the hour, until we can see thousands of geese at once. Finally, by late midafternoon, the flocks are so high each bird looks like a little gray speck, and then they all leave, heading off over the mountains to the south. Now that the family and crew are gone, and even the geese are leaving, Berry Creek is beginning to feel like a very lonely place. It doesn't help that, now that the nights are getting dark, wolves sit up on nearby hilltops and howl mournfully at each other.

We have no radio, and no one else is around, so Dad and I have no awareness of world events. We do not know that while we watch geese rise in our sky, the residents of Hiroshima and Nagasaki are watching atomic bombs fall from theirs. Then, on August 10, a jeep races into the camp, and a young soldier yells gleefully, "The war's over, the war's over!" He is the first new person I have seen since we stopped to eat at Silver Fox Lodge two months ago and he is about the happiest person I have ever seen. He is so excited he is jumping up and down. He gives us a few details that include something about the new bombs. "They're made out of some strange thing called uranium," he says, and then, "I got to go now so I can tell everybody else along the road." He jumps in his jeep, spins it around, and heads off at high speed down the highway toward Tok Junction.

"Uranium, huh?" Dad says with a thoughtful look. "That's why they were so interested back then in Gateway."

Not long after that, we finish up at Berry Creek and move into town so that Lewie and I can go to school, and Mom and Dad both can hold jobs. They have to get jobs because, although the Berry Creek operation was reasonably successful, it has not been profitable enough to pay all the debts piled up from the purchase of machinery. Dad even sells the sawmill. Next year we will concentrate on farming and get rich that way.

Finding a house to stay in is not easy. Mom tries again to rent one of Mrs. Ford's empty houses, but has no luck at all. Mrs. Ford still does not want any men or boys around. Mom and Dad finally locate a two-bedroom log cabin on lower Third Avenue, convenient to both the town's library and the Fourth Avenue Line. I spend a lot of time in one but almost none in the other.

FAIRBANKS HIGH SCHOOL

WINTER 1945–46

IGH SCHOOL IS A FRIGHTENING experience for me. Except for Lewie, and of course he doesn't count, I have not exchanged a word with another young person during the past year. And during the year before that I was in the little one-room school in Iowa where I was alone in my class, and the only older boy in school. The school also had girls, one older than me and some younger, with whom I played at recess—games like fox and geese, hide and seek, and anty-over. They did not bother me too much, but now that I am a thirteen-year-old freshman, any young female terrifies me. I cannot bring myself to talk to a girl or even look one in the face. Fairbanks High School is a big place, too; it has 132 students and half of them are girls. All of the students seem to know each other, and all are self-confident and knowledgeable about things of which I know nothing. If a teacher happens to call on me in class, I freeze up and have difficulty stammering out any kind of answer.

Toward the end of the first week in school, as I sit in last-period study hall doing my schoolwork, Mr. Scott, the school superintendent, walks up to my desk. "Come with me," he says. I know that I have done something terrible, but what can it be? As we walk down the hall, he says, "From now on, you will not attend study hall. Instead, you will take dramatics class."

He then leads me into the lion's den: a room filled with girls, a female teacher and only one other male student. My ears and face burn red as I walk into that room with all those girls watching my every move. No question about it, this is the worst day of my life, ever.

That night I tell Mom and Dad what has happened, and ask them to go see Mr. Scott and try to get me back in study hall. They refuse; I am stuck with it.

The next week is miserable, the next week after that, bad, and the next not so bad. I almost begin to look forward to dramatics class because all of those girls actually are pretty nice once you get to know them.

A setback occurs when the teacher assigns me a part in a school play. The part is not big, but it requires the performance of an action that sends chills through me every time I think about it. I am playing the role of a girl's father, and I have to kiss her on the cheek. Any girl would have be bad enough, but this girl is Jeannine Persinger, a sophomore, and in my eyes just about the most beautiful girl in school.

The speech teacher is an understanding sort, so our play practices never require me to kiss Jeannine. But the day of reckoning comes, and for that event the teacher arranges a special practice that is without observers and involves only the teacher, Jeannine and me. Jeannine is really swell about it. She doesn't laugh or anything when my lips brush her cheek. She just smiles sweetly at me as I came close and quickly back away.

A few nights later, I kiss Jeannine right up there in the glare of the lights before a full house, and nobody laughs that time either. I am over the hump on this dramatics business, and it is starting to be a lot of fun. One thing I learn about actresses during this play is that they are not very shy backstage. Girls change their dresses right in front of me, just as though I were not a boy. Actresses also tend to hug a lot, and I get so I didn't mind that either.

That semester I win an award for my dramatics work. It is a nice scroll with my name on it and the words "Most Improved." I am proud of it, but I also realize that when you start small, even a tiny bit of progress looks immense. By this time I also learn that drama class is an optional that nobody has to take. Mr. Scott outfoxed me that first week in school. I don't care about that any more; in fact, I sign up for the second semester of the dramatics class. I am beginning to think that someday I might become a great actor, always surrounded by beautiful women who don't even care if you see them in their underclothes.

All this has nothing to do with sex. I understand all that stuff pretty well because we have this book which I began reading back on the mountain when I was eight. It is called "Living a Sane Sex Life," and it tells more than anyone would ever want to know about men and women and having children, including pictures of everything.

One weekend in late winter another boy, a junior whose family is Mormon, and I drive our pickup out to the homestead to set beaver traps in 14-Mile Slough. He sees the book on the shelf and is fascinated by it, especially the pictures of how women are put together. "Gosh," he says, "I've never seen anything like this before. Your folks let you read this stuff?"

That night he reads part of the book and then asks if he can borrow it. The next time I see the book is about a month later, as one junior girl takes it out of her locker and surreptitiously passes it to another. When the book finally comes back home at the end of the year, it is in terrible shape. I get the impression that practically every girl in Fairbanks High School has been studying the book. Interesting, I think; these girls always look like they know everything, but I have become an expert on sex long before them.

Mom used to go to church back when we lived in Hanna, Wyoming, but she and Dad never belonged to any organizations except the unions. Other than groups like the United Mine Workers, Dad has never liked organizations, especially big moneyed ones like the Union Pacific Railroad. The army is even worse, Dad says; it is an organization that should not even exist, and everything the army does is wasteful. People in the army do not think, they just follow orders.

Dad really is right about this, I conclude one Saturday. That morning several other freshman boys and I want to play basketball. We go to the school gym and find that other groups have signed up to use it all day. The gym is always busy in winter because it is about the only place in Fairbanks for indoor sports, and it also serves as the school auditorium and the stage for plays.

"Hey, I know what we can do," one boy says, "Let's take the bus out to Ladd Field and play in one of their gyms."

"How will we get through the guard at the gate?" somebody asks.

"Heck, we'll just tell them we're the high school basketball team. Everybody carry a bag, and I'll carry the ball under my arm. It'll work; you'll see. Those guys are stupid."

The boy is right. When the guard comes on the bus to check everybody out, we say we are the Fairbanks High School varsity team, and he believes it. We then go to a hanger in which several basketball courts are laid out, none in use. We play a while, and then look around.

In one corner of the building are large bins, each about ten feet square, eight feet high, and open at the top. One bin contains baseballs, one softballs, one bats, one catcher's mitts, another fielders' mitts—and one is completely filled with basketballs. The army has more basketballs than it needs, we think, so we hoist one boy up into the bin, and he throws some out. That afternoon, the "high school team" rides the bus back out the front gate, each member bouncing a basketball and carrying several more deflated ones in his equipment bag. Nothing is wrong about this, we know, because the army is a total waste, its guards are stupid, and we are just saving these basketballs from being thrown away someday.

It is about this time that I decide another similar organization is not much better. It is just a juvenile version of the army, although I do not think about it that way when I first join the Boy Scouts. Full of enthusiasm, I go to my first meeting where I am told about the things I have to memorize to become a full-fledged scout, and also about a contest that the troop plans to enter.

Rats are a real problem around Fairbanks, especially at the city dump. To help alleviate the problem, Wien Airlines is offering a free round trip to Fort Yukon to whoever can kill the most rats. The scoutmaster suggests, and all the boys agree, that we will buy a whole bunch of rat traps so we can win the contest. We are doing this mainly as a service to the community but, by some means not yet specified, one of us will be chosen to make the trip to Fort Yukon.

At our next scout meeting we talk a lot, and we collect the money for the traps. The meeting after that we spend discussing organizational matters and what to do with the traps as soon as we get them. The two boys on the committee assigned to buy the traps have forgotten the task, but they assure us that the traps will be available at the next meeting. Although we all talk about it a lot, somehow we never do set the traps. They just lie in a big box in the Presbyterian church basement where the troop meets. Then we see in the newspaper that the contest is over, and that it has been won by a boy in school named Angus Carter. While we were sitting in our Boy Scout meetings, Angus was out at the dump with his rifle shooting rats. He has killed an incredible number of them.

Dad was right about organizations. One thinking person who works hard and does not waste things can accomplish a lot more than a whole bunch of people who like to sit around and talk. And as an organization gets bigger or more powerful it starts doing more evil and less good. The Boy Scouts is just a teen version of the army, and the less you have to do with either the better off you are. The incident with the rats causes me never to attend another scout meeting.

Angus Carter, the boy who won the contest, is a different sort of guy. He has a stern, craggy face that almost makes him look too old to be a high school boy, and he doesn't behave like most of them either. Angus just walks silently from class to class, usually neither looking nor smiling at anyone else, while most of the older boys laugh and talk loudly to each other and to the girls as they walk through the halls. Some of what takes place between the louder of the boys and one or two girls is so bad that it really embarrasses me, and once when I am walking up the central stairwell near Angus I see that he is embarrassed too. Two of the older girls, ones wearing tight sweaters, are standing up at the top of the well leaning over the railing there when one of the louder boys in a group on the basketball varsity calls out, "Hey, girls, give us a yawn," and another echoes his words. Just as Angus and I come to the base of the last flight of stairs, the two girls up above us smile lewdly as they pretend to yawn with elbows and shoulders thrown back. The fronts of the girls' sweaters come way out over the rail, and some of the boys hoot words like "Hey, hey." Angus is silent, and as he turns his face away I see that it is just as red as mine feels.

Angus has big wide shoulders and his whole body seems stiff and squarish. When he walks it is like a block of wood—a two-by-six, maybe about a foot long—leaning slightly forward and rocking along on its two front corners. It is an uneven jerky motion because one of Angus's legs is not quite like the other one from his having had tuberculosis when he was younger. Even so, he is a fairly good basketball player, not good enough to be on the high school team, but better than many of the boys on the intramural teams. As far as I can see, that is the only group thing that Angus does because of sticking to himself so much. Perhaps some of the reason for that may be that Angus is part Indian, having been born at Stevens Village, over on the Yukon. Angus's father was white or mostly white but he died, so Angus's mother moved to Fairbanks where she works in a bakery.

Perhaps Angus's being part-Indian might not be the whole story because there are several other part-Indian or part-Eskimo boys in school who are as outgoing and raucous as anybody. We have only one full-Eskimo boy in our class, and he is adopted into a white family. All the other Native high schoolers go to a school in southeastern Alaska, but a number of students in our school are, like Angus and the others, part-Native. Mostly you can't tell them from anybody else, except that the Native girls tend to be prettier than other girls, have more musical voices, and are generally more friendly towards people like me who they can see are sort of outsiders, too. It may be for another reason, too: the white boys and girls seem to go for having groups that you are either in or out of, but the Native kids seem to accept everybody the same, like we're all in it together.

Aside from his tendency to stay off to himself, Angus does things that no other older boy would do. Like go out and shoot rats. Even more strange is that Angus, although a junior in high school, stands down at the corner of Second and Cushman every afternoon selling newspapers. Boy, you wouldn't catch me or any other high school boy doing a kid thing like that. Angus does not even have a good coat; at forty or fifty below he looks awfully cold standing out with the bundle of newspapers under his arm, exhaling plumes of frozen breath as he calls out "News-Miner; getcher News-Miner."

But then all of a sudden, Angus becomes the envy of almost every boy in school. With the money he has saved up he has gone over to the salvage yard on Garden Island and bought, for only $50, a military surplus truck that runs. The purchase ignites all sorts of dreams and discussion about how the rest of us can go over and buy real cheap equipment like that, trucks or even bulldozers—if we just had the money.

Along about midwinter, Angus does another unusual thing, one that many people think is pretty ridiculous. He starts accumulating a dog team by picking up stray dogs around town. He is quite a sight driving his dogs through the streets because the dogs are all different sizes and kinds. People laugh when they see his team go by, Angus usually humping along behind or riding with one leg on the runner and kicking with the other. "God, look at that bunch of mutts that fool kid has got. There's even a poodle in there, and see that skinny one that looks like a bloody greyhound. He's gonna freeze his balls off in weather like this. Ha, those dogs will never amount to anything," I hear one man say to another as Angus and his dogs run down First Avenue in front of the Northern Commercial Co. store. I sort of laugh to myself too, but it is kind of an uneasy, envious laugh because I have a dog team too that looks better than Angus's but does not, by any stretch of the imagination, run half as well.

MY DOG TEAM

1945–46

I HAVE ALWAYS LIKED DOGS and other pets, too, even though I never had much luck with them when I was little. Grandma Davis had a nice dog named Pooch when I was born, and I guess Pooch thought I was his pet. Mom said he used to guard me and would not let anybody except her get near my baby carriage. I really liked Pooch but he started chasing cars and got killed. I had another dog for a while, but he ate broken glass and got cut up inside so much he died, too. Then one of Grandma's neighbors in LaSalle gave me two chickens to take home to Hanna, and those chickens almost got me a really swell pet.

While driving home, we stopped at a big open lot outside of Greeley where people were selling fruits and berries and trading things. You could buy almost anything there for nearly nothing because people who did not have any money were selling their furniture and anything else they owned just to have enough to buy something to eat. We didn't have much money either, but we never went hungry like some people did then. You saw a lot of people who did not have homes. They just drove around in old cars that carried all they owned. Many of them were headed west to California, and others were following the harvest north so they could have work.

While Mom and Dad were off buying some fruit and I was watching the chickens in the car, a gypsy boy my age came up with a monkey on his shoulder. That was the first monkey I ever saw up that close, so it was pretty interesting. Even better, the boy said he had to get rid of the monkey because his family could not afford to feed it any longer. He wanted fifty cents for the monkey, but he agreed to trade for my two chickens. I could see he was sad to have to give up his monkey, but he said, "My mom be happy 'cause we eat dos chickens." My mom was not happy, though. When she got back, she made us trade again.

"You're going to have a baby brother or sister soon, so you don't need a monkey, too," she said. We got the chickens back to Hanna, where a dog broke into their pen and killed them. Then Lewie came along. He was sort of like a pet, but at the time I thought a monkey would have been more fun.

The next pet we got was Bear. When Dad took over the uranium mine in Colorado, Bear came with it. One of the men at the mine had shot Bear's mother and brought him home when he was just a little cub. He was pretty cute and a lot of fun, but as he got bigger you had to be careful with him.

One of the games we played with Bear was to try to get him in a little trap like you use to catch foxes. Lewie and I would set the trap and put food on it. Bear was not very smart. Time after time, he would come along and catch his nose in the trap, and then jump around pawing at it until he got the trap loose. Sometimes he would even step in the trap and then shake his leg real fast until it fell off.

Bear always chased after you if he thought you had any food, but he was so clumsy that if you dodged around, he could never catch you. We used to hold food in front of him and then climb up a tree and go out on a limb. Bear always went up after us, and when he got close we would jump to the ground. Bear was afraid to jump, so he just climbed back down the tree. Then we would do it to him again.

The funniest thing that ever happened with Bear was when he got into Mom's sugar jar, which she had left on the kitchen table. The man who owned the uranium mine told Mom that if she ever had any trouble with Bear, she should hit him on the nose with a steel bar he gave her for that purpose. He said that bears can't stand being hit on the nose.

One day, Mom walked in the kitchen, and there was Bear up on the table with his nose and most of his head in the sugar jar. As Lewie and I watched, Mom picked up her steel bar, and since she could not get to Bear's nose without breaking the jar, she just pounded on his hind end. Bear paid no attention to her until he suddenly raised up, turned around, and dragged his front paws down her body. Bear didn't hurt Mom any, but he tore her dress and brassiere right off, and pulled her panties almost down to her knees. She got a shocked expression on her face, and I think Lewie was just as stunned as I was. We'd never before seen our mom stand by the kitchen table without any clothes on. Bear seemed to be the most surprised of all. His front paws came back alongside his head, he let out a noise that sounded like "Raaoowh," and he somersaulted backwards off the table and ran out the door. Bear had never seen a naked lady before, and I guess it scared him pretty bad.

We lost Bear the day Mom gave Lewie two pieces of candy, one for him and one for Bear. Lewie was not much smarter than Bear. He went outside, gave Bear his piece of candy and then sat down beside Bear to eat his own. Bear gulped his candy, then tried to grab Lewie's. Bear caught a claw in the corner of Lewie's eye and ripped it open, and he bit down on Lewie's arm hard enough to poke tooth holes in it. That night, when Dad came up from the mine, he went outside with the gun, and we never saw Bear again. So that Lewie would not feel so bad about losing Bear, Dad told him that Bear had gone into hibernation under the house.

As far as pets are concerned, it has gone a lot better since we came to Alaska. Well, maybe except for the half-wolf named Wolf I got from Nellie Kelley, but the three young husky sisters we got from Zehnder Camp are fun dogs. Of course I have weaned them off their former straight diet of T-bone steaks, but they still eat well on scraps Mom or Dad bring home from restaurants, and I've given them some dried salmon and cornmeal, too. I named the dogs after the three nearby rivers—Chena, Salcha and Tanana—but the names have not stuck. Tan-colored Chena, the most lovable of the pups, quickly became Che-Che. Her black sister became Blackie, and the brown one, Brownie.

At first, the dogs ran loose around the cabin, and Lewie and I had a lot of fun playing with them. Even before the snow came, I started making harnesses so the dogs could pull the old dog sled I fixed up with babiche and a few new wooden pieces.

Early on, we discovered that the dogs had a fourth sister that had been taken to the messhall out at 26-Mile Camp where the military had built a dirt emergency airstrip, and which someday would become Eielson Air Force Base. A friend of Mom's who was cooking out there brought that sister to me, and I named her Yukon. That name stuck.

Yukon is a beautiful black and white dog with glistening hair, one flop ear, and a bushy tail that curls up over her back, slightly off-center. Curiously, she always runs a bit sideways, as though she wants to see where she has been. That stance and her twitching tail made her look coquettish when she runs ahead of you, like she is a saucy young girl begging you to chase her. When I first got her I decided right away that Yukon would be my team's lead dog.

The main reason for Yukon's beautiful hair when she came to the homestead was her diet. At 26-Mile, she ate only eggs, three dozen of them every day. Yukon was the smartest of the litter, but it seemed that she might starve to death during the days after she arrived because she refused to eat anything but eggs. Yukon turned up her nose at steak for nearly a week, but she finally gave in.

We still give her eggs once in a while just to watch her eat them, because she is an expert egg eater. Taking one in her mouth, she lies down and puts her nose between her front paws. She rolls the egg around with her tongue until the small end is upright, and then somehow breaks the shell in half so that the bigger round comes out into her paws with the yolk contained. That part of the egg remains there until Yukon has removed the white from the half of the shell still in her mouth. She then spits the shell out and carefully laps up the rest of the egg from the shell held between her paws. She performs this ritual very slowly, like she was in a movie playing the part of an elegant lady at high tea nibbling daintily on an eclair. Never does Yukon lose even one drop of egg white or break the yolk.

But when it comes to rabbits, Yukon is a killer, as are all her sisters. That first year on the homestead, if one of them chanced to see a rabbit while the dogs were out in the woods walking with Lewie and me, she might give brief, half-hearted chase, seemingly well aware that she would never catch the animal. This was just for fun. When the dogs really wanted to catch rabbits, they went at it together in a carefully planned way.

We soon learned that the dogs held war councils, during which they stood silently facing each other in the semblance of a circle. When you saw the dogs do this, you knew they were up to something—usually a rabbit chase. Then Yukon would lead them out onto the old Richardson Trail, and three of the pack would skulk off into the brush. They spread themselves in a line that angled back from the dog farthest off the road to where one dog, usually Yukon, stood on the road. They then started running parallel to the road. Before long, a rabbit would pop out of the brush onto the roadway where Yukon would grab it. She rarely missed, and when the rabbit was dead she would drop it on the road as the others came out to share the feast. Someone at Zehnder Camp had claimed that these dogs were quarter-wolf. That probably was not true, but when you saw those dogs hunt rabbits, you could almost believe it.

Usually the four sisters behave as stupidly as any other dogs, but one day they pulled off a trick that suggested that they could be smart and had a sense of humor. It happened while Dad and I were building the bridge over 14-Mile Slough. Lewie was playing around in the rocky gravel alongside the stream when we noticed that the dogs were going into a war council. It lasted only about thirty seconds, and then the dogs slowly moved into a big circle around Lewie. Suddenly, Blackie and Yukon ran at him full tilt, bowling him over onto the ground. Che-Che raced up and tore the stocking cap from his head. She carried it off a ways and dropped it. Lewie got up and went for his cap, but just as he was leaning over to pick it up, the cap skipped away in Brownie's mouth. Dumbfounded, Dad and I watched as the dogs continued to tease Lewie like that for a minute or two. Then some silent signal passed between them and they all sauntered off to do what dogs usually do.

When the first snow came, I began working the dogs. The first task was to catch them, since they all ran loose. These may be smart dogs, but they had a hard time understanding what they were supposed to do. Whenever I went to harness Che-Che, she looked at me lovingly with her soft brown eyes, wagged her tail, and lay against my leg. Brownie and Blackie thought harnessing was a signal to run in tight little circles that tangled the ropes, and the harness insulted Yukon. She would lie down in the snow and pout.

Lewie and I eventually would get the dogs running down the Richardson Trail—to wherever the first fresh rabbit track crossed over the road. Then, working together, Lewie and I would have to pull the sled and dogs backward out of the brush, and get the team going as far as the next rabbit crossing. But gradually, the team started to shape up. The dogs really did know what they were supposed to do, as I learned the first time I fell down and lost my hold on the sled. Yukon sped them off down the Richardson Trail like a trained racing team, ignoring all rabbit tracks. I chased them all the way out to the Alcan at 15-Mile, where they must have actually seen a rabbit and tangled themselves up trying to chase it through the brush.

On those few occasions when the dogs did run well, I was thrilled. Leaning forward over the sled basket, I was Sergeant King of the Royal Canadian Mounted Police chasing a criminal across the snowy Canadian wilderness, or Leonard Seppala delivering the serum to Nome behind his lead dog Balto. I was beginning to think I might become a famous dog musher instead of a farmer.

But that was more than a year ago. Now that we are living in town and going to high school I keep just Yukon at the house and have her sisters and several other dogs tied up alongside the city dump, down on the river below town. Once each day I use Yukon and a little sled to haul food out to the other dogs, but other than that, I am too busy with school, dramatics and basketball to run the dogs. Someday I will get around to running them more, but they sure are a lot of trouble because I still have a hard time getting them to run at all, and rarely in the direction I want, like Angus can with his team.

Angus's dogs look bad, but they sure run fast, and as the winter wears on he is able to make them turn whenever he wants just by calling out "Gee" or "Haw." A friend who knows Angus says that he spends many hours with them each weekend and after school. He will take the dogs out on a trail and tell them to lie down. If a dog moves, Angus beats the dog with a whip, and he has them all trained so well that he can walk away from the sled and the team will stay wherever he leaves them for hours. I never whip my dogs like that; I just talk to them nice. I'm afraid though that it may be necessary to do things more Angus's way.

All of us who laughed at Angus earlier in the winter are not laughing now that the spring races are well underway. Angus's team still looks like what it is, a Heinz "57 Varieties" mix. "They look like purebred Nordales to me," said one of the more clever guys in school, coining a new breed named after the famous old Nordale Hotel in Fairbanks. The thing is, though, that Angus is winning or placing in races regularly. People are even saying that he might win the big North American Championship race.

I think Angus possesses characteristics that I lack. He does not seem to care if people laugh at him. He works hard at everything, including running dogs, and it is obvious that he knows a lot more about dealing with animals than I do. Still, I am accumulating dogs, and the dogs are having pups, lots of pups.

The only dog I have gottten rid of is Wolf. What Nellie Kelley said about Wolf's father being a wolf obviously was true. I spent a lot of time trying to tame him but the older he got the wilder and more vicious he became. When he was young I could pet him, but if I tried to play with him like a normal dog, his eyes turned green and he started biting. Once when I cut my hand on the wire of his run, Wolf smelled the blood and went for me. He also did that when I turned my back on him. He would jump up and try to bite the back of my neck. Mike Agbaba thought he was nasty, too. When I went to pick up the dogs after we got back from Berry Creek, Mr. Agbaba told me the river had flooded while we were gone. He was afraid the dogs would drown in their fenced-in kennels, so he moved them all to high ground—all except Wolf, because he wasn't about to let a dog that mean out to where he might get a kid. He seemed to think Wolf was about the worst dog he'd ever seen. I couldn't get Wolf to run in front of a sled so I sold him to a man who thought it would be fun to have a real wolf on his dog team, and since Wolf was so big the man believed he would make a good wheel dog. I warned the man what Wolf was like, but he said he could handle any dog. The first time the man harnessed Wolf up and walked away, Wolf reached out and clamped his jaws around the butt of the dog in front. He completely ruined that dog's hind end, and the man had to kill the dog. He was so mad he shot Wolf, too.

SUMMER ON THE HOMESTEAD

SUMMER 1946

NOW THAT SCHOOL IS OVER, we have all moved back to the homestead. I have dogs tied up all over the place, and I have built a fenced-in area for the many pups born this spring. Soon after I put them in their pen I noticed that the pups seemed to be awfully whiny. The next day they whined so much that I thought they must be hungry so I gave them extra food. The pups did not eat the food, and the next day they whined continuously. Almost by accident that morning I discovered what the problem was. The answer came when I set down just outside the pup pen a bucket of water I was carrying to give the adult dogs. When I saw how frantic the pups were to get at the bucket I felt awful. How could I have been so cruel to them by failing to recognize that they too needed water? No one else knew what had happened, but I felt terribly ashamed of what I had done to those poor pups.

I am still feeling low about it—and about a lot of things, too. I have an uneasy feeling that nothing is going right, and that coming back to the homestead is a let-down all around. Several of the other boys in my class have summer jobs as stewards on the Alaska Railroad sternwheelers that run out of Nenana on the Tanana and Yukon Rivers. The pay is not much and the hours are long, the boys say, but it sure sounds like fun to travel up and down the rivers like that. I was going to apply to be steward or maybe try for a truck-driving job with the Alaska Road Commission, but I never did, partly because I was thinking of another plan that seemed exciting, too.

The stepfather of another boy in my class has a placer mine on Faith Creek, sixty-six miles up the Steese Highway north of Fairbanks.

The stepfather of another boy in my class has a placer mine on Faith Creek, sixty-six miles up the Steese Highway north of Fairbanks. Having seen the truck that Angus Carter bought so cheaply at the salvage yard, this boy and I came up with the plan to buy a tractor there and then take it up to mine at Faith Creek. We heard that you could get an operable little tractor called a Cle-Trac Model 15 for $50 or $100. We were fired up about the idea, and we made all sorts of plans for the mining enterprise that summer. We did not spend a lot of time thinking about exactly how to go about the actual mining—that would just come about naturally once we got to Faith Creek—but we did have most of the meals doped out. Grouse, rabbits, grayling, fried potatoes and hotcakes figured heavily in the menus. It all came to naught at the last minute when we failed to come up with the money for supplies and the tractor, and it turned out that the boy's stepfather had made other arrangements for operating his mine this summer, anyway.

After losing out on all those exotic possibilities, it isn't much fun being back at the homestead where the only planned activity for me is to help Dad with his farming effort. I have the feeling that even Dad is a bit subdued this spring, although he perks up when he starts thinking and talking about how well we will do with the farming. As near as I can tell, Mom and Dad are nearly out of debt, since both of them worked all winter long in the restaurants. I know they feel lucky to have held jobs all winter because postwar Fairbanks is winding down. Two restaurants have closed their doors. Three others, also in financial difficulty but with enough money for fire insurance, have gone up in smoke, including the one in which Dad was working. He got another job and is continuing to work at it during the summer, but Mom has engineered a lay-off for herself so that she can collect unemployment for at least a while. I don't think it is quite right for Mom to do this because unemployment is for people who can't work, not for those who don't want to. It is supposed to be a system where the lucky people with jobs help the unlucky ones, but if everybody takes all the unemployment money that they might be entitled to, then the whole thing falls apart.

I guess Mom's case might be a little different, though, because the work and her asthma really wear her down. The greasy air in the restaurants tends to bother her, and the house we lived in this winter was heated with an oil stove which put out fumes that made her choke up and wheeze pretty badly at times. Out at the homestead she can get away from all the bad smells and doesn't have to do anything except cook our meals. She can just lay around and do what she likes best when she is not feeling good: read mystery magazines and love stories, or maybe go out and sit on a bank of 14-Mile Slough and do some grayling fishing. Then when berry picking time comes she can spend endless hours at that. She loves to pick berries so much that last fall she sold berries to the Model Cafe by the fifty-gallon barrel.

How anybody can enjoy picking that many berries is beyond me. I hate doing the same thing over and over again, but Mom actually enjoys it. I think maybe that is one of the differences between men and women. Men are always looking for new ways to make things go easier while women have so much patience that they will knit, crochet or pick berries forever. Mom actually prefers to pick berries with her fingers rather than use one of those little berry-pickers that looks like a scoop attached to a little pitchfork and that makes the work go about ten times faster.

One day last fall when Lewie was sliding down a tree he kicked over Mom's two-gallon berry bucket which she had just filled. The berries all tumbled out and most of them disappeared down in the moss. Knowing how long Mom had worked to pick those berries, I was furious at Lewie for being so careless and I started chewing him out. "Leave him alone; he didn't mean to do it. I'll just pick some more," Mom said, smiling and reaching out to tousle Lewie's hair.

This spring as soon as the weather warmed up enough for the pickup to run, Dad started going out to the homestead frequently. On weekends, I, and sometimes Mom and Lewie, went out to help too. Under Dad's supervision, we built flat boxes from scrap wood, filled them with soil dug out of a hole below the floor of the new cabin, and planted cabbages and tomatoes. Every window of both rooms of the cabin soon was filled with growing plants.

We went out and dug the snow away from a cabin-sized area and constructed a greenhouse out of poles and a plastic-like material Dad had purchased from a catalog. With fittings bought at the N.C. Co. store, we built another barrel stove. It sits in the center of the structure, throwing out heat while consuming prodigious amounts of wood. Now in early June, the greenhouse is filled with tomato plants, some more than three feet high.

Dad has also hired a man with a large tractor—a Caterpillar D-8—to clear land. He now knows that the best way to clear land is to scrape off the brush and trees while the ground is still frozen enough to retain most of the moss and roots. In just a day or two the tractor scraped off 20 acres of the homestead, the amount required to be planted in crops in order to prove up on the 160 acres. Once the ground thawed, Dad and I managed to plow up a third of the cleared land well enough to plant row crops like potatoes. The rest we scarred up well enough to plant an oat crop that Dad thinks will pass land office inspection to qualify as "in cultivation," which is what is required. We also have built a shed for hogs and another for chickens. Dad bought two young hogs and ten chickens from a farmer out north of town so now we are really into farming. All Mom and Dad have to do now to prove up is live on the homestead another year and the place will truly be theirs. Sometimes I get wound up enough in these projects that I forget the uneasy feeling I have about how life is passing me by and how I can't do anything right, even take care of dogs.

All of a sudden everything has really gone to hell. Mom and Dad are going to lose the homestead. We just got the word that the army is planning to take over the area that includes our homestead to use for winter training maneuvers. This is one of the few times that I've seen Dad really discouraged for very long, and he and Mom are having long discussions about what to do when the army kicks us out. Maybe they will move to town and both get restaurant jobs; maybe they will start a new restaurant, or maybe they will go someplace else and go into the sawmilling again. Mom does not seem very happy about any of these ideas and she is having repeated asthma attacks. She hasn't done much the last few days except lie in bed because Dad drove her into town to see Dr. Haggland and he gave her some extra-strong medicine that really has knocked her out.

The only good thing to happen to anybody in the family all spring was what happened to Lewie while Dad and I were out working away from the cabin. All his life Lewie has been a little brother, and a small one for his age at that. When I was born I weighed eight pounds, but Lewie was premature and had only weighed four. Seems like it has been that way ever since, with Lewie always being too small or too young to do whatever I might be doing. And Lewie so much wants to be around other people that any job he has to do by himself is a double agony for him. He would have much rather stayed in town where there were other kids to play with than come back to the homestead where he mostly has to entertain himself.

The contrast between what Lewie and I are doing, and about how differently we appear to others and even ourselves, really came home to me one day when we had a visitor. While Dad and the man stood outside the cabin talking, I was working away with an axe and a saw building a new frame for sawing up firewood, and Lewie was just sitting around listening. When the man got ready to leave he made some comment about how strong I was and how much work I was doing. Dad picked up on it and said a whole bunch of complimentary things about how much help I was around the place; it was just like having another man, he said. Of course, these comments made me feel pretty good, but I was used to having things like that said about me.

The man got in his car, rolled down his window so Dad and he could exchange a last few words, and he started his engine. Just then Lewie, who was standing by silently listening to everything that had been said, reached up to tug on Dad's arm. "Hey, Dad, why don't you say something good about me, too?" Lewie said plaintively. It was too late by then so the man drove away without hearing anything good about Lewie. That was the way it has been just about all the time: Lewie never hearing any bragging on him, and that is sad. That's why what happened to Lewie that day was so great all around.

It started when Mom looked out the cabin window to see a black bear climbing up in the pickup to get at its load of feed for the pigs and chickens. Dad and I were gone, so Mom told Lewie about the bear. "I'll go shoot it," he said, picking up our grouse gun. It is a .22-hornet in which we use ordinary .22 shells that are slightly too small, so the rifle rarely shoots straight. Mom suggested that he take out Dad's big gun, the single-shot 30-30, or the old 30-06 military Enfield that I traded a dog for last winter. Lewie refused, saying that he did not know how to shoot the big guns very well. Actually, I think he was a little afraid of the little single-shot 30-30 because it kicks like heck when it goes off, and my gun is so heavy he has to prop it on something for aiming.

The bear heard Lewie come out, so he ran off and stopped about 70 yards away. Lewie said he thought he would just shoot the bear in the butt, like he had seen us do up at Berry Creek last summer when we wanted to chase bears away. Lewie aimed and fired, and the bear

fell dead on the spot. Instead of hitting the bear's hind end, the little bullet entered his brain through his ear.

Now Lewie had done something to brag about. Everybody who has come around after that has heard the story about how Lewie killed the bear—at 70 yards with just a .22 rifle—and with just one shot, too. If Mom, Dad or I forget to tell the story, Lewie always remembers. One neat thing about the event not mentioned by anybody is that it shows Lewie is plenty capable of taking charge if Dad or I are not around. As small as he is and like a little kid in lots of ways, Lewie is tough in other ways, and he has never been afraid of bears or anything else, either. Once when he was not yet quite four years old he saw a bully and some other boys starting to beat me up. Lewie came running over, jumped up in the air with arm stiff and fist clenched, and he hit that bully under his chin. Everybody was so stunned, even the bully, that they laughed and quit pounding on me. "That little kid's got guts," one of the boys said, and everybody agreed.

We skinned the bear, and found that it was good eating. Lewie insisted we save the hide, and as soon as it dried out a little, he nailed it on the wall above his bed. Up to that time, he still slept with a favorite blanket as both he and I had done when we were real little. But now he doesn't need that blanket any more. All he has to do when he is feeling low is to look at that scraggly bear hide on the wall, or sometimes reach up and fondle it, and he usually goes to sleep with one hand laid against the black fur and the thumb of the other hand in his mouth.

TAKING STOCK

EARLY SUMMER 1946

RIGHT AFTER LEWIE SHOT THE BEAR, and while we are still reeling with the news that the army is going to take away the homestead, we get another dose of bad news. Not only is the army maybe taking away our land, the Civil Aviation Authority and the City of Fairbanks are also considering putting in a new airport that might require most of our homestead and other land nearby. This is more than just talk, but it might not happen because two other sites are under consideration for what is already named the "Fairbanks International Airport." One possible site is atop Chena Ridge just west of town, and the other is nearby in the valley almost where the Chena runs into the Tanana.

A large caterpillar tractor arrives one day to clear swaths through the trees in preparation for a soil survey of the potential nearby runway sites. They are across 14-Mile Slough from our homestead, so not actually on our property. Even so, if that area is chosen, the plan is to take away almost all of our homestead to use for access and other purposes.

The engineer in charge of doing the site testing negotiates with Dad to have me make the soil survey and to use the Farmall H in the work. The engineer is willing to pay the incredible price of $25 per day for me and the H, and he will furnish the one other piece of equipment required, a prospecting boiler. I figure that $10 a day would be fair pay so I think that the engineer is giving us this extra to keep Dad from objecting to the testing work. I suggest that Dad take most of the money, but he says I can have the whole amount.

The engineer brings the boiler out the next day, and we mount it on our go-devil so that I can pull it along the survey lines behind the

H. He shows me how to run the boiler and tells me what to do. From then on I am on my own, quickly getting rich by driving holes in the frozen ground to find out how far below the surface the gravel lies.

Each morning I go over to the site and build a fire in the boiler. This is a small boiler, light enough that two strong prospectors can carry it. It is just a big metal box with a water pan on its top, and a hand pump to force water into the internal pipes that generate steam. When steam is up, I drill my first hole, using a hollow steel pipe attached to the boiler with a strong rubber hose. Each hole goes rather quickly; the steam jetting out rapidly thaws the ground ahead of the point and blasts away the silty dirt. Things slow down considerably when the point hits gravel, but that is as far as the point has to go. I record the depth, and move on to the next hole, another hundred feet down the proposed runway.

With two week's work I amass a fortune: more than $200. That is more money than I have ever had before. As soon as I cash the check in town I buy an old pump and a used one-lunger diesel engine to run it. My idea is to pump water out of 14-Mile Slough to use for irrigating our crops. The two purchases added up to $186.

"Oh, why did you spend your money on that," Mom says in an anguished tone as she watches me unload my pump and engine when I got home. "If you were going to spend the money you should have bought something you wanted for yourself."

Her remarks smart, partly because I am not sure myself if the old pump and motor really will run. Maybe I have wasted the money. Her tone bothers me, though, and as I ponder that I begin to think I know why she is distressed. Mom is thinking that I am getting too much like Dad when it comes to spending money. If any is available it goes into equipment or something else needed for work—but never into purchases that add to personal comfort or make the family's living better. It has always been like that for Mom, and here I am doing the same thing. I wish that I had spent some of that money on something nice for her. Something that she needs, or maybe just something pretty for the cabin.

The fun of doing the soil testing work, and of earning and spending all that money so quickly all seeps away as I mull it over. I can see that what I have bought is a total waste because that pump and motor will never run. They will just lay in the brush alongside the cabin until they rust away because I do not have the knowledge or the ability to make them operate. Everything is bad: the folks are going to lose the homestead, either to the army or the airport; Mom will never have a house that she really owns, and I can't do anything right. I can't fix machines right, I can't spend money right, I can't train dogs and I can't even take care of the pups right.

I cannot help but keep coming back to thinking about the pups, and that leads to more thinking about the dogs. Counting pups and adults, I now have fifty-four dogs altogether, and they are chained and penned up all over the place. We used to let the dogs run loose, but now I have too many of them for that. I realize that those dogs really did not have very good lives. All summer long they lie there on their chains, and most of the winter, too, because I am not good about running them. And fifty-four? How can I ever use that many dogs?

Having been around farms and ranches, our family has always been practical about animals. When the time comes to eat them or to get rid of them for some other reason, the animals are supposed to be done in without much if any agonizing. But one rule I've heard over and over is that animals should not suffer when being killed, nor should they ever be allowed to suffer in their normal lives. When he was young, Dad had once worked in a packing plant in Pueblo, Colorado, and he'd told about how bad it was on the day once each month when the rabbis came in to kill cattle for kosher meat. The workers had a method for knocking out the cows instantly so that they never suffered at all, but the rabbis used knives to kill the cows slowly. That made the plant workers both sad and furious, Dad said.

Thinking about that and my dogs also reminds me of the rancher Bart Scott who lived a few miles from us when we had the uranium mine in Colorado. I hardly ever saw him, and even then he was usually on a horse some distance away. Aside from his having such a neat strong-sounding name, Mr. Scott was a dashing figure to me because he was a genuine working cowboy who I knew had a lot of guts. The proof of that was the little black cloth bag on his wrist where his left hand should have been. Our friend Charley the trapper told me why Mr. Scott wore the bag instead of a glove. One day, just four years before, he had roped a big steer and his horse had reared back on his haunches like he was trained so as to hold the steer. Unfortunately the lariat had looped around Mr. Scott's left wrist as well as the saddle horn, and the tugging by the steer and the horse stripped the hand away from his arm until it was attached just by a bit of gristle. Bart

Scott knew what he had to do then: he reached out with his pocket knife in his right hand and lopped the left one off. He never even went to see a doctor afterwards, since the closest one was sixty miles away, and ten of that had to be on horseback or walking.

Mr. Scott was a real decisive man for sure, and he also had strong opinions about animals, especially his riding horses. He believed that his personal riding horses, always stallions, should be as perfect as possible and never be kept beyond the time of peak performance. Mr. Scott decided that ten years was as old as his riding stallions should get, and it was his rule that each one had to be destroyed on its tenth birthday. It seemed to me that it was foolish in a way to kill a fine stallion in his prime like that, but I could see that Mr. Scott's scheme insured that he would always ride a first-rate horse.

I will never forget that day I was at Charley the trapper's when Bart Scott came slowly riding up on his favorite horse, a beautiful big white, and with another nice-looking stallion in tow. While Scott was still a quarter of a mile away Charley told me what was going on: it was the white horse's tenth birthday, and Mr. Scott was bringing the horse to Charley to use for trapline bait. Mainly it was because Scott thought so much of this particular horse that he could not bear to shoot the animal himself.

"Howdy, Charley," Mr. Scott said without a smile.

"Howdy, Bart," Charley replied.

Silently, Bart Scott dismounted, stripped the saddle off the white stallion and put it on the other horse. Then he exchanged the halter on that horse with the bridle on the big white. Fascinated, I watched how the rancher's black-bagged left wrist assisted his right hand throughout the process almost as well as if it were another hand. Then with his back to us Mr. Scott reached up under the horse's neck with his left arm and held it tight, his own face buried in the horse's mane. He stood there like that for a few seconds and then backed away toward us. As he did so, Bart Scott gently swept the black bag down over the top of the horse's head and held it briefly on the horse's muzzle. I remembered then Charley's telling me that this was the horse on which Mr. Scott lost his hand. A tear rolled down the rancher's cheek as he turned to us and handed the halter rope to Charley.

His voice cracked as Bart Scott said, "Wait until I am gone, then make sure it happens fast." He rode off up the valley, and when he was out of sight Charley and I took that magnificent white horse out to where Charley planned to set a mountain lion trap. Charley aimed his gun so perfectly that the stallion was fully dead when his huge body collapsed to the ground.

Thinking of Bart Scott and Angus Carter as I worked today at my daily chore of cooking a big tub of cornmeal and dried salmon for the dogs, I suddenly knew what had to be done. I was never going to be a dog musher like Angus, so my childish accumulation of dogs without proper training or care must come to an end. And no government agency or Charley the trapper was around to accept what I knew was my own responsibility.

I put nearly all the dried salmon I had left in the food mix and fed and watered the dogs well. The rest of the afternoon was awful tough. Out a long way from the cabin, I went through nearly three boxes of 30-06 shells and I hugged, petted and cried over 52 pups and dogs before it was finally over. Only saucy Yukon and the lovable Che-Che, Mom's favorite, survived. The little pups were extra hard, but not as hard as old friends Brownie and Blackie.

When Mom, Dad and Lewie came home this evening, Yukon ran in circles and howled a greeting, and Che-Che came over to rub against Mom's leg, but the usual din that announced the arrival of a vehicle was absent. "Sure is quiet around here," Mom said. "What's with the dogs?" I explained what had happened, and she came over and put her arm around me. "Oh, Neil," she said almost choking, then added, "It had to be done," with a note of pride in her voice.

Tonight, I know I have done the right thing, the adult thing, and part of me is proud that I could do it—but the rest is miserable. The older I get, the harder it is to kill animals.

HAULING WOOD

LATE SUMMER, 1946

DAD'S MAIN PUSH RIGHT NOW seems to be the farming, and in a way it is a necessity if he is going to be able to prove up on the homestead—if the army or the airport will let him. He is really about the first one out along the Alcan south of Fairbanks to try to prove up by actually farming. Others in our area proved up years ago by exercising their World War I veteran's rights. All they had to do to get 160 acres of free land was build a cabin and maybe live in it a few months. Dad has never been in the military, so he has to go the whole route of building a cabin, living in it a few years and then putting one-eighth of the land into cultivation.

Dad talks up farming, and of course we putter at it, but I don't think Dad likes routine things enough to ever be a real farmer. He keeps coming back to things like wanting to make money out of trees, either by sawing them into boards or cutting them up into firewood. And even with the farming, it is obvious to Dad that he and Mom either have to keep working in town or have some other way to make money. I think he was more eager to work for himself than Mom is, but they both like being their own bosses.

With the idea of possibly selling cordwood, Dad now has a timber permit on land out six miles beyond the homestead, near 21-Mile. He figures that the place, Jensen's Island, just across a little slough of the Tanana from the Alcan, has at least 1000 cords. Since all the trees on Jensen's Island are green, he can't sell them as firewood until a year after they are cut. So Dad and I go out and spend a few days on the island, knock down a bunch of trees, and leave them to dry.

We now have a truck, the one Ed Blair used to haul all the lumber from Berry Creek last summer. Dad actually bought it, but he says that it is my truck in payment for the work I have been doing. I guess he recognizes that I have been feeling lost and restless all summer, and he figures my having the truck will help. It does, too. I am pretty pleased that, like Angus Carter, I now own a working truck with which to make money.

Dad also helps me arrange to buy dry firewood from several of the old woodcutters who live within a few miles of us. I pay them $8 to $10 per cord, depending on where the wood is located. The wood, in either four-foot or sixteen-foot lengths, is worth $17 per cord delivered in Fairbanks. Most of the people who buy the wood then hire a man with a buzz saw mounted on a little Allis-Chalmers tractor to cut it to burnable length. For this task they pay $3 per cord.

Dad is still working a job in town, so the plan is for me to do all of the actual hauling work. One hitch in the scheme is that people in Fairbanks do not burn much wood in summer, so I have trouble getting orders. Several men have been hauling wood for years and have regular customers already lined up. My few orders come about only because of personal contacts of some sort, or because someone who needs wood sees me deliver to a neighbor.

Right off, I do make a fair inroad toward supplying one particular block called the Fourth Avenue Line. Twenty-three ladies operate there, each in her own little wood-heated two-room log cabin that faces backwards on the street. Primary access to the Line is a boardwalk located where an alley would normally be. Most of the cabins have big picture windows on that side, and if a potential customer sees a lady sitting inside the window he knows she is available for business. I know all this because another boy and I got up enough nerve to do a little window shopping last winter when I was in high school. We did not go inside any of the houses, of course, but the other boys my age claim that you can. Furthermore, they say that some of the ladies seek to build clientele by giving free introductory offers to school students. A sufficiently detailed and funny description of one extremely brief interaction between a classmate and one of the ladies gives me good reason to believe it's all true.

The man who runs the buzz saw arranged for my first delivery to the Line. "Now don't let her try to take it out in trade," he chuckled, and that embarrassed me no end. He had me convinced that my customer would make this suggestion, so I was almost trembling when I knocked on her back door, the one facing out on Fourth Avenue. Instead of haggling, the lady took one quick look at my loaded truck, handed me $34, and told me where to dump the two cords of wood. I was relieved, and perhaps slightly disappointed. Nor have any of the other women done differently; they all treat me with the courtesy that one professional normally awards another.

Except for the wood dealings, I have never talked with any of the women on the Line, but Mom and Dad know some of them from having met them in restaurants. Mom says the prostitutes are better tippers than almost anybody else, and Dad thinks that they are generally honest. Both agree that the Line and its occupants serve as a useful part of the community, and if it comes up Dad usually launches into a long tirade about all the talk by the Fairbanks city fathers about wanting to get rid of the Line.

For one thing, Dad argues, where the ladies are they can be their own bosses. They need no one else to drum up trade for them, so that tends to limit any criminal element hanging around. Also, by being in one confined location as they are, it is possible for the local military to exert some control. Dad said that the military has agreed to keep the Line "on limits" as long as each lady reports weekly to the Ladd Field doctors for a medical examination, and that this procedure helps limit the spread of venereal diseases. The women all sell liquor to the customers, but they charge fair prices, so Dad sees no objection to that. In addition to minimizing the problems that come with having a large population of single men around, Dad says that the ladies contribute much to the economy by acting as bankers to some of the small miners and others that the town's banks refuse to help.

From Dad's overall discussions of the Fourth Avenue Line, I see that what goes on there is probably not all that much different than in married life. Without the hanky-panky there would be no Lines or marriages, but in the long run other things like companionship, trust, financial dealings and personal responsibility are important enough that you can see how the sex almost submerges into the background. Maybe.

Folded in with the wood hauling, I embark on another venture that is short-lived but profitable. In payment for a debt, Dad has acquired a building lot in a new subdivision called Hamilton Acres. This is a popular place for people who work on Ladd Field to build homes because the subdivision is near one back gate to the base, and the land is not expensive. Dad, in turn, passes the lot and also a set of building logs on to me, in payment for some of the work I have been doing.

On my truck I haul the logs to the lot, dig a shallow outhouse pit, and set up a tent to stay in. My next task is to put in a foundation for the cabin I intend to build, but there I run into trouble. Just a few inches below the surface, the ground is frozen solid. About two weeks go by before the ground thaws enough for me to put in concrete footings. In the meantime, I am beginning to think that building a cabin is perhaps more work than I bargained for. Nevertheless, I plunge ahead—until a man walks up with an offer to buy me out. We negotiate only briefly before I agree to sell the lot and the logs to him for several hundred more dollars than I had paid Dad in labor equivalent.

Although I have not made a huge profit on the deal, I think a person can make money doing things like this. The combination of a lot, some building materials and a foundation is attractive to the many soldiers and workers who want to build their own homes, and I can put the combination together with little work or skill. With the thought of trying it again, and with Dad's help, I begin accumulating another set of logs. Then just as I am looking around for a second lot to buy, the house of a friend of Mom's and Dad's burns down. He is a nice guy who is having a string of bad luck, so we talk it over and decide to give him the set of logs. I also go to his homestead and spend several weeks working for free to help him get some land in cultivation. Before I know it, the summer is almost over. However, unless the army or the airport throws us out, Mom, Lewie and I are staying on the homestead, and Lewie and I again will take correspondence courses.

TOM WADE

CA. 1857–1947

MY WOOD HAULING during the summer of 1946 has caused me to learn more about the several interesting old men who have been our only neighbors within several miles. They all came here before us, and they all live in the woods, well off either the old Richardson Trail or the newer Alcan. Three of them came into Alaska by way of the 1897-98 Dawson gold rush, and two others are Russians who came to escape the 1917 revolution in that country. I actually met all of them my first year in Alaska, but in summer 1946 I am seeing them frequently.

Tom Wade is the oldest, and one of the first to start living in the immediate area. His cabin is off in the woods about a half-mile from 17.5-Mile on the old Richardson Trail, three miles beyond our homestead. Dad first met him while driving out to the homestead soon after Dad homesteaded. At about 10-Mile Dad saw the old man walking along, the brown main canvas pouch of his wood-framed Trapper Nelson packboard filled with groceries. Dad's was the first civilian car to come by since Wade started out that day from Fairbanks, and of course Dad stopped to offer a ride (no military vehicles ever did). Learning where Tom lived, Dad drove out past our homestead to deliver Tom to his door. Tom invited Dad to bring the family for a visit soon, but he also handed Dad a five-dollar bill to pay for the ride.

"Why, Mr. Wade, I can't take that," Dad said. "I'm your neighbor."

"You will take it, or I don't want you to set your foot on my place ever again." Dad took the five dollars, and soon we all came for a visit.

Tom is an unusual woodcutter for the area in that he keeps himself and his surroundings spotless. He also is a reader; his cabin contains shelves of books and magazines. Tall and spare, white of skin, and with a sparse shock of pure-white hair, Tom looks frail and almost ghost-like. He speaks grammatically in a firm, quiet voice, and his pale blue eyes never waver. I always have the impression that whatever is going on at the moment occupies only a fraction of Tom's mind. Hidden away behind those probing eyes seems always to be thoughts of other places and times. I try to learn more about him, yet he tells me little.

I have learned that Tom followed his brother Jack to Alaska. Jack Wade was one of the really early-day prospectors, coming north even before the Klondike gold rush. After Tom arrived, he and Jack had mined over in eastern Alaska, in the Fortymile, at a place named Jack Wade, on Jack Wade Creek. Way over in western Alaska, not far from Nome, Jack Wade had a gulch named after him, too. I wondered why things got named after Jack instead of his brother Tom, but Tom never enlightened me. It seems to me that Tom scowls slightly whenever I mention Jack's name, and I can't tell if Tom has bad memories of him or misses his now-dead brother.

Tom's cabin is as immaculate, airy and white as himself. Its high-peaked ceiling of carefully peeled and whitewashed poles creates a feeling of spaciousness in the small structure. He has built two large windows on the south side of the two-room cabin, and both doors have glass windows as well. Sunshine floods in and reflects from white-washed log walls and a light-colored linoleum floor. Other than several shelves loaded with copies of the *New Yorker*, a few other magazines and books, and a battery-operated radio, the only decorations and furnishings in the main room are the stove, food cupboards and a calendar on the wall, straight-backed chairs and a small table covered with a clean red and white checkered oilcloth.

This is far and away the most charming home down the highway from Fairbanks for many miles, maybe all the way to the Canadian border and beyond, for all I know. No use to compare it to structures off in directions away from the highway because none are there. A person might go a hundred miles in those directions without seeing a cabin, and if he does see one it is probably falling down beneath its sod roof.

Out in front of Tom's house is his carefully tended garden, lush with cabbages, celery, carrots, turnips, potatoes and onions. Each time we visit him, he sends some home with us. Rabbits stay out of Tom's garden because he has built a fence formed of intricately woven willow wands. Above the garden and above his roof, little miniature cabins stand atop tall poles, the homes of many swallows that make a heavy inroad on the mosquito population.

On our first visit Tom took great pleasure showing Lewie and me his little grayling stream out in back of the cabin, one of the prettiest places I'd ever seen. The stream really is an old cut-off portion of 14-Mile Slough, separated enough not to receive any of the slough's somewhat silty waters that come in from the Tanana through Moose Creek Dike. Thus the little brook is absolutely clear all the way to the bottom. Numerous large grayling scattered away from the near bank as we approached, and a bevy of immature mallard ducks paddled quickly off around a bend. Tom said that Lewie and I could come back to this secret place to fish, but we could not take more than two grayling apiece each time. Tom usually ate several fish each week, he said, and wanted to make sure enough were always there. He was catching them in a little fish trap made of willows, and all he had to do to get a fish was reach into the trap and pull one out. I visited Tom many times after that. Sometimes Lewie and I walked to his place, and later I drove my truck over to haul wood.

Visits to Tom or any of the other old-timers always mean that you have to drink a cup of tea, whether you like it or not. They offer the tea, and you know it is an insult to refuse. If you happen to be at Tom's at news time, all conversation stops. Precisely at the time the news is to begin, Tom switches on the radio, and precisely when the news stops, the radio goes off. Tom never listens at any other time.

Tom seems awfully interested in some kinds of politics, not Alaska's so much as what happens back in the States and elsewhere in the world. Whenever the radio tells about anything to do with the new organization called the United Nations, Tom listens intently, and he obviously thinks that its leader, Trygve Lie, is a great man. Dad says that the United Nations is a bunch of nonsense, that nothing will come of it, just like nothing came of President Woodrow Wilson's League of Nations back after World War I. Tom likes Trygve Lie so much that I wondered if he knew him or was related to him. "No," said Tom when I asked him about it. "He's from Norway; Wade is an English name, just like yours."

Tom comes as close to lecturing me about going to school as anybody ever has. He is somewhat subtle about it, never saying more than

165

a few words at any one time. Just things like, "The world is changing fast; you are going to have to work hard and learn all possible just to keep up," or, "A young man like you needs to get all the education he can. This country needs people who are smart and well educated."

My very last visit with Tom is on a brisk fall morning. A light snow has fallen during the night, and a low almost fog-like cloud cover still gives the sky that grim appearance hinting of the colder days to come. A minor breeze tickles fluffs of light snow from the limbs of willows and alders where they lean over the old Richardson Trail out ahead of me as I drive my truck along. Jutting up above the truck's cab, the big wooden forward bed rack whips the snow off the overhanging brush, causing the limbs to snap upward in my wake. They pop up out of a snowy comet tail that hides the view behind.

As I turn into Tom's long driveway, the moving air wafts the biting aroma of overripe highbush cranberries across my nose, a pleasant smell but one that presages winter in interior Alaska. Few spruce trees stand here, for this is an area that Tom has cut over to earn his living these past ten years.

Smoke curls up from Tom's cabin, but I see no sign of him. Usually when he hears my truck coming, he comes outside to greet me, but not today. He knows I am coming, too, because this is the morning I agreed to haul in his winter's wood supply.

Tom does come to the door as I shut down my engine and walk over toward his cabin, but he just stands there leaning against the doorway until I enter. He soon has the tea ready, and we sit down before the checkered tablecloth. Tom steers the conversation to what I am doing and planning to do, so I do most of the talking. Tom is not a talker anyway, but he does seem quieter than usual.

The tea finished, I prepare to go to work. "Which piles do you want me to haul from, Tom?" I ask.

"It doesn't matter; take from whatever is easiest."

I drive out to Tom's cutting area and select the first pile I come to, one containing 16-foot spruce poles and logs up to about eight or nine inches in diameter. Like all such piles the old woodcutters assembled, this one is neatly stacked with all log butts evenly placed at one end. Tom and the others take pride in doing it this way, but more than neatness is involved because this stacking scheme makes it easiest for a wood hauler to load by himself. Like the wood cutters, the haulers are all loners who work alone. They have figured out an effective scheme for solo loading, and I follow it.

First, I park the truck directly beside the pile with the front of the truck's bed just a few inches forward of the butt end of the pile. I then carefully placed a six-inch diameter fulcrum log crossways in between the bed and the truck's frame. It needs to be just back of the center of gravity of the logs to be loaded, and to stick out toward the pile about eighteen inches beyond the truck bed. With the aid of the fulcrum—if I do everything just right—I will be able to load two cords on the truck while standing down at the tail of the pile, and I will never touch any piece being loaded except right near its small end.

The key to easy loading is to develop a rhythmic movement that involves picking up the small end of a pole and then laying the pole on the fulcrum piece with a downward push that will cause the pole to flex down at each end. Then as the far end of the pole rebounds upward I lift the small end and throw it up on the truck. If all the motion is perfect, the pole jumps up on the truck as though it were alive and falls in the intended place on the load. For that to occur I have to move smoothly and exert just the right pressures at the right times, letting my actions be guided by the feel of each pole as it flexes when picked up and laid on the fulcrum, and also an initial mind-set as to where on the load I want the pole to land.

It helps that few of the pieces in a pile of sixteen-foot firewood are likely to be larger than eight inches in diameter because the old wood-cutters can't move the heavier sixteen-foot lengths into a pile. Instead, they usually saw those up into four-foot lengths and pile them separately. I can still manage the larger sixteen-foot pieces and in fact can load any log if I am strong enough to pick up its small end. The big ones are awkward to load because they are too heavy to move rapidly and they will not bend under their own weight. It is necessary to lever the butt ends of these up on the load slowly and so no help comes from flexing or momentum. Also, it is wise to reserve some space low in the load to accept those bigger pieces.

In a way it is kind of fun, sort of like an athletic contest where I am the only player on my side going one-on-one against a team of sixteen-foot poles on the other, each with a personality of its own that has to be judged and dealt with effectively if I am going to win the game. As usual, a few bobbles occur, but within the hour I have Tom's first two cords on the truck and am pulling up alongside his cabin to unload. Tom comes out and stands in the doorway to watch as I unchain the load and flip the pieces out into a pile beside the stand where he will cut them up into firebox lengths. I am getting ready to go back for another load when Tom calls me to the door.

"That's enough wood," he says in a soft, quiet voice, and he hands me a $20 bill.

"But, Tom, you will need at least one more load to get through the winter, maybe two, and twenty dollars is way too much pay even for that."

"No, you will haul no more wood," Tom, his voice now gruff, "and you will take the twenty dollars. Good-bye. Now go home."

I drive off, trying to understand what I have done to make Tom so unhappy, and why he has insisted I accept that much money. I did not plan to charge him anything at all, and $5 is more than fair pay. I am sad and uneasy as I drive off, and as I reach a bend in the trail I look back to see Tom still standing in his doorway watching my departure. Something, I know, has to be very wrong.

And of course something is, but I have had nothing to do with it. Tom is dying of cancer, and he knows he will not live long enough to burn even that one truckload of wood. Proud and independent to the last, Tom closes up his cabin two months later; Dad drives him to the hospital in Fairbanks, and there he dies. He is almost ninety years old.

MIKE BEDOFF

CA. 1867–1947

THE YOUNGEST OF OUR NEIGHBORS is
Mike Bedoff, who for a while was Dad's part-
ner in the sawmilling operation. Only in his mid-sixties, he is Tom
Wade's opposite in every way. Mike is short, dark complexioned, and
generally unkempt. Beneath his black mustache he displays a tooth-
less grin when he speaks his broken English, an accent difficult to
understand and seemingly always hinting of guile. He wears the same
tattered clothing day after day, and rarely if ever washes any of it. Open
sores fester under the rags that he wraps around his lower arms as a
normal part of dressing each morning. Nor is Mike one to discard
anything before it is worn out. I once watched him put on a sock,
carefully rotating it until the one remaining inch of material joining
the foot with the upper part could drape across his heel. Unlike Tom,
who never smoked, Mike continuously puffs away on homemades that
are even more sadly constructed than Mom's, and that make his fingers permanently yellow.

Mike acquired his property from some earlier resident skilled at
building with logs. The cabin and several outbuildings are attractively
sited on a wide bend in 14-Mile Slough. Here, the stream banks are
far apart and the pools deep, almost as though the stream were a cres-
cent-shaped lake. The previous owner had cleared all brush and smaller
trees away from the larger spruces to create a pleasant, park-like atmo-
sphere.

The cabin is a classic structure of the old style, its walls made of
massive logs hewn square and carefully jointed at the corners. Uni-
formly sized spruce poles leading from wall tops to ridge form a low

169

pitched roof covered with metal sheeting, sod and a lush growth of grass. Light enters the cabin only through one small pane of glass set in the door and two modest windows, one beside the door and one on the opposite wall, facing out over the stream. The interior walls and the ceiling poles are a rich dark brown, the result of a many-year accumulation of cooking grease and lamp soot. After stooping down to enter the low door of Mike's cabin, a person is not inclined to move rapidly inside until his eyes become dark-adapted sufficiently to navigate across the single room. It sports two bunks and an open closet along one windowless wall, and across from that a barrel heater and a cook stove. Mike's wood box covers a portion of one lower wall, and above it open shelves support containers of food and other possessions. His table on the opposite wall and several nearby Blazo boxes used for chairs complete the furnishings. Not a single magazine or book is in evidence because Mike cannot read. Unlike Tom Wade, Mike does not give the impression of possessing deep thoughts, but, like Tom, he listens to the news on his radio and is interested in what is going on in the world.

Mike has a large garden area, but he grows only potatoes and cabbage in it. His diet consists mainly of heavily sugared coffee or tea, sourdough muffins made each morning, eggs, and cooked cabbage. To cook his eggs, Mike uses a greasy skillet that he never washes, and it is the same with his muffin tin. His other cooking utensils are a coffee pot and a large boiling pan used for cabbage.

Mike often rises late in the morning, so he is sometimes still in his aged gray long johns when I arrive. He always offers me breakfast, but I never accept anything but coffee. The eggs do not look very appetizing, and I cannot conceive of eating the muffins. Mike ladles the thick batter into his muffin tin with a large never-washed spoon that hangs on the wall beside the sourdough vat. Below the spoon's hook, a coating of hardened sourdough spreads down across the wall to the floor. Mike cooks his muffins in a muffin tin set on the stove top, so it is possible to watch the cooking dough expand upward as though it were toothpaste squeezing from a tube. Each little mound grows until it slowly falls over against the pan or another muffin. The main reason I never want to eat Mike's muffins is their color. Instead of turning brown as it cooks, the cream-colored dough transforms into a rubbery green mass, slightly translucent. Mike eats several of these disgusting green objects every morning, and the rest of the tin later in the day, along with his cooked cabbage. I don't know, but I suspect that Mike's muffins are green because he uses cabbage broth in his sourdough mix. Mike thinks that cooked cabbage is the perfect food for man as well as beast.

Over a year ago he bought a bunch of little white pigs from a farmer. "I gonna bee reech, someday. Gonna grow lotsa cabbage and grow lotsa pigs," he said. "I sell dos pigs and bee reech. You watcha see." Mike put the pigs in his root cellar which was pitch dark, and he never let them out. Each day for a year he kept them there, and each day he fed them all the cooked cabbage they could eat, but nothing else.

Dad tried to tell Mike that he should build a pen for the pigs outside, and that he should feed them raw instead of cooked cabbage. Mike refused to listen, if he even understood what Dad was telling him. Finally one day he said, "Dos pigs, dey no dam good. Day not grow. I quit. I gonna turn dem loose and dey can go to hell. You come see."

We went out to the root cellar where Mike opened the door. A terrible smell emerged, followed by a bunch of staggering, blinking little pigs, all white as a sheet, and only slightly larger than when they'd been placed in the cellar many months previously. Mike slammed the door shut and walked away in disgust. "I not gonna feed dem anymore," he said disgustedly, "Dey can just die."

During the following weeks, the pigs ranged around everywhere, digging up the ground near Mike's buildings and in the nearby woods. Each of them put on an incredible growth spurt and quickly grew into a 200-pound porker. "I dunna unnerstan it," Mike said, shaking his head, "Dos pigs got no good cabbage to eat, and dey grow anyway. I donna unnerstan—dey not like goats."

The reference to goats mystified me until just recently, as did Mike's many earlier references to these animals. He was always talking about goats, but I never could quite understand what he was saying, partly because of his poor English, and partly because when Mike talked about goats he mentioned foxes, too. "You needa goats ona your place, und fox. Nice fox. Goats maka milk, good milk. Needa fox, too," he said again and again in one version or another. Then just the other day when I met a man who knew Mike back in the 1930s I finally understood. The man said that back then Mike had a herd of goats that wandered around his place, often jumping atop his buildings to eat grass, or just for the fun of it, as goats are wont to do. But Mike also had acquired a pet fox, and this fox thought he was a sheep dog. The fox spent much of his time keeping a watchful eye on the goats as they pranced around, and he herded them back whenever they tried to stray from the immediate area.

When Mike talks he is so difficult to understand that I have never figured out if he merely trying to con Dad when he claimed to have huge forests of large trees on his homestead, or if he simply did not know. On several occasions that spring, Mike led me and others of Dad's crew on what seemed to be snipe hunts as we searched for trees big enough to saw into boards. Mike walked out in front, his double-bitted axe on his shoulder as I followed along riding the Farmall H. Mike did not think much of the H; he believed it to be a poor machine for logging. "You needa horse," he would mutter, "We usa horse in woods always. Dat best way. Get 'tween trees better, und horse strong, pull beeg logs." Mostly, I think, he was trying to keep my mind off the fact that we couldn't find any big trees. Eventually, though, we would come to a tree that Mike had felled, usually one marginally big enough for lumber. I would hook my cable on it and drag it back to the saw-mill, with Mike tagging along behind repeatedly muttering, "You needa horse."

However, Mike was happy as could be to have Dad put the saw-mill on his place because the sawmill meant activity and people around. Mike loves people. Yet he has no transportation, and he rarely goes into Fairbanks. He once returned from one of those trips in a military four-by-four loaded with Russian pilots, the men who picked up Lend-Lease fighters and bombers at Fairbanks to fly them on into Siberia. That began a series of visits that quickly evolved into wild parties some-times lasting several days. The pilots drank and sang at night and then they staggered around in the daytime, still drinking and often firing off pistols at vodka bottles or just shooting them off in the air. They had an endless supply of both vodka bottles and ammunition. During these visits Mike was in his glory. He smiled continuously as he ban-tered in Russian with his former countrymen, and did his best to con-sume as much alcohol as they did.

KRILL (KRIM)

CA. 1870–1947

MIKE'S PLACE IS THE CONTACT POINT with civilization for three other old-timers who live off in the woods and earn their living by cutting firewood. One is another old Russian who calls himself Krill, and sometimes Krim. A short, stocky man with a normally sad face that can suddenly break out into a pleasant grin, he lives in a miserable little cabin set in a dark wood over beyond 14-Mile Slough. He does not own the property; he is just squatting there, and he has almost no possessions. His location and his cabin are so depressing that I usually skirt around it when in that general area.

When he does see me, Krill insists that I come in for tea. He likes me, but he sure hates the Russian fliers. Krill stays away from Mike's place when they are around simply because they are Soviets. They were the ones who had killed his mother, father and sister back during the revolution, he said. Krill's English is far worse than Mike's, so he is determined to teach me Russian so that we can converse better. This is a useless effort, and one reason I often skirt around Krill's cabin is to avoid these painful, unending lessons. I might pick up a few words after a long session, but never well enough to remember until the next time.

I feel badly that I often avoid Krill, because I know how much he enjoys company, and he is a gentle soul. I think his diet is worse even than Mike's. All around his cabin are many grouse, and I have wondered why he does not eat some of them. I quit wondering on the day I was walking behind him along a trail that led through the dark, wooded, almost swampy area near his cabin. Trees crowded in on all sides, and the ground was covered with deep, wet moss. Hunched over, Krill looked pathetic as he shuffled along ahead of me, his sockless feet clad only in an old pair of unlaced shoepacs cut off just above the rubber foot part. What a sad way to live, I thought, all alone in such a gloomy place. Then, off to the side of the trail I saw a hen grouse walking a path that would intersect Krill's track. Clucking, she walked directly toward him and then passed just under his upraised shoe. He paused and held his foot high until the eight little grouse chicks following single-file behind the hen had also crossed the trail. Krill clucked at the hen grouse, she clucked back, and we all continued on our way.

I know that grouse are pretty dumb about trusting people, but I have never seen it go anywhere near this far. The hen that day even trusted me, but of course it was only because I was with Krill, and she obviously knew that he would protect her. I feel good about what I saw that day. Perhaps it is because I now know that Krill has friends other than me—and ones more faithful, I hate to say. But ever since that day I have not enjoyed shooting grouse much, and I certainly am not about to shoot any that live near Krill's place.

HENRY SPALL AND JAY LIVENGOOD

CA. 1867–1947

IT'S ALL OVER NOW, but the two men I have enjoyed visiting the most have been Jay Livengood and Henry Spall. They were partners, but their partnership was a strange one for sure.

One neat thing about Jay was that he knew my grandfather when he was in the Klondike during the gold rush. He did not know him well, but saw him enough to recognize that my dad looked like his own dad. Hearing Dad's name and seeing him the first time, Jay realized that a family connection must exist.

How Grandad Davis learned about boats, I don't know, but I guess he was a fair boatman, as well as an inventor. He had made some money by taking people's boats down through Miles Canyon and Whitehorse Rapids in the fall of 1897, and that was where Jay Livengood first met him. Jay even looked like my grandfather, too. They were both slightly stocky and nearly the same height, about five foot eight. Even their voices were similar, I thought, but maybe that was my imagination.

Before he came to the Klondike in 1897, Jay was a prosperous wheat farmer back in North Dakota. He left his wife to run the farm when he went north. After the Klondike, Jay had gone to the Nome rush in 1902, and to other gold camps in Alaska. He then returned to North Dakota and found that his wife had been running the farm pretty well. Jay thought gold mining was more fun than farming, so he left the farm in his wife's capable hands, and went back to Alaska.

In 1914, Jay and a man named N. R. Hudson discovered gold on a creek northwest of Fairbanks that came to be called Livengood Creek. The town of Livengood grew up there, and Jay even had a nearby mountain named after him. All the old miners knew who Jay Livengood was, and he knew most of them. Jay had never gone back to see his wife and farm in North Dakota, but he said he was going to someday. Jay was more than eighty years old when I first met him in 1945.

Sometime before World War II, Jay had taken on his current partner, Henry Spall. Henry was about fifteen years younger. He was over six feet tall, red haired and powerfully built. But Henry was badly crippled, and could barely move his legs. When he walked, he used two chest-high sticks to drag his lower body along. Jay told me that one day they were mining in a cut up at Livengood when a large rock rolled down on Henry and hurt his back. After that, Henry could not walk very well.

Jay and Henry were still mining at Livengood in 1942 when the government stopped all gold mining because of the war, and also confiscated Jay's and Henry's equipment. Since gold was not necessary to the war effort, you could understand why the War Production Board shut down the mines, but it was a terrible thing to do to the sourdoughs because it destroyed their way of making a living, and most of them were too old and too used to living alone out in the wilderness to do construction work or anything like that. Like a lot of the others, Jay and Henry were essentially dead broke, so they had come to Fairbanks to become woodcutters. They had a timber permit over in the woods near Piledriver Slough, about two miles out behind Mike Bedoff's place.

Trucks could drive there only in winter, along trails that Jay and Henry had cut through the trees so that the trucks could reach their cordwood. That was part of the deal; for a woodcutter to sell his wood for $7 to $10 per cord it had to be properly piled alongside winter-drivable trails. Most woodcutters sold sixteen-foot wood, but Jay and Henry produced only four-foot wood because that was all they could handle. Jay was too old and weak to move the longer pieces into piles, and Henry could not walk well enough to do it either.

The odd thing about their partnership was that, while they called themselves partners, Jay and Henry never worked together. Each had his own cutting area in which he worked strictly by himself. Nor did they live together.

All year-round, each man occupied an eight-by-ten double-walled tent made of light-weight white canvas and that had a dirt floor. The first year I knew them, Jay and Henry had located their tents on the edges of their cutting areas, several hundred feet apart. Later, the two tents sat corner to corner, less than ten feet apart.

That Henry and Jay did not communicate daily came clear one day when I walked up to Henry's cutting area. Even before seeing or hearing him, I knew he was there because my nose caught the pungent scent of oil of citronella. Instead of repelling mosquitoes by rubbing it on his hands and face, Henry soaked his clothes with the oil. That procedure worked much better; it even kept the mosquitoes off me when I was near him, but you could smell Henry quite a ways off. He was resting when I got there, sitting on a log and puffing on his bent pipe that hung down over his chin. "How's Jay doing?" I asked him as we chatted.

"I don't know; I haven't seen him for two weeks." Looking over towards Jay's tent area, I could see a plume of smoke rising up, so it was obvious that Jay was over there. I went to see him, too.

Because it was always like this, a visit with them could take several hours, especially if both were in their tents. Each man then insisted on having tea, and of course neither offer could be rejected. Nor would it have been proper to visit one without seeing the other.

Much to my surprise, the double-walled tents were cozy inside even in the coldest of weather, far cozier in fact than our two-room cabin over at the homestead. To erect the tents, each man had built a framework of light spruce poles. The inner tent hung on the poles and the other covered the array to leave an air space of about two inches. The air space was the key to warmth, that and the little box-like Yukon stove each man had just inside his doorway. When the tents came from the store they had just flaps for doorways. Jay and Henry modified the entries by making up little wooden door frames and doors constructed of canvas and Blazo box wood. They hung the doors on hinges so that they opened like normal house doors. Henry's even had a little isinglass window in it near the top. Other than that, the tents had no windows, but since they were white, plenty of light came through.

Each man's bunk was located so that if he choose to sit up on it he was facing a little table right alongside the stove. It was also possible for him to put wood in the fire without getting up. Jay and Henry stored their food under their bunks, and their other few possessions in or on Blazo boxes at the far ends of the tents. One Blazo box was always available to seat a visitor for tea.

Twice each year, Jay and Henry went to Fairbanks to buy food. Each bought a case of eggs, a side of bacon, tea, sugar, flour and assorted canned goods. These trips were major expeditions that lasted at least three days, and sometimes as much as a week, depending on the availability of transportation between Mike Bedoff's place and town.

Initial preparation for the trip involved dressing up in the town set of clothes. These were identical to Jay's and Henry's work clothes, but cleaner, and Henry's town set was not soaked in oil of citronella. They both always wore "Alaska tuxedos," the matched woolen twill pants and jackets, sturdily made and with plenty of pockets on the jackets, including a large game pocket across the back. Manufactured by the C.C. Filson Co. of Seattle, Alaska tuxedos come in gray or green; Jay's were gray, and Henry's green.

The journey over to Mike's place occupied most of each expedition's first day. Henry and Jay started out at the same time, but they leap-frogged past each other, like the tortoise and the hare. Jay could walk fairly fast, but not far at a time. Two hundred yards was about his maximum between long periods of rest. Henry, on the other hand, never stopped, but his progress was agonizingly slow. While Jay sat on a log to rest, Henry poled past him, his sticks probing into the ground out in front of his shuffling feet. Then Jay got up and sped past Henry, only to stop again a short distance down the trail. By early afternoon, they would be in Mike Bedoff's cabin, visiting over tea and resting.

If we were aware that the time had come for one of these excursions, our pickup or truck would happen to arrive at Mike's the next morning, and it would be just stopping by before heading to town. Alternatively, Jay and Henry stayed at Mike's until some other vehicle was going into Fairbanks. When Jay and Henry arrived back at Mike's they always had more food than they could carry. Of course each man's case of eggs was impossible for him to transport more than a few dozen at a time. In winter, when trucks could get into their wood cutting areas, a wood hauler would deliver the entire six month's food supply to the tents. Otherwise the bulk of the supplies remained in temporary storage in Mike's cabin. That gave Jay and Henry the excuse to come back every few weeks during the warm part of the year. While they were content to be alone most of the time, they obviously did enjoy the trips out to Mike's place where they could visit with whoever might be around, and also listen to the radio news. Neither had a radio at home. As over at Tom Wade's, the radio at Mike's only came on for this purpose.

One day when I was there, the time came and Mike flipped the switch on at the precise moment. " . . . and now the news. The Manhattan Project has reported that its underwater nuclear explosion at Bikini Atoll two weeks ago was highly successful. Forty-two thousand men participated in the tests, along with hundreds of pigs, goats and rats, and a number of ships spread over the 25-mile lagoon. The detonation sank nine ships and estimation of the damage to others is suspended until they become less radioactive. This will be the Manhattan Project's last effort because today President Truman signed a bill creating the Atomic Energy Commission. The commission will oversee all further testing and the development of the atom for the welfare of all mankind. . . ."

"Harumph!" said Jay.

"The sonsofbitches. . . ." muttered Henry, shaking his head and reaching over to knock his pipe empty on Mike's big barrel stove.

"Also in the news....It has been announced that philanthropist John D. Rockefeller, Jr., is making available eight and one-half million dollars to purchase a permanent site for the United Nations Headquarters in New York City...."

"Rich bastard...." moaned Henry, and this time Jay said nothing. And so it went. Henry and Jay never said a harsh word about anyone they knew, but they enjoyed spitting out disparaging comments about whatever the announcer had to say. I guess for them, listening to Mike's radio was like going to the movies for most people.

Neither Jay nor Henry cut very much wood each year, typically about fifty to seventy-five cords apiece. The income from that amount was all each needed to buy food, candles, files and saw blades. Rarely did they come back from Fairbanks with anything else other than an occasional new pair of shoepacs or horsehide moccasins for cold weather wear.

Henry and Jay lived frugally, and the frugality extended to the bodily effort each man put out to accomplish whatever task was at hand. Toilet areas near the tents were located adjacent to woodpiles so that a trip back brought in, in Jay's case, an armload of stove wood.

Because he needed both arms for walking, Henry carried his in a battered, almost threadbare Trapper Nelson.

Both men worked in a highly efficient manner when out cutting; for them it was a matter of necessity. Small and frail, Jay used a little double-bitted axe for trimming the limbs from trees, and he kept it and his Swede saw razor sharp. Henry had a large axe, a Swede saw and a pickaroon. This pickaroon, a device akin to a mountaineer's ice axe, had an unusually long handle.

When felling trees, Henry tried to position himself so that he could work on several at once. His first step was to trim each tree as high as he could reach, and then peel the bark from two opposite sides to speed the drying process. To make a tree fall in the desired direction, he made a small axe cut on that side near the base of the tree. A few strokes of his sharp Swede saw then brought the tree down. With five or six trees fallen in a compact nest, Henry worked his way along with the axe, trimming and debarking at times and at others cutting the trees into Swede saw lengths, exactly four feet. Then came time to use the pickaroon. Standing in one place, Henry reached out with it to spike all wood lengths within reach and drag them into a pile. Henry's wood piles were always much smaller than those of other cutters, and sometimes not directly alongside drivable trails. That caused the wood hauler extra work, but none complained, partly because Henry charged one dollar a cord less to compensate. Jay got $9 to $10 for his cords, and Henry $8 to $9, depending on pile size and trail proximity.

Everybody who heard about it was amazed by something that happened to Jay the winter before he died. That was a very cold winter. Our outside thermometer never registered warmer than fifty below for six weeks, and sometimes it was down below minus seventy, which was as far as ours could register.

A month into the cold spell, Jay got sick with dysentery and could not get out of his sleeping bag. One night he stoked his fire so hot that a spark fell on the top of the tent. The resulting fire burned out both the outer and inner tent panels near the chimney, leaving a three-foot by four-foot hole open to the sky. Henry, located in his tent ten feet away, was unaware of what had happened because Jay did not call out. He lay there another two weeks until the cold spell broke. His illness was mostly over by then, but he was still very weak. He also needed a new sleeping bag, which Dad made a special trip to town to get.

Jay never really recovered from that incident. Because of it, he had been unable to write his one annual letter, a Christmas message to his wife back on the farm in North Dakota. He had not seen her for more than 30 years, but Henry said that Jay wrote such a letter each Christmas, and that the letter always had the same last sentence: "I will be home in the spring."

Jay was too weak after his illness even to write the letter, so he dictated it to Dad as the two of them sat in Jay's now-patched tent. The letter ended as usual, "I will be home in the spring."

Several months later on, Jay rode into Fairbanks with Mom for his semiannual food-buying spree. On her way home, out beyond Big Bend, Mom suddenly remembered that she was supposed to pick up Jay. She drove back to their meeting place at the corner of Second and Cushman, only to discover that while Jay was visiting with another old-timer on the Post Office steps he had collapsed and died.

I think Jay's death really tore Henry up. During the days to follow he was morose, and he soon decided to go back to New England to stay with relatives that he had not seen in many years. The ground had not yet frozen enough to get a truck into the cutting area so I took the Farmall H and a go-devil over to help Henry move out.

We hardly talked at all as I helped him take down his inner and outer tents, and while he began to disassemble the pole frame I loaded all his things on the go-devil. He had one trunk and a suitcase that he was taking with him, and the rest was going over to Mike Bedoff's for storage. I helped him finish taking the frame down and lay its poles on the ground in a neat pile, along with the poles and boards from his bunk and table. Lying there in the tromped-down eight-by-ten rectangle, they were the only remaining sign of Henry's residence of the past two years.

Even less was in the nearby rectangle where Jay's tent had been, only a small pile of ashes right in the center. When I first drove the H up I had seen what else was left of Jay's, there in a pile beside the ashes: a Yukon stove, a Blazo box containing letters, a gold pan and a few other things that Henry wanted to send to Jay's wife, Jay's sleeping bag, his snowshoes and his axe and Swede saw. Those things remained there until we had taken care of all of Henry's gear, and then he dragged himself over with his walking sticks to stand beside the little pile.

Henry stood silently with his back to me for a few moments, much as though he was saying good bye. Then he leaned down, picked up

Jay's little axe and his snowshoes and handed them to me. "I think Jay would like it if you had these. You can give the rest of the stuff to your dad."

The snowshoes are too small for me to use in soft snow, but they are great on a packed trail. I enjoy walking on them but they are wearing out, so now I just keep them to look at. It's the same with the axe: I used it until its handle broke, but I rebuilt it, and now I keep it with the snowshoes. I guess I know that these are the last, very personal, physical reminders I will ever have of the romantic era when the early-day sourdoughs like Tom Wade and Jay Livengood roamed the land.

ON JENSEN'S ISLAND

1946–47

D AD'S ENTHUSIASM for cutting cordwood gets a big boost when in at the N.C. Co. he sees a new tool for sale. Made in Canada, it is called a chainsaw, and it is the first one to show up in interior Alaska. It is just a little aluminum-colored thing weighing about twenty pounds that you can carry around in your hands, and it cuts wood like crazy. A quick pull or two on a cord starts its engine, and you just lay it on a log and its sharp-toothed chain whips down through the wood in seconds. This thing is expensive, close to $600, but Dad buys it anyway.

The chainsaw is swell for cutting up trees already fallen, but preparing it to cut trees down is a different matter. This machine has a carburetor that always has to remain upright whenever the engine is running, and the engine can be started only when the saw is upright. Then, the operator has to loosen a ring that holds the carburetor, and quickly rotate the chainsaw relative to the carburetor by 90 degrees, and then retighten the ring. The maneuver is tricky; unless you do it just right, the engine dies, and you have to start all over.

Dad says that we will soon learn how to run the saw well, and with it we can easily cut 10 cords of firewood a day. Somehow, it doesn't seem to work out that way. We have discovered that the adjustment of the carburetor is critical. Unless the settings are just right, the saw will not start, and if it does start, sometimes the engine quickly overheats and has little power. We spend a lot of time adjusting the carburetor, pulling on the starting cord, and sharpening the chain.

During cold weather, we have even more problems making the chainsaw run. The worst thing, though, is that a person can't keep warm himself while operating it. Steady work with an axe and cross-cut or Swede saw keeps a person going pretty well, but at forty below that chainsaw leads to cold hands and feet quickly. One cold day like that, Dad and I try to get the saw going until we are both frozen. "Aw, to hell with it," Dad says, "Let's forget that damn thing and get some work done." I agree, and soon we are dropping trees the slow, steady, warm way.

Dad tells me I can have the saw, and I can throw it away for all he cares. I play around with it a few days, trying to get it as well adjusted as possible, and then I take the saw to town to a store that sells used things on consignment. Even before I leave the store, a man walks in and gets just as excited over that chainsaw as Dad did when he first looked at it. The man wants a demonstration, and that causes me some concern. "Yeah, start that thing," the owner of the store urges because he too has never seen a chainsaw operate.

"Right here?" I ask, hoping he will say no because several people are standing around watching, and I know they will razz me when the engine fails to start, which is highly likely.

"Yeah, go ahead; and cut one of those pieces of firewood there by the stove," the owner says, so I gave the starting cord a hard pull. A cloud of smoke erupts as, surprisingly, the engine roars to life, so loud in that room that it sounds like a Norseman airplane taking off. The chain whizzes around at high speed; I put the blade through the piece of firewood quickly, and the store owner yells, "Jesus, shut that thing off."

I quickly comply, and the prospective customer, his eyes wide, says, "Wow, that's great. I'll buy it." That poor fool, he'll soon be sorry, I think, half guiltily and half gleefully, as I walk out with $250.

Another good thing that has happened is that, as near as we can tell, the army either has dropped its plan to take over our homestead to use for a training ground, or its attempt to acquire the land has been somehow blocked. Perhaps it is because of the possibility of the airport coming here, but even that is not going to happen. Somebody has figured out that putting Fairbanks International Airport midway between Ladd Air Force Base and the big military airfield that is being built up at 26-Mile might not be too shrewd. That would create three big airports all within a few miles of each other and all with their runways lined up in the same general direction. Since airplanes are likely to get bigger and faster, the idea is to spread things out more by putting the new city airport at the site down below town near the mouth of the Chena.

So it looks like the only thing we have to do to get title to the homestead is finish proving up by putting in one more year of residency. Therefore, Mom and Dad have decided that we will base at 14-Mile this fall. Lewie will take a grade school correspondence course from the Calvert School again, and I will take sophomore-level high school correspondence courses from the University of Nebraska. Dad will continue to work in a restaurant in Fairbanks in order to bring in some money, and will stay in town part of the time. As soon as he saves up enough money, he is thinking about buying another sawmill. With what extra time we have, he and I can cut some trees from his timber permit up on Jensen's Island, out beyond the homestead. By spring, we ought to have a bunch of logs hauled from there to the homestead, where Dad plans to set up the new mill when it comes.

In late November, Mom takes Dad and me to Jensen's Island in the pickup and drops us off. We plan to spend about a week there, cutting trees while living in a tent. We start out by erecting the tent but we sort of screw up the measurements when building a frame for it, and the bottom of the tent fails to come down to the ground by about two feet. Rather than cut the frame down, we just leave it that way because the weather is still fairly warm.

A few mornings later, I leave the cutting area to go back to the tent to put wood in the stove. While walking along carrying my double-bitted axe beside my leg I trip on a log down under the snow and fall against the axe. The blade goes right through my pants and into the side of my leg, leaving a shallow cut, but one that opens up a good half-inch wide and bleeds a lot. I head back to the tent where we have a first-aid kit, and wrap a bandage around the wound. That stops most of the bleeding, but as I walk back to the cutting area, the bandage slides down to my ankle. The bleeding has mostly stopped, so I think to hell with it, and I just keep going.

We work out there the rest of the day, and we notice that the temperature is dropping rapidly. While cooking supper, we estimate that it is about 20 below, and getting colder. I put a fresh bandage on my leg, and we crawl in our sleeping bags.

Some time in the night, I wake up really cold, especially down around my knee where the bandage has fallen off again and my sleeping bag has gotten a little wet. Dad soon wakes up cold too, and we know that it is at least 40 below outside, and about the same here in the tent. We finally both get in Dad's bag, which is bigger than mine. Huddled together like that, we warm up some. We know the temperature is probably going to get worse, so Dad asks me if I think I will have trouble walking back home. The leg is bothering me some, but it sure is no fun lying here freezing to death, either.

We make the big decision, jump out of the bag, and dress as quickly as we can. By two o'clock in the morning we are out on the Alcan, hot-footing it down the road as fast as we can walk under a heck of a good aurora that helps take our minds off our trouble. Two hours later, we are happy to see the 15 milepost which signals that we only have to go another half mile down the old Richardson Trail to our nice warm cabin. My lower leg is a bit of a mess and somewhat sore, but the sight that awaits us as Dad and I turn off the Alcan makes me forget all about the leg.

DEALINGS WITH THE MILITARY

WINTER 1946–47

IT MUST BE AT LEAST FORTY-FIVE below as Dad and I walk off the Alcan onto our loop of the Richardson Trail and see the parked convoy of army trucks, jeeps and tanks half on and half off the snow-covered roadway, not quite blocking it. If we were driving instead of walking we would not be able to get through because of the many small tents set up beside the parked vehicles. Even though not one a single engine there is running and most of the tents are quiet, all is not silent because a few soldiers are stirring around in the predawn darkness. As we approach we see four heavily bundled-up individuals huddled together in a pathetic attempt to start a fire atop the packed snow, using military toilet paper and green alder twigs broken from the nearby bushes. They are so engrossed in their hopeless task that they pay no attention to us as we walk up. And when they finally realize we are there they do not seem surprised to see us, even though our dress clearly marks us as civilians. I get the feeling that they are all terribly cold, and what they are doing brings Jack London's "To Build a Fire" to mind.

In response to Dad's question about what they are up to, one of the soldiers, who looks to be not much older than I, says they are camping out on their first night of "cold weather maneuvers."

"What happens next?" Dad asks. "What are you going to do when it gets light?"

"Beats the shit out of me, sir," the young soldier replies. "We're freezing our asses off out here. It's too damn cold even to sleep so I hope the colonel gets back from the base soon so we get moving somewhere." Dad and I can sympathize with that thought, in view of what

187

has happened to us this night, so Dad suggests that they ought to scrape the snow away and find some dead branches for fuel before they burn up their entire supply of toilet paper. By this time it has occurred to the soldier to wonder what we are doing out at five o'clock on such a cold morning.

"Oh, we're just out to enjoy the scenery and get some exercise before breakfast," Dad says, his voice bland.

"Jesus, you folks actually live out here, suh," another soldier drawls in an accent that suggests he is from some place like Alabama, "and you walk 'round fo fun when it's this cold?"

As we head on home past the long row of vehicles all pointed down the Richardson Trail in the direction we are going, Dad says, "I guess they have just as much right as we do to be here, but after we get some sleep I think if we can get the pickup going I better run into the land office and see what's going on with the army's wanting all the land around here."

It turns out that we are never again going to get that pickup running. While we sit at the breakfast table we hear a roaring noise and then a terrible crash. We run outside to see a big army truck with its bumper against the back bumper of a jeep which has its front bumper against our pickup. Almost the entire pickup is mashed in under the back of my truck, which had been parked a few feet in front of the pickup.

What has happened soon becomes evident. After sitting out in the cold all night, almost none of the army vehicles would run. However, the soldiers had managed to get one big truck started and were using it to push-start others. The truck had been pushing this particular jeep at high speed down the Richardson Trail, and the jeep's driver had cleared only a tiny hole from his icy windshield. He had not even seen our pickup parked in the road before he hit it. That the accordioned pickup will never run again is obvious, but we all agree that the jeep driver is lucky because he would be dead if the positions of our two vehicles had been reversed. As they untangle and turn the army vehicles around, the jeep driver and the other soldiers seem to view the freak accident as just one of those funny things that sometimes happens and is of no concern.

That and what they did to our pickup is bad enough, but what the army does to our homestead and some of the land around during the next few days is absolutely infuriating. When the soldiers finally get their tanks running, they run them everywhere, over our fields and through our woods. They also find several old woodcutters' cabins that are still around from the early days. These cabins were not really livable before, but now they don't even exist. With great glee, the soldiers have repeatedly driven their tanks through and over the cabins, totally destroying them all.

Dad's attitude toward the military has rubbed off on me already, but now I am developing a real hatred for the army. Dad, I think, is amazingly calm about it. A trip to the land office has revealed to him that the army's land grab has been squelched somehow and that no permission has been granted by any authority for the maneuvers now taking place on what is a combination of both private and public property. "But there is nothing we can do," Dad says, "other than try to get paid for the pickup. The trouble is that you can't sue the government unless it agrees to be sued, so I don't know what chance we've got."

It takes three days, but the army sates its appetite for knocking down trees and cabins, and finally rumbles back down the highway to Ladd Field. Dad also heads there and puts in a claim for $1000 to pay for the destroyed pickup.

Days, weeks, and finally months go by with nothing happening. Then Mom takes over. As I had learned when I let that turd in the tub years ago, Mom is nobody to fool around with, and the commanding officer of Ladd Field is about to get the same lesson.

"I don't know how long this is going to take, but I am going to sit in his office every day until we get paid," Mom says.

She heads into town one morning on the bus that runs in from 26-Mile Field, and that night she comes home in the back seat of an army sedan flying a flag on its front bumper. The driver pulls up beside the cabin, jumps out, opens Mom's door, and throws her a nice crisp salute as she gets out.

Mom has gotten some attention, that's for sure, but no pay. The commanding officer says that he has no authority to give her any money for the pickup; that has to come from an office back in Washington, D.C. Mom isn't having any of that, so the next day she is again off to Ladd Field.

That night, three soldiers bring her home in a larger vehicle, which also carries a brand new steering unit—steering wheel, steering column and gear box—for a big army truck. Mom got the unit by telling Ladd's commanding officer that the steering column in my truck is worn out, so that we cannot drive the truck. Therefore, since the army has destroyed our pickup, we are totally without transportation.

"Go get this woman a steering column, and take her home," the officer told one of his aides at the end of that second day.

Mom lied a little about the steering column. It is worn out, like she claims, but I can still drive the truck. Down at the bottom of a steering column, in the gearbox, is a bearing with little steel balls in it. In my truck, that bearing is completely shot, and all of the little balls have fallen out. Thus the bottom of the steering column rests on a cap that screws into the bottom of the gearbox. If you turn the truck's steering wheel to the left, no problem occurs, but a turn to the right tends to unscrew the cap.

When driving the truck, I start out with the cap screwed all the way in. Each right turn unscrews the cap a little bit, giving the wheel more play. I find that I can keep the truck on the road until I have more than one full turn of play. Then I have to stop, crawl under the truck, and tighten that cap again. I can usually get to Fairbanks on only three or four cap tightenings. Sometimes I have to stop if I meet another vehicle, because when that cap is really loose, I swerve around so much that I need most of the road for myself.

I guess Dad does not have faith in Mom's attempt to bring the U.S. Army to its knees, or maybe what she is trying to do embarrasses him. He goes to town and hires a lawyer to pursue the matter. Mom keeps right on going back to Ladd Field, and coming home in the command car every night. A few days later, the payment comes through. The army has decided that our pickup is worth $400, and that is almost exactly what the lawyer charges Dad for his services.

I am glad I'd stolen the basketballs from Ladd Field. I think anything you can do to even up with the damn military is just fine. Dad, though, never believes in doing things like that. He is so honest, it is irritating. When he sells a cord of wood, he always made sure that it is a big cord, and if a board is not sawed right on one end, he knocks more off the price than he needs to. Dad says that you always have to be fair, and never take advantage of anybody or any group, even something like the army.

So I never told Dad about one thing I did to Ladd Field. That was the time I helped a friend of Mom's and Dad's—I'll call him Willie—steal one of their buildings. We took it on a truck, right out past the guards at the front gate. Actually, the building wasn't worth much of anything, just one of those prefab things made out of panels that the army was probably going to burn up someday anyway.

Willie has a contract to haul garbage off the base, so his truck is a familiar sight to the guards. That day, we just loaded the building in the truck and put some garbage on top, leaving some hanging over the edges of the box on the guard's side so he'd be sure to see that we were hauling garbage.

We took the building to Willie's place near Fairbanks where he erected it and used it for a house. Soon after that, he got married to a real perverse lady. The marriage did not last, and when she left, the woman sawed the building in half and took her end away with her.

Many other things went out the front gate of Ladd Field on Willie's truck like that building did. Willie is not the kind of guy who will steal things to sell or anything like that. He just believes that useful things ought to be used by whoever needs them. He gives all sorts of things to his friends, and he hauls quite a bit of stuff out to our homestead. Dad will not let him bring in tires or valuable things like that, but we do get a lot of good food.

The army cooks actually throw away unbroken cases of cereal packed in serving-size boxes because they take up so much space and nobody on the base wants to eat that stuff. We have thousands of little boxes of Kellogg's Corn Flakes and Rice Crispies.

When the army men finish eating, they are supposed to sort out their eating utensils from actual garbage, but some of them just dump trays and all in the garbage cans. Willie takes the garbage to a big lot where he keeps pigs and lets them eat whatever they want. Mom goes out in Willie's feed lot and picks up all the plates, cups, spoons, knives and forks she wants. She leaves thousands of others lying on the ground but she also collects a lot to send to friends she knows in some of the Indian villages, people she has met while working in the restaurants in Fairbanks.

Seeing things like that—damaging or throwing away things that other people need and can use—helps make you realize how bad the army really is; it wastes everything, and what the army does not waste, it destroys, just for fun. I am getting so upset that I do not even like to see military people on the streets of Fairbanks, and I know I will do everything possible to stay out of the army, even if they draft me.

A WALK TO TOWN

WINTER 1946–47

WHEN MY CORRESPONDENCE courses arrive, I have a hard time getting interested in most of them; the things like geometry, English and history. I spend much of my time on just one optional course called "Gasoline Engines." I am now almost 14 years old, and I can see that life is getting away from me. Most of this schoolwork, other than the gasoline engines course, is a big waste of time.

Then within a few weeks, the engine in my truck really goes bad, so Dad arranges for a mechanic who has his own garage in town to work on it. Part of the arrangement is that I get to help do some of the repairs. This experience, plus all the interesting stuff I am learning in my engines course, decides me to become a mechanic. One nice thing about that line of work is that you didn't need any more schooling than I already have.

I go back into town whenever I get the chance to work for free for the mechanic. He says that if I get good enough, and if he has enough business, he might hire me later on. Mom and Dad see that I have mostly stopped doing schoolwork, and so we talk about it some. I tell them about my plan to become a mechanic, and they say the idea is fine with them if that's what I want to do. Everybody has to make his own decisions, Dad says, and I am getting old enough to do that. Nobody is going to make me go to school if I didn't want to.

Dad says he will help me as much as he can. If I can find a mechanic's job in town that pays enough to live on, I can do that. Or if I can't, I can stay on the homestead and help run the new sawmill that he is going to buy soon.

I am happy that the folks are seeing things my way, but somehow life seems empty this winter. I can do whatever I want, but nothing seems really satisfying. I putter at the schoolwork, get the wood in every day, and do a lot of reading. Mom, Lewie and I play cards a lot, and if Dad is around, he plays too. Sometimes we play cards when we first get up in the morning, and play all day into the night.

When beaver season comes, I put out a long trapline down along 14-Mile Slough and several miles up and down Piledriver Slough. It takes me two days to make the rounds of the traps on snowshoes, but it isn't much fun because the weather is cold and I am not catching any beaver. Some days, I do not even want to go out, and so after a few weeks I pull the traps.

Then comes the long cold spell, the one during which Jay Livengood gets sick and burns up the top of his tent. Day after day, the thermometer stays 50 below or lower, occasionally going down beyond 70. Dad is working in town, staying there in the hotel in which he cooks. We now have no vehicle that runs because the truck has broken down again. It quit about half a mile from the house, and there it sits with our wood supply on its bed. Lewie and Mom stay in the house, but I am out each day, if for no other reason than to haul wood in from the truck.

We have plenty of food, at least of certain kinds, but after a month, we run out of Blazo for the lamps. The few candles we have last only two more nights. I rig up a lamp made of a wick dipped in a tin pan of motor oil. It just barely burns, and it makes a lot of smoke. The wall above my bed is starting to turn black, and the smell is making Mom's asthma kick up, so I quit using it.

The next day, the temperature rises from about 60 below to near minus 50, so there is a chance it might be even warmer tomorrow. I decide that if it gets above 50 below I will go to town to get Blazo.

We cannot see the thermometer from inside the cabin, but the next morning the normal pinkish blue of the sky near the horizon has what I think is a warmish hue. As I dress up to go out, Mom suggests that I wear a pair of Dad's wool pants which she thinks will be warmer than mine. Confident of the day's warmth, I walk out the door, telling Mom that I will be back either tonight or tomorrow. Fifty-two below, the thermometer reads. Darn, I'm really in the mood to go. What difference does two or three degrees make, anyway? I'm going.

I head out the Richardson Trail toward 15-Mile. That is the long way around, but I have a good trail to walk on, which I would not have by taking the shorter route to 14-Mile. I have learned that even when it is cold, soft snow clings to pants legs and the uppers of moccasins, making them eventually freeze. Since I might have to walk all the way to town, I know I'd best stay as dry as possible.

Before I am even out of sight of the cabin, my upper thighs get cold. Dad's pants are not near as good as Mom thinks, so maybe I ought to go back and change into my own. Naw, that is too much trouble, I'll just keep going, and soon my legs will warm up.

They do not warm up by the time I get to the highway at 15-Mile. I head toward Fairbanks, rationalizing that a vehicle might come along at any minute, and of course its driver will give me a ride. My legs are getting cooler out there on the open road where no nearby snow-covered brush helps to still the air. Soon I find good reason to walk along with my mitten over my crotch for a few steps every hundred yards or so. The scarf I am wearing over my mouth and nose is creating a minor problem with my eyes, too. My breath deflects upward and freezes my lashes together so that I cannot see without frequent swipes of the back of a mitt to wipe the frost away.

As I approach 14-Mile I toy with the thought of heading back on the Richardson Trail there to the cabin. No, I can make it, and so I head on down the Alcan. While walking along, I am seeing bits of coal fallen off the truck that hauls the fuel out to 26-Mile Field. I begin filling my pockets with these and occasional splinters of wood lying on the roadway, knowing that if things get too bad I can build a fire. Plenty of wood is off to the side of the road, if I want to go through the deep snow to get it. Only as a last resort will I take a chance on getting wet by doing that.

Not a single vehicle has come in sight by the time I get to 10-Mile. My legs are really getting cold now, and I walk with one mitten between my legs most of the time. Then I come around a curve, and with great glee, see a large cardboard carton filled with paper, well off to the side of the road. Unmindful of the waist-deep snow, I run over to it and set the papers and box ablaze. As I straddle over the fire I feel like Robert Service's Sam Magee that night he was cremated on the marge of Lake LaBarge. Like him, I am wearing a smile you could see a long ways off, and the similarity does not end there. As with Sam's whole body, a certain important part of mine is warm for the first time since I left home.

Good luck comes in bunches. Just as the box is burning out, I see a military six-by-six truck coming down the road toward Fairbanks. I run over to the roadway, waving my arms in a signal to stop, but the truck shows no intent of even slowing down. What the heck—surely not even a dumb soldier would pass somebody by at 50 below! Just as the truck whizzes past, God or somebody intervenes. The hood of the truck pops open, blinding the driver. He slams on the brakes, and the truck slides to a stop on the ice-covered roadway.

I run up to the truck just as the driver, a young soldier, fastens the hood down and prepares to drive off. No, I cannot ride with him, he says, it is against the rules. Civilians cannot ride in army vehicles. I point out to him that we are the only people within miles, and who is to know. Reluctantly he gives in, saying that I can go with him as far as 6-Mile as long as I get off before we came in sight of the guardhouse there.

I feel so warm inside the cab of that truck that I strip off my mittens and scarf to better savor the hot air. That turns out to be a big mistake, I discover as I prepare to leave the truck at 6-Mile. Both the mittens and the scarf are frozen stiff because the air in that cab is far colder than it feels. But I have to get out, so I open my shirt and tuck my mittens and scarf in under my armpits until they thaw enough to wear.

As I walk on down the road toward Fairbanks I feel colder than ever, partly because evening twilight is starting to fall. I make 5-Mile, 4-Mile, 3-Mile, and then as I approached 2-Mile, a civilian pickup comes along. Of course it stops, and a few minutes later I am in Fairbanks.

I immediately go to the home of a man named Staley who hauls firewood in from 18-Mile, just out beyond the homestead. He does plan a trip for the next day, but if I am willing to help him load up his truck at his wood-collecting site, he will go out this evening, and then deliver me to 15-Mile. That is great. Two of us can transfer two cords of wood from a pile to his truck in no time at all, I figure. I'll be home almost by supper time.

I scurry over to the Northern Commercial Company store for a five-gallon can of Blazo, and I also buy a dozen eggs. We have been out of eggs for weeks, and I know Mom really misses them.

The adventurous part of my day is over, I think, as I sit in the warm cab of Staley's truck on the way out to 18-Mile. Still, I have learned my lesson about how cold it can be inside a seemingly warm truck cab, so I carefully carry the eggs inside the front of my coat as we drive along through the darkness.

Near 18-Mile, the Alcan curves up onto the dike that holds the Tanana River out of 14-Mile and Piledriver sloughs. We come to the dike and proceed along it for a short distance. Then, somewhat to my surprise, Staley wheels his truck out onto the ice that covers a wide slough running along the upstream side of the dike. We drive along past a network of other little sloughs emptying into this major one, and then come to a small portable building sitting near the slough. Little more than a large wooden box about six feet square, this is Staley's warm-up shack. First we will build a fire, he says, and I wonder why because we'll need only a few minutes to load his truck.

A thermometer in Staley's shack registers fifty-six below as he lights the fire. Just then, we hear a "kerplop." We look down at the floor beside my foot, and there is an egg, frozen to the floor with its yolk intact, and looking exactly as if it had been perfectly fried sunny-side-up. "What the hell, how did that get there?" Staley exclaims, giving the egg a quick kick that does not even dent it. He is mystified, but of course I know what has happened. Very carefully, I unbutton my coat and extract the rest of the eggs before any others fall out the broken end of the carton.

The fire starts, we go outside, on our way to Staley's woodpiles. When none appear, I began to comprehend what Staley is up to, and I realize why he has been so willing to bring me home tonight if I would help him load up. This is going to take a while, because we are going to go out and collect standing dead trees, those killed by the water backed up from the dike. Hours will go by before we get the job done.

The task is not as difficult as I first imagine. The trees are rotted enough at their bases to push over easily, and they are mostly bare of limbs. A hard shove against a tree usually bowls it over, and the trees are small enough that one person can drag them to the truck for loading.

It is a strange, unearthly place, though. Evening twilight left hours ago, but we can see with clarity because a full moon reflects from the almost bare ice along the slough network and the deep snow on the little islands between. All is white and an ethereal blue-gray, except for a tinge of green aurora off in the northern sky. Everywhere around us, stark tree skeletons reach silently upward as though begging the cold heavens for a return to life. It is not to be, for those trees will soon be chopped in little pieces and consumed by hellish fires.

I quickly learn that the easiest trees to get are those that stand right at the very edges of the sloughs, within a few feet of the ice. One tree up on a slight bank looks inviting so I began to step off the ice into the bordering snow to get it. Everything happens at once. I hear the sharp loud rifle-shot noise that cold ice makes when it breaks and the soft whoosh of falling snow as my footing gives way beneath me. In panic, I know what I will feel next: icy water closing in around me. But instead of that happening, I plunge downward, spinning and sliding on my back along a dry slope for more than twenty feet to the very bottom of the slough. It contains no water at all, I realize in amazement, and as I look around I am surprised at the amount of light coming through the ice roof high over my head. I can see for many yards up and down the channel. Light even glints from hoarfrost crystals that cling like beards to the underside of the ice.

I scramble to my feet, still frightened by what has happened, and wondering if I can get out alive. Yet I am struck by the beauty of the ice roof and awed by its ability to stand in place unsupported by water. Migawd, I think, not only have I been walking on this stuff, Staley has been driving his truck over it. I crawl back up the slope, delighted to see stars and bare sky again. Then I began to shake, partly from relief and partly because a lot of snow has got into the neck of my coat when I fell, and it is melting.

Recovering back in Staley's warm-up shack, I think more about it and realize why the slough network is dry. After the ice froze in place, the water in the Tanana has fallen drastically, and that has drained out the slough network. Staley just laughs when I tell him about the dry sloughs. Oh yes, he knows all about it, he says. He has fallen through himself several times where the ice broke away from the slough shores. No problem with the truck though, he says, as long as he makes sure to drive it only along the centers of the sloughs. I guess he's probably right but I am uneasy until we finish and Staley drives the loaded truck off the ice and back onto the roadway atop the dike.

I finally get back to the cabin about midnight, triumphantly walking in from 15-Mile with my can of Blazo, and still with 11 eggs safely warm inside my long johns. This had been a heck of a day, and I am tired and hungry.

BACK TO SAWMILLING

SPRING 1947

THE FEELING OF UNEASE that began in the spring after my year in high school has continued all summer, and hangs on into the winter. I want to get on with life but I can't quite seem to get a handle on how to go about it. For me, schoolwork has always been, if not fun, at least not onerous. Now it is a drag, and it does not have any real value that I can see. One consequence of what I am feeling is that I fail to finish half of my correspondence courses by the time spring rolls around. The hope of going to work in an auto repair shop in Fairbanks is remaining just that, a hope. Nothing seems to be working out right, whichever way I turn.

I am not even very enthusiastic when Dad's new sawmill arrives. Why he keeps coming back to the idea of making a living running a sawmill is more than I can understand. This new sawmill is not much either. Called a Belsaw, it is just a few boxes of metal straps and little castings so light that Dad was able to have the whole thing shipped into Fairbanks by air. If he was going to get it any time soon he had to do that because a longshoremen's strike in Seattle has blocked all sea freight to Alaska. When we unpack the sawmill it is hard to see how the thing can ever saw up any logs, even the little ones we have around the homestead and on Jensen's Island.

There isn't anything else to do other than help Dad assemble all this junk and build the wooden platforms that are supposed to support it. So we go at it, and after a few weeks we have this thing that is supposed to be a sawmill set up near the cabin.

Surprisingly, the Belsaw does saw nice boards. They are a lot truer than those put out by the old sawmill Dad had, or even the army sawmill out at Berry Creek. This mill's little carriage runs up and down the track just about as fast, too. I guess the best part of it all is that as Dad begins hiring a crew, he appoints me official sawyer. That means that I am boss when Dad is off in town taking orders or delivering lumber. For a fifteen-year-old boy to be the half-way boss of two or three older men is kind of exciting, I have to admit.

The only catch with my age comes when Dad somehow learns that the government has rules saying that no one under eighteen can work around dangerous equipment, and also about having certain safety guards installed. In deference to the one rule, Dad has us build a board protective frame over the long belt that drives the sawmill. That keeps the person who carries off boards and slabs from getting his pants caught in the belt, or maybe getting a board wound up in it. Dad solves my age problem by instructing me, if any official-looking government car happens to drive up, to have someone else shut the mill down while I quickly disappear.

We've all heard the joke about how you can tell if a man works around a sawmill very long because of his lack of fingers, so all of us who work on the mill are pretty careful. The only thing you really have to worry about is the big saw itself. If you keep out of it, you are not likely to have any other serious problems.

It was for that reason that when Earl Hirst was our sawyer he always had a little stick laid by his foot for cleaning out any bark that might get stuck in the saw guide. If that bark remained there, it could cause the saw not to run true. He would reach down with the stick and flick the bark out, keeping his fingers well away from the whirling teeth nearby.

I do the same thing when running the mill, but instead of a stick, I use a little roll of stiff wire about four inches in diameter, with one end of the wire sticking out about a foot outside the roll. I learn one day it is a dumb thing to do.

Dad is in town on a delivery when we start the mill up after lunch, and I know Mom is about to leave also to go shopping. I cut but one slab off a log before bark catches in the guide. Then as I stand in front of the saw using my roll of wire to clear the saw, I suddenly feel a terrible impact on the right side of my face, and I go down flat on my back on the sawyer's platform. My right eye is blind, and I know why when I put my hand up to my face to touch only bare bone across my forehead and cheek. My eye is gone.

"Shut 'er down," I yell as I jump up and start running toward the house, hoping to get there before Mom drives off. Once she leaves, the only way to get to a doctor is for someone to go out and flag a car down on the Alcan. I run as hard as I can with my right hand clamped over the bare bones of my face, thinking that maybe my eye is still in there where it was supposed to be. One thing that surprises me is that I do not seem to be bleeding much, but I do not even think of that until I see that Mom and the car are gone.

Only when I get inside the cabin and look in the mirror do I understand what has happened. My roll of wire caught in the saw and went around once before coming off the blade, all stretched out into an oval about a foot long. That oval hit me on the face with enough force to warp the wire into a shape that conformed to my forehead, eye socket and cheek. The bare bones I felt when putting my hand up are nothing but that roll of wire, still lying there plastered across my forehead and cheek. I peel it off to discover that my eye works just fine when it was not covered up with wire, and that my only injury is a series of wire marks across the forehead that are bleeding slightly. By this time, the rest of the crew arrives, all white-faced, and we have a good laugh as I show them what has happened, and I resolve to quit using wire to clean the saw guide.

The summer goes well for Dad because he gets a big order for three-sided house logs. I don't think the idea of making them originated with us, but we are the only mill in the area producing them this year. People like the three-sided logs because they are easy to put up, and they make a wall that is smooth on the inside but rounded like a regular log cabin's on the outside. The logs are a good deal for us, too, because they require trees only of small size, and they are fast to saw.

If the round log is the right size, seven and one-half to nine inches at the small end, it becomes a three-sided log with only three passes through the saw. The removal of three slabs leaves a log six inches thick between the sawed faces, and six inches wide as measured from the third sawed face to the remaining unsawed face. With additional passes through the saw to remove one or more one-inch boards, logs larger than nine inches also become three-sided logs.

The production of three-sided logs goes so fast that soon I am far exceeding Earl Hirst's record on the number of logs sawed in a day.

He could do sixty at best, but now we are turning out a hundred on a really good day—and with only a three-man crew.

When Earl Hirst sawed, we always set both of the mill's hook-like steel dogs in every log to keep it from twisting, and he never did any of the log turning. Earl left that up to the dog setter. I soon learn that one dog set in a log is good enough to hold the log steady until it enters the saw, and by that time the back upright standard carrying its dog comes alongside the sawyer's platform where I stand. Thus, if I turn my own logs, and set the dogs one by one as they go by my position, we can get away with one less man. Especially when we are producing the heavy three-sided logs, it takes two carry-off men to remove our output.

Using the new procedure, I can just barely keep up with the two carry-off men, so things balance out well. I roll a log onto the empty carriage and set the front dog. As the log goes into the saw, I reach over and set the back dog as it comes by. Then when the carriage comes rolling backward after a cut, I reach over again and grab the back dog to pop it out of the log on the fly, and do about the same with the front dog. Only seconds later, I have the log turned for the next cut, and it is rolling back into the saw.

Even if we are sawing only boards, we are beating Earl Hirst's daily production records, and of course that makes things more fun. The two men on the crew and I keep careful count of the logs going through so we can sit around and brag on ourselves each day that we beat an old record. Dad, of course, does not mind at all seeing those boards and three-sided logs rapidly piling up at the foot of the mill.

The big order for three-sided logs comes from a man who is building a bar that he is going to call the Squadron Club. He has acquired the hulk of a C-46 airplane which he has set up on blocks alongside Cushman Street in south Fairbanks, essentially at the edge of town. He plans to use this as the front wall of the bar, and to build the rest of the bar out of three-sided house logs. The Squadron Club is to be a big bar, so it will take a lot of logs.

The best part, though, is that the man has asked Dad if he is willing to deliver the logs already peeled for an extra five cents per foot. Dad is getting 25 cents per foot for the logs with the six-inch-wide strip of bark still remaining on the rounded side, so this extra five cents is a heck of a deal. What the man does not realize is that we can remove the strip of bark from green logs in only a few seconds. When a three-sided log is brought to size, I merely flip it over so that the round side is out toward the saw and redog the log. Then one of the carry-off men slips an axe-head in under the bark at one end of the log to get the bark started. He grabs the bark in his hand as I roll the carriage away from him. This usually peels the entire strip of bark off in one piece. For this simple task, we are doubling or tripling the profit Dad is earning from each log.

Even so, Dad is having a tough time meeting the payroll each week, and I can see that he, and sometimes even Mom, is under a lot of strain. When Dad gets like that, his face looks pinched most of the time, he does not smile much, and he is not good about lining out work for the crew when we are not actually sawing. With Mom, it is usually a matter of her asthma kicking up. She has a hard time breathing, her hands shake, and it is about all she can do to cook for the crew.

Saturdays are the worst, because that is payday. Dad heads off to town early Saturday morning to work on collections. That night after work, the fellows clean up and I drive them into Fairbanks in the truck. I usually park off on a side street, and we all go to the fire hydrant at the corner of Second and Noble. This hydrant, like others in downtown Fairbanks, is inside a large wooden box that helps keep the hydrant from freezing up in winter, and that box also serves as Dad's pay table. He usually shows up around 7 p.m., and then he spreads the cash out in piles for each man.

I can tell by the way he walks up how it has gone each day. If he walks quickly, he has enough to pay everybody. When he walks more slowly, he first takes one or two men aside and asks a question. "George, can you ride with me another week? I can give you ten now." George or Ed, the ones usually chosen because they are oldest and not big spenders in town, nod and usually refuse the ten-spot.

Unless I have lumber on the truck and need to make a delivery with Dad, I always go to a movie after he finishes paying the men, and most of them drift into bars. If we do not deliver lumber, Dad might go back to his collecting, and sometimes he just drives on home. At midnight, the rest of us assemble again near the truck and head back to 14-Mile. Most of the crew does not work on Sunday, but one or two of the men might help Dad plane lumber, while I spend some time doing upkeep on the mill, and maybe Lewie and I do a little fishing in 14-Mile Slough. If Mom is feeling up to it she usually joins us. She always enjoys fishing, and it doesn't matter if she catches anything or not.

WORKING FOR WIEN AIRLINES

LATE 1947

M Y ROLE AS SAWYER ON DAD'S MILL is improving my spirits this summer. I really am working like a man and that makes me feel better about how things are going than I have for a long time. I am enjoying what I am doing enough that I spend most of my evenings around the sawmill, sharpening teeth, doing general upkeep and often helping Dad plane lumber or load up the truck for his next-day lumber deliveries.

Daytimes are so busy and Dad is away so much then that we rarely talk, but the evenings are different. When we do our after-supper loading or other work we usually go at it slowly and sometimes sporadically. The soft yellowish light that spreads down through the trees in late evening makes a person feel good and not want to do anything very fast. Once in a while we just sit and talk, and it seems that these conversations usually come around to what I plan to do.

My main plan is to avoid going to school any more; beyond that I have no real goal other than to be a mechanic or something like that. When Dad and I are talking I might say something like I think a person can do just fine as a mechanic without spending a lot of time in school. When I make statements of this kind Dad never disagrees, but he sometimes has a commentary of some sort that is about what you would expect from someone who had been to college and used to be a teacher. Despite that, both he and Mom are really good to talk to about this kind of stuff because they never really argue or preach, and they always seem to be able to see things my way.

My truck has grown awfully tired during the last few months. The steering column is still in bad shape and the connecting rod and main bearings are now even worse. Each time the engine gets too noisy I pull the oil pan off and then file off the flat surfaces where the two halves of each bearing fit together. I know that this is not a good thing to do because it changes the bearings from what are supposed to be circles into ovals. Nevertheless, the engine sounds better when I do it, and if I am careful to keep the rpms low I can run the truck to Fairbanks two or three times before having to pull the pan again and do more filing. But now the tires are starting to go flat so I have moved the truck in by the sawmill so we can use it for hauling slabs out into a nearby field. A few flat tires don't hurt much for that purpose—as long as the load isn't too big. Amazingly enough, that truck continues to start, and as the engine hammers away at those oval bearings it noisily moves the truck off under a load of slabs.

On the day the end finally comes, only two of the truck's six tires still hold any air. After a hard life spent entirely on Alaska's gravel roads, the tough old Jimmy goes out fighting. The event occurs as the truck cripples along slowly, its engine choking and gasping as it struggles to haul a load of slabs out to the dump. It gets there, but then the truck settles into a minor mudhole and that extra bit of strain is just too much. The engine both clanks and roars loudly for a brief instant, and then I hear a muffled explosion as the oval bearings finally collapse and the oil pan and various assorted other objects fall out on the ground below. The truck is now dead, and it will never run again. I have learned a lot from it, mainly that if you treat a machine carefully, it can run for a long time even if it is in bad shape. The GMC's ability to keep going proves the old saying, "If it ain't broke, don't fix it."

I am now without a running vehicle of any sort. It would be fun to have a car, but I actually do not need one. The only place to go is Fairbanks, and to get there I can drive whatever vehicle Mom and Dad might have around or take the bus that occasionally runs between town and 26-Mile Field. Once in a while I just start walking, and only once in several times have I had to walk the whole way because not a single civilian car came along while I was on the road.

Then one day I suddenly become the happy owner of a 1932 Model A sedan in excellent shape. Dad has been paying me for my work on the sawmill this summer by means of entries in his record book, and allowing me to draw whatever cash I need, at least when he has the cash to give me. I have spent almost no money at all this summer so I have plenty of credit built up. My getting the car was Dad's idea, and he said that he would put up the $250 needed to buy the car from two of his employees. Brothers, they drove the car up the Alcan this spring from Michigan just for the trip and have worked for Dad all summer. They now plan to fly home, and of course I am tickled silly to get their car. But I wonder why Dad has suggested this purchase when I see how much trouble he has coming up with the money to pay the two men off and also buy the car.

Then one evening after returning from town Dad tells the few remaining men on the crew that we will not operate the sawmill the next day. He takes me aside and says that he has talked about my interest in mechanics with Forbes Baker, a World War I veteran who homesteaded on 14-Mile Slough long before us. He now is an aircraft engine mechanic who serves as a foreman in the Wien Airlines engine overhaul shop on Weeks Field. It seems that I might have a chance of getting something like an apprenticeship in that shop. That is a pretty exciting possibility.

Dad heads off to Fairbanks early the next morning to attend to business, and he suggests that I drive my car to Fairbanks and meet him at the Model Cafe for lunch. From there we drive over to Weeks Field to see the overall boss of the Wien shop, a man named Eldred Quam.

We meet Mr. Quam outside the shop, standing near a pile of airplane engines ready for overhaul. Dad says little, and I haltingly tell Mr. Quam that I want to work for him but have no experience except for the gasoline engines course from the University of Nebraska. After a while, with what sounds like a tone of reluctance in his voice, Mr. Quam says, "Well, I guess we do have to train new mechanics somehow. O.K., you can go to work here. Your first job will be to tear down that Franklin engine over there." He points to a complex-looking engine with a long snout and a lot of complicated wires and tubes sticking out of it here and there. I am so pleased with his response that I do not in the slightest mind when I learn the rest of the arrangement. Both Mr. Quam and Dad think it important for me to continue with some schoolwork, and it seems that Dad has already set it up that morning during a talk with Mr. Scott, the high school principal. As soon as school starts I will work thirty-four hours each week for Mr. Quam, six hours on each weekday, and four hours on Saturday morning. I will also spend two hours each weekday at Fairbanks High School taking two academic courses of my choice. I really prefer to avoid the courses, but, what the heck, if that is part of what it takes for me to learn to be an aircraft engine mechanic, I'll do it.

And so I enter my new career, and what an exciting one it is. I am pleased just to have a paying job that is not family-connected. This of course is not just any job like being a riverboat steward or a road commission trucker. It is a special job not only involved with airplanes but with Wien, the territory's oldest airline. From having listened to Tundra Topics on radio station KFAR night after night, I know what a major role Wien Airlines plays in the lives of everyone who lives in the top half of Alaska. Wien is a famous name in Alaska and extra-special to me because I already know Noel Wien, the man who founded the airline in 1926. He and his wife Ada were also passengers on the airplane that Lewie and I rode from Seattle to Fairbanks back in 1944 when I was only twelve. Since then every mention of the Wien name has made me proud that I know someone that famous. Now I not only know Wiens, I actually work for them.

Wien Airlines is a big outfit. It has some 300 full- and part-time employees scattered around central, western and northern Alaska. The main base is here in the Wien hangar on Weeks Field, a jumble of interconnected wooden buildings. Next door to the east is Alaska Airlines, another bush outfit that operates into the Kuskokwim and other points southwesterly. The Pan Am hangar, that airline's northern terminus, is off to the west, near the airfield's tower.

I am here to learn how to overhaul engines, but right from the start I am immersed in all the day-to-day operations of a bush airline. This is partly because my workplace, the engine overhaul shop, is so close to everything else. It occupies the back of the Wien hangar, and out front is the passenger waiting room and the dispatch office with its chalkboard listing the day's flights and the crew members. The main hangar area, barely big enough to hold a DC-3, is attached, and various add-ons beyond contain areas set aside for specific purposes. One area is the propeller repair shop, another the fabric shop and yet another the ski shop where men actually manufacture the skis used on the bush airplanes. The capability exists here to build an airplane from scratch if the mechanics had a reason to do so. All this is here for me to see, everything involved in the operation and maintenance of a major bush airline.

Another reason for my sudden immersion into all aspects of the flying business is that the engine shop is a social hub, not only for

Wien employees, but also for a collection of pilots and others connected with flying. Eldred Quam's personality contributes, but I sense that there is more to it than that. Perhaps it is something to do with engines being such crucial parts of airplanes.

The intimate connection between the engines we are working on and the actual flying is particularly obvious each morning at eight o'clock when the shop opens and start-up noises begin erupting from those airplanes sitting outside that are scheduled to fly that day. During the night or on the late afternoon of the day before, ground crews have serviced and loaded the airplanes, so all is in readiness for the pilots arriving in early morning. Most wear heavy military-surplus flight jackets and each carries his bag of maps and emergency gear. Their faces all look serious, and none are inclined to do much talking, unless it is a new man seeking information about a route he has not flown before. The focal point for such discussions is the big yellow aeronautical map of Alaska glued to a wall near the dispatch chalkboard. Some small parts of this map—mainly mountain sections north of Fairbanks—are blank, so first-hand route information is valuable. Those morning take-offs are serious business for all concerned, including those of us in the engine shop. We are well aware that the pilots and their passengers will soon be flying out over uninhabited wilderness buoyed up by the hammering of pistons in the reciprocating engines we have put together.

The men in the engine shop also are inclined toward silence during the times when the pilots fire up engines outside the hangar each morning. The mechanics' attention is mostly on the whining sounds of starters being energized, the coughing when the starters engage, and then the throaty roars as the engines settle into a steady rhythm. The men all know the sound of a cylinder head popping off, and only after all the engines are going smoothly do the men in the shop begin to concentrate fully on the normal work of the day.

I learn right away that a licensed mechanic in the shop has to sign off on every engine, and if the engine fails and kills somebody because of an improper overhaul, then the man who signs off is liable for a manslaughter charge. I do not have to sign, of course, because, at fifteen, I am three years too young to hold a license. Nor do I have even a good start at the experience required to apply for one. Nevertheless, anything I do has to be done right and with great care—day after day, Eldred Quam, Forbes Baker and the other mechanics drill that lesson into me. That saying about not fixing unbroken things does not hold here; instead the idea is to fix it before it breaks, and to do it right every time. Eldred Quam would have kicked my butt, or at least probably not have hired me, if he had known about my fixing up my GMC engine by filing off its bearing flats.

Right from the start, I am thrilled by my opportunity to work at Wien. This is not like working for Dad on the sawmill, this is work in the real world, and in about the most exciting business you can imagine. No question about it, my future lies in aviation. That line of thinking gets its biggest boost along about three o'clock each afternoon, the time when the pilots on the bush runs are returning. They have been out to exotic places like Wiseman, Arctic Village, Stevens Village, Rampart, Fort Yukon and Ruby.

The faces that looked so serious in the morning now wear smiles as the pilots check in to the office and then come back to the engine shop to detail the war stories of the day. I have a hard time concentrating on my work as they tell about flying up the wrong canyon in the Norseman on the way to Old Crow, a difficult landing with a Stinson at Venetie, and how the engine caught fire at Bettles, but the pilot got it out before it burned up his Bellanca. I soon come to learn all their names, too, Sig Wien, Noel Wien, Don Hulshizer, Randy Accord, Bill English, Cliff Everts and a dozen other bush pilots. They are all heroes in my eyes, yet I sometimes sense that some of them are almost scared when out in the air alone far from town, and happy each day to make it back to Fairbanks.

Of course pilot Noel Wien is a special figure in my eyes. I now fully understand what a famous bush pilot he is, partly because I have purchased and repeatedly devoured a copy of Jean Potter's book *Flying North* which tells about him and other earlyday pilots. In addition to being a pilot, Noel is a photographer, and his darkroom is in a little room opening off the engine shop. He no longer uses the darkroom, but it is filled with copies of his pictures and also many negatives that Noel has never bothered to print. I usually eat my lunches in that room while looking at his pictures and negatives. They show images of old airplanes, airplane crashes, aerial views of the Alaska countryside, and scenes depicting distant villages and their people. Sitting there in that windowless black-walled room, I soar out into the wilderness each noon with Noel Wien, seeing through his camera a quarter-century of his experiences. Perhaps Noel and I are the only persons to see those images he has not bothered to print, for as near as I can tell, no other person ever comes into this room.

I start out at Wien doing only engine disassembly, totally dismantling each engine and placing all its parts on a portable wooden rack. That rack then goes into the cleaning room where one man, who is somewhat mentally incompetent, spends a week soaking the parts in horrible-smelling solvents to remove all oil and carbon. After that, Eldred Quam or Forbes Baker use micrometers to measure the parts for wear and order whatever might be needed to overhaul the engine. Cylinder overhaul can begin right away, and since the man who does this work leaves a few months after I arrive, I take over his job. Eldred Quam machines the cylinder bores on his big lathe, but I do all the rest of the work: grinding valves and valve seats, and replacing valve seats and spark plug inserts when necessary.

The replacement of bronze or brass valve seats and spark plug inserts in the aluminum cylinders is a tricky process. The most crucial task is playing the flames of two blowtorches over the cylinders to expand the aluminum away from the inserts without getting the cylinder so hot that some of its fins melt. If a fin folds over, the cylinder is ruined, and that is a big loss. It is demanding work that elevates me in the eyes of the men in the shop. Before long, I also am helping the men do final assembly. Each man specializes in one or two types of engines. Paul, the youngest man in the shop, does the big fourteen-cylinder Pratt and Whitneys that power Wien's two DC-3 airplanes. Forbes Baker does the Continentals used in small airplanes; another man does the Lycomings, and another yet the larger nine-cylinder Pratt and Whitneys used on the intermediate Norseman aircraft.

Nobody wants to overhaul the Franklin engines used in Sig Wien's Seabees, so I inherit most of the job after getting some training from Forbes Baker. These are terrible motors, sort of glorified automobile engines that vibrate badly and wear out quickly. But Sig Wien is the president of the company, and he loves the Seabees. He spends much of his time flying them up around Barrow where lakes are plentiful, making it possible, when the weather gets bad, for him to put down and keep right on going. But the Franklin engines are not designed for propelling airplanes across great expanses of lake; they overheat and quickly destroy themselves.

Eldred Quam often chews the pilots out for misusing engines, but of course President Sig is exempt from Quam's harsh words. One of the first Franklin engines I disassembled was in Sig's plane for only six hours before it quit. When I opened up the engine, I found a one-inch hole burned right through the center of one piston. Eldred Quam grimaced when I showed it to him. "That Sig's a crazy bugger," he said with a smile, shaking his head and walking away.

When Eldred Quam allowed me to go to work for Wien, he did not mention pay, nor was I about to ask. Not until receiving my first paycheck do I learn that my salary is 50 cents an hour, which I think is reasonable in view of how much training I am getting. That level of pay, however, is inadequate to keep me going. During the first weeks I boarded with a family in town, the parents of a high school friend, but my hours were such that it did not work out well. Now, one of the mechanics I work with, Cliff, lets me stay in the little shack he rents in south Fairbanks. I have to pay half his oil bill, and I have to sleep on the floor in a sleeping bag because the little building is too small for any other arrangement.

That takes care of housing, and for meals I buy a meal ticket at the little High Spot Cafe on Ninth Avenue, right alongside the Fairbanks school. Each meal ticket costs $20, and I if I am careful about what I eat I can stretch it to cover the meals I need in a week. During the first week, I figured out the best buys on the menu for each meal, and I now have settled in on a diet that never changes. For breakfast, I eat hotcakes and eggs; for lunch, a carry-out ham sandwich; and for supper, breaded veal cutlets. It is a far cry from going downtown to enjoy the meals and atmosphere of the Model Cafe, but that is not a possibility.

I am even still a few dollars short, so every Saturday afternoon I go out to the homestead where I can eat for free that night and the next day, and I can earn additional money hauling trees in from the woods to Dad's sawmill. That is a job I can do by myself using the Farmall H. My pay for each weekend stint is at least $15, plus the tops of the trees I am hauling in, everything smaller than six or seven inches. My plan is to use these tops to build a cabin. In payment for past work I have done, Dad has agreed to give me a site at one end of the homestead.

The work at Wien Airlines, the weekend tree-hauling and my two hours of high school each weekday totally occupy my time. I have two back-to-back classes, one in biology and one in history, that I can take by leaving the engine shop during the noon hour and returning soon after 3 p.m. These classes both require some homework that I can easily do in the evenings after work.

One midwinter night while I am doing my homework at Cliff's house, we hear a knock. In walks a man Cliff introduces only as Jack. I soon learn that Jack is a former military pilot who owns a little plane with which he is trying to make a living. Cliff tells me not to mention Jack's arrival to anyone because Jack is flying illegally. He comes into Fairbanks only at night, and tries to keep his airplane out of sight so that the Civil Aeronautics Administration will not impound it or have him arrested. Jack is in town because he has just badly bent his landing gear from a rough landing at Ruby with an overload of dried salmon. He usually flies with an overload, I comprehend from his conversation with Cliff. His airplane is still flyable, Jack says, but because of the bent landing gear one wing tip droops much lower than the other when the plane is on the ground.

Jack is strange. A slender dark-haired man in his late twenties, he wears a thin black mustache. He acts nervous and looks furtive, and he even carries a pistol in a shoulder holster beneath his jacket. Other bush pilots also carry guns for emergency use, but they normally keep them in their flight cases.

Jack's arrival soon leads me to the realization that Dad does not have a corner on wild schemes to make money. Cliff and Jack come up with two propositions. The first is really Cliff's idea. Cliff suggests that, since I now own a bunch of logs from my weekend work at the sawmill, he and I go into partnership with Jack and other bush pilots like him. Cliff and I will build a hangar with my logs, and then he and I will rebuild crashed airplanes in the hangar. When we get our first plane built, we will offer it to Jack. His plane and ours will be enough to keep Jack in the air—he can be flying one while we repair the other one from his most recent crash. Cliff says that pilots like Jack crash a lot of airplanes, but Cliff thinks he and I might be able to keep up with three or four pilots in similar arrangements.

Cliff's idea sounds pretty good to me. Actually, I become excited enough about it to begin designing a hangar. Then Jack gets into the act, and the whole business escalates into a proposal that is fun to talk about, but close to ridiculous.

Jack suggests that the hangar should have three extra rooms, one to be used as a bar, and two others that will contain beds equipped with girls. He points out that the prostitution business in Fairbanks now has a profitable new dimension because the city fathers and mothers have now managed to abolish the Fourth Avenue Line by outlawing prostitution within the city. The result is that the ladies on the Line have dispersed themselves around the fringes of the city limits. Cab drivers and others are now making more money than the ladies because of the need to transport customers to the outlying places of business. The ladies are still getting about $5 per customer, but the transporters are getting $15. Thus, the total price is $20, and Jack figures that he, Cliff and I can retain a fair portion.

Jack got his idea from what went on with the young Eskimo girl that he flew in from one of the villages a few weeks ago, and who was without a place to stay. While I slept out on the floor in the little outer room, this girl slept with Jack and Cliff in the shack's bedroom, all three in one bed. The girl stayed in the bedroom for over a week, during which time I rarely saw her, and we never spoke. She seemed like a nice girl, and I did not really like what was going on in there. Jack and Cliff kept her occupied, and they at least kept her well supplied with food. The girl's apparent satisfaction with the arrangement evidently convinced Jack how easy and cost-free it will be to provide customers with one of the attractions of the proposed establishment. Jack has another, similar, plan for furnishing our new bar with wares. He claims to know a source of bootleg liquor somewhere on the other side of the Canadian border. He will make a night flight over as often as necessary, without, of course, filing a flight plan.

The Eskimo lady is now long gone and it seems that Jack also has disappeared. Since he never files any flight plans, it is hard to know what may have happened to him, but in any case the combination airplane repair shop, bar and whorehouse has fallen through. Jack's disappearance is part of the problem, and another part is that since the new Fairbanks International Airport is a sure thing, the city will not allow us to erect a new building here on Weeks Field. Cliff and I might be able to rent a small hangar, but the idea of operating just a simple airplane repair shop seems so anticlimactic after all our grand scheming that we are giving up on that, too. Also, I think I may not be as impressed with Cliff as I was earlier—I guess it's partly the business with the Eskimo girl—so I am looking for another place to stay.

Spring is on the way, and I now have been in the engine shop for about six months. Eldred Quam is busy boring out a set of DC-3 engine cylinders on his big lathe, and I am over across the room grinding valve seats on another set when he calls me over. "How much are we paying you?" he asks. When I tell him, he shakes his head in disbelief. "You take off work right now and go downtown and see George Rayburn at the business office. You tell him how much you are getting." Rayburn is the company's comptroller; he is a rather crusty guy that I have seen a few times when he comes around the hangar. Since Sig Wien is usually off flying some place, I think George Rayburn probably really runs this airline.

I walk down to Rayburn's office on Second Avenue and enter with trepidation. What am I going to say to him? Actually, I do not have to say anything. Rayburn has received a telephone call from Quam while I was in transit, and he is ready for me. "You now make $1.25 per hour," he says, as I walk up to his counter. The other mechanics at Wien are making much more, some $2.25, but I am elated. I can use the additional money, but more than anything else, this huge raise signifies that I am doing well in the engine shop.

Now that the weather is getting warmer and I have been here long enough to feel as if I am a proper worker, not just a kid apprentice, I muster up enough nerve to ask Eldred Quam if it might be possible for me to go out on some of the Wien flights. I have learned that employees can do this if they have the pilot's permission. Quam says he will look into it, and about a week later he says, "There's a flight tonight right after work headed for Nome and Kotzebue. You can go."

That flight turns out to be quite an eye-opener into the ways of pilots. I am still in my mechanic's coveralls when I walk out to the plane, a DC-3, and stand by the door as the pilots and passengers enter. When all are aboard, the copilot comes back and tells me to close the door. I try but I can't see how it operates, so the copilot does the job. I start to sit in the one remaining passenger seat when the copilot says, "We've got a CAA inspector aboard; you'll have to ride in the cockpit as a crew member." I know then that this flight is going to be even more fun than I have anticipated.

The cockpit has only two real seats, so the pilot tells me to squat down just behind the pilot and copilot and sit on a little jump seat that folds out into the narrow passageway. Right after we take off, the copilot says, "Hey, I can't get the gear up. Oh, oh, we've got a hydraulic leak. I suppose we better go back."

"Naw, this plane's been leaking like that for days," says the pilot. "Our guest here can pump the gear up by hand, and, Joe, put some more fluid in from that spare can we've got behind the seat." While the copilot takes out the five-gallon can and pours its contents into a hole behind his seat, I work away at the laborious job of pushing back and forth on a handle that raises the landing gear, the chore taking me the better part of ten minutes.

I then listen to a discussion about how we no longer have any spare fluid because the can is empty, and maybe we really ought to go back to Fairbanks. The pilot decrees that we will keep going, but we may have to bypass Kotzebue because the runway there is short. Since we are low on hydraulic fluid, the brakes are not going to work very well, so we might just roll off the end of the strip.

The reason we are continuing the flight, I realize, is that flight crews only get paid for time in the air. If we go back to Fairbanks as we should, the flight will probably terminate, and the pilot and copilot will receive pay only for a few minutes of work. From what I have heard around the hanger, I know that Wien has more pilots than needed, and each is eager to get in as many flight hours as possible.

We continue westerly as I stand looking over the shoulders of the two men, torn between wanting to give full attention to what is going on inside the cockpit and an equally strong desire to look at the countryside beyond the windows. With my feet and my hands I can feel the steady, comforting vibration that says this silver DC-3 is alive and healthy as it sails through the air, a giant gull with stiffly outstretched wings. My ears hear the sleepy purring of the engines and the regular "ruum, ruum, ruum" snore caused by the slightly different rotation speeds of the two big Pratt & Whitney 1830s and their attached propellers. When the sound gets too bad I see the pilot's hand reach out beside his thigh to close over the throttles. Almost imperceptibly, his hand rocks sideways on his wrist as he jiggles one throttle relative to the other until the snores lengthen out and almost go away. The sound likely will come creeping back in a few minutes, and then the hand again will reach out to squelch it. My eyes also take in the complex array of instruments mounted on panels dispersed around the front of the cockpit. Some of their white-tipped needles quiver and some don't, but all are happily nested in the green portions of their dials, well away from the worrisome yellow and red.

Out beyond the flat sloping front windows, the Tanana River weaves back and forth across swampy flats, breaks sharply left to skirt around the Tolovana Hills, and then off almost to the horizon its dirty brown waters turn to metallic gray as they stretch out in an eager final dash to empty into the river of countless adventures. Yes, there it is, the mighty

Yukon, a wide ribbon of mercury roiling along between swamps on the left and low mountains on the right.

I am so entranced by this first glimpse of the river Grandad Davis rafted down from Dawson to St. Michael exactly fifty years ago this summer that I almost fail to see that the pilot is up out of his seat and is trying to get past me. "Excuse me," he says, "I'm headed back to do some visiting." I move aside, and he disappears from the cockpit.

"Like to sit down?" asks the copilot, motioning to the pilot's seat.

The copilot obviously thinks I know more about airplanes than I do, because a few minutes later he tells me to take over the controls so he can get some coffee. "Keep it on the same heading as we're on," he says, and he too leaves the cockpit.

For the first time in my life I am holding onto the steering column of an airplane in flight, and I am looking at a vast array of instruments that I do not understand. I at least recognize which one is the compass, and I gingerly toy with the column and the foot pedals, trying to hold the heading and to keep the airplane from going up or down. Migawd, I think; this is a fully loaded DC-3 passenger plane with a CAA inspector aboard, and the only person in the cockpit is a sixteen-year-old boy who is too dumb even to know how to close the airplane's door, never mind fly the thing.

By the time the copilot comes back fifteen minutes later, I have gained enough of a feel for the controls that I am able to keep the plane level, but I am not yet doing well on heading. "Dammit, you're five degrees off course," the copilot says as he sits down and takes over.

Relieved from my piloting duties, I slowly recover from the excitement of that responsibility and focus more attention on the vastness slowly unfolding before us as we drone on westward. The sky above and below our four-thousand-foot flying level is absolutely cloudless so only the distant mountains limit how far we can see. Mountains do show in all directions but between them and us are extensive swamp-filled lowlands cut by little streams that wiggle and wind around on themselves like snakes before they join to others or the Yukon itself. Except for the white grandeur of Mt. McKinley way off to the left, the river dominates the view until we finally reach the Nulato Hills, a strong barrier that shunts the water off to the left on a straight-arrow detour down to Holy Cross. There, out of our sight, the Yukon again turns sharply to resume its westerly course on out another two hundred miles to the Bering Sea.

Up to this point the landscape has not been all that different from what I have seen around Fairbanks and down along the Alcan to Berry Creek, but, boy, there sure is a lot of it. The swamps and hills and mountains seem to go on forever. Even though we are speeding along at about one-hundred-forty miles per hour, we seem to be just crawling across the vastness. But now as the Yukon peels away from our course and the Nulato Hills reach up beneath us, everything looks different. Even though it is summer, the low mountains below look cold. Only moss and lichens cling to the rock rubble on the higher slopes, and scattered stands of wiry brush show in the lower swales, but I see not a single tree. Then as we crest this range I see the gray waters of Norton Sound extending out to the horizon, ahead and to the left. The sea adds to my sense that all below is cold and desolate, for a strong onshore breeze is lifting whitecaps and spraying their froth in long streamers toward where waves are breaking against the shore. This is a world like I have never seen before, and I almost shiver as I suddenly remember that right down there, below where we are now flying, Leonard Seppala in 1925 took the big chance and crossed the bay on the ice in order to speed the diphtheria serum to Nome. I can almost see him down there, the tough little man dressed all in white helping push the sled across the snow. I've never met Seppala but now-dead Wolf was the offspring of one of his dogs, and I have watched Seppala run his beautiful all-white Siberian Husky team in the dog races at Fairbanks.

It looks like it ought to be the end of the world out there, but it is not. The mountains continue along to the right of our path, and we still have an hour to go to get to Nome. From having studied the maps, I know that Alaska extends out northwesterly another hundred miles, and just beyond that is Siberia.

We finally get to the Nome airport, a collection of forlorn buildings, mostly military leftovers, alongside the long blacktopped airstrip. Not a bush or a tree is in sight, and the wind is as cold as I thought it would be. As we climb out of the airplane the pilot decrees that I, the mechanic, should fix its leaky hydraulic system. I have not the foggiest idea of what to do, since my entire knowledge of airplanes is confined to the internal workings of engines. Were I asked to mount one of those engines in an airplane, I could not even accomplish that task.

Not wanting to disillusion the pilot, I walk around the airplane as I have watched real mechanics do, and in the process see hydraulic oil

dripping out the bottom of one of the engine housings. That is a start, but the next step probably is to remove some cowling, and I do not know how to do that. Fortunately, I spy a little cap near an opening in the cowling. Its safety wire is not properly attached, and the cap is loose, allowing the hydraulic oil to escape. And so I fix it, using a combination crescent wrench and pair of pliers that I happen to have in my pocket. Rummaging around in the airline building, the local Wien agent finds another can of hydraulic fluid, and so we are in business again.

We fly on to Kotzebue and back home to Fairbanks, arriving too late for me to get much sleep before going to work that morning. I don't mind at all. I have just flown my first airplane, then repaired it, and I have seen a huge exotic part of Alaska with my own eyes—not just through the lens of Noel Wien's camera. I now am totally, absolutely hooked on aviation. I too will become a bush pilot, and I wish I had the money to start taking flying lessons right now.

GETTING BACK IN PHASE

·

T HAT FLIGHT, MY FIRST as an employee "dead-header," has opened the door to other similar trips, mostly on the DC-3s headed into western Alaska, to Nome and Kotzebue. I also have been going on test flights, short trips around the Fairbanks area to check out new engines and sometimes to give new copilots practice in instrument approaches and landings.

An additional option for me opens up from the impending resignation of one of the flight engineers who flies on C-46s, Wien's largest aircraft. Used mainly for hauling freight to the North Slope, these planes carry a crew of three, and have three regular seats in the cockpit. I take several trips to Umiat and Barrow in the capacity of an apprentice flight engineer, with the expectation that I might take over the departing man's job. A Wien flight engineer requires little technical knowledge because his main function is to load and unload the airplane. The pilot and copilot do virtually all of the work involved in the actual flying, and about all the flight engineer does is look at gauges and lower and raise the landing gear.

I come away from these flights with several unexpected impressions about commercial aviation, at least as conducted in Alaska by Wien Airlines. One surprise is the discovery that almost every takeoff is in an airplane that has one or more operational defects. Before each flight, the pilot inspects the set of records carried in each ship that detail what maintenance has been performed, and what faults still remain. If the pilot thinks the faults minor, he goes ahead with the flight, but he always has the option to refuse to take the airplane up.

But as I saw on my first flight, the pilots' desires to build up flight time often shade the decision in favor of going.

Another surprise is to learn the great range in level of concern over what is going on during the different portions of each flight. The pilots and copilots conduct preflight checks in an unsmiling, precise fashion, and as the take-off roll begins their mental alertness goes into high gear. Everybody knows that the take-off is the most critical part of the flight because the engines are running at full power and rapidly heating up. In a DC-3, 500 near-explosions are occurring each second inside those 28 big aluminum jugs mounted radially around the engine casings, and any one explosion might blast a cylinder head away. If that happens at just the wrong moment during the take-off, the sudden loss of power can be disastrous.

As tense as is the mood of the pilots during take-off, it is even worse, occasionally verging on panic, during most landings. Statistically, the take-offs are more dangerous, but the rise of that hard runway surface up toward the heavy multi-engined airplane prior to touchdown seems to put an unreasoned fear into the men at the controls. The pilot always maintains a calm expression—it would be bad form for him not to—but sweat often appears on the forehead of the copilot, whose only duty is to call out the airspeed. The pitch of his voice invariably rises as the plane mushes in toward its stall speed.

That the pilots take their jobs seriously when their airplanes are near the ground makes good sense, but I am shaken by their lackadaisical attitude when in level flight out away from airports. For hours on end, when I am deadheading in the cockpit, I am the only one who ever looks outside the airplane. It is common for one pilot to sleep and the other at the controls to read a book as we lumber along through the empty sky. It is empty, too, for we rarely if ever see another airplane, other than the occasional little bush plane skittering across the hills and valleys at low altitude.

Thrilled as I am with flying, I slowly develop a disillusion with the thought of taking up a career as a flight crew member. The members of the Wien flight crews lead difficult lives, I conclude. To get in their allotted 80 hours of air time each month, the flight personnel put in far more hours than anyone in a normal job. It looks to me that one paid hour in the air is accompanied by two or three more hours waiting for planes to be repaired or loaded, or for the weather to improve. A person really has to be in love with flying to put up with the erratic life and the low pay. I am having a lot of fun now, but what will it be like in a few years when I will be flying over the same routes day after day in airplanes that I can drive as easily as a car or Dad's Farmall H?

The same gnawing feeling comes over me about my future as an aircraft mechanic, although I am advancing rapidly under the tutelage of Eldred Quam and the others in the engine shop. Quam has now assigned me to work almost exclusively with Paul, the specialist on the Pratt and Whitney 1830s used in the DC-3s.

Wien's two DC-3s are putting in a lot of hours flying up to Barrow and into western Alaska, so many that the aircraft mechanics are giving each a 25-hour check every other day. Since we are getting about 800 hours from each engine, the DC-3s are going through overhauled engines at a rate of one or two per month. Paul is working hard to keep up, but more is in the wind than that. He is planning to leave in midsummer to attend college, and Eldred Quam is hoping I can take over his job.

I really like working with Paul, and I much admire him. That he is thinking of doing something better than being a mechanic is also having an effect on me. Perhaps I too should go to college and follow Paul's plan to become an aircraft engineer. First though, sadly enough, I will have to finish high school. I could do it by correspondence; on the other hand, maybe it would be fun to go to a regular high school. This past winter I have seen enough during my two hours each day at Fairbanks High to appreciate some of the things I am missing by not being a regular student—most of them being objects with two legs and skirts, I grudgingly have to admit to myself.

As soon as school was out this spring, I got my Model A fired up after its winter of idleness and moved from Cliff's place out to the homestead. That was pretty interesting at first because of the flood, the worst Fairbanks has had in years and bad enough that school let out a week early. That meant no final exams, which of course did not break anybody's heart. The strange thing about this flood is that all the water causing it came into Fairbanks from the Tanana. Of course that is the way it used to be every spring before they built the Moose Creek Dike, but this year the Tanana was so high that it flowed cross-country into Fairbanks, the water moving essentially at right angles to its normal direction. For about a week much of the town was under water.

Only two vehicles were navigating the Alcan during the flood, the bus to 26-Mile Field and my Model A. "Navigating" is the right word, too, because between town and the homestead virtually the entire roadway was under water. The only exception was a stretch less than a hundred yards long near 10-Mile where the highway went up on a little rise that had been manufactured from material taken from a gravel pit during the road construction. The homestead itself was totally dry, verifying that Dad had selected well when he picked this property. Beyond the homestead the road was mostly dry so the 26-Mile bus was able to make it through to Moose Creek Bluff, and from there the passengers were put in a boat and taken on to the base.

The water running sideways across the Alcan on the way out to the homestead was in most places only a few inches deep, and never deep enough to stall out my Model A unless I drove too fast and splashed water up into the distributor. I tended to drive pretty slow so as not to go off into the ditch in places where I could not see the road through the water or where no snowplow markers lined the roadbed. Even so, I usually did stall out two or three times each trip. I then crawled out onto the front fender where I could raise the hood and dry the distributor with a rag. That done, I could stand out on the bumper and crank the car without getting my feet wet—well, most of the time.

Since the flood I have been putting all my spare time after work and on weekends into building the cabin I have been planning. It seems that all our agony over the army or the airport taking away the homestead was for nothing because Dad now has obtained title to the homestead. He and Mom are thinking of subdividing a part of the property, the portion that lies down near where the Richardson Trail intersects the Alcan at 14-Mile. He says I can have one lot there for a cabin site.

Dad is off into a new business venture again. Fairbanks, he has decided, is in sorry need of low-cost housing. Dad has designed a house that he can build almost entirely of materials off the sawmill and that can be hauled to town on a truck when completed. Little more than eight feet wide and 14 feet long, each has a two-by-four framework covered inside and out with felt paper and rough one-inch boards. Insulation consists of sawdust poured into the floor, walls and ceiling. Other than felt paper, roll roofing and nails, Dad needs to buy only a roof jack, a little window, and door fittings to complete one of these small dwellings, so labor is his main outlay. He is selling these wanigans for $700 each, usually on credit, because anyone who will buy one of them typically lacks money for a cash payment.

One advantage to Dad's scheme has been that the work could progress during last winter's cold months. He has constructed a heated shed large enough to hold one of the wanigans up on a high platform to make it easy to load onto a truck. On those winter days that were not too cold, Dad and his crew of two men ran the sawmill, cutting up the trees I had been hauling in each weekend to make whatever boards he needed. These were fresh-cut trees, solidly frozen, and mighty tough to saw. Sawmilling in the dead of winter is no fun at best, and last winter I was glad I was not involved. I thought it was kind of funny that Dad and his crew found that they had to let the boards thaw inside the warm shed before driving nails into them. Otherwise the green boards just split.

Dad's wanigans are crude, but even though constructed of green lumber and filled with green sawdust, they are warmer than a lot of little shacks around Fairbanks. They also are sure as heck warmer than the homestead cabin which still has a roof consisting only of roll roofing over three-quarter inch boards. The little wanigans actually sell like hotcakes because many people who first came to Alaska during the war as soldiers or construction workers are now returning, and they are desperate for housing they can afford. But Dad is in his usual financial straits because he is selling the units on credit. As when he was selling just boards, he has been having a hard time collecting from buyers.

Dad let me use his crew for a few days this spring and we have quickly sawed my pile of tree tops up into two-sided logs five inches thick. It took us only a couple more days to lay the logs up into a sixteen- by-twenty-foot cabin. After another week goes by, I have the roof up and am moved in. My spare money and time this summer is going into finishing up the cabin, building an outhouse and driving a well. The latter turns out to be a simple matter because the water table under the homestead is shallow. In the Wien shop one night I weld a point on a piece of pipe, and when I get home that night I crawl up on top of my car and bang the pipe into the ground with a sledgehammer, hitting water about ten feet down.

All summer I work full time in the engine shop, overhauling the 1830s with Paul until he leaves. Then I am on my own, doing final assembly on the big engines.

This process is always done in the exact manner Paul has shown me. Before assembling any section of an engine, I lay out all the parts in precise rows on the bench, and then follow the assembly manual page by page as I put the parts in their proper places. One of the crucial jobs is to make sure that gears line up properly, a task made easy by little red dots set into those gear teeth that have to line up. Before closing up a section of an engine, I follow the practice we all use of having someone else look the section over to verify proper gear alignments and that all the parts formerly laid in rows have actually gone inside the engine.

I have done final assembly on three engines by myself before the first one goes into a DC-3. The airframe mechanics install the engine and then fire it up. The airframe foreman then comes to me and says, "This engine runs pretty rough, like the valves might not be set right. You better come out and take a look."

I go out to the plane and remove the covers from all the rocker arms on the newly installed engine. By gosh, he is right; some of the valve rocker arms on the front row of seven cylinders are so poorly gapped that I can't believe it. On the other hand, those on the back row are perfect.

I go through the whole engine, resetting the gap on each of the valves that needs adjusting. The airframe foreman and a pilot start up the engine. It still seems to be a little rough, but they think it good enough for a flight test, so they take the plane off. The DC-3 wheels up to the hanger a few minutes later, its one engine coughing erratically. "Hey, something is radically wrong with this engine," the foreman says in agitated fashion, "We damn near didn't get back from our turn around the field."

I am completely mystified, so I go to Eldred Quam and Forbes Baker to talk things over. "Are you sure you got all the timing marks lined up right?" Eldred asks.

"Yes he did," replies Forbes, "I checked everything over myself. He didn't do anything wrong that I could see."

Quam ponders the matter for a few minutes, then he smiles. "Aha, I bet I know what's happened. The front half of that engine is 360 degrees out of phase with the back half. A complete cycle on an engine is two revolutions, or 720 degrees. Think about it, you guys. That engine has two rows of cylinders. The back cam ring drives all the valves on the back row of cylinders, and the front cam drives all those on the front. It is possible to have all the timing marks lined up and still have those two cams out of phase by one revolution. When that happens the magnetos will send spark to half the cylinders at the wrong times, and half the valves will have been improperly set. Let's check the manual and see what it says."

We check the manual, only to discover no mention of the matter, and I know that Paul has never said anything to me about it either. "Well," says Quam, "I think we better go out and pull the front housing off that engine and rotate the front cam one full turn."

The task is fairly simple, and three hours later that engine is running just fine. We all go back to the shop, where Eldred and Forbes watch me do a reenactment of the process of putting the front cam in an engine. We then conclude that the reason Paul has never had this problem is that he—quite by accident—always rotated an engine's internal workings in a certain set fashion that resulted in proper phasing of the two halves of the engine. I have done it a little differently, but at least I am consistent. We tear open the other two engines I have assembled and find that both of them are also out of phase. "Well, I guess we all learned something, didn't we?" Eldred Quam generously comments as we finish up.

He was so good about it, and he has been so good about everything this past year, that I hate to tell him I am quitting to go back to school. He is good about that, too. "You are doing the right thing," he says. "You don't want to spend the rest of your life working on these damn engines. Don't feel bad about leaving, either; you have paid your own way here." Eldred Quam is one swell guy to say something like that when he really wishes I was staying on.

RETURN TO HIGH SCHOOL

FALL 1948

MY DECISION TO GO BACK TO HIGH school is almost rational. I know that I do not want to spend my life doing like Dad. He jumps from one scheme to another, never sticking at any one thing quite long enough to be successful, and that is tough on both him and Mom. I am bothered with the thought that I am doing the same thing by quitting Wien. In two more years I will have the training and be old enough to hold an airplane mechanic's license. Maybe I should have stuck it out.

Even though I am leaving, I know the stint at Wien has been very good for me in many ways. Like that on Dad's sawmill, the work in the engine shop has put me in close daily contact with older men who take their jobs seriously and are not about to put up with any smart-aleck behavior from a young boy. Eldred Quam and the others at the shop have taught me how to behave on the job, and they have drummed into me the need to work carefully and in a precise fashion. Best of all, I no longer have the burning desire to get out into the real world; I know that I am already in it, and now all I need is more education.

I wish that I did not have to go to high school before going on to something better. I really have no other good choice, I rationalize, but the truth is that something else is working on me to cause me to want to go back to school—but not to Fairbanks High.

Ever since I left the one-room school back in Iowa, I have been corresponding with the girl who was one year ahead of me. She is a gentle, calm girl, and rather shy. The last time I saw her before coming to Alaska, she asked me to write to her, and as the words came out, she blushed beet red and quickly walked away. She's pretty nice, I thought to myself then, and so I have written several letters to her during these three years in Alaska. This past year, the letters have become more frequent, and I am having some very kind thoughts about this young lady. It is because of her that I have sold my Model A, rented out my now-completed cabin at 14-Mile, and bought a ticket to Iowa. Uncle Irwin and Aunt Phena have agreed to let me come stay with them on the farm again and attend the high school in the nearest town.

My entry into Panora High School is nearly as scary for me as my start into Fairbanks High School. I again feel awkward and ill at ease, and I do not come across too well to the other students at first. I convey an air of self-importance that is part bluff and part real. Nor do I really enter into the social life of the high school very much for the first six months I am there.

My girlfriend from the one-room school is the reason for that. Now out of high school, she works in Des Moines. Each Friday night, she boards a bus and rides the forty miles to the intersection of a country road with the main highway that forms one corner of Uncle Irwin's farm. I borrowed his car to pick her up and drive her to her parents' farm a few miles distant. Then that night and the next night, I have a date with her, usually taking her to a movie or a sporting event, followed by an hour or so of gentle necking in the car when I take her home each night. We don't do anything but talk, kiss and hug.

This goes on for several months. Then one day while we are doing farm chores, Uncle Irwin has a talk with me. He says, "You know, you really ought to be spending more time with the other kids in high school. At your age, you are making a mistake spending all your time with one girl, and don't forget, she is older than you. She is of an age where she will want to get married soon, too."

I deeply resent his advice. He is talking to me like I am a kid, and he should not be interfering in my life. But about this time, probably mainly because of this talk, I begin to realize that both the girlfriend and her mother indeed have serious designs on my future, justified by my own behavior toward the girl. I continue to meet the bus every Friday night, but as time passes, I look forward to weekends less and less.

My last date with this girl is not a happy one for either of us. She is shocked by what appears to be a sudden change in my attitude, and I feel pretty bad about it too. Once it was over, though, I perceive that a great burden has been lifted from my life. I am so happy to be alone on weekends that I push it even farther by spending endless days when not in school out looking for fossils that lie in the creek beds in this area, and I decide that maybe I will become a geologist. What a great life that should be; you can spend months by yourself out in the wilderness, away from girls and the cares of the world.

My urge to be in seclusion lasts the better part of a month. I begin to attend all the school dances, and I even go out on a few dates with various girls from our school. These are girls that most of the boys have known all their lives, and I know some of them from long ago, too, back in the days of the one-room school. They are all nice girls so I, and I think the other boys also, generally behave well toward them. But it's different with the girls from other towns. Sometimes a couple of the boys will go together in a car and arrange dates with them, and when the guys do that they have just one thing in mind. Some of the guys tell lies about what goes on during these dates but my experience suggests that if a boy is lucky enough to get his hand inside a brassiere he thinks he is really making out.

I go out for football when I arrive at Panora High, but cannot play in any games because competition rules require a student be in a school for one semester before playing on its teams. My role on the team is the equivalent of a tackling dummy since I am part of the opposition that the team runs its plays against in practice. Basketball is underway when the second semester starts, so I began to play, and do well enough to be on the starting five.

When basketball ceases it is time for track. My interest is minor, but the coach talks me into learning how to throw discus and shot. Still, I do not care for it much, so I tell Coach Russell that I want to quit. He says I can, but he wants me to go to one track meet first, and I agree. Coach is a cagey bugger, I comprehend at the track meet, where I place second in one event and third in another. Collecting medals is fun, as Coach knows, and so he has me hooked on track. I do well enough that spring to qualify for the state track meet, and Coach Russell predicts that I might take second place in the discus at the meet. Events, though, preclude my attendance.

In addition to becoming a geologist, I am still thinking of becoming a bush pilot, at least temporarily to help finance more education. So whenever I can spare the time and the cash, I go to a little dirt strip near the next town and take flying lessons. Each lesson lasts an hour and I sometimes walk the full ten miles each way just to put in that one hour of air time. The walking takes a lot of time, and because of that it occurs to me that my ratio of air time to ground time is even worse than that of a Wien Airlines pilot back in Alaska.

Nevertheless, my interest in flying accelerates when I get word from Dad that he is planning another new endeavor, since by this time he has abandoned the construction and selling of wanigans. Dad is planning to put in a sawmill on Hess Creek, a tributary that enters the Yukon some miles above Rampart. Mom and Lewie are already in Rampart, where Mom has taken over the operation of the Northern Commercial Company trading post there. She is having the time of her life, it seems from the few letters I receive from her, and I am pleased that she has gotten away from the homestead and into something she likes to do. Dad is still in Fairbanks, trying to collect money from the numerous people who still owe, and planning the new operation on Hess Creek.

With great optimism, I suggest to him that if he can come up with the $2000 I will need to buy a new Piper airplane, I will fly it to Alaska this spring and take care of all his logistics problems at Hess Creek. No roads are in that part of the country, so the only other access is by riverboat. I can fly in the groceries, any needed repair parts and members of Dad's work crew. It sounds like a heck of a fun summer to me, and Dad says he might be able to come through with the money.

My other great thought this spring is to see if I can avoid going to high school another year. I contact Iowa State College at Ames to see if I might get in without a high school diploma. Yes, it is possible, I am told, if I will come to Ames for a day of tests to check on my preparedness.

When the tests are over, the registrar says I can enter. "However," she says, "we will require you to take several noncredit courses to bring you up to acceptable level." She points out that, since I am not an Iowa resident, a year of taking noncredit courses will be rather costly. "You might want to consider taking another year of high school," she says. "And by the way, why is it that you want to become a scientist? The tests show that your aptitude may lie elsewhere. You might think about switching over to literature."

What a surprise that is. English always has been my toughest subject. I am not very good at it, and my penmanship is nothing to write home about either. I leave Ames pondering what to do. Again, the decision is not quite totally rational. On the day I drive up to Ames for the tests, a girl from my class accompanies me, just for the ride. I've had several dates with her, and she is going back to Panora High next year. I think I will too. She is a slender girl named Rosemarie, and she is sharp as a tack. Besides, I like the way her butt wiggles when she operates the pencil sharpener on the wall over beside my seat in political science class.

ANOTHER SUMMER IN ALASKA

SUMMER 1949

DAD DOES NOT COME THROUGH with the $2000 for the new airplane, but he says he will send me money to come to Fairbanks so I can work for him this summer. He has a new sawmill operation going on the old Horn place, downstream on Piledriver Slough about six miles from the homestead. Even though it is only six miles, it is a situation of not being able to get there from here. To drive to the Horn place from the homestead, a person has to go along the Alcan down to 6-Mile and then follow Badger Road from there to its end, and on a bit farther along a dirt track to the Horn place. The drive is about seventeen miles. It is also possible to walk along the game trail that runs beside 14-Mile Slough and continues down along Piledriver Slough. Either way, the trek is so time-consuming that Dad has moved his whole operation from the homestead to the Horn place where there is a large building that can be used for a mess hall, as well as several smaller outbuildings for housing those of the crew who do not have their own places to stay.

Dad now has two sawmills. The Belsaw mill has worn out, so he has purchased a used American Sawmill Co. mill that he has set up on the Horn place. In addition, he has acquired use of the original American mill he and Mike Bedoff had previously owned. This mill is set up on the Salcha River, at about 40-Mile on the Alcan, and with it is a pile of logs that the sawmill's owner brought down the Salcha last year.

Dad writes that I should come to Fairbanks as quickly as possible when school is out, because I am badly needed. He already has fourteen people hired for logging and sawmilling operations on the Horn place, and he wants me to take part of his crew out to Salcha and operate the mill there.

Eager to go north, I arrange to finish up my tests and leave school a week early—and for that reason, I miss the state track meet. Dad is supposed to have mailed me a ticket, but it has not arrived by the time I am to leave. Grandma Davis is visiting in Iowa, and Dad knows that I plan to take the train with her back to LaSalle, Colorado, and then continue by train on to Cheyenne. From there, I will fly to Seattle and Fairbanks. An exchange of telegrams tells Dad that I already have bought my ticket to Cheyenne, and tells me that he has arranged to have my air ticket waiting for me in Cheyenne.

I say good-by to Grandma as she gets off the train in LaSalle, and continue on to Cheyenne with what money I have left, less than $10. Dad has not told me where in Cheyenne I can expect to find my ticket, but that doesn't bother me. Having lived there the summer I started the third grade, I know the town, and figure I'll have no trouble.

I am wrong. The ticket is not at the downtown office of TWA, right near the train station. Perhaps it is at the airport, the agent tells me, so I walk out to the airport. The ticket is not there either. After I make several walking trips between downtown and the airport, the ticket arrives, just an hour before my scheduled flight time.

I am greatly relieved until I discover that the ticket is written only to Seattle. What the heck is going on? I think, and then I realize what the problem is. As usual, Dad is having a cash flow problem. I can only hope that while I am in transit to Seattle, he will have collected enough money to have another ticket waiting for me there.

Trans World Airways' Seattle agent has my reservation for the flight to Fairbanks, but no ticket. I explain my problem to him, and amazingly enough, he agrees to give me a ticket to Fairbanks by way of Anchorage if I promise to pay for it later.

So that night I arrive in Anchorage, having spent all except 65 cents of my money for food in Cheyenne and Seattle. I already know that I have to stay in Anchorage overnight, and am not quite sure how I am going to manage it with the current state of my finances.

The airplane lands at Elmendorf Air Force Base instead of at Merrill Field in town because the plane we are in is too big for that airport. All passengers will be bussed to Anchorage, we are told, the cost to be but one dollar. I can walk the few miles to Anchorage, but then I will have to walk back the next morning to catch my next flight. And of course my 65 cents is not going to buy much in Anchorage, so I decide to remain on the base for the night.

I am hungry, but nothing can be done about that. I'd best just try to find a place to sleep. After wandering around for a while, I locate a pile of tumbling mats stored on a baseball diamond, just under the bleachers back of home plate. The time is approaching ten o'clock in the evening, but it is still broad daylight, as it will be all night at this time of year. Almost as soon as I lie down on the pile of mats, people began arriving, and they start a baseball game. I crawl out from under the bleachers and watch for a while, and then walk back to the airport terminal. There, I find an empty room marked "International Passenger Lounge," and therein, I realize, is the solution to my sleeping problem. As far as the airline is concerned, Alaska is considered an overseas destination, so my ticket says that I am an international passenger.

I stretch out on a sofa in the lounge and go to sleep, awaking soon thereafter to the tap on the bottom of my shoe from an MP's nightstick. "Hey, kid, you can't sleep here," one of the two men standing over me says.

"Why not?" I reply, "This is an international passenger lounge, and I am an international passenger." The MPs inspect my ticket, scratch their heads, and finally come to the conclusion that they can't kick me out. That I have just confronted the military and won the battle pleases me no end.

I am really hungry when the snack bar opens the next morning, an hour before flight time. The prices are terrible, but I manage to get two doughnuts and a glass of milk with my remaining funds.

Dad meets me at Weeks Field when I arrive there in early afternoon. "We've got to make this delivery right away," he says after a brief hello, and as we crawl into his truck which is fully loaded with boards. Dad is so unusually quiet, even brusque, that I tell him only briefly about my trip up. He seems more under duress than at any time in the past, and although I do not quite comprehend it that afternoon, he probably is near to mental collapse.

Things are not going well out at the Horn place, he admits. He has hired Earl Hirst again as the sawyer, and Earl is not doing a very good job. Dad has three other men on Earl's crew, but Earl is sawing only about 60 to 80 logs a day, and some of the boards he is turning out are so varied in thickness that they are unsalable. Dad also has a foreman hired to run the logging crew, and he has hired a cook. Still, Dad is having such a tough time delivering enough boards and collecting for them that it is nip and tuck if he can meet the $1500 payroll each week.

Dad figures he has enough logs on the Horn place to run the mill there for another month or so, and in a few days I will be taking part of the crew out to the Salcha and I should finish sawing the logs there in about a month. Dad then plans to move the main crew and the sawmill from the Horn place over to Rampart in midsummer.

Dad tells me all this as we unload the truck, and then he says he has to stay in town to make more collections, so he would like me to take the truck out to the Horn place where the foreman can load it again and bring it back to town that night. As I get ready to leave him, I notice that the gas tank on the truck is nearly empty. "If you will give me some money, I will gas this thing up before I go out," I say.

Dad reaches in his billfold, pulling out two dollars, evidently all he has. "Here, this will be enough to get the truck out there and back," he replies, and he seems to be mad at me for asking for the gas money.

Wow, I think as I drive out toward the Horn place, Dad must be in sad shape. When I arrive there, things look even worse to me. I locate the foreman, turning over to him the truck and the lumber order Dad has given me, and then I watch Earl Hirst saw a few logs before quitting time. Earl is not doing well at all; his hands are shaky; he is moving slowly, and he seems to be having trouble seeing. I notice that the mill is badly out of line. Earl appears to be showing his age, somewhere in the high seventies.

Supper that night is a total disaster. Dad's cook, an unkempt potbellied man with a foul temper, dishes out the plates for each man. Each contains two burned sausages, some potatoes and a few green beans. "Nobody told me we'd have an extra guy to feed tonight," he grumbles. "No seconds for anybody." I am hungry as all get out by then, and I can see that everybody at the table wants more to eat.

When Dad arrives that night, I waylay him for a hard talk. You better get rid of both Earl Hirst and the cook is the gist of my remarks. Never before have I been so outspoken to an adult, and I feel badly about it when Dad just sits there listening with his shoulders hunched and his head bowed—looking almost like a little kid being berated by his parent. I expect him to get mad at me, and although I can see that his face is burning, he says almost nothing at all. I walk away feeling a bit foolish for my outburst, but Dad lays off Earl Hirst the next day, and he fires the cook the day after that. He had also sends a message over the radio to Mom at Rampart asking her to come to Fairbanks as quickly as possible to help on collections and cooking. I guess my discussion with him has helped him realize that he has gotten in over his head.

It is too bad that Mom has to leave Rampart because she is doing well there. When she took over the store at Rampart it had extended large amounts of credit to people along the Yukon, and over the winter she has reduced the amount owing by nearly $10,000. Mom gets along with the Native people very well, and she has not just been sitting in the store. She has seen that a major problem for both the store and the people is that fur traders take whiskey out to the villages to exchange for furs. The result is that people do not buy what they should, and are unable to pay their bills at the trading post. So Mom has been traveling around, trying to beat the traders into the villages so she can collect furs against bills owing and take grocery orders. She does not get Dad's message right away because when he sends it she is off on a flight to Stevens Village, and is coming back down the Yukon to Rampart in a rented boat, picking up furs from people who live along the river. But a few days later Mom and Lewie arrive. She makes no complaint as she takes over the cooking duties on the Horn place, but I am sure she is not happy about leaving her work at Rampart.

Earl Hirst's departure puts the plan to send me out to the Salcha on hold. As soon as he is gone, I tear the sawmill's carriage tracks loose and realign them. Several days pass before I am fully into the swing of sawing again, but our production picks up remarkably. By noon one day, I have sawed 75 logs—about as many as Earl had been doing in a full day—and when we quit that night the tally is 147 logs for the 10-hour shift. Lewie's arrival helps too. He is not strong enough yet to do heavy lifting, but he is able to replace the man at the tail of the saw, whose duty is to flip slabs and boards coming off onto a set of rolls and send them down to the end where one or two men carry them off to the proper stacks.

We are putting in some pretty heavy days. I try to have the mill running soon after seven o'clock, and to do the midmorning and midafternoon tooth-sharpenings as rapidly as possible. By eating lunch quickly, I am able to get the noon sharpening out of the way by one o'clock, the scheduled afternoon start-up time. After supper each night, I work the saw teeth over carefully, squaring them up with a hammer and swaging tool, filing them, and when needed putting in a new set

around the perimeter of the saw. Then I and one or two others, sometimes including Lewie, work at bringing up logs out of the pond and
loading them on the ways in preparation for the next day's sawing.

One night while doing this, I accidentally let a cable slip between
the two drums of the log hoist. The cable winds down into the frame
of the hoist, suddenly breaking the frame in half. This is a disaster,
because once we saw the seventy or so logs already lifted from the
pond, the sawmill will be out of business. Dad does not need such a
terrible thing to happen right now, just as things are starting to pick up.

With the man who's been working with me, an energetic fellow
who is not much older than I am, I load the broken hoist on the truck
and head for Fairbanks. We arrive there about eleven in the evening
and began going around various old machinery piles and garbage dumps
looking for another hoist like the one we have. If we can find an identical device, we hope to rob it of its frame. Our foolish optimism de-
clines with the passing hours. It finally bottoms out for me about 5
a.m. when I walk around an old car in one dump and come face to face
with Mrs. Ford. She is dragging a gunny sack that clanks with metallic
objects. As I approach she adds one more, a badly battered graniteware
plate. Then Mrs. Ford, the richest woman in town, the hater of men
and boys, almost smiles. Is she smiling at me in recognition that I am
a kindred soul, a fellow connoisseur of cast-off objects? No, probably
not; more likely it is because she has just found another treasure to
stash away in one of her many unlived-in houses. Wordlessly, we each
go our own way, Mrs. Ford intent on adding to her possessions, and I
now giving up on my search for what I know I will never find, a particular model of a certain make of hoist with its frame in perfect condition. My objective is a little too narrowly defined, I decide as I leave
the field to Mrs. Ford.

Shortly thereafter, about 6 a.m., we drive to the High Spot Cafe,
my old Wien Airlines days eatery, which now serves as the pickup
point for several members of the crew. They congregate there for breakfast and to meet the foreman who drives them out to the Horn place
for the day's work. He looks at the hoist and says that he thinks that
there is a chance it can be welded, so I leave the truck and hoist with
him, and drive his car and the crew out to the mill.

We fire up the mill at the usual time and work on the logs available. As the log pile gets smaller my apprehension increases, and I am
really mad at myself for breaking the hoist. To my great relief, the

foreman shows up with the repaired hoist just as we are running out of logs. He locks the hoist into place and begins bringing up more logs, so that we end up with almost no downtime because of my mistake of the evening before.

But having been up since early yesterday morning, I am getting a bit groggy when, in midafternoon, we have a minor breakdown. A bolt has come loose on an axle, and in order to fix it I have to lie down on my back beneath the log carriage. It feels so good to be in that position that I promptly fall sleep. Not for long, though, because as I doze off, the wrench I am holding falls on my chest and wakes me up. We manage to meet our average production of 125 logs, but I sure am beat when quitting time comes. I have supper and immediately go to bed.

Even though we are all working hard, it is fun to be with the family again. Mom's arrival has taken a big burden off Dad, yet he still is having a hard struggle bringing in enough money to meet the payroll. Lewie is contributing well by replacing one paid hand, and that is no small thing.

I have not seen much of Lewie these past two years, and I recognize that he has grown up a lot. He is still a tough little bugger, and as always, unafraid to try anything. He really scared Mom this spring at Rampart. On the day the ice went out in the Yukon, he took a canoe out in the river where he paddled around among the churning blocks of ice. Not a smart thing to do, really, but that is Lewie; he just can't resist water, and I am still chagrined that he learned to swim long before I did. Last winter at Rampart, he also worked with dogs, and he has acquired one of the best-trained dogs I have ever seen. The dog was the leader on the mail run between Manley and Rampart before planes took over the job. One day Lewie took the dog out skijoring, and before they turned around to come back, they had run thirty miles up the Yukon. That impressed the heck out of me. Lewie has the dog here with him on the Horn place, and he keeps on running him in summer, now using him to pull a bicycle rather than skis.

Lewie and I are having a lot of fun this summer playing logger on the storage pond. The trees we are sawing really are too small for the sport, but we have log birling contests almost every evening. Lewie is so good at it that he is dumping me in the water as often as I flip him, maybe even more often. We also are talking up the idea of him coming back to Iowa with me this fall to attend school.

Then one day an event occurs that, to Lewie's chagrin, pretty much curtails the birling. It is late afternoon and all is well with the crew and the mill. All day we have chewed through the logs at a fair pace, and if I can saw four more logs before quitting time we will have a new record. Partly because of my eagerness to keep things moving I pay little attention to the old pickup coming into the mill yard, other than to notice that a man is driving and he has a passenger. Furthermore, I have no particular reason to give the vehicle any thought because the foreman takes care of anyone coming in to buy a few boards or to place an order for lumber.

A year or two earlier I would have been keenly aware of any visitors simply because of my pride in having them see me, the hotshot boy sawyer heroically doing his thing as good as or better than most grown men. In my dreams the best of the observing visitors were always beautiful women. Of course now that I am seventeen, I am over that foolishness, although I admit that even now it is kind of fun to have an appreciative audience once in a while when the mill is running especially well. Right now, this afternoon, I am just interested in getting those next few logs sawed before we shut down.

I am aware that the man from the pickup is having a long discussion with the foreman, and I have a vague feeling that I have seen him before. His passenger seems to have disappeared. I make the final cut on the last log of our record-breaking day, turn to move off the sawyer's platform, and there before me, watching my every move, are two lovely dark brown eyes. They are wide-set in a beautiful face surrounded by long black hair that cascades down over the shoulders of a most shapely young lady not much over five feet tall. Now I know who the visitor is: Mr. Cornwell, the man who, five years ago, walked into our homestead with his little ten-year-old daughter Shiela. Shiela is no longer a little girl.

"Hello, Neil," she says in a deep melodious voice that hints of both shyness and warmth.

"Shiela...you...remember me?" I stammer, standing there with my hobnailed boots locked to the ground because the sight of Shiela has made my legs quit working.

"Of course I do. I have not forgotten you since that day I first saw you. And you remember me; I was afraid you might not. You know we live just two miles from here, off the main road and right on Piledriver Slough."

"Would you like to go fishing after supper? I could be there at seven o'clock." It's the best thing I can think of right at the moment.

Several weeks have gone by since Shiela and I spoke our first direct words to each other, and during those weeks many more words have passed back and forth. I will never forget that first night Shiela and I sat shoulder to shoulder, knees drawn up, in a little mossy clearing on the bank of Piledriver Slough, surrounded on three sides by dense brush that shielded us from the rest of the world. We did have our fishing poles, but they lay unused beside us as we sat there basking in the warmth and soft light of the sun crawling across the low northwest sky. Sometimes we glanced at each other as we talked, but mostly we looked out at the water swirling in a slow eddy beyond our feet. For a while we watched a cow moose and her calf browse through a stand of willows on the far bank. She knew that we were there but she paid us no mind.

As the moose left, Shiela laid her head over gently on my shoulder and I touched my head to hers. Over the strong odor of the Six-Twelve mosquito dope we both wore I could smell Shiela, and she smelled very good. Silently we sat there a long time like that, both wishing, as we told each other later, that we could sit like that forever.

Shiela and I went fishing almost every evening after that. One exception was the Saturday night Shiela invited me to take her to the Eagles Hall for a dance. We could go because her father belonged to the organization, she said, and she loved to dance. In her long, full dancing dress, she looked extremely lovely that night, like a debutante going to a ball in a Hollywood film. I picked her up in Mom's green Model A coupe roadster, and that pleased Shiela because she thought it a classy car. Just after we got past Big Bend and were on the straight part of the Alcan leading into town, Shiela said , "Stop! I want to ride in the rumble seat." so I stopped, folded open the seat and helped her up into it. Then, feeling like a chauffeur, I drove slowly down Cushman Street to Eagles Hall with Shiela up there behind me, giggling and smiling, like she was the queen on the way to the coronation.

Shiela was disappointed in me that evening because I was not much good at the schottisches and polkas, the mainstay dances of the evening. Later, on the way home, I parked the roadster in a place where we could look out over the valley at the sun painting yellow tips on the mountains to the south. As we sat there it occurred to me that, unlike Iowa, Alaska is not a good place for high school kids to neck in cars. In winter it is too cold to do it, and in summer the midnight sun takes away much of the romance.

Maybe it was the bright light in the car or maybe my poor dancing performance, but Shiela seemed a little distant that evening as I drove on out Badger Road to take her home. "You are awfully serious; I'm not sure I want to be that serious yet," she said just before I dropped her off. "By the way, I'll be gone for two weeks. Mom and I are going down to Anchorage to visit her sister. See you later."

I haven't seen Shiela since, and I guess I know down deep that we probably will never get together again. For a while it was great to be with her, but she really is still a young girl, too young to be interested in the things I am. Also falling apart is Dad's plan to move the sawmill to Hess Creek near Rampart. Nor will Mom be going back to run the trading post. I promote the idea of her coming to Iowa with Lewie and me in the fall. She is still, as always, having serious asthma problems, so I think that if she can get away from all the hassle of the sawmilling business it might be good for her. I am hoping Dad will get out of it too. Almost anything ought to be easier than this continuous struggle to meet a payroll. He is toying with the idea of taking over some mining ground on the Tolovana River, up to the north of Fairbanks, and I encourage that, but urge him not to hire anybody if he decides to go into the gold mining business. It does seem that almost everyone who works for Dad makes more money than he does.

Since we will not be going up on the Yukon, Dad starts laying off the crew as we move toward the end of the log supply on the Horn place. Dad is sending three men with me out to the Salcha to saw up the logs stored there, keeping only one other man and Lewie to help plane up the lumber still remaining on the Horn place. Some of the lumber we will be putting out on the Salcha will also come here for planing.

Dad's trucker hauls the three men and me out to Salcha where we set up two tents for sleeping. Since the mill is only a mile from Aurora Lodge, Dad contracts with that roadhouse to provide our meals.

We go at it with a vengeance. I'd like to finish up in time to go back to school, and the other three are eager to get back closer to town. Two of them are young men who much prefer some nightlife.

I run the mill as many hours as possible, and we all work seven days a week. At least once each day, we have to shut down to load a truck with our production, so we are lucky to keep the mill running more than eight or nine hours. Still, we are working twelve to fourteen hours because, in addition to actually sawing the logs, we have to cut the trees in half with a crosscut saw and move them over to the ways. A plan to roll the logs onto a go-devil for transport falls apart because the two young men think that procedure is too slow. If the four of us pick the logs up with cant hooks we can carry most of them to the go-devil faster. Before a week is over, my back is giving me trouble from all that heavy lifting. Even though I am the boss of the operation, I cannot convince the guys that we ought to roll the logs instead of carrying them. So we do it the hard, fast way, and by the end of three weeks we have the entire pile of logs sawed up, some 70,000 board feet of them, and I go back to the Horn place. The nights are getting dark now, and it is almost time to go back to school.

The next evening, I shoot a bear, the second this summer. Bears are a problem around the Horn place because, a year ago, the previous occupant raised pigs. Many of them died and were left where they fell, so the bears have been coming in all summer to chew on the carcasses.

One night before I went out to the Salcha, the first bear came into the cook house where we were sleeping in the loft overhead. Hearing the bear, Mom woke up. She looked downstairs to see the bear up on the main table, eating a ham she had left there. That really ticked her off, so she yelled, and the bear rushed out the doorway, carrying away the door and the door frame with him. In my shorts, I went running out after the bear, swatting mosquitoes off my thighs with one hand and shooting my 30-06 with the other. I hit him in the butt three times before I killed him with the fourth shot.

This second bear is really a tough one, and his killing is a little tough on Mom, too. She, Lewie and I are playing cards around a Coleman lantern when this bear tries to come in through the door that the earlier one broke. I grab my gun, and Mom picks up the lantern. She carries it over to the door, and holds it out in front of her as far as possible. Standing beside and slightly behind Mom, I fire the gun, and the bear goes down. He gets back up, so I fire again. Mom is doing her best to hold the light so I can see better, but even with the bear only a few feet away, I am not doing well. I knock the bear down again and again, and finally, on the seventh shot he stays down.

"Thank God you finally got him," Mom says, "because now I can't hear." Not until the next day does she recover from having that big gun go off seven times, its bolt just inches from her head.

247

THE END OF AN ERA

LEWIE AND I FLY TO IOWA, arriving just in time for school to start. In the meantime, Dad has contracted to build a log house in Fairbanks for Bob Byers, a pilot from Manley Hot Springs, so Mom stays on to help him and the one man still working. During this job Dad becomes a recognizable sawmill man.

He has a big Skilsaw, a huge saw with a blade large enough to chew through a six-inch log. The saw is so heavy that a person has to use both hands to pick it up and lay it on the log to be cut. Then, because the saw has a sticky guard over its blade, you have to reach down under it with your left hand and pull the guard back before the cut is made. On this particular day, Dad makes several cuts using the standard procedure. But then he reaches down to move the guard, only to receive what is, by his own statement, a severe manicure. The guard sticks up inside the saw housing, and so Dad's hand hits the spinning blade. The cut runs all the way from the base of his little finger to the first knuckle of his pointer finger, thereby removing parts or all of the four fingers on his left hand. A wild ride to town follows, with Dad's hired man driving the car as far as the Territorial Troopers' base in south Fairbanks. The troopers load him in one of their cars and drive him on over to the hospital where Dr. Haggland cleans things up.

The accident puts quite a crimp in the folk's finances, but Mom does manage to get away about Christmas time for a trip to Colorado to see her mother for the first time in years. She also stops by to see Lewie and me in Iowa before going back to Alaska. Mom and Dad are supposed to be sending money to Uncle Irwin and Aunt Phena to help pay for our keep and for Lewie to have spending money. However, the money orders that do come are infrequent and usually too small. I am not pleased about that, because it does not seem fair to my aunt and uncle. To ease the burden on our adopted parents, I give Lewie some of the rent money I receive each month from my house at 14-Mile. For a while it is so bad that if Lewie is to have a school lunch, I have to do without. My stomach feels pretty empty some afternoons, but it is better to do that than go without gas money for dates on the weekends. I am leading an active social life with Rosemarie, the girl who sharpens pencils so attractively.

I now have given up on the idea of becoming a bush pilot—I am going to become a geologist for sure. What I'm not sure of is how to cover the cost of the necessary education, but I apply to enter the University of Alaska back in Fairbanks, and am accepted.

This is my last year in high school, and I am serious enough about my studies to make good grades. I also participate fully in sports. Although I play tackle on offense and linebacker on defense, Coach Russell has me calling the offensive plays for the football team, and when basketball season comes, I am the play-maker guard. Track is a repeat of the last year; I again collect various medals and qualify for the state meet in shot and discus.

Physically, I am a good athlete, but I lack the ability to peak myself mentally in the fashion of an outstanding competitor. That becomes evident the Saturday of the annual county track meet.

The coach repeatedly warns us to eat well, and to get plenty of sleep the night before any sporting event. Earlier in the year, I followed his advice faithfully, but on the evening before the county meet Rosemarie and I have a date. She keeps me out until five in the morning, so I get little sleep that night. Then the bus that takes us to the meet arrives so late that I am barely able to enter the shot-put event. The other participants have already completed their first round of four throws when I come running up. Even though I am late, the official says I can throw, so I enter the ring. Standing there, I count out the markers placed each five feet from the ring, and I aim at the spot that I know is my throwing limit. When the shot falls three feet short of my aiming point, I know that the coach is right: I should have gotten more sleep last night. I make my next three throws, the shot going a bit farther each time, but never as far as my usual distance.

I did not understand why several bystanders applauded my throws until after the official says, "Congratulations, you just broke the county record." Dumbfounded, I count out the markers again and realize that I miscounted the first time. Each of my throws has exceeded my previous attempts by several feet, the last by nearly five. When we all come back for our final three throws, I know what the distances are, and am unable to throw farther than I had on previous days, nor do I ever again throw beyond my usual range. It is quite a lesson, and it convinces me that I can never become a truly first-rate athletic competitor. Not that I really care because, as far as I was concerned, sport is just something you do for fun.

I am much more serious about Rosemarie, the girl who is keeping me out so late at night. We decide we have a lot in common, and the fact that we have virtually identical grades that make us class valedictorian and salutatorian at graduation helps our bonding. Fortunately, I beat her out for the top spot, and that is good because no young man wants a female around who is smarter than he is. Unfortunately, down deep I suspect that she is the smart one, but she does not work at it as hard as I do.

The school superintendent and some of the men teachers are displeased with my obvious deep interest in a girl. They are afraid that, like many of the farm students, I will get married right after high school instead of going on to college. The funny thing about this is that they have the wrong girl picked out for me. Rosemarie has a close friend who spends a lot of time with the two of us, and the teachers all think I am hot for her. She is extremely well stacked, and I think that tends to obscure these teachers' observational powers.

The academics are wrong on both counts. Not only do they have the wrong girl, but I do head off to Alaska by myself as soon as school is out, again too early to attend the state track meet. Rosemarie and I agree we will get more education before any deeper involvement.

I am eager to get north as soon as possible so that I can find a job to earn money for school this fall. The air ticket consumes my remaining finances, so I need to find a job in a hurry. A little looking around after arriving at Fairbanks produces nothing, so, with Dad's help, I follow in his footsteps. He no longer owns a sawmill, but the first one we had, the one that Dad put on Mike Bedoff's place back in 1945 and which I had used on the Salcha the year before, is for sale. Dad loans me the $300 needed to buy it.

I take out a timber permit on school lands near the homestead and go to work by myself. One thing I have learned is that paying someone to work for you is a loser. Whatever money I will be able to make this summer will stay in my pocket for school—once I've paid back the $300. For six weeks, with axe and Swede saw in hand, I walk into the woods every morning to cut trees. My daily goal is to knock down and trim twenty trees, and by early afternoon I have done that and worn myself out. Then I go back to the homestead and spend the remaining part of the day setting up the sawmill, arranging it as best I can for a one-man operation. Normally a mill like this can handle logs up to twenty or twenty-four feet long, but this mill has several sections of spare track so I assemble it all to create a machine that will saw logs up to forty feet long, just in case the need arises.

That turns out to be a good decision because just as I finish up, a man comes along who has a set of thirty-six-foot logs that he wants slabbed off on two sides and some other logs he wants to convert to boards. A week later I am able to hand Dad a check for $300 that pays him back and puts me in the position of turning profit from now on.

By late July I am working on several orders for lumber, the machinery is all running well and I am feeling pretty good about everything. Then one day just as I shut the mill down and am washing up for lunch with Mom, a jeep bearing a spiffy-looking air force officer shows up.

The last jeep that drove up like this under its own power bore a happy private with the message that the war was over, but this one carries a solemn lieutenant with the message that a new war is just beginning. And with a vengeance, it seems, because the lieutenant tells us that South Korea is under invasion, and we in Alaska may be next. Communist bombers are likely to show up overhead at any time, the man says, so both nearby military bases are on full alert and we must prepare for evacuation. He tells us that if we hear a continuous siren out on the Alcan that everyone between Ladd Field and 26-Mile Field—what they are now starting to call Eielson Air Force Base—must be out on the highway within fifteen minutes for pickup. Military trucks will take us to one or the other of the air bases and we will be flown either to Canada or the States.

As a final punctuation to the lieutenant's words, one of those new jet fighters flies by, over the Alcan just above the treetops, and as it comes abreast of us we first see and then hear what to me is a chilling incident. The sleek black ship's afterburner kicks in and the machine suddenly flips upward at high angle into a knifing attack on the sky above. It is frightening and unreal. The only time I'd ever seen anything like this was years ago in a Buck Rogers comic strip, and it makes me remember with a touch of nostalgia those other fighters and bombers that used to plod through the sky over the homestead, on their way to Russia. They were impressive then, but the world is changed, and now such airplanes are just quaint. I was a twelve-year-old boy when those propellered aircraft flew over. Now I am a healthy eighteen-year-old young man—and that puts this war business in a whole new light.

The days go by with no invasion nor any bombing, but my mind remains full of turmoil as I plug away at my one-man sawmill operation. I know that my chances of going to college for very long look bleak. Perhaps the thing to do is forget college altogether. Hell, I probably will not even be alive in a few years; why fight it? Maybe I will just keep sawing boards as long as I can, or maybe I will use this sawmill to make enough money to buy an airplane so I can become a bush pilot after all—if I ever get out of the military.

All this is terribly depressing. I ponder the future as I work away, and I keep coming back to the thought of modifying the obvious course of events with an accident like Dad's. Damn, I bet that hurts a lot, though, and a person really does need his fingers. Toes would be better, and a 30-06 accident sure would be fast. Trouble is I could bleed to death before I get to town. It would be smarter to take the gun in and have an accident on the front steps of St. Joseph's Hospital...St. Joseph's Hospital, that's where Tom Wade died. And thinking of him brings to mind Jay Livengood who always said he'd be home in the spring but who died over on the front steps of the Federal Building, and thinking about that makes me think of something else. Maybe it's Henry Spall and the smell of oil of citronella, the pleasant smell of fresh white spruce sawdust coming off the saw, or how silly that Canada jay sounds over there as he scolds the squirrel for carrying such a big mushroom up that tree.

One thing I've been thinking about as I work is this homestead and what it has meant to all of us these past few years. I've learned a lot living here, by working for Wien Airlines, and by going to high school. The homestead is the only thing Mom and Dad have ever owned, and it's the only thing Dad has stuck to year after year. But now that the long battle to prove up on it is over, he seems tired of the whole business, and of course Dad is no farmer. He has already exchanged a few small pieces of land over on the Alcan for debts owing, and he's talking with a real estate guy in Fairbanks who wants to buy a large chunk and subdivide it. Another thing is that other people have been homesteading along the highway between 10-Mile and 18-Mile, so the whole area is changing and feeling more crowded. The old-timers are all gone now but there must be at least ten families within a few miles of the homestead. Enough people seem to want to live here that I think Dad could make quite a bit of money with this place, but I have a feeling it is not going to go that way. Of course the war screws everything up, too. After the Russians drop their big nuclear bombs on this place, there might not even be any trees or houses left.

One good thing about laboring by yourself like I'm doing is that you can work on whatever it is but think about something else without any interruptions. Your mind can just wander around at will, and you can work at your own pace. It doesn't matter if you want to work slowly, or even just sit down and do nothing at all except think. Sawmilling is good thinking work, too, because it is routine enough not to occupy a big piece of your mind, yet still not boring. Each log is different, and no two boards are quite alike either. The big saw's teeth cut their own marks across the wood grain and through the knots to produce intricate patterns. If you use your imagination a bit you can see all sorts of landscapes or pictures of animals, but what I recognize mostly are peoples' bodies and faces.

In the long wavy grain pattern of the board coming off the saw now I see Grandma Sappenfield's hair...sweet-faced Grandma Sappenfield whose persistent goody-goody preaching contributed so much to my aversion to gods and organized religion of all sorts. "Kneel down and say your payers, and God will always take care of you," she used to say with her ever-present beatific smile. Like hell, Grandma, I don't think prayer is going to hack it when the guns start going off. You pray, and I'll put my whole effort into dodging bullets.

And that long, thin, almost featureless one-by-six is her tall, gentle husband who I almost never got to know but who gave me the hammer, nails and block of wood. He spoke little but he understood a lot. Now if he said "Pray," I might do it.

A stout six-by-eight coming off the saw, its grain tough and twisted around large tight knots, is Grandma Davis who walked the better part of a thousand miles across the prairies as a young girl and in her later years supported her inventor husband, the Kansas legislator and Klondike gold rusher who on his deathbed told me to be a good boy. Of the four grandparents, she is the only one still alive, and she is still strong.

As the boards come away from the saw and move into the stacks, various thoughts go with them, some generated totally within my mind and others triggered by the shapes and shadowy silhouettes within the boards. Most of the thoughts are fleeting, half-formed and without conclusion, and they tumble one upon the other as I struggle with my uncertainty of the future and what I am going to do about it.

Every so often, I think about stable Uncle Irwin and Aunt Phena back there working day after day on the farm and frugally preparing for a comfortable old age before death. Over and over again, though, I think about Dad always battling away against success with his strange combination of hard work, unwarranted optimism and lack of persistence—and about Mom's whole body heaving with raspy, hacking asthma coughs as she patiently goes along, and then repeatedly becomes enthusiastic about each new venture...and Lewie, tough little sociable Lewie, born short and in my shadow but gutsy like Bart Scott with the black bag, and the dog-mushing rat-killer with the gimpy leg, Angus Carter.

These people and others have purposelessly threaded their ways back and forth through my mind these past two uneasy months, right up to this moment. And now as I sit here on this pile of newly sawn boards, enjoying the low evening sunlight filtering through aspen leaves already turned yellow, I suddenly feel very good. It is exactly the same feeling I had that day back in LaSalle those many years ago when I comprehended that I could avoid having to make a grown-up's decisions by not growing up. But this time, the good feeling is because I have made a decision.

I really do have a good life, and the best way to make it even better is to get rid of this stupid sawmill and head off to college next month. It's as simple as that. If the Russians or the army try to interfere I will fight them to the end—and I'll do it with ten fingers and ten toes.

EPILOGUE

A LL THAT WAS LONG AGO, and if I'd been smart I would have saved myself a lot of anguish by just remembering what I'd learned early on: don't worry about future events because most of them won't happen anyway.

The Russians never did show up, but the army did its best to nab me until it discovered during my pre-induction physical that I was slightly asthmatic, not enough to give me any problem but enough to qualify for a 4-F card. By then I was in my second year of college and was married to Rosemarie. She was pregnant with our first daughter, and we were living near the University of Alaska in the first house she and I built together. When our daughter was born, Grandma Davis drove with my mother up the Alcan in the dead of winter to see her. Grandma, the lady who walked across a big piece of America behind a covered wagon, headed back to her home in LaSalle, Colorado, in a Boeing 707. It was her first airplane ride. She became a major league baseball fan in her later years and a fan of NASA. She watched Neil Armstrong step on the moon.

A slow learner, I remained in college for eleven years, but I did have a Ph.D. when it was all over. Lewie actually *volunteered* to join the United States Air Force and served for six years before his four years in college gave him a bachelor's degree that prepared him for a teaching career.

Much to my surprise, Uncle Irwin and Aunt Phena moved away from their Iowa farm after paying it off. They went to a fair-sized city where Uncle Irwin became the head sociologist for one of the state prisons and Aunt Phena returned to her first love, teaching grade school.

The homestead went about like I thought it would. Mom and Dad sold one big chunk and then another, until none was left. Lots that they sold for $500 were worth $5000 within a year because a new city was building at that location. Before long the original cabin was torn down to make room for a church's paved parking lot. Mom's and Dad's take from all this was enough to pay off all their debts, and that pleased them because it was the first time in years that they had no money owing.

Like Uncle Irwin, Dad went into the prison business. He began as a guard at the Fairbanks Federal Prison, and before long he was the assistant director. He and Mom moved to Nome when Dad was appointed director of the Nome Federal Prison. Mom took over the hardware section of Nome's Northern Commercial Company store. The Nome jail's clientele was almost all Eskimo, and Nome had a high percentage of Eskimo residents. Mom, especially, seemed to feel much at home with them—perhaps in part because, like her, they tended to be nonjudgemental. Dad also fit in and he had always claimed that only a very fine line separates those who stand on the opposite sides of a row of prison bars. If you visited to his jail, he made sure that you shook hands with every guard and every prisoner. Dad even earned some acclaim within the federal prison system by writing a manual on how to deal with Native prisoners that was adopted system-wide.

Mom and Dad were successful and happy in their jobs, and it seemed that they had worked themselves into long-term situations. But then came statehood and the transfer of Alaska's seven federal prisons to state government. The new government established a rule that the director of a state prison must have a college degree, and since Dad only had a two-year teaching certificate, he lost his job. The head of the federal prison system offered Dad the directorship of one of the federal penitentiaries in California, but Mom and Dad could not bear the thought of leaving Alaska, so Dad turned that down.

Mom and Dad liked Nome and its people, but the real reason they did not want to leave is that they had purchased a collection of gold claims out some sixty miles north of Nome, and fourteen roadless miles across the tundra from Teller. Now in their fifties, Mom and Dad still were not content to work for someone else on a steady basis. The homestead used to be their excuse for not working too long at any one thing, and now the mining ground became an improved replacement for it.

Nobody ever gets rich quick from farming a homestead, but it is possible if you have a gold mine.

They spent their winters in Nome working at one thing after another. Dad spent one winter as the area's parole officer, and another winter he and Mom operated a restaurant. Then Dad settled in as the cook at a boarding school for Native children, just outside Nome. The seasonal nature of the job fit in well with gold mining.

Each winter as they worked, Mom and Dad dreamed of the fortune to be made the following summer. Each summer they were out at Igloo Creek, alone in a windblown expanse of low hills covered only by moss and a few short bushes, looking for gold—and playing cribbage. They played a lot of cribbage, always keeping a tally of games won during each season. One seasonal tally in their log showed that Mom came out ahead that year by more than one hundred games. They played cribbage every evening, and sometimes all day long when, as often happened, not enough water was available for sluicing. They also had one long cribbage stint when a robin came along and built a nest in the top of the tallest object she could find: Dad's tent-covered equipment sled. That brought mining to a halt for some time, until the day the young robins were able to fly.

When the birds were not interfering, and enough water was running for sluicing, Dad pushed dirt into the box with his little Caterpillar D-4, and Mom stood by, kicking the bigger rocks down over the riffles with a shovel. They always found a few nuggets, but never so many as to quite pay the summer's bills. That was just fine, for had it been otherwise, what would have been the challenge in life?